A Story of My Travels with…

Joseph Shepherd

by

John Jung

New Creation Publishing, Tipp City, Ohio.

Joseph Shepherd is a historical novel. Some of the characters are easily recognizable as important philosophers, inventors, writers, and even geniuses. Care was given to be true to the events of the time period, and most events are essentially historically accurate. Interactions between the historical characters are part of the fiction, although many of these contemporaries did actually have a relationship and had correspondence or interacted with one another.

Published in the United States by New Creation Publishing, Tipp City, Ohio.

Foreword

     This journal of my adventures with Joseph Shepherd has been in the making for many years. I have compiled years of my own diaries, journals, letters, as well as notes from others, to try to accurately describe this amazing journey I have had with my friend, Joseph Shepherd. Indeed, some of the descriptions of Joseph's journey, where I was not present, are quite detailed. I urge the reader to follow this chronicle to the end to see how that information was preserved for this account.

     Joseph changed my life and the lives of many others – indeed perhaps the course of history. Certainly, he has influenced generations since our adventures began. While he told me of his journeys prior to meeting me, I suspect that there is much he left out. His journeys seemed to encompass much of the world, for there were few places with which he did not have some familiarity. He had met some of the most amazing people – scholars, scientists, theologians, philosophers, etc., and he felt at ease discussing with each of them their particular area of knowledge. At the same time, he could feel just as at ease talking with poor, ill, broken people, and be completely engaged in their world.

     I have compiled this journal and committed it to the form of a book in the hope that the reader may see that life is richer when the travelling companion is a person of trust, one who challenges us beyond our comfort, and one who helps us in the most difficult of circumstances. I trusted Joseph Shepherd as my travelling companion, and I am glad that I made that choice…

Dr. Luke Greene

Part I

Chapter 1

The small boat seemed to dance in the moonlight. Seen faintly off the starboard bow of the man o' war HMS Intrepid, the small craft appeared to be empty. Boatswain Thomas Kent was the first to see the boat, and he seemed strangely excited by the sighting. He was on his first voyage, as were many of the seamen aboard the *Intrepid*. "Captain Braden," Kent yelled, "there's a boat off starboard." Kent peered into the moonlight with eyes squinted, but concluded, "I can't see a soul on it."

Captain Braden was an unusual commander of a British fighting vessel. He was a veteran of several campaigns, including the historic battle with the Spanish Armada over thirty years ago. He was only a seaman at that time, but that encounter had changed him in many ways. He was a very astute leader, tough when he had to be, but generally much calmer than most of his counterparts, and for this he had suffered the indignities of fellow officers. Yet he maintained a dignity and grace that had won his crew's allegiance over the years.

"Steer to starboard, Mr. Ross," Braden commanded to the wheelhouse. The great ship heaved to the right, making slow progress in the calm water. As the *Intrepid* approached the little boat many of the crew came on deck and strained to see what the change in course was about. Rumbles went through the ranks of superstitious sailors. While a little excitement might be nice for a mission that was nothing but a shakedown for the new warship, several of the crew, mostly the veterans, questioned the idea of approaching an unknown vessel, no matter what the size.

As the *Intrepid* crawled closer, silence gripped the lumbering ship. The little boat, which had appeared to be empty, did indeed have an occupant. A man lay face down in the boat, motionless, bloodstained, and tattered. He appeared to be dead. "Board the boat Mr. Kent!" Braden ordered. Turning to me Captain Braden said, "And you too, Doctor Greene." I was not surprised that he had asked me to board the boat. The poor devil in the boat was probably dead, and he wanted me to verify the fact. Besides, Kent was just a young fellow and might be a bit taken aback by the sight of a violent death. Several of the *Intrepid*'s sailors had tasted death up close, but not Kent.

1

Mr. Kent and I struggled over the side of the now bobbing *Intrepid*, and we boarded the smaller craft. The seas had picked up a bit, and there was a breeze, which was making the little boat jump in the waves. This action must have shaken our poor victim in the boat, for he suddenly lurched up as we boarded his boat. Mr. Kent went for his dagger to subdue the stranger till I screamed at him to stop.

"Mr. Kent," I said, "this man is no danger to you; put down your knife."

Embarrassed, Kent sheathed the dagger, but he grabbed the stranger and pinned him to the boat as he rolled him over on his back.

"Who are you?" demanded Kent in a voice that was at once harsh and frightened.

The dazed stranger looked up at us and tried to determine where his senses were. The man had been in the boat for some time, maybe several days. His clothes were ragged and torn, his face and hands burned terribly from the sun. The blood was dry, and his hair was caked with it. His lips were parched white. His beard was caked with salt that had dried in the sun. This man had been through an ordeal of exposure, and he had sustained a serious blow to the head. He might have other injuries too, but he could die from what I saw without a further examination. There was a sack next to him that contained a jug, some bread and a few salted fish – the kind that most sailing ships carried as provisions.

"We need to bring him aboard the *Intrepid* if he is going to have any chance to live," I said.

Mr. Kent looked at me and said, "The Captain will make that decision."

"I know that, Mr. Kent," I said with growing anger. "Captain, permission to bring this man aboard," I yelled up to him.

Captain Braden did not hesitate to order the man brought aboard the ship. Kent glared at me, with an expression that reflected some of the odd superstition that prevailed on ships. Findings such as this were seen as bad luck. Adding another soul on board, a stranger found in the middle of the night, was surely a bad omen. I sighed as I stared at Kent and I said, "You will obey the Captain's order now, Mr. Kent."

The man was hoisted up onto the *Intrepid* and brought to the infirmary, which was next to my quarters. The stranger seemed to be coming to his senses as I slipped a cup of water to his lips. He tried to drink heartily – a good sign, but a bad idea, for he would surely vomit it out if he continued to gulp as he did. I pulled his clothes off, and he was even able to assist me some in that endeavor – another good sign. The man was of slight build, bearded, with very dark hair, which was rather long and unkempt, matted with blood. It was

2

difficult to determine his age given his disheveled and broken appearance. He was not the most attractive of men, but his eyes were expressive and piercing. His dark, ruddy complexion was evident despite terrible sunburn from exposure in the boat. He was somewhat small in stature, but muscular. I finally judged him to be in his early to mid-thirties, about my age, but it was a little hard to determine. As I looked him over I saw bruises over much of his body and a few telltale marks of a lash on his back. The blow to the head had not fractured his skull, and I could not determine any other external injuries. If there were internal injuries, I suspected that he probably would already have died from them. I also determined that he had not been unconscious the entire time he was on the boat, because he had been drinking water from the jug. Even though he was dehydrated, he had obviously drunk some water over the past several days.

"What is your name, sir?" I asked, hoping to determine his level of clarity of mind as well as to find out more about him. He looked blankly at me for a moment as if I had asked him to name the stars.

"Shepherd," he said softly. "Joseph Shepherd."

"Where are you from, and what were you doing in that boat?" I inquired. He struggled to come up with the energy to speak. "No," I said, "you do not need to talk. I'm sorry that I asked you so much so quickly. You just rest now, and in the morning I will bring you something to eat."

I spent the rest of the night in the infirmary with him to make sure that he would make it until the morning. I had seen cases before where men had looked like they were going to recover, and then they just slipped away into a coma. Where was this man from, and what was he doing in that boat? I was very curious about this man's past. Was he a criminal? What did he do to get such a beating? He had apparently been cast from a ship, but what had he done to deserve this fate?

The *Intrepid* had proceeded smoothly through her maiden voyage up until this point. The seas had been calm through this summer cruise into the mid-Atlantic. The *Intrepid* had performed well as the crew put her through her paces. The guns had been fired without incident, and the sailors were awed at the firepower of these new cannon. The larger sails and the sleeker hull design of this ship made her the fastest of her class of warships. The latest navigation equipment was on board, including the latest clock design, which allowed more precise guidance from the stars to better determine longitude. Her crew was beginning to gain confidence in the performance of this vessel. The *Intrepid* could hold her own against any ship on the sea. Now it appeared that she would have to show her ability to handle her first storm.

The crew was growing wary of the brewing storm, but they only talked about the new passenger. It was not good luck to discuss a storm, so they talked about Mr. Shepherd, though they, and I, knew nothing about him. As I came into the mess, I heard the crude remarks of Seaman Pratt about the addition of our passenger. "I been sailing for twenty years and never seen good out of picking up the dregs of another ship," he snorted. "I say we should have let the bastard die like he was supposed to!"

"Mr. Pratt," I called, "do you know where Mr. Shepherd has come from?"

"Who is Mr. Shepherd?" yelled Pratt.

"I see you do not even know his name, but you know where he is from and what he did!" I said. Several sailors laughed at Pratt, as I had hoped. Pratt was a rather loathsome sort, and in need of someone to occasionally remind him of it. I enjoyed this job greatly, and the crew often enjoyed it as well.

"Doctor Greene knows something about this new man," said Pratt. "Tell us what you know!" he demanded.

"I know that his name is Joseph Shepherd and that he is an injured man. It is my duty to treat him, and that is all I know about him. The difference between you and me, Mr. Pratt, is that when I do not know something, I do not make up wild tales about the things of which I am ignorant." At that I left the mess area to the laughter of the crew and the curses of Pratt.

I went back to the infirmary on the lower deck, and found the footing a little harder due to the pitch and roll of the ship. Upon entering the infirmary, I found Shepherd vomiting up the little water I had given him. I had seen this before with men who had sustained blows to the head. Mr. Shepherd was suffering, but he was silent, and was not calling out to me in curses as other sailors I had often treated. As I approached Mr. Shepherd, I saw Captain Braden enter the infirmary. He looked pale, and he complained of aches and a fever. I bid him to sit for an examination. He was indeed warm to the touch, and he winced as he lifted his arms for my examination for swelling in the limbs. I told him to lie down and rest, but he declined, stating that he had no time for rest as a storm approached. He asked me for some medicine to relieve the pain in his neck. His neck was swollen, and he appeared to be glazed in his eyes. "Captain Braden, I believe that you would do well with a night's rest. We can ride out this storm."

He looked at me with a strange glance, rose from the chair and said, "I have no time for that man; I must be back up on deck!"

I knew that something was dreadfully wrong. Captain Braden was a man of clear-headed logic, not given to impulse and whimsy. He was, I presumed, becoming delirious with fever. He had not shown any symptoms prior to this, so this illness, whatever it was, had come on very quickly.

As I was thinking about this latest of concerns, the ship rocked violently as she was hit by a wave. The storm appeared to be approaching gale status, and the ship was being tested very quickly on her first voyage. Cargo was shifted on the lower deck as I heard a tremendous crash of barrels and crates below ship. The crew had evidently failed to secure the provisions and ammunition properly. I hoped that this mistake would not prove to be fatal.

4

Swamped food and cannon balls rolling around under me gave me a chill as I thought about it. What kind of crew did we have on this ship?

The ship continued to be slammed by the storm, and the curses and yells of fearful and angry crewmen filled the air. The crew was now working hard to keep the *Intrepid* from being torn apart by the storm. I heard Mr. Pratt screaming to Captain Braden.

"It's that man Shepherd that you brought on board that's caused this! As soon as he was brought on board, this ship was doomed!"

Pratt was now raving, and I wondered if Captain Braden was able to bear up under this madness in his condition. Others of the crew were starting to believe the story of the frightened Pratt. They would be ready to throw Shepherd overboard if they thought that would calm the storm. Suddenly, the wind died down and the rain, which had been driving sheets, settled into a steady downpour. This storm, which just seconds before looked to be disaster, was now just a rainy night at sea.

As I looked up at the crew now beginning to pile in below deck, I saw them staring at Mr. Shepherd, who was standing with his hands raised near the entrance to the infirmary.

"Mr. Shepherd!" I blurted out. I was dumbstruck to see Mr. Shepherd up and about. He had put on an extra set of clothes stored in the infirmary, looking to be greatly recovered from his recent ordeal. He was standing straight, and I noticed that he was rather short of stature, since this was the first time I had ever seen him on his feet. His beard was rather scruffy from all the time in the small boat. Yet he carried himself with dignity, despite his bedraggled appearance – unshaven and in clothes not even his own. He seemed oblivious to the stares of the crew, and he appeared to be talking to himself. "Good God," I thought, "has everyone on this ship gone mad?"

After a few moments, Mr. Shepherd turned and walked toward me. "Mr. Shepherd, how is it that you are walking around? I was not sure that you were going to be able to get out of bed for some time!" I said.

"I am feeling much better, Dr. Greene," he said calmly. He called me by name, which surprised me no less than his amazing recovery.

"And you know my name as well," I said.

"Yes," he replied, "I heard Captain Braden address you just a little while ago."

"Where are you from?" demanded Mr. Pratt.

"I fear that I have had a serious blow to my head and I cannot remember very much of anything until this past hour," Shepherd replied softly.

"We picked you up off a little boat floating in the sea. We reckoned that you was thrown off a ship and left to die," Pratt said.

"You may be right, sir," replied Shepherd, "for I cannot remember anything until I was taken aboard this vessel."

I surmised that he was from England, given his command of the language – an educated man, and not a seaman. What he was doing in that little boat was a mystery, but so was everything about this man. He seemed to be a gentle man, but not afraid of this situation which confronted him. His behavior during the storm was most curious – rising from his sick bed to standing up on a rolling ship in the middle of very rough seas. For not being a sailor, he seemed to have sea legs, and a calm that belied his disposition and his physical state. Truly, this man was a curiosity.

Chapter 2

Captain Braden staggered into the infirmary once again, but this time he did not appear to be able to go anywhere else. Having dutifully gone back to the top deck during the storm to lead his crew, he now retreated to a sick bed. The purple splotches appearing on his neck and chest were a grisly omen of disease unchecked. His fever was rising, as was his now nearly complete delirium. Barking orders to no one in particular, he seemed convinced that the ship was going down. I assured him that the storm, which had so frightened us, was over, and that we would soon be seeing the light of dawn.

"Not so, surgeon Greene," he said, "this ship is in trouble. Our mainsail was torn before we could haul it down during the storm, and repairs will take some time. We are drifting toward Spanish waters and the pirates who wait there. We must be preparing straightaway for a fight!"

With those words he slipped out of consciousness. Thankfully, the rest of the crew had headed to the rum supply for a dose of cheer to celebrate the end of the storm. I sensed that the storm was really about to begin if Captain Braden were unable to lead the ship. Judson North, the second in command, was an able man, a fighting commander who could not really lead a crew in a time of peace. His anger always seemed just below the surface, and his face seemed to reflect it. He rarely smiled, and rarely looked a person in the eye. He seemed to be able only to rise to command when he was in a fight. In the midst of a fight with a French frigate or a buccaneer galleon, he would be in his glory. Indeed, he had received the nickname "Bloody North" for a victory over a privateer in the Indian Ocean. He had seized the vanquished ship and personally saw to it that each pirate's throat was slit before they were heaved overboard. Mr. North, it appears, did not care for prisoners. However, taking charge of a group of sailors such as we had, a few grizzled, war-seasoned veterans and a larger number of raw young seamen new to the rigors of sea life, was more than he was built for. He was not disciplined himself, nor could he impose discipline on others.

I went to see Mr. North after I checked on Captain Braden. Captain Braden was breathing steadily now, and appeared to be sleeping. Whether he was sleeping or was in a coma, I could not tell, but I knew that Mr. North needed to be apprised of the situation.

Mr. North was calm upon hearing the news of Captain Braden. "Thank you, Dr. Greene, for your information about the Captain," he said. "I will be taking command of the *Intrepid* until the Captain is able to resume his duties."

"Very well," I replied. "I will keep you informed of the Captain's condition." I was not convinced that the Captain would recover, nor could I stifle my growing concern over the symptoms that the Captain presented. "Could it be the plague?" I asked myself. "Could it be anything else?" I reasoned. God save us if it were the plague, for we would all surely be doomed. Even if the plague did not kill us, we could never be received in any port if word got out that plague was on board.

Thankfully, no other man on board showed symptoms. Maybe the case was confined to the Captain. Maybe it really was not the plague. As I wrestled these things in my mind, Mr. Shepherd came into my quarters.

"Good morning, Dr. Greene," Shepherd said. "I see that Captain Braden has taken ill and is at the infirmary."

"That is where you should be, Mr. Shepherd," I replied. "You still have a nasty lump on your head, and I have not had the chance to give you a thorough examination."

"Dr. Greene," said Shepherd, "I am not the patient you should be worried about. I saw Captain Braden, and I fear that he has the symptoms of the plague," he said almost calmly. I was amazed by his observation, and also shaken by what sounded like a second opinion of my diagnosis.

"Are you a physician?" I asked.

"I am," he replied.

I did not know whether to be relieved or frightened. If Mr. Shepherd was a physician, his observation was much more valid, and would confirm my worst fears.

"I thought you did not remember anything of your past?" I said.

Shepherd answered, "I do not recall how I got here, but I do remember my profession. I am a physician."

"You must not tell anyone of your opinion about Captain Braden," I said. "If the crew hears that he may have the plague, we will have panic on this ship. They have already been through enough this past day."

"I would never tell anyone else about this," he said. "The crew would hardly believe me anyway, Dr. Greene. They would want to throw me overboard for such a statement. In fact, I think they would like to cast me off anyway. They must believe that I am bad luck."

Mr. Shepherd – Dr. Shepherd, if you please – was quite perceptive of the situation he faced. Indeed, he hardly seemed disturbed by the fact that he was not a welcome part of the ship's crew. Perhaps he had been in this situation before. Perhaps Pratt, God forbid, had been right about Shepherd.

"I have no time to worry about how you are received on this ship, Dr. Shepherd," I said. "I am very worried about Captain Braden, and even more worried about this ship."

"Yes," replied Shepherd, "you have very good reason to worry, but what we need is proper action. Worry will not add a thing to this situation."

8

"You are a physician," I replied, "What is your opinion of how to proceed?"

"Well," he said, "the first thing I do in such cases is pray."

I noted that he was a man of faith. A good thing, to be sure, but out of place on a ship full of hard-living men, many of whom had never seen the inside of a church.

"Fine," I said. "Pray about what to do, and pray that word does not get out about Captain Braden. Maybe God will bless us with only one case of the plague."

Dr. Shepherd went off to his bed in the infirmary, having no other place to call his own, and he bowed down, evidently in prayer. I went over to Captain Braden to check on his condition, which seemed to have gotten worse. He had slipped into a coma, as I was unable to rouse him despite vigorous efforts to do so. We would be losing the Captain soon. Perhaps Shepherd was right to pray, for surely we would need more help than we presently had available.

The sun was now beginning to rise, a beautiful scene that belied the terrible weather of just hours before. The ship had sustained some damage to the mainsail, as the Captain had noted even in his delirium. The *Intrepid* had managed to come through the storm otherwise relatively unscathed, however, and the crew was already working on repair of the mainsail. Mr. North had assumed command, and the crew at this time seemed to be responding well.

"How is Captain Braden, Doctor Greene?" yelled seaman Samuels.

"He is resting well right now," I lied. Samuels nodded and mumbled something to several men nearby. They seemed satisfied at his report.

Mr. North, however, was restless as he bustled along the deck inspecting the work. He wanted the repairs done quickly so as not to be vulnerable to attack. He was convinced that we were heading straight for the pirates who plied the coast off Spain. Those pirates had the protection of the Spanish fleet as long as they preyed upon only English or Dutch ships. Catholic Spain felt no need to protect the heathens of England and the Low Countries. Indeed, Mr. North would just as soon be going to battle as leading the *Intrepid* back to England from a routine cruise – no glory in that. He needed the smell of powder and the clash of iron to feel like a real leader of men.

The repair work was interrupted by the report of Mr. Kent from the lookout nest. Glass still in hand, Kent screamed out, "There's a ship to the east; I cannot make out who she is!"

Kent was looking into the sun, and many of the crew were not sure he was really seeing another ship. Surely the sun was blinding him, and giving him an illusion, not an uncommon occurrence. Mr. North asked him to look away for a few moments and resume his watch. Kent complied, and a few minutes later he yelled again, "I see a ship. I cannot tell her colors. It looks like she is headed north."

Mr. North responded immediately, "Turn to port."

That put us on course due east, toward the unknown ship. Surely, Mr. North was hoping for some action. The crew was starting to buzz. Most of them had not been in combat, and they might be getting a chance for it now. The mainsail was not yet completely repaired, but the rest of the *Intrepid* was seemingly ready for action. As we turned to port, we could see the brilliant sunlight glare off the calm sea. There was a slight breeze from the west, which quickly picked up our speed. The tranquil sea and deep blue sky behind us was a picture of calm, but everything else about the morning had taken on an air of excitement. The unknown vessel toward which we sailed was still not visible from my vantage point. I began to think of Mr. North's rash decision to pursue this ghost. He did not hesitate for a second to look for a fight, and I was sure that he would be deeply disappointed if we could not engage this ship in action. This was his chance to lead the ship the only way he knew how.

Soon we began to make out signs of a ship in the distance. It was indeed heading north, as Mr. Kent had noted. I decided to slip below to check on the Captain and Dr. Shepherd. I saw Dr. Shepherd sitting next to Captain Braden's bed, applying something to his forehead. Captain Braden began to stir, and he started to respond to Dr. Shepherd.

"Dr. Shepherd, are you treating my patient?" I called.

"Dr. Greene," replied Shepherd, "I thought that you had asked for my assistance. Please forgive me if I have overstepped my bounds."

"He seems to be better. What did you do?" I asked. I was not really upset over Shepherd's assistance; I was more curious that he would expose himself to a man with the plague for whom he was not responsible. As ship's surgeon, I was the one who was to take such risks, not a stranger – especially one so recently injured, and one whom the crew would not accept. This man was different indeed.

"His fever seems to be down, and his delirium is gone. He is still very ill, though, and I am quite certain that this illness is the plague," Shepherd replied.

I came near to talk to Captain Braden. His neck was swollen, and he was barely able to speak above a whisper, but he seemed intent on asking me about the welfare of the ship. I told him that Mr. North was in command until he could return, fully knowing that the captain would not return to command the *Intrepid*. I told the Captain that he needed his rest, and I withdrew to my quarters with Dr. Shepherd.

"What did you administer to the Captain?" I asked.

"I just anointed him with oil," replied Shepherd. "I had also fed him a bit of bread I had with me in my sack. I think the bread was stale, and maybe had a bit of mold on it, but that will certainly not hurt him. He told me that he was hungry, and I wanted to be sure to respond. That was so encouraging that I wanted to get him some food quickly. My sack was available, and..."

Mr. Shepherd seemed apologetic about feeding the Captain. I was quite certain that the bread did not hurt him. Besides, if the Captain had the plague, he would die no matter what we did. A little compassion was a good thing to have in any case.

The *Intrepid* was heading straight for a confrontation with a pirate ship. Mr. North was having the ship move full speed to the conflict. The pirate ship was now in view, but was still at a great distance. The crew was preparing for battle. The *Intrepid* was equipped with thirty-two cannon, sixteen on each side. As the seamen went below decks to load shot and black powder for the gunners, they found the horrible disarray left by the storm. Food, cannon balls, and black powder sacks were strewn from bow to stern. Water swirled below decks, spoiling a fair amount of the ship's provisions and weaponry. This ship was not really prepared for a fight, but Mr. North would not be aware of this problem until it was too late.

The gunners were securing their cannon to the ship in preparation for battle. English gunners were the best trained in the world, and were able to fire their cannon at least twice within a five-minute period, often three times. Given the number of cannon on the Intrepid, the ship could produce steady volleys of fire at the interval of a shot every ten seconds. The gunners had a supply of powder and shot stored in the magazine deck, and they were not aware of the problem below. They were confident that they could perform well under fire. They also knew that pirates wanted to board the ship, relying on cutting in close to the vessel under attack, boarding her, and utilizing their brutal hand fighting tactics to subdue the enemy. These gunners would let nothing of that sort happen to the *Intrepid*.

The vessel appeared to be a captured Dutch ship. It flew no colors, a pretty sure sign that it was a captured ship, likely pirates, perhaps from the Barbary Coast. As it came into closer sight it appeared that the pirates wanted nothing to do with a fight with a British warship. Merchant vessels were one thing, but fighting ships were not a desired target of these brigands. Mr. North would have none of a retreat, neither his own nor that of his enemy. He called for his sailors to pursue their victim, and indeed they did; for the next three hours they pursued the pirate ship. Strangely, it seemed that the pirates were playing cat and mouse with us. They would seem to slow down, and then they would make a run to stay out of our cannon's range. Mr. North was becoming enraged at the cowardice of these pirates, these dregs of the seagoing world. He would shout and curse at them, as would the rest of the crew, taking his lead. By mid-afternoon the *Intrepid*'s crew was tired and hungry, having chased this elusive enemy for much of the day. The nerves of the crew were getting raw, and disputes arose about why this chase was even underway. As tempers flared, Mr. North knew only how to attack. He threatened those malcontents who were so cowardly as to complain with a time in chains before being hanged. As these little exchanges were taking place on the *Intrepid*, Mr.

11

Conner, who was now in the lookout position, shouted an ominous warning, "Ships to starboard, ships to starboard!"

Two Spanish warships were indeed heading for the *Intrepid*'s right flank. Just as they were spotted, Mr. Kent yelled from the bow, "The pirates are turning toward us!"

Mr. North suddenly realized that this was no coincidence – he had fallen into the trap set by the pirate ship. The *Intrepid* was no longer the pursuer; she was the pursued. Sleek and fast as the *Intrepid* was, she was slowed by the incomplete repair of the mainsail. The *Intrepid* was trapped. She could try to make a run west and hope that the Spaniards would not pursue further. During the storm and the pursuit of the pirates, the *Intrepid* had come within one hundred miles of the Spanish coast – far from her original cruise plan. In his desire to make a fight, Mr. North had neglected to take note of his position. England and Spain were not in the midst of a declared war, but an English warship so close to Spain was enough to justify an attack from the Spaniards. The pirates would simply be glad to seize the vessel for their own use. Those new cannon and provisions, not to mention the price that might be gotten for these sailors as seamen to be impressed into a foreign navy, made for great motivation for the pursuers. The fight was on.

Chapter 3

Mr. North decided to fight. The pirate vessel was now bearing down on the Intrepid, and Mr. North decided to close the distance quickly. He would engage the pirate ship as quickly as possible, believing that the Spaniards would only be interested in a fight after the pirates did some damage. Maybe the Spanish would not even move in on the action at all unless they saw that the *Intrepid* was in trouble. North felt that the Spaniards were opportunists, and may not be committed to bloodshed. Mr. North was committed to the fight; that was sure.

As the *Intrepid* sped toward the pirates, Mr. Pratt delivered the news to Mr. North that much of the powder had been fouled during the storm. The Intrepid would be going into the battle with only half her available amount of black powder. North did not flinch upon hearing the news. He almost seemed to welcome the adversity, perhaps to add to his legend after the battle that he had won despite a grievous handicap. Mr. North, to be sure, was not lacking in confidence, though I suspected he was lacking good sense at times. But North's confidence and decisiveness seemed to have a galvanizing effect on the crew. They seemed to share his confidence in a quick victory despite the circumstances.

"We are closing on them, Mr. North," yelled Conner from atop the mast. "It is a Dutch frigate with twenty-four guns."

North sent word to his gunners to fire a broadside as soon as they heard a musket fire. First Officer Swailes stood by North's side with a loaded musket. This served as the signal to fire, and was also a bit of protection for North if the fighting became close enough for small arms fire. In pirate fights, that was usually the case.

The pirates came close enough now that North could almost hear the clamor and shouting on their ship. As North had hoped, the Spaniards had not yet committed to the fight. They were drawing closer, but had not made a run on the *Intrepid*. If the *Intrepid* could knock out the pirates quickly and decisively, he may not have to face the Spaniards. He would not have enough powder to fight them in any case.

The musket shot rang out, and immediately the *Intrepid*'s gunners let loose with a broadside of eight cannon, followed seconds later by another eight shots. The sound of cracking timber split the air as the *Intrepid*'s gunners found their mark on the enemy ship's mast. Cursing could now be heard clearly from the pirate vessel as they scrambled to avoid the falling tower of sail. The pirate gunners were now firing their own broadside, and cannon balls whistled through the air. The *Intrepid's* gunners continued their fire as Mr. North led the ship away from the pirate vessel's approach. Taking advantage of the *Intrepid's* easier maneuverability, Mr. North pulled the *Intrepid* away from the enemy ship and lined up his starboard side on the stern of the pirates. The pirate ship, disabled by the first burst of fire, which had split the mast, had trouble responding to the *Intrepid's* move. The *Intrepid's* gunners continued their murderous fire on the floundering enemy. Cannon balls raked the stern of the pirate ship, smashing through the rigging of the mizzenmast. The enemy, now reeling, could not maneuver enough to turn for a good shot at the *Intrepid*.

Mr. North burned in his soul to finish off the despised enemy ship, which lay helpless before him, but he turned the *Intrepid* quickly to the north, hoping to avoid the Spanish ships that lurked nearby. He knew that an engagement with them would be a disaster given the *Intrepid's* powder shortage.

As Mr. North had hoped, the Spanish ships did not pursue. Perhaps they were intimidated by the quick work the *Intrepid* made of the hapless pirates. More likely, it was as North had suspected – the Spanish were only interested in a fight already won, or one with a very disabled opponent. Neither situation being the case, the Spaniards turned east, presumably heading toward home. The helpless pirate ship, now drifting aimlessly, was left to its own fate, a fitting conclusion to its voyage.

I went below to tend to the wounded. Captain Braden seemed to be sleeping peacefully. I was encouraged by this, feeling that his death might be without the misery usually attendant with the plague. As I walked by the Captain I saw two gunners dragging in one of their companions. The poor fellow was bleeding heavily from his right leg. As I looked closer I saw a large piece of wood protruding from the blood-soaked leggings he wore. The most ghastly injuries of such naval encounters were just that – splinters of wood blasted from the ship flying into the bodies of helpless gunners.

As they lay him down, his friends begged me to save his leg.

"Gentlemen," I said, "I will be most fortunate to be able to save his life. He will be lucky if he leaves this ship with one leg."

The victim was delirious with pain. The splinter of wood was deep in his thigh, probably not through to the back of his leg, but close, I suspected. I asked the steward to fetch a large draught of rum for the wounded man, Mr. Kelley. Sean Kelley was a fairly large man, an experienced sailor despite his relative youth. I suspected him to be in his early thirties. Kelley was thirsty from the loss of blood, and he drank deeply from the cup offered to him. As I waited for the rum to start its numbing work I heard Dr. Shepherd call out to me.

"Dr. Greene, if I may be of some help," he said.

"Yes, Dr. Shepherd," I said, "I could use some help holding him down, but in your weakened condition, I suspect you could be of more use to me in assisting me with a knife on that leg."

Some of the crew asked why I called the stranger Shepherd "Dr. Shepherd."

"He is a doctor by training," I replied, "and if he can be of help to your mate, I want him to help."

"He better be good, or we can throw him back into his little boat!" snorted Kent.

"Maybe that's why he was thrown off the other ship!" said Mr. Merck.

"Before you use the knife, I think it would be good to use this approach I have used before in such cases," Shepherd said. Shepherd took a length of cord and proceeded to tie it around Kelley's thigh, above the site of the dreadful injury. Kelley screamed in pain.

"Get him off of me!" Kelley screamed.

Before I could respond, Shepherd said, "I know it hurts terribly, but this will save your life."

Kelley looked at me, expecting me to stop the odd procedure.

"Give him more rum," I ordered, "and give him a cloth to bite on."

Kelley gobbled another large draught of rum, and was then given a thick towel to bite down on. Slowly he settled down on the pallet. Perhaps the rum was starting to work or the pain and loss of blood was getting to him.

I was puzzled by the work Shepherd was doing. Not only did he tighten the cord by hand, he had a stick to help twist the cord very tightly on Kelley's leg. I noticed that the blood flow had stopped as I stripped away Kelley's leggings. I poured water over the wound to clear away the blood, and I saw the depth of the wood in the wound. I told Shepherd that I was preparing to remove the wood, but he stopped me.

"Dr. Greene," he said calmly, "I believe that leaving it in a bit longer might be good. It is helping to stop the bleeding by being in place. It will also help if we pour rum into the wound. It will help to keep it clean."

The men standing by us began to react to this odd suggestion by Mr. Shepherd.

"You are going to pour rum on this man?" they said in disbelief. "Get the splinter out of his leg. That will help him!" they screamed.

"Dr. Greene, who is the surgeon on this ship, you or this madman we picked up?" said Mr. Kent. "Get Captain North," Kent yelled. "He will put a stop to this nonsense!"

I was fascinated with the results I was seeing from Mr. Shepherd's actions. I also believed that Mr. Kent and the others were less interested in maintaining my authority as ship's surgeon than in seeing Mr. Shepherd discredited and thrown off the ship.

15

"I will make the decisions about the medical care of this crew!" I said sternly to Kent. "And I do not need you or Mr. North to interfere. Dr. Shepherd is trying a new medical procedure which seems to be effective."

I really do not know why I defended the actions of Shepherd as actively as I did. I barely knew the man, and I certainly did not know of this procedure he was doing. But there was something about the demeanor of the man, his compassion toward people he did not know – indeed toward people who detested him – that I found engaging. So I found myself defending him at my own possible peril.

Kelley was more subdued now, and I decided to try to let him rest as the alcohol was taking effect. Surely I would need to remove this splinter of wood, which measured about nine inches long and almost two inches wide. The cut of my scalpel into the thick muscle of Kelley's thigh would require force, and it would require several men to hold him down, as the pain would break through the sedation of the alcohol.

It was then that Dr. Shepherd made another suggestion.

"Dr. Greene," he said, "may we have some privacy with Mr. Kelley? I fear that these men around us are a distraction."

Dr. Shepherd said this calmly and without anger, but the suggestion was met with great anger from the several men gathered around us. They had, of course, great interest in the welfare of Kelley, a fellow gunner and shipmate. He had apparently been the only casualty of the brief conflict with the pirate ship. His gunner's port had been hit by a pirate cannonball, which had sent splinters of wood flying. Mr. Kelley was the only unfortunate one to be hit and seriously wounded.

I agreed with Dr. Shepherd, even though I had usually wanted several men present in such situations to hold down the unfortunate patient for the inevitable surgery or procedure to be attempted.

"Mr. Kent," I called, "take these men to Mr. North to await his orders."

Kent glared and said, "Captain North had sent us to you to assist with Sean. I am just obeying orders."

"You can assist me best by leaving," I said.

"I will be telling Captain North about this," mumbled Kent. "God help this ship with a surgeon such as you."

"That will be all, Mr. Kent," I said.

The crew left with some reluctance, but they followed Kent's order to report to Mr. North. I turned to Dr. Shepherd and asked his reason for privacy, especially in light of the likelihood of the need for some strong men as assistants.

"I do not believe we will need men to hold him down," replied Shepherd. With that, he knelt directly over Kelley and looked into his eyes and began to speak to him, softly, almost melodically in tone. Shepherd put his hand in front of Kelley's face, and with his other hand put pressure on a spot

16

just below where he had tied the cord tightly around Kelley's leg. Kelley's eyes were fixed straight ahead and began to take a look of distance. He seemed oblivious to our presence almost, although he responded to questions from Shepherd – slowly and calmly.

"Dr. Greene, I think you may begin to remove the splinter from Mr. Kelley now. He will be calm, and he will not feel pain from your surgery."

As Shepherd said the words he seemed to be talking to Kelley and not to me. Kelley's lack of response to the idea of having his leg cut upon gave me the confidence to begin the surgery without men to hold him down. Dr. Shepherd continued to kneel above Kelley and to talk with him as I took out my scalpel and began to make an incision near the wood splinter. I worked quickly, cutting away as little muscle as I could in order to free the splinter. I was amazed to see how the muscle did not tighten around the splinter as I had seen in other cases such as this. In a few seconds I had secured enough space around the splinter to begin the ordeal of pulling it out of Kelley's leg. I gave a quick tug and the wood slid out. It was at this point that I feared that the pain would be unbearable, and that Kelley would violently jerk his leg away, causing damage to me as well as to himself. I removed the splinter cleanly, and with very little loss of blood, although blood poured forth upon the removal of the ghastly spike of wood. Dr. Shepherd advised that I pour more rum into the gaping hole in Kelley's thigh before I bandaged it. I did as Shepherd advised, and I bound the wound tightly. Shepherd then loosened the cord he had tied above the wound. Kelley's eyes were still fixed on Shepherd, and then he abruptly fell unconscious – from the pain, I presumed, even though he had not uttered a sound during the surgery.

I was almost too amazed to speak to Shepherd after Kelley passed out. "I have never seen anything like that in all my years as a surgeon! What did you do to Kelley to keep him quiet?" I demanded to know. "How could he endure this surgery without screaming in pain?"

"The mind is a powerful thing, Dr. Greene," he said. "There are times that a person can overcome physical pain."

Just then Mr. North burst into the infirmary and asked what was going on with Mr. Kelley.

"He appears to have survived the surgery well," I noted. With that I picked up the bloody, angry-looking spike of wood that I had removed from Kelley and showed it to North. "I removed this from his thigh with the assistance of Dr. Shepherd," I replied.

North mumbled his approval and asked if Kelley would lose his leg. North, too, had seen many such injuries, which had often resulted in loss of the limb.

"I do not yet know, sir," I said. "I will know better in the next day or two, but I trust that he will recover and keep the leg as well."

Mr. North left us to tend to our patient. As the thought of this amazing surgery began to sink into my mind, I began to have more concern over Captain Braden, my other patient. Certainly his condition was much more critical to the wellbeing of this crew than anyone suspected, and not just because he was the captain.

Chapter 4

Captain Braden seemed to be resting comfortably as I approached his bed in the infirmary. His neck seemed to be less swollen, and the purple patches on his body seemed to be smaller and less colorful. He looked even older than his years, and he was now near his sixties. Until this voyage he had kept his age well. Now his stubbled gray beard just made him look even more feeble. I spoke to the Captain, and he stirred somewhat upon hearing my voice.

"Captain Braden," I called, "can I get you some water?"

"Dr. Greene," he said, "what medicine did you give to me?"

"I gave you no medicine," I replied. Captain Braden looked at me quizzically.

"Well, it must have been a dream," he said. "I was floating on a large, beautiful ship, heading west toward a spectacular sunset. I could feel no more pain. In fact, I seemed to be as healthy as a child. I felt a tremendous sensation of warmth as we neared the horizon, but the sun did not set. The sun kept getting brighter and larger, becoming more brilliant. I was about to give the order to keep heading toward the sun to see what would happen when I heard someone give the order to turn about away from the sun. I tried to countermand the order, but I was unable to speak. I must have fallen asleep at that point, but I was filled with a feeling of warmth and peace like I have never felt. I did not awaken until I heard your voice."

I believed that the Captain had simply been in a fever-induced delirium, and I was glad to hear that he seemed to be calm and peaceful. Death by plague is an awful thing, and I felt that God must have given him this dream to calm him before such a horrible death. I then noticed that Captain Braden seemed cooler to the touch, and that his eyes appeared to be clearer. His breathing, while somewhat shallow, was steady and not really labored. In fact, I felt that he did not look like a man dying of the plague.

"Get some rest now captain," I advised. "You will have a ship to command in a few days."

Captain Braden replied, "Thank you for saving me, Dr. Greene. Whatever medicine you gave me saved me."

I smiled at the Captain and walked away. He was convinced that I had saved his life. Indeed, his life may have been saved, but not by my efforts.

I went to report the news of the Captain's turn for the better to Mr. North. North met me as I hastened on deck to tell him about the Captain.

19

"Dr. Greene," he began, "can you tell me what happened to Mr. Kelley? The men tell me that some very strange things happened while they were with you and Shepherd."

"Yes, I think that would be true to say," I replied. "I cannot explain all that happened during that surgery, but Mr. Kelley has benefited from the new techniques I saw demonstrated by Joseph Shepherd."

North flashed a look of anger as he asked, "Why does the ship's surgeon allow some stranger to assist in the surgery of a seaman on my ship?"

There was no mistaking his emphasis on the words "my ship." The *Intrepid* now apparently belonged to Mr. North.

"Mr. North" I said, rising to his anger, "may I remind you that surgery on this ship is under *my* command. I have no need to answer to you about how medical procedures are carried out on this ship!"

My bluster seemed to have taken North by surprise. He was not used to having someone under his command talk to him in such a manner. Indeed, I would not have done so had I not really believed that people like North must not be given the idea that they can dominate others by such intimidation. Mr. North had no business in medical affairs, and he needed to be so reminded. I believed at the same time that he would find a way to destroy me if he could. I was now entering dangerous ground. Further, I began to see that he would not welcome the news of the recovery of Captain Braden. North was convinced that the *Intrepid* was his ship, and the crew, after a victory, his also. God save us from those who would rather command than lead.

I left the top deck and went below to my quarters somewhat shaken from my encounter with Mr. North. As I was lost in my thoughts, Joseph Shepherd approached me.

"Dr. Greene" he said softly, "may I speak to you about Captain Braden?"

"Why, yes indeed," I said, "in fact, I meant to ask you about him. He appears to be improving. Can that be true?"

Shepherd looked at me and nodded.

"Yes," he replied, "not only can it be true, I believe it is true. Captain Braden is recovering. And he has the plague; I am convinced of it," he continued.

I had to sit down as I began to think about this latest turn of events. I had heard of people recovering from the plague, but I had never seen it before. I was again seeing a medical cure that I had not experienced before. Why was this happening? How was this happening?

"Mr. Shepherd," I said, "you have been a part of some amazing things aboard this ship in the past day. How do you explain it?"

Shepherd paused briefly and then replied, "There are many things that we do not know about healing and the human body. I have seen many things which have puzzled me over the years, and I have come to understand that I

20

will never know the answers. I have also come to see that the body can heal itself if given the chance. As physicians, we are only able to help the body to heal itself." Shepherd paused again and said, "I myself have been a witness to the fact that the body heals itself. I had all the symptoms of the plague, and I was near death at one time. I recovered, perhaps only by the grace of God, but I recovered."

"Is that why you were cast aside from your last ship?" I asked.

"Well, I do not know that, Dr. Greene," he said. "Perhaps," he mused. "Those memories are still a little hazy."

"I did not mean to pry," I apologized, "it just might explain some things."

No one else on board the *Intrepid* knew of the diagnosis of Captain Braden's plague except Shepherd and myself. Should he recover and be able to assume command of the *Intrepid* again, this whole amazing voyage could be concluded favorably. But I had not fully understood the depth of Mr. North's frenzy to command the *Intrepid*.

Mr. North bounded into my quarters and demanded to discuss the medical condition of Captain Braden.

"I am told," North said, "that Captain Braden is dying of the plague. Is that true?"

"No," I replied, "Captain Braden is not dying of the plague."

"Don't lie to me, Dr. Greene," North said, "I have been told that there were purple marks on him. He has the plague, and I will not have my whole ship die for one man, even if he is a Captain!"

"He is not dying," interrupted Shepherd.

"Throw *him* in irons!" said North. "I will have no more of this stranger's interference. All of our problems began with his appearance on this ship."

I stepped forward to defend Mr. Shepherd, but I was met by Mr. Kent and Mr. Dooley, who restrained me and gagged me. While Kent was a man of somewhat low intelligence, and low moral character as well, Dooley was a bit brighter, but strange in his thinking and actions. Dooley was one who the other sailors avoided. He believed himself to be special, gifted, and above the other sailors. Many of the sailors had told me that Dooley would talk to himself, grimace angrily for no reason, and threaten to kill anyone who looked directly at his face. Fortunately, most of the crew happily avoided looking into the contorted grimace of Mr. Dooley.

Shepherd was also attacked and thrown to the ground. He was immediately shackled and led away. This entire sordid event was planned by North and several crewmen who had now become thugs and brigands. The ship was being overcome with a very ugly mutiny led by Mr. North and a few of his closest commanders, and it appeared that no one could stem the tide. Mr.

North was now "Captain" North, and I feared that Captain Braden would be killed in the process of the mutiny – all in the name of saving the ship.

North was now working quickly. He ordered Mr. Kent and Mr. Pratt to take Captain Braden and set him adrift in a small boat with enough provisions for three days. He reasoned that the Captain would be dead in that period of time, but North would not be directly responsible for his death. The plague would do its ugly work out of the sight of the *Intrepid's* crew, and Mr. North could be the savior of the crew if the plague did not spread to the rest of the ship.

Pratt and Kent picked up Captain Braden who, though weak, was becoming more alert. North had ordered them to lift him into the same small boat that had been the rescue vessel of Joseph Shepherd. When Captain Braden realized that he was to be set adrift, he saw it as the act of mutiny it was. North had cautioned Pratt and Kent to do their deed quickly and quietly so as to not frighten the rest of the crew. He had explained that such a rumor would cause a riot. The sooner Braden was adrift, the better. There would be no debating or arguing over the order; it would simply be accomplished, his reason being the very safety of his men.

The rest of the *Intrepid's* crew was starting to realize that Mr. North was now in total command of the ship. Pratt and Kent had managed to load poor Captain Braden into the small craft that had served to save Joseph Shepherd. That same little boat would now be the last command of Captain Braden.

Mr. North gathered the crew of the *Intrepid* and informed them of the events of the past day. He proceeded to remind them of their glorious victory over the pirate vessel, and he told them of the mutinous behavior of the ship's surgeon and the newly arrived "Jonah," Joseph Shepherd. He told the crew of the strange behavior of Dr. Greene, who had allowed the stranger, Joseph Shepherd, to assist in the surgery of Seaman Kelley. North added that but for the intervention of himself, Seaman Kelley might not be alive today. Finally, he sadly told the tale of poor Captain Braden, who had indeed come down with the plague. He added that, because of the quick response of their new Captain, and the unselfishness of Captain Braden, who had given his last order to have himself set adrift to protect the crew of the *Intrepid*, the ship was now safe and on its way back to England.

The crew let out a thunderous cheer for "Captain" North. Mr. Shepherd and I were now companions in the brig, bound and gagged, and awaiting transfer to England where we would undoubtedly be hanged as mutineers. While I was pondering the unfairness of my plight, Shepherd appeared to be calm. I started to feel ashamed of my own self-pity when I began to consider what Shepherd had gone through in the space of the past several days. He had been set adrift himself, suffering from exposure and various wounds. He had been instrumental in ministering to Captain Braden

22

and Seaman Kelley, and found himself labeled as a "Jonah," awaiting his death in England. He had done no wrong on this ship, yet he was awaiting a criminal's death. Shepherd had said that he believed in God, but no God I could think of would allow such suffering for having only done good.

The next few days were very uncomfortable. We were allowed to have the gags removed only to eat. Two seamen were assigned to feed us and to accompany us to toilet. We were strictly forbidden to talk. When we did speak we were cuffed in the mouth with the back of a rough seaman's hand. We were told that the next infraction would end in a flogging.

The brig was damp and dark, and we lost track of time. I was cramping due to the rough confinement of the shackles, and I found myself hearing and seeing things which were both frightening and beautiful. I was near complete breakdown within the first three days of this confinement. If Shepherd were experiencing the same things as I, one could not tell it. He appeared to be lost in thought much of the time, but his eyes were not as frantic and full of fear as mine must have been. His calm demeanor amazed me.

It must have been about the fourth day of confinement that Mr. Kent came to see us. "Greene," he barked roughly, "I am going to take that gag out of your mouth and I am going to take your shackles off. If you say one word that I don't like, or Captain North don't like, I'll have you flogged."

I nodded that I understood and he began to loosen the shackles and he removed the gag.

"Why are you setting me free?" I asked.

"You ain't free. You're still a prisoner who started a mutiny. I'm taking you to see Captain North, and you better keep that tongue of yours respectful to him!"

My heart raced as I was taken to see North. He held my life in his evil hands, and he could easily find a reason to have me set adrift or hanged, just as he had treated Captain Braden. He had no reason that I could see to keep me alive, especially since he knew that I knew the truth.

"Dr. Greene," North began, "sit down over here." He beckoned for me to sit next to him. "Dr. Greene, you were treating Captain Braden for the plague – I know that. You lied to me when you said he was not dying of the plague, didn't you?"

"No, Mr. North, I..."

"Captain North," he interrupted. "I am Captain of His Majesty's Ship *Intrepid*."

"No, Mr. North," I said, "I was not lying to you. Yes, Captain Braden had the plague, but he was not dying. He was starting to recover when you had him set adrift."

"How do you know that?" he asked sharply. "He looked very sick to me – like I've seen men before, ready to die of the plague."

I was now again getting angry at the insolence of this pompous windbag. I began to get flushed, and I tried to calm the rage that had been building the past few days.

"Mr. North, I can tell, too, when a man is about to die. I have seen more dying men than you have, and Captain Braden was going to live until you set him out to die!"

North did not respond as I thought he might. I figured that he might have me flogged for my own insolence, but he softened as I finished my accusation of him.

"Dr. Greene," he said, "I have two men who are sick, and I think that they have the plague. That is why I called you up here. I need you to examine them and see if it is the plague."

I sank in my chair. Mr. Shepherd and I had feared that this might happen, hoping against hope that Captain Braden's case was isolated.

"Yes," I responded, "of course I will examine them. But I will only do so if you also free Mr. Shepherd."

I could hardly believe that I had said such a thing. I was duty-bound to treat those seamen whether or not Mr. Shepherd were freed, yet I somehow made that a bargaining point to North. Perhaps when in the presence of evil, I responded in kind. Perhaps I was still not thinking clearly after my days of confinement.

North looked at me and said calmly, "Can he be of help to you?"

"Yes," I said, "he is a physician of the first order. I have already learned from him."

"Then he will be allowed to assist you," North said. "But if you begin to say anything that could incite a mutiny, I'll throw you overboard myself."

North said this almost matter-of-factly, with little discernible anger. He seemed to be shaken by the idea of plague on his ship, and all he wanted was medical help. He seemed to acknowledge the risk of having Shepherd and me about on the ship and in contact with the crew, but he also made it clear that he would have us killed if he felt it necessary.

Chapter 5

Captain Braden had been afloat for almost four days when an English merchant ship came upon his tiny craft. Braden was quite ill when he was spotted by the *Elizabeth*, a ship owned by the British East India Company on her way back from a journey to Italy. The *Elizabeth* was laden with wine and olive oil, but more fortunate for Captain Braden was the fact that the *Elizabeth* also carried a passenger who was returning from a scholarly mission to Padua where he had been studying with Italian scientists, (heretofore usually called natural philosophers) about anatomy and the properties of human blood. William Harvey had always had an interest in medicine, and he was excited about the latest discoveries, which were leading him to radical (and unpopular) ideas about anatomy.

As the *Elizabeth* came upon Braden's boat, the crew saw that he was an English Captain. Braden was too weak to call out for help, but he managed to wave to the approaching *Elizabeth*. The crew of the *Elizabeth* was not used to seeing such a sight as a small boat floating on the calm waters off the coast of Spain. Word quickly spread through the *Elizabeth* that a small boat with one survivor had been spotted. Rumors of this man being the lone survivor of a shipwreck quickly spread through the ship. As Captain Braden was helped aboard the *Elizabeth* he was very weak. He was taken to the quarters below deck and William Harvey was asked to examine him.

Captain Braden was able to relate to William Harvey that he had not been part of a shipwreck, but that he was Captain of the *HMS Intrepid*, and that he had been deposed in a mutiny. As Harvey continued his examination of Captain Braden he noticed some faint splotches of purple on his thighs. He also noted that Braden had some swelling in his neck and armpits. Harvey had some suspicions about these symptoms, but he was more concerned over the fact that Braden was weak, pale and dehydrated.

"He will need rest," said Harvey. "He cannot be subjected to interrogation about his current state of affairs."

Harvey felt that his patient would be able to relate his tale of woe in good time, but a stream of inquisitors would be of great harm at this time. Besides, he was not so sure that people should be exposed to this man with an unknown illness. All the while, he pondered the symptoms he saw in the curious survivor.

On the *Intrepid*, Dr. Shepherd and I began to examine the men who had started to show symptoms of illness. As we approached the suffering sailors my heart sank. The plague had indeed been visited upon the *Intrepid*. I began to believe that this ship truly was cursed, and that God had somehow singled us out for destruction of the fiercest type. Any of the men on the ship would much rather die in battle than die the horrible death of the invisible plague. Yet, these men would have no chance for battle. They would die gasping for breath, their skin having turned almost black, and their bodies covered with terrible purple buboes. Worse still, the rest of the crew would panic, and general disorder would rule this renegade vessel until the entire ship became a ghost ship.

As my mind raced far ahead to this terrible scenario, Mr. Shepherd turned to me and asked how I would treat these men. I had seen people bled as treatment for the plague, but I had never seen much success from it. Perhaps it hurried death for them, so, in an odd way, it helped them to cheat the awful Black Death. I had also seen mercury compounds used, but also to little avail. Supportive measures which helped to comfort the patient seemed to have, at best, a palliative effect.

"I have several ideas, Dr. Shepherd, but no answers," I replied honestly. Shepherd then began to tell me of the way he had treated Captain Braden. Not treated, really, but how he had ministered to him. Shepherd said that Captain Braden was a religious man, and that, as he believed he was near death, he asked to have someone administer communion to him. No one else being present, Shepherd had taken it upon himself to give "communion" to Captain Braden. Shepherd reported that he had just fed the Captain some of the stale, moldy bread, and that he used the same bread as "communion elements," along with a cup of rum. While these were no ordinary communion elements that I had ever heard of, it had given comfort to a dying man. If communion were of any value or not, I do not know, but there is value in making death more peaceful.

"Are you suggesting that we give a religious service, Mr. Shepherd?" I asked whimsically.

"No," said Shepherd. "I scarcely think that religion is very well known on this ship. But I do suggest that we use the bread to feed to the sick crew. Who knows but that some healing may have come to Captain Braden from it? Besides, we have no real treatment other than the supportive measures you had suggested."

Shepherd was correct about the sorry state we were in.

"Well, Dr. Shepherd," I said, "let us give them your bread."

Shepherd went to fetch the remaining bread left in his pouch. It was covered with mold – most unpleasant to look at. As Shepherd removed the last part of the loaf from his pouch, he broke it and said some sort of prayer. He then went to each man who was sick, and fed him a bit of the bread. He also

26

gave them a bit of rum, duplicating the methods he used with Captain Braden. The men were weak and desperate, and they did not question this odd medical care. They ate and then seemed to slip off into a coma.

"Their fate, and ours, now seems to be in the hands of your God," I said to Shepherd.

"That is all we can ever hope for," replied Shepherd.

Captain North was feeling uncomfortable with the latest turn of events. He knew that plague was on his ship, and if word got out among the rest of the crew, he might not be able to retain control. He wanted to make for the nearest port, and he needed to do that while his crew remained healthy. He decided to sail immediately toward Plymouth. He figured that with good weather, he could reach port in less than two weeks, perhaps ten days.

On the *Elizabeth,* Captain Braden was slowly recovering. The commander of the *Elizabeth,* Edwin Carr, asked to speak to Captain Braden to inquire about his story. Mutinies on English warships were unsettling for merchant seamen. They depended on English rule of the seas, and anything that eroded this mastery posed a threat. Was this Braden a fraud? Or was he such a poor leader that he was dumped by his crew? What leads sailors to do such a thing? Discipline on a ship is imperative, and Carr wanted to know exactly what had happened.

Captain Braden relayed his story. He explained his illness, his care by Dr. Greene and the stranger Joseph Shepherd, and the encounter with the pirates off La Coruna's coast in Spain. He was not at all sure of the details of that attack, but he knew that the *Intrepid* had repulsed them. Carr was most interested in the thing Braden knew least about – the existence of pirates near where he would be sailing in the coming week.

William Harvey was interested in Braden for another reason. He believed that Captain Braden had the bubonic plague, yet he appeared to be gaining strength, not dying. Harvey asked Braden about his treatment.

"I know very little about how I was treated," said Braden, "only that I was treated with great kindness. I remember eating some stale bread, moldy bread. Moldy bread and rum. That is all I remember before being set adrift by Mr. North – the scoundrel!"

"So was there plague on your ship?" asked Harvey.

"Plague!" said Braden. "You think I have the plague?"

Braden knew that the plague had ravaged London in 1606, the last major outbreak in England. He knew nothing of the plague on his ship.

"I don't know, Captain," said Harvey, "but I see some signs in your body of the disease. Strangely, though, you seem to be recovering, and I was interested in what type of treatment you received."

Harvey went to Captain Edwin Carr to inform him of his observations. He cautioned Carr to isolate Captain Braden until he could see the progress of

27

his disease. No need to expose the rest of the crew to disease just because they had been good Samaritans.

Joseph Shepherd and I were concerned about our patients. We believed that other sailors may be stricken, and we anxiously awaited the response of the men we had "treated" with such odd methods. Within two days we had our response. The men we had treated were rousing out of their lethargy. Fevers were down, swelling was down, and they asked for something to eat. They too were recovering!

I asked Mr. Shepherd about the treatment.

"Tell me, my good Dr. Shepherd, how did you learn of this treatment? It is nothing short of a miracle! Indeed, moldy bread and rum. Sailors eat that often at sea. Imagine that healing people of a dread disease."

Shepherd responded by saying, "Dr. Greene, don't you recall stories in the Bible about Jesus using his own spittle to restore sight to the blind? Sometimes the most common of elements can be used in uncommon ways. God can use anything for his purpose, even a talking ass to Balaam, lamps to Gideon…"

"Enough, enough!" I said to Shepherd, smiling. "I suppose you could give me many examples from the Bible. You obviously know much more of that book than I."

"I did not mean to belittle you," said Shepherd. "I simply meant to say that God heals; we simply provide our hands to Him."

"Perhaps God can tell us how we can save ourselves in the coming days," I countered, a bit irritated with the talk of God.

Honestly, Mr. Shepherd spoke like he knew God personally. This was more than a little disconcerting to me, and it would be of no help at all with a tyrant like Mr. North. North would only keep us alive as long as he believed that we could keep his crew healthy. Long enough to reach Plymouth – that was all he needed.

As I was talking to Mr. Shepherd, Seaman Kelley came limping into our quarters. He looked remarkably well considering his injuries in the past week. Often, sailors with such injuries survive the initial injury only to succumb to killing infections within a few days.

"Mr. Kelley," I hailed him, "you look well."

"Well?" he said. "My leg hurts like hell's fire!"

"Mr. Kelley," I chided, "you are then fortunate to feel hell's fire while still alive. Many sailors with your injury face life with one leg, then find hell itself after infection kills them. Perhaps," I added, "you could thank the good Dr. Shepherd for your life *and* your limb!"

"I beg your pardon, Dr. Greene," he said. "You and Shepherd done your jobs with me, didn't you?"

"Yes, Mr. Kelley, we did our jobs."

28

Chapter 6

William Harvey was a man becoming known in scientific circles in Europe. He was studying the heart and blood, and challenging medical principles that had been accepted since Galen. Harvey was not one to shy away from criticism, and he did know how to play the political and power games so necessary for support of scientific pursuits. His brilliance was unquestioned, and he was also adept at winning friends, quite a profound combination of talents.

"Captain Braden," began Harvey, "how are you getting along today?"

"I feel much better, Doctor," said Braden. At this point, he was nearly back to his normal vigor. Harvey looked again at the purple splotches, which had almost completely disappeared. Harvey was sure that this man had suffered from plague, and he was also sure that he was recovering.

"Amazing," breathed Harvey, nearly inaudibly. "Captain Braden, you are one fortunate man. Whatever treatment you received is far above any medical procedure I know of short of a pure miracle."

"It was a miracle, Doctor," said Braden. "It was."

Still, Harvey did not want Braden exposed to the other passengers on the *Elizabeth,* so he told Captain Carr to continue the isolation. At the same time, Harvey told Carr that he could speak further with Braden to gather whatever information might be important to help the *Elizabeth* in her final leg home to England. Braden could offer only the sketchiest information to Carr about the location of the encounter with the pirates, but it was sufficient for Carr to help plot a course that could keep the *Elizabeth* clear of trouble.

Mr. North was confiding to Mr. Ross that he was glad the pirate victory was behind him. At this point, he was short on powder, had a damaged mainsail, and considered the possibility that plague was still on his ship. The sooner he reached Plymouth, the better he would feel. Besides, he could now return as a victorious ship captain. He would relate that Captain Braden had died of illness while on the cruise. His crew better damned well back up that story, and as for Shepherd and me, well, we could turn up dead too, as far as he figured.

Just as he was turning over in his mind how this all could play out, Mr. Crowell, the lookout, barked, "Pirate ship to starboard!"

"Another pirate ship?" screamed North.

"Are you sure it isn't a Spaniard?" North barked to Crowell.

"She flies nothing but a black flag!" screamed Crowell. North was puzzled, but began to be resigned to another fight.

The second pirate ship had evidently been lurking near the first fray, unseen by the *Intrepid* in the excitement of the moment. The privateer probably had seen that the *Intrepid* had put forth a small boat some days earlier, and they may have surmised that this could mean mutiny. Mutinous ships made nice prey, since they could fold at the first sign of a real fight. At any rate, these pirates from North Africa were daring opportunists. They were willing to engage any ship that they believed could be in any way crippled. They had not failed to notice that the *Intrepid*'s crew was continuing to work on a mainsail, which never seemed to fully unfurl.

The pirates began to close on the *Intrepid*, and North did not hesitate to respond.

"Make ready to fight," he screamed. Immediately, sailors began to race to the cannons, while others started to secure powder and shot from below. The sun was low on the horizon, and the setting sun silhouetted the *Intrepid*. The pirates were now closing fast, less than a thousand yards away. The pirate ship was a captured English ship, the *Bristol*, smaller than the *Intrepid*, but faster than the now crippled *Intrepid*. North believed that the pirates would not attack into a broadside blast, but would drift to the rear of the *Intrepid* to pursue for boarding. North chose to use his slowed speed capability to his advantage. He ordered the sails tacked to slow the *Intrepid*, maintaining his starboard to the pirates as long as possible as they tried to creep behind his crippled vessel. He would, by God, get at least one broadside volley into the teeth of the pirates.

As the *Intrepid* slowed, the pirates found themselves closing too quickly on their prey. As the pirates steered to the south to get behind the *Intrepid*, they were going to be, for a brief time, starboard to starboard, the *Intrepid* facing north, the *Bristol* south. Just as the pirates started the turn south, North knew he had a window of opportunity. He ordered his men to fire when they heard his pistol shot.

The pirates drew closer, and as they made the anticipated turn, North fired his pistol. The *Intrepid*'s entire starboard side erupted in fire as cannons discharged. The pirates were raked with a deadly volley of heavy shot. Screams could be heard as splintered wood flew into the air. Cursing pirates swore withering oaths at the *Intrepid*'s crew. The jib mast of the pirate ship cracked as it received a direct hit. The pirate captain apparently was undaunted by this first volley. He assessed the damage, and he found no other sail damage, some damage to the front deck, and the loss of four crewmen. The distance between the ships had saved the pirates. The pirate captain may also have realized that he was still vulnerable to another volley. Despite the distance, now about eight hundred yards, he ordered his men to fire a starboard volley of their own.

The pirate guns let loose with a roar. Inferior cannons on the *Bristol* yielded no hits on the Intrepid as the shots mostly fell harmlessly short. The *Intrepid* was now turning east, exposing another starboard approach to the *Bristol*, which was now running with its aft facing the *Intrepid*. Another volley of cannon fire belched from the *Intrepid*, but now from even closer range. Shots whistled past the *Bristol*, which had been outflanked by the *Intrepid*. Two cannon shots found their mark on the *Bristol* with devastating effect. The rear cabins, exposed to the murderous fire, caved in. A gaping hole in the *Bristol*, framed by shattered windows and shards of wood, stared at the *Intrepid*. As the *Bristol* made no turn to return fire, Mr. North assessed his situation.

The *Intrepid* had sustained no damage in the brief exchange, but she was low on powder. The earlier failure to secure the kegs below deck would now cause North to disengage from a fight he could easily win. His bluff of letting everything loose on two broadsides belied his low stock of powder and shot. The *Intrepid* had never been outfitted to fight on this maiden voyage. She was only to test out the equipment. She had surely done that under very trying circumstances, but she was not prepared for two extended battles.

At the very moment of likely triumph, North gave the command to break off the fight and head north. The pirates, not sure of the *Intrepid*'s motives, nonetheless chose to continue south. Pirates generally did not prefer a fair fight with a healthy enemy. They much preferred trader ships, which could not put up a fight. A few well-placed shots by the *Intrepid* had convinced the pirates to seek easier prey. The *Bristol* continued to limp south, wounded by a superior enemy.

As the *Intrepid* proceeded north, Mr. Shepherd and I discussed the brief but powerful encounter we had just witnessed from below deck.

"Dr. Shepherd," I said, "Mr. North is a savage scoundrel, but he is a fine fighting commander, I'll give him that."

"Yes," said Shepherd, "he has a gift of battle strategy. Too bad that talent is wasted on a man who cannot fully appreciate it."

Chapter 7

The *Elizabeth* was now heading northwest, having long passed the straits of Gibraltar, under full sail and perfect weather. She was making excellent time, about seven knots. At this rate, the *Elizabeth* would be on course to reach Plymouth about three days after the *Intrepid.* Both ships were headed there, but for very different reasons.

Mr. North was hoping to reach port quickly to repair and re-provision the *Intrepid*. Given his triumphs over the pirates, he believed that he would retain command over the *Intrepid*. Captain Braden, poor devil, was probably dead by now. North's crew would be loyal to him after having seen him in action. North believed that he could come back after those pirates with a repaired fighting ship, and he would surely bring glory to himself, and prizes to his men. He cared very little for England's interests, but if he prospered, he didn't care if it helped the English cause in Europe either. That would be nice for England, but that was not his highest concern.

Captain Carr was interested in bringing his cargo home safely. The faster he got his ship home, the faster he was paid. He also did not relish the thought of having to fight his way past the Spanish coast. He had planned to alter his course slightly west to avoid the Spanish coast after having heard of the presence of pirates. He also was considering the possibilities of finding the *Intrepid.* What would one find if he happened to encounter that ship? The crew of the *Intrepid* had set their captain adrift. It could have been for fear of the plague, or perhaps the crew had simply mutinied and had set the captain adrift rather than kill him. Maybe they didn't even know he had a disease, or maybe he developed it after he was adrift. Maybe he didn't even have the plague.

Carr pondered these thoughts as evening slowly exchanged places with the setting sun. The *Elizabeth* was now heading due west into the setting sun, taking advantage of a change in winds. The beauty of it was startling on this evening. Orange and purple hues enveloped wisps of clouds. This evening would be calm and pleasant.

"Better enjoy it now," thought Carr, "for next week may bring trouble."

"Captain Carr!" hailed William Harvey, "I have some good news."

Carr turned and inquired of Harvey his good fortune.

"I am confident that Captain Braden is fully recovered of his illness. Based upon such recovery, I rather doubt he had the plague. He probably had some other illness which mimicked the plague," Harvey concluded.

"That is good news!" responded Carr. "I trust that Captain Braden can join me tomorrow at the helm to discuss our voyage home. He may be of help in navigating by the pirates he spoke of."

Harvey agreed. "Yes, I think he would be most happy to join you. He probably wants to get back to sailing as soon as possible."

On the *Intrepid*, Dr. Shepherd was asking if we could check the rest of the crew for signs of plague.

"Dr. Shepherd," I countered, "I think the ones with symptoms will be coming to us if it still persists on this ship."

"Perhaps you are right, Dr. Greene," said Shepherd. "I suppose that if there is no more sickness on board, we may be of no further use to Mr. North. I also believe that if we are of no further use, we too shall be set adrift...or worse."

I had to agree with Shepherd on this point, painful as it was to face. We would be a liability to North's story about Captain Braden. The crew was solidly behind North, if for no other reason than that they feared him. Truth was, many of the crew actually were willing to follow his leadership. Wherever North was, action would follow. Many of this crew wanted just that – action of any type. While there were several veterans, many were very young, sixteen and seventeen years old, some of them. Adventure was getting into their blood, and a few more battles would seal them forever as fighting sailors who would need that fighting to feel alive. North could provide that for them, because that was who he was, and that was all he knew.

"What do you suggest?" I asked Shepherd.

"I suggest that we pray," Shepherd said calmly. I was not a praying man, and I thought that we should do something a bit more helpful, hatch some plan to escape perhaps.

"Pray?" I repeated. "You go right ahead, Mr. Shepherd, you pray. I will try to find a sailor or two who might be inclined to help us," I said sarcastically.

"Then that is what I shall pray for," said Shepherd, "a sailor or two who might help us."

With that he smiled and turned over in his straw bed.

"Imagine that," I thought. "Sailors on this ship who will want to help Shepherd and me!" I laughed at the thought. Joseph Shepherd was still thought to be a Jonah, maybe even a madman. His unusual ideas, his calm in the face of storms, his confidence that was seen as arrogance – none of those attributes had won him a friend – except for me. I was his friend. I had come to respect his intellect and medical knowledge. It was beyond me, and I knew it. His willingness to help those who had tried to harm him was truly an amazing thing. Yes, I liked this man, but I could not imagine anyone else on this ship who might do anything to help him. Actually, my own insolence toward this uneducated, superstitious group of bounders and thieves had not won me many friends among them either. Up until this very moment, I had not really cared. Now, my life could be in this group's hands. Yes, Dr. Shepherd, may God help us!

Chapter 8

The sea was beginning to get a little rough as the weather turned quickly. It appeared that another storm had popped up – nothing unusual for late July, but such storms cause sailors to act in strange ways. The men aboard the *Intrepid* reacted quickly to the rising wind and waves. They trimmed the sails to minimize damage, and they began to lash down everything on deck that moved. As the rains began to pelt the ship, winds tossed her about the waves. Between curses and oaths, some again remembered the presence of Joseph Shepherd, who had brought no luck at all, save his uncanny knowledge of the medical arts. Some of the sailors began to accuse Shepherd of using the power of the devil. He did not practice medical arts, they surmised, he practiced the black arts of Satan himself. The storm was raging now, so there was no time to worry about Joseph Shepherd. Let him and Dr. Greene rot below, they probably figured.

This storm seemed particularly cruel. Rain was coming down in sheets, bent sideways by the wind. The ropes on the masts were singing with the wind, and the ship was pitching wildly. Lightning was piercing the sky in every direction, and the moon, which had previously been the sky's light, was now obscured by storm clouds. As the *Intrepid* was pitching in the sea, one of the lightning bolts struck the already damaged main mast, splitting it from top to bottom. The sound of the splitting wood and the sight of the blue and orange flames shook the crew. Panic spread through even the toughest of sailors, and they huddled below deck, tossed by the storm. Fear is usually masked by anger in such men, so the rage turned to anyone available.

Joseph Shepherd once again became the target of their wrath. Bouncing in the lower deck of the ship, Mr. Kent began to berate Shepherd.

"We've had nothing but disaster since we took on Shepherd," began Kent. Others joined in the railing. People have a need to find reasons for their misfortune, and Mr. Shepherd was an easy target. A foreigner, not prone to fit in with the coarseness of the crew, Shepherd did not even try to raise his voice in his own defense. Instead, he looked aside and fixed his gaze away from the gathering din of discontent. Several of the men took this as arrogance, and became even more enraged.

"Thinks he's better than us, he does," said Kent. Others followed, and I began to sense that they might take him up to the deck and push him overboard. The only thing that may have prevented this was the continued rolling of the ship, which restricted much of the possibility of upright movement at the moment.

Suddenly, Mr. Kent lunged at Shepherd with a knife. Before anyone could make a response, Kent was on Dr. Shepherd, and he plunged the knife into Shepherd's side. Shepherd made no attempt to move away as Kent came at him again. As Kent drew back for another attack, the ship heaved violently, throwing Kent backwards into a barrel of black powder. Kent seemed to bend in half at the waist as his lower back crashed with a sickening thud on the barrel rim. I heard his spine crack as he let out a muted scream. The knife fell from his hand, and a muffled groan followed. As I got over to him, I saw his eyes rolling back in his head. He could barely breathe for the pain he was suffering. While I was getting ready to offer some assistance, I saw someone pick up the knife and drive it into Kent's neck. Blood squirted all over me, and covered those who had gotten near to Kent. He was dead in seconds. I looked up to see Mr. Kelley kneeling over Kent with a knife dripping blood.

"He was a dead man anyway," said Kelley. "I just moved it along a little quicker, saved him the pain."

Sailors were quieted by this grisly scene, and attention was no longer on Joseph Shepherd. Shepherd was now my main concern. It looked as if the wound he received was not as deep as I had feared. It appeared that Mr. Kent had missed his aim because of the rolling ship, and he had delivered a glancing blow to Shepherd. The knife skimmed off one of Shepherd's ribs, opening his side but leaving no serious damage.

Kelley had made a show of ending Kent's suffering with his swift stab to Kent's neck, but I thought it to be something different. I believed that Mr. Kelley was just returning a favor to Dr. Shepherd, and Kent was the recipient of some seagoing justice, swift and sure.

Mr. North came bounding down to the mob of sailors. He saw blood pouring out of Mr. Kent and a group of rather quiet sailors.

"What happened here!" he shouted.

"Attempted murder," I said more softly than I had expected given my excited state.

"Looks like actual murder to me, Dr. Greene," countered North.

"Mr. Kent went after Joseph Shepherd," I said, "and he paid the price for doing so."

"Well then," said North, "who killed Mr. Kent?"

"Actually, I believe that Mr. Kent was close to death when Mr. Kelley took compassion on him and finished the deed," I said. While I did not believe that to be quite so true, I did not want Mr. Kelley hanged for taking the life of worthless scum like Kent.

As the conversation continued, we heard a heavy crash on the deck. The remainder of the main mast finally succumbed to the wind and crashed down into the ship. Water poured in, the mast fell onto two sailors, and confusion ruled the hour. The ship was reeling about in the heavy seas, and I was convinced that we could not take much more pounding from this storm. If the storm did not abate soon, we were doomed.

Joseph Shepherd, bleeding from his wound, began to speak to the men assembled in the chaos of the lower deck.

"This storm will pass soon," he said calmly. "You need not fear."

With that he raised his arms and appeared to be speaking, maybe even praying. His white shirt now drenched in blood, he looked gruesome and tortured, yet strangely calm and in control. He stood amidst the rocking of the ship and was able to maintain his balance. Soon, the wind died down, and the squall passed. The hole in the deck where the mast had crashed through now gave us a view of the heavens, which were filled with stars. The black clouds were gone and calm was restored.

"Don't be telling me that the storm calmed just because he prayed," said Mr. North.

"I don't know why the storm calmed," I said. "Let us just be glad it is over."

The rest of the men slowly returned to their duties, the first of which was to extricate the bodies of seamen David and Michael Clark, who had been crushed by the mast. They were twin brothers, just seventeen years old. They had signed on to the ship together, and they died together in her service. Some of the men saw this as another omen of ill fate for the *Intrepid*. They had believed it to be bad luck to have twins on the ship. This was proof enough for them that God was punishing them for the foolishness of allowing twins to serve on the ship.

I began to tend to Joseph Shepherd, wrapping his side tightly with clean strips of bandage.

"Dr. Shepherd," I whispered, "do you believe that your prayers really calmed this storm?" I could hardly believe that I was even asking the question.

Shepherd answered, "I have no special powers, if that is what you are asking. I simply trust in the Father, and He supplies our needs. You decide if it was an answered prayer. I am also certain that I was not the only one praying a few moments ago," he smiled.

I had to agree with that statement, because even this unbeliever was crying to God in that situation.

Chapter 9

The sun rose brilliantly beside the *Elizabeth* on her starboard side as she began to turn north again. The open Atlantic spread before them, and this turn caused some discussion on board the *Elizabeth*. The Spanish had grown wealthy with New World plunder, and Captain Carr began to speak with Captain Braden about his encounters with the Spanish.

"The Spaniards," began Braden, "are a greedy lot. I have heard stories of how they stole gold from the people they found in the New World, then simply murdered them. I think they baptized them first to be sure that they would go to heaven, then they sent them on their way there pretty quickly."

Braden spoke like a veteran of Spanish wars. He hated the Spaniards, their greed, their religion, their sense of superiority.

"Well," said Captain Carr, "I do not care one way or another about the Spanish as long as they leave my ship alone. Do you think that they are using pirates to raid commercial ships such as ours?"

Braden hesitated, then replied, "No, I do not think that the Spanish are really enlisting pirates to raid shipping. Pirates may well be preying on some ships, they always have, but the Spanish are too arrogant to use the pirates that way. And most pirates do not want any connection with any civilized government, not that I consider the Spanish civilized."

Carr pushed further. "Wasn't the *Intrepid* attacked by pirates, and didn't you say that Spanish ships were nearby?"

Braden replied, "If a pirate ship engaged the *Elizabeth*, and Spanish vessels were nearby, they would do nothing to help or hinder the action. As far as they care, one less load of cargo to England probably helps the Spaniards. But the Spanish fleet does not care to tangle with England again. Your worry is pirates, not the Spanish."

Captain Carr asked directly, "What course should we take to avoid those pirates who attacked the *Intrepid*?"

"There is no proper course," said Braden. "Speed is what you want. Get back to Plymouth as fast as you can. The only thing on your side is luck. Luck and good speed."

Carr had already decided that traveling further west to avoid pirates off the Spanish coast was futile. He would heed Captain Braden's advice, and he would take the fastest route back home. Good weather had been aiding the Elizabeth all along, and he would take advantage of it by looking for the best winds to get him back to Plymouth.

Aboard the Intrepid, the crew was trying to make repairs as best they could. The storm had completely wrecked the main mast and much rigging on the other sails. The top deck was splintered with the remains of the mast, and a gaping hole stared clear below decks. The crew was now jettisoning any cargo deemed unnecessary. There was very little powder for cannons, and the Intrepid was now nearly defenseless. We had been less than ten days out from Plymouth, but with this sail damage, who knew how long it might now take. Further, the food supply was dwindling, and we would need to catch fish to live. Fishing took time, but we would live on whatever fish the men caught. There was a good deal of rainwater captured and stored in casks. The trip back home would be slow with only mizzenmast and aft sails available for the little wind they would encounter. If the pirate ships fought in the past week came back, the Intrepid would be completely incapable of defense.

The Elizabeth, I was later told, was making good time now, plowing north with the coast of Spain receding to the east. Captain Braden seemed to be completely recovered from his illness. William Harvey, enjoying the time to himself, was reading voraciously. He was fascinated by the action of the human heart, and he was reading books by the ancient authors, all the while wondering what new learning could be done through experimentation on human corpses. This practice, while known, was disdained by most scholars, and it was forbidden by the Church. Harvey was also fascinated by the recovery of Captain Braden. He had heard from Braden about the efforts of Joseph Shepherd and me to save his life. When Braden talked about the treatment, Harvey discounted it as the recollections of a man in delirium. The treatment with moldy bread and rum was bizarre at best, but Harvey continued to keep an open mind. If Harvey had any outstanding attributes, it was that he kept an open mind to everything. Such is the inquisitive nature of a true scientist.

Several days after Captain Carr had his conversation with Captain Braden, and had decided to plot the fastest course as his safest course back to England, the *Elizabeth* encountered a ship to her north. Dusk was turning into night as the ship came into sight, and what a sight it was. The ship was lacking her main mast, and much of the rigging was in tatters. The ship was barely moving, and it appeared that it was in trouble.

Captain Carr hailed Braden and asked him to join him by the helm. Braden shuddered as he squinted into the eyeglass offered by Carr. It was the *Intrepid*.

"Did you call me up here to verify that this ship is the *Intrepid*?" asked Braden.

"That was my suspicion. What do you suggest, Captain Braden?" said Carr, continuing to show deference and respect to the senior captain.

"I suggest that we sail by her as quickly as possible!" said Braden. "If Mr. North is in command, we do not know what he may do, especially if he would have any idea that I was on board. He led a mutiny and set me adrift. If he does get back to England, I'll see that he hangs!"

"There is another reason to get away from that ship," interrupted William Harvey. "I must apologize for the intrusion," he offered, "but that ship looks like she is just adrift herself. Who knows but that she is now a ghost ship with bodies of plague victims on board. Even if the ship does have survivors, we cannot afford to offer help lest we expose our people to plague."

Carr did not need to think long about his decision. He would stay clear of the *Intrepid* at all costs. It was quite evident that the *Elizabeth* would be long past the *Intrepid* by morning. As the evening deepened into night's darkness, the moon exposed an eerie outline of the *Intrepid*. The Elizabeth got as close as a thousand yards to the doomed ship. Lights did appear on the ship, so Carr knew that the crew was not all dead. He would take no chances. His crew worked all night to secure the light wind from the lee side, and the *Elizabeth* quickly moved well past the stricken *Intrepid*. By morning, there was no sight of the *Intrepid*. It was now time, Carr hoped, for a clear and uneventful trip home. He should reach Plymouth in less than a week.

Chapter 10

The Plymouth, England toward which Captains Carr and North were headed was a bustling seaport. It also was abuzz with political foment and discussion. A group of Puritans were heading toward Plymouth from Holland, with a final destination of the New World. The New World for them would be more than the opportunity for wealth, it would be a haven of religious freedom. It would also be an escape from a land, or perhaps just a king, which no longer supported such ideals. Religious freedom was tied to a philosophy of simplicity of life and worship. Promise of available land, and economic and religious freedom, fueled hope in the hearts of this simple but determined people.

John Ward, a spokesman for this group, was in London, meeting with King James for one last time to plead the case of his people. Ward was a strong and idealistic leader. Integrity was his life's theme, and so was a steadfast determination to do the right thing and to tolerate nothing less. He was single-minded and unshakeable in his zeal. He was not particularly tolerant of anyone who had less vigor than himself in such matters.

"Your majesty," began Ward, "I beg you hear our concerns about our freedom to worship God without the interference of the Crown."

"Interference of the Crown?" James thundered. "Mr. Ward, the Crown is ordained of God for the protection and direction of the people of England. How dare you make accusations about God's appointed leader of your country!"

"With all due respect, your majesty," countered Ward, "my only Lord is Jesus Christ, the Son of God, appointed for my salvation and the salvation of His people. We worship Him in Spirit and in truth, and with no vestige of papist ceremony. He is the King of Kings, and you would do well to heed Him also."

At this point James was willing to tolerate no more from Ward.

"Do you intend to preach to your king?" inquired James. "Indeed, even calling your divinely appointed king a Papist! Take him to the Tower, and let him find time to learn respect for the king of the realm!"

At that, Ward was led away by two royal guardsmen. Ward did not protest, and he did not seem surprised. It was almost as if he had provoked such a response, and now had found the conclusion he had anticipated.

Word quickly spread through the Puritan and Nonconformist communities. Other leaders, not of any particular religious persuasion, also took note and spread the word – the king had banished a leader of the people who dared to request a simple freedom long a part of English tradition. Freedom of dissent and limits on royal authority were well-established English principles. Ward had simply provoked this diffident king to an action that could foment trouble down the road. Right now, it simply sent a message to his people that Ward was willing to die for his faith. Let the king be the one who starts the flames of rebellion.

It was a hot day for London, and the crowds, which had gathered at the Boar's Head Tavern, were in a restive mood.

"Ward's in the Tower!" yelled one of the runners on the street, "Ward's in the Tower!"

Several of the men gathered in the tavern resolved to use this as a reason to cause some mischief.

"Tonight," they whispered to one another, "tonight the king feels the bite of the snake."

Jacob Carr was one of the crowd at the Boar's Head that day. He had no particular concern or sympathy for John Ward or the Puritans. He was an opportunist. King James' popularity was waning, and there were those who had a mind for revolt. They had a need for financial backing, and Jacob Carr might be able to secure some funds for the right favors.

The economy of much of Europe was in shock due to the loads of gold and silver coming from the New World. Prices were rising, and wages were not keeping up. This was causing a greater and greater gulf between the rising commercial and industrial class and the workers. Peasants had no standing whatsoever, nor even any actual money. They survived one day at a time scraping what they could from the land, begging for food, and stealing if they must. Poverty was an increasing problem for those who came to the cities to find work of any type. The restlessness of poor men, unskilled and uneducated, was displayed in shocking acts of crime. Public executions of common thieves were a regular occurrence. Debtor's prisons were overflowing, to the point that King James was willing to send these debtors overseas to the New World, or to remote places in the kingdom. He had little use for those who could not pay their debts. Some religious people saw this as the hand of God's judgment on those who were not "elect." Therefore, some of these "religious people" were content to let them starve and attributed it to God's plan.

Jacob Carr was not a poor man. He also did not believe that hard work was a value that he wanted to endure. His brother, Edwin, was the captain of the *Elizabeth*, and Jacob would find a way to sell some of the cargo, which had not totally been accounted for by the ship's log. He and some dockworkers knew that markets existed for the fine Italian wines and Tuscan olive oil that may have escaped the East India Company's inventory. That inventory often could get distorted by a few well-placed guineas in the hands of the right people. Jacob Carr knew the right people.

Parliament had not been meeting regularly because King James had simply ignored them. English history had long recognized the right of the people to limit royal power, but James seemed immune to such thought, and disdainful of the people who proclaimed it. He had no real idea of English political realities, having come from Scotland to assume the throne upon the beloved Elizabeth's death. The Puritans and other pietistic movements were only interested in having the freedom to worship their God. Others in England believed that royal authority had simply grown too much.

That night, Oliver Craft met with Jacob Carr by the royal stable. It was a rather warm evening, and the fog was beginning to become formidable. Torches around the stable had large, hazy orange halos around them. Cricket songs were just picking up volume, and bats were screeching hunting sounds as they gorged themselves on the numerous bugs in the air.

"Good evening," hailed Craft to one of the royal guards.

"What's your business here?" the guard replied.

"Why, I'm here to make sure you have a nice evening," said Craft. He handed the guard a bottle of Madeira, the kind the guard was not used to seeing.

"What do you want?" demanded the guard.

"Do you want my gift?" asked Carr.

"Looks like I've got it now, doesn't it?" he grinned. "Now get out of here and let me enjoy your little gift!"

Carr signaled to several men in the shadows, and in a moment, the guard was knocked to the ground with a blow from a club. Two of the men uncorked the wine and drizzled a fair amount around the face and clothes of the guard.

"I believe he would rather have been conscious to enjoy that wine. Pity it is, too. That is too fine a wine to be wasted on such a lout."

Craft then grabbed a torch nearby and threw it into the stables. Several others of the mob did the same, and soon the stable was ablaze. Frantic horses, awakened by the smoke, strove at their collars and shrieked into the night. Fire was the most feared event in the town. Watchmen nearby raised the sound of alarm, and townspeople, guards, and passersby joined in the impromptu fire fight. Water buckets were secured, and a line to the nearby canal was formed. This would be a fight for life. If the blaze could not be contained, the western part of the town, at least, was doomed.

People were now running to the scene to help fight the fire. Young boys, excited by the adventure, ran to help. In the midst of the growing excitement, Craft's mob, which now included Jacob Carr, roved into the merchant's section of the town, and helped themselves to some prizes. A nice gold watch from Tarleton's Shoppe, a couple of fine firearms from the blacksmith, and expensive perfume from the trading company agent's private larder. He had always kept some back for his mistresses, and Jacob Carr knew such secrets, and the places where they were kept.

The townspeople were successful in fighting back the blaze in a short time. They had become accustomed to such drills, and had become proficient at protecting their city from deadly fires. Nonetheless, Craft's mob had been able to disrupt the town long enough to secure what they wanted. Carr could have bought all these things, had he not wanted something else even more – to cause trouble for the king.

Early the next morning, the stable guard, having survived the fire and the nasty blow to the head, was hauled in front of his commander.

"Mr. Key," barked the royal army's commander, "you are a disgrace. Asleep at guard, drunk, and unable to protect the royal stables. You are not fit for service to His Majesty!"

Key was still reeling from the concussion he had sustained, and the previous evening's activities were not registering to him. The last thing he remembered was holding a fine bottle of Madeira, then his world became dark.

"Drunk again?" chimed in Jacob Carr.

Carr knew most of the royal guard, and he was acquainted with commander Mills through some exchanges of fine goods.

"Yes," said Mills, "Key smelled like he drank a whole bottle of wine. Passed out, and he didn't notice that the stable was on fire. He probably fell down drunk and got that nasty lump on his head."

Mills then said, "I understand that there was some mischief in town last night. Tarleton told me he lost some watches. There were more than watches stolen last night, Jacob. This is not the first time that we have had some mysterious things going on."

"Well," said Carr, "there is a lot of unrest in the whole kingdom. If the king would not be bowing to the papists, and putting men like John Ward into the tower, perhaps there would be less mischief."

Mills looked quizzically at Carr.

"When is it that you became interested in religious affairs and affairs of the kingdom?" asked Mills.

"When it involves the amount of money that I can make," said Carr.

"I think you are doing well just the way things are," replied Mills.

"A man can always do better if he is close to power," said Carr, "and that is my aim."

"And just what does that mean?" asked Mills.

"Someday you will see, Commander Mills," said Carr.

Chapter 11

The *Elizabeth* made good time on her way to Plymouth. The rest of her journey, nine days of good weather and fair winds, brought her into Plymouth on August 29th. Captain Carr supervised the unloading of his ship's cargo, and his brother Jacob was on hand to greet him. Jacob was usually on hand when Edwin's ship came into dock, and Jacob's dockworkers always seemed to land the contract to unload Edwin's ships. Edwin was pleased to see his brother. Jacob was six years Edwin's junior, and had always managed to travel to see him, even when their paths were not close.

Captain Braden asked to be taken to the Lord Admiralty as soon as possible to tell his tale of mutiny and the scurrilous acts of Mr. North. William Harvey was anxious to see his wife, Elizabeth, daughter of one of the royal physicians. This is primarily how he secured his position as court physician to King James. He would seek a ride to London as quickly as possible.

The *Intrepid*, limping along, was also helped on her journey by the good weather and fair winds. Some repairs on the rigging, and adding some extra cloth to her remaining masts, helped to restore some speed to the ailing ship. On board, the tension was diminishing, but hostility remained toward Joseph Shepherd and me. The story of exactly how Mr. North came to command the ship was changing. Would anyone believe that there was plague on the ship that was cured? How could they explain the expulsion of Captain Braden? Mr. North did have a plan that could deal with all of his problems.

"Mr. Swailes," summoned North. "Come here, I have need of you."

"Yes, Captain," said Swailes, "I'm here."

Swailes was loyal to North, and he believed him to be just the kind of tough officer that a warship needed. North had brought them through peril, two battles, and a near disastrous storm.

"Swailes," North began, "you must help the men to understand that our safety was secured only through the strong leadership and difficult decisions that we made as officers on this ship. When we reach port in Plymouth, we need to be all of one mind about decisions we made at sea, including having to set Braden adrift. He was diagnosed by Dr. Greene as having the plague. We acted on that information, and saved the ship by our quick actions."

Swailes seemed unsure of why he needed to convince the men of anything. Had the story changed a bit? Yes, Braden had the plague, or so we thought, he reasoned, but there were two other men who had the plague, and they recovered. Furthermore, Captain North had told the crew that Captain Braden had voluntarily asked to be set adrift so as not to infect the crew.

"Swailes!" said North more sternly to get his attention. "Did you hear me?"

"Yes, Captain," said Swailes, "I was just wondering why…"

"Stop wondering and just follow my orders," interrupted North. "I know how people think, and you just need to be clear that Greene diagnosed Braden, his doctor friend Shepherd was in agreement, and we decided, for the safety of the ship, to set him adrift. If we say that some of the crew had the plague, people might panic, and they might not allow us to stay in port. We need to get to Plymouth quickly, and we need to be together on what happened. Remember, this is a crew of heroes who fought off pirates, and returned to tell of it."

Swailes agreed with North. This was a fine fighting crew, which deserved recognition. What would it hurt to tell the story just a bit differently than what it appeared to be? People just do not understand what it's like on the ocean in battles and gales. Mr. North should be supported if that is what he orders. No harm done, he reasoned.

North would tell a darker tale of Shepherd and me. He would say how we had convinced him that Captain Braden was dying, and that by setting him adrift, North had saved the ship. He would say that we had predicted that Braden would die quickly on the little boat, and that if he stayed on the *Intrepid*, the rest of the ship was doomed.

I had surmised as much on my own. I was aware that if Joseph Shepherd and I were able to survive until we got to port, we would be blamed for the decision to set Captain Braden adrift. If we all held to the same story, no one would be held accountable. Braden was dead, we presumed, and the *Intrepid* would have made it safely to Plymouth. In fact, Shepherd and I could even take credit for the safety of the crew. It was a tidy story, if only it were true. When Mr. Swailes came to me with the story, I decided not to refute it. To do so might be fatal to Shepherd and to me.

When I talked with Joseph Shepherd, he was not so compliant. Recovering nicely now from his stab wound in the side, Shepherd was able to get around reasonably well, though he was still in some pain. Shepherd had been meticulous to wash the wound with fresh saltwater every day, and he had done another curious thing. He had put some of the sulfur, which we used to help preserve apples, on his side after cleansing the wound. It was another trick I learned from him that I would surely incorporate into my medical practice.

"Dr. Greene," said Shepherd, "am I to believe that a man of your character will go along with this lie of Mr. North?"

Shepherd had a way of piercing through to my conscience that I had never before experienced.

46

"Joseph," I said in a more familiar way than I had ever addressed him, "Captain Braden is surely dead, and we will surely be dead if we do not go along with this story. I cannot see much harm in it, really."

"No harm in a lie?" he asked. "The real harm," he said, "is the harm it will do to your soul. You are only worried about the harm it will do to your body."

He had a point there, but when it came to saving my body, or saving my soul, I would go with the one that I could see and feel.

"Perhaps you do not care about your body, Dr. Shepherd, but I care very much for mine," I said. I did not feel very noble in this line of reasoning, but I could not see who would be hurt by this plan. Yes, it was not actually true, but Braden was dead, we were all alive, and no amount of truth telling would bring Captain Braden back to life.

"I ask you, Dr. Greene," Shepherd continued, "what if Captain Braden is not dead? Does that make your lie any different?"

I thought about that for a moment. If Braden were alive somehow, we would still be justified, in a way. If he lived, then we would not be responsible for his death. There would be a chance that we could be caught in our lie, and that would not be good, but it was certainly not likely either.

Then again, if he were dead, it could be because of North's actions, but Shepherd and I had not been in agreement with that plan. We had no choice, even though it very much appeared that Braden was recovering. So, by lying, we would be allowing a murderer to go free of his crime. It could also be that Braden died of the plague, despite his presumed rally of health. Then, it was a good decision to let him adrift to save the ship.

While all of this was tumbling in my head, I understood Shepherd's point. No matter the outcome, truth is truth, not to be changed by the life or death of Braden. I could participate in the lie to save my skin, or I could hold fast to the truth, and risk death – death in defense of nothing more than honor.

Captain North broke into our conversation with a more pleasant than usual greeting.

"Good afternoon, Dr. Greene," he said. "I trust that Mr. Swailes has spoken to you about Captain Braden's unfortunate death at sea. You know, I have been thinking about good Captain Braden, and I think that we might actually help his memory, and perhaps the lot of his wife and children, by saying that Braden ordered himself off the ship to save it. What do you think of that?"

"Isn't that what you told the crew after you set him adrift?" I asked.

A shadow came over North's face and his demeanor changed markedly.

"Greene," he said, "you will promise to say whatever I tell you to say or I will throw you overboard before we reach Plymouth, so help me God!"

He turned and left without even acknowledging the presence of Joseph Shepherd, who witnessed the increasingly outrageous behavior of Mr. North. I believed that North would not hesitate to throw both Shepherd and me overboard. In fact, I believed that Mr. North was in danger of being completely out of control. In fact, he seemed to be showing signs of being deranged.

"No harm in a lie, Dr. Greene?" asked Shepherd.

"He is becoming mad, Joseph," I said. "I fear for the whole crew."

"Then we must not allow the lies to continue," said Shepherd. "North must be stopped now."

The *Intrepid* would be making port in Plymouth any day. I could see the gulls at a distance, so I knew that we were closing in on land.

"Mr. Swailes," I said as I saw the tall lean figure of Swailes approach, "tell me which story we will be telling about Captain Braden's departure when we reach Plymouth."

Swailes was not amused at my question. "You will tell whatever story Captain North says you'll tell," he said rather smugly. Mr. Swailes, while an officer on the ship, was not known to be of the best and brightest stock. His sister was related to North by marriage, her husband being North's nephew. Mr. North tried to surround himself with people he trusted, and when the summons came to man the *Intrepid*, North engaged Swailes to sign on. North arranged to have Captain Braden name several of his friends as officers on the ship. This managed to engender some of the crew's loyalty to North. Captain Braden had failed to recognize this troublesome pattern when staffing his ship.

"Mr. Swailes," I continued, "don't you think that if we keep changing the story that someone will get confused and accidentally tell the truth?"

Shepherd saw the humor in this and laughed out loud for the first time since boarding the ship.

Swailes glared and said, "I don't know what the truth is anymore, and I do not care! You just say what we tell you!"

He walked off muttering to himself. Mr. Kelley came by at that moment and saw the end of the exchange.

"Swailes is a fool, isn't he, Dr. Greene?" ventured Kelley.

"I rather think so, Mr. Kelley, but the rest of the crew, save yourself, are just as foolish. I believe that such behavior might just have us in irons after we land," I said.

Kelley led us into a corner and began to speak in lowered tones.

"That is why I came by," he said. "I heard that Mr. North is planning to have you both killed before we reach port."

While I had felt this to be very possible all along, the words chilled me to the bone as Kelley breathed them.

"When is this to happen?" I asked when I could get my thoughts collected.

"Probably tomorrow," said Kelley. "I will help you if I can, but I am not sure how to do so. Keep alert, and I will try to warn you if I hear more."

"Shepherd," I intoned, "you are a praying man. Pray for an answer to this!"

Mr. Shepherd was calm, as usual, and said, "God is in control. I need not worry."

I was at once comforted, then incredulous that he could trust so completely.

"Do you understand the danger here?" I asked.

"Yes," he said, "I am well aware that our lives are at stake, that there are those who would have us killed for no good reason other than to save themselves. I have faced this before."

I began to wonder if he had been thrown off the last ship he was on before the *Intrepid* saved him some weeks ago. Perhaps he really was a Jonah, and anybody that touched him was bound for trouble.

"What happened to you in the past?" I asked, "Do you remember any more about what happened before you came aboard?"

"Yes," he said. "The last few days much of my memory has been coming back. I was not thrown from a ship for having the plague. I was living in Egypt before I set sail. I was aboard an English trading ship, the *Herald,* which was bound for the West Indies. I was told that this was an English voyage, but the truth was that Portugal wanted to avoid any interference from Spanish ships, or pirates loyal to Spain. Hiring an English ship for Portuguese trading in the New World was a trick that the Portuguese felt might enhance their waning position in the New World.

"I had a desire to see this New World, and I had hired on as a ship's physician. The ship was to stop in West Africa for some provisions of food and fresh water before our trip across the ocean. We had loaded a fine supply of ivory as well when the captain told us that the rest of the cargo was going to require every man to keep his senses keen and his guard up. I then saw that the 'cargo' was human slaves. About fifty black men, women, and children, chained together, mostly naked, looking wide-eyed and frightened. They were packed into the lowest deck chained together, and laid on wooden shelves, just like we had loaded the ivory.

"I was shocked at the sight of this. When I refused to participate in the loading of the slaves, I was beaten by several other hands, and then put into chains myself. I was thrown right beside the slaves, and they were even more fearful of my presence than of being packed like ivory into the ship. They had kept me on board to try to keep as many slaves alive as possible. Usually, about half of the 'cargo' of slaves dies on those voyages. When we set sail, the ship was blown off course by a storm. We ended up just off the coast of Spain. I complained to the captain that God was punishing the ship for the evil of participating in the slave trade. The captain laughed at me, and told me that he

49

would 'spare me that punishment' by setting me adrift in the ocean. A number of the crew took it upon themselves to mock me, beat me, and then set me adrift with a week's supply of salt fish and water. They were convinced that I would die on the little boat they set me on. I was given a hard blow to the head before I tumbled onto the little boat. The next thing I remembered, I was being picked up by the *Intrepid*."

I was amazed at Shepherd's tale. However, he now had a bigger problem than before. Mr. North was fully capable of murder, and we would be his victims unless we could find a way to save ourselves.

Chapter 12

William Harvey took his position as a court physician very seriously, and he felt obliged to report to the port master in Plymouth that there had been plague on the warship *Intrepid*. Indeed, the *Elizabeth*, making good sailing time, had beaten the *Intrepid* into Plymouth by more than seven days at this time. Harvey relayed how Captain Braden had been stricken, and subsequently recovered, and that Braden was even now seeking travel to London to discuss the mutiny on the *Intrepid*. Harvey felt obliged to protect the residents of Plymouth, even though he was doubtful that the *Intrepid* would seek port at Plymouth. The port master, a stout, ruddy man of some advanced years by the name of Alvin Toll, allowed as how this port was under his authority, and that no plague ship would be allowed entry. Harvey then felt satisfied that he had done his duty, and he made arrangements for a carriage to London.

Edwin Carr had finished overseeing the unloading of his ship, and he had, as usual, delegated some of that chore to his brother Jacob. Edwin believed that Jacob was meticulous in his oversight, and that he usually had ensured that the job was done promptly and with little waste of cargo or time. Edwin and Jacob then decided to spend the evening together in celebration of another successful voyage.

"There has been some unrest here since you left," said Jacob.

"Has King James found new ways to enrage the people?" asked Edwin, smiling.

"No," replied Jacob, laughing, "he uses the same old ways."

Edwin joined in the laughter, and together they hoisted a pint of ale to the King.

"All hail the King!" toasted Jacob. Several of the men drinking nearby replied with, "The bastard King of Scotland, may he rest with his head on a pike!"

The whole tavern erupted in song about the old days of Queen Elizabeth. Nostalgia was playing well these days, even though the queen was not far removed from the throne. She was sorely missed. This papist-leaning (as some thought) King James was not well appreciated.

"I've heard that a group of the Puritan people are heading to the New World from Plymouth," said Captain Carr.

"Yes," replied Jacob, "but not for treasure. They leave for religious freedom. I don't think that I'd travel to America for religion, but I might go to find some silver."

"Jacob, Jacob, always looking for the silver," said Edwin, shaking his head.

"Yes," said Jacob, "I will always be looking for more silver. I can count on silver, and very little else."

Alvin Toll entered the pub and walked over to Edwin Carr. He had always liked Captain Carr, and he had never been able to see how two such opposite men as Jacob and Edwin had come out of the same womb.

"Edwin," hailed Toll, "how was your voyage?"

"Most enjoyable, Mr. Toll," replied Carr. "Some adventure, good company, fair weather, and, all in all, a successful trip."

"You always seem to have a good trip, Edwin," said Toll. "Good captains have good trips. I hear that you picked up a Captain Braden who had the plague."

"Who told you that?" asked Carr.

"Why, none other than William Harvey," said Toll, proud to have spoken to such a man as Harvey. "If the *Intrepid* tries to dock in Plymouth, she will meet with a hundred cannons fending her off!"

Toll was now swelling with pride over his well-protected port, even though he had grossly exaggerated the number of cannon in the port. He would make sure that no breach was found on his watch.

Joseph Shepherd was praying when I walked in on him. Mr. North had allowed us to stay out of our shackles so as not to arouse undue suspicion and morale problems, or to divide sentiments on the ship. There were those among the crew, chiefly Mr. Kelley, who felt some loyalty toward us for the medical care they had received. Mr. Crane and Mr. Elliott, the two sailors whose symptoms of the plague were successfully treated by Joseph Shepherd, had also naturally felt kindly disposed to us.

"Joseph, we are now just a few days out of Plymouth," I said. "What do you think our course of action should be?"

I asked this in some despair, believing that we would be summoned to Mr. North any moment and heaved overboard. North would make up some tale of our disappearance, the crew generally would not ask too many questions, and they would sail into port, heroes of some victories over pirates at sea.

"I have been praying about our situation," replied Shepherd, "and I think that we should go to Mr. North and ask him to do the right thing by us and by the ship."

"Oh, how wonderful!" I exclaimed in mockery, "Of course, that is the best solution, sure to work!"

Shepherd endured my naturally cynical response and continued.

"Our job is not to convince him of anything; our job is to tell him the truth. God will take care of the rest."

So simple a solution in Shepherd's eyes – just tell North the truth and trust in God. I wished it were that simple.

"Think about it," continued Shepherd. "We have little to lose in the venture. If he hears our pleas, he can either accept them, or reject them. As it stands now, we are destined to die for his sins. If he rejects us, we are no worse off for having asked him to do right."

Shepherd had an odd but true point. There was little to lose; it was just a fearsome thing to do. Shepherd's courage never ceased to amaze me.

"Your plan is better than anything I have come up with," I said. "Proceed."

We gathered ourselves and went to the top deck and to the helm where North was standing. He looked so proud commanding his damaged ship on her final leg home to Plymouth.

I interrupted North's reverie by asking, "Mr. North, may we have a word with you?"

North looked around and saw Shepherd and me standing to his side. The wind had almost completely died down, and the weather was beautiful. I wondered if this would be the last few moments of sunshine I would ever experience. I was taken by surprise when Joseph began to speak. I had felt it to be my place as the ship physician, but Shepherd started boldly, yet softly, to address North.

"Mr. North," Shepherd began, "we believe that we must ask what your intentions are for Dr. Greene and me."

North looked a bit surprised at the directness of the question. He replied, "I intend to have you say what I tell you to say when we reach Plymouth. There will be an inquiry about what happened on our voyage, and I intend to make sure that you two say the right things."

"We will indeed say the right things," said Shepherd.

"What do you mean?" asked North.

"I mean," said Shepherd, "that we will tell the truth."

North was in no mood to banter back and forth over semantics. "The truth is what I tell you it is!" he thundered.

"Captain North," began Shepherd, "surely as His Majesty's representative on this vessel, you have a high responsibility. Would you have us lie to His Majesty's inquiry?"

North seemed increasingly uncomfortable with this line of thinking. He started to turn red from his neck to his ears, and he ordered the nearest sailors to seize us and throw us in irons. Mr. Crane and Mr. Kelley were nearby and had heard the exchange. North pointed to them and ordered them to seize us. They hesitated, and North was now fury itself. He started to jump down from his elevated perch on the helm when a gust of wind slammed into the ship. North tripped on his way out of the helm booth, and the wheel spun into his shoulder, knocking him down with some force. He let out an oath, and tried to clamber back up. As he stood, I saw his left shoulder noticeably drooping down, horribly separated from the socket. The pain was searing, and he staggered toward us. Crane and Kelley stood motionless, unable to move.

"Seize those bastards!" he shouted.

No one moved. Time seemed to be frozen as North tried to steady himself, but the pain was more than he could stand. He fell again, heavily onto his left side. He screamed in pain, and then quickly passed out.

I looked at Joseph, then at Crane and Kelley. Joseph responded first.

"Help me get him below deck so that we can minister to him," Shepherd said. Crane and Kelley grabbed his limp form and took him below deck to the infirmary.

"Dr. Greene, we will need to assess if the shoulder is broken or separated, or both," said Shepherd. I began to question my Hippocratic Oath very seriously at this time. I was not convinced that I wanted to help the man who would have me killed as soon as I helped him to feel better. While I was musing, Shepherd had placed his hand on the shoulder and determined that the shoulder socket appeared to be in place and unbroken. He asked if I concurred, and after a cursory examination, I agreed with Shepherd. Joseph then asked if I wanted to jerk the shoulder back in place, or if he should proceed. I told Joseph that it was my place as ship physician, and I commenced to work on the shoulder to jerk it back into place. There had evidently been a great deal of damage to the sinews of the shoulder, and I could not budge it. Joseph then placed his hand behind North's shoulder blade and lifted. At the same time, he rotated the shoulder forward and then out, and I saw the shoulder slide back into the socket.

At that moment, North came back to consciousness. Crane and Kelley were now joined by a number of the crew who was asking what had happened to Captain North.

Kelley spoke up, "Captain North took a nasty fall and broke his shoulder. Mr. Shepherd and Dr. Greene got him fixed up, I think."

North was still in enormous pain, but now somewhat relieved by the procedure done by Shepherd.

"Seize these men," North said, but much more weakly than before. The crew began to mutter, questioning the reason for such seizure.

Before anyone could respond, Kelley continued, "Captain North is still a bit out of his head from his fall. I think he needs some rest."

Mr. Swailes came bursting in at that moment and asked about the confusion.

"Captain North was hurt," Kelley said, "and the doctors have patched him up."

Swailes was not totally satisfied with this answer, but he did not know enough at that point to recognize Kelley's clever cover of what was happening. I then interrupted.

"Dr. Shepherd," I said, "I believe that Captain North is in need of some pain relief. Please get him a large draught of rum."

At that, Shepherd put a mug of rum to North's lips, and North gladly drank. Shepherd kept the mug in place till North drained it. Shepherd then refilled the mug with more rum, now laced with tincture of opium which I had secured while North was drinking his first mug of rum. North drank this mixture with some prodding by Shepherd, who seemed to have a strange quality of calm and persuasion that paralyzed resistance. North came away from the drinks quiet and at ease. He seemed to forget his orders for Shepherd and me, and he slowly drifted away into sleep.

Swailes then took charge.

"Captain North had ordered me to put Shepherd and Dr. Greene back into chains," he said. "Mr. Jenkins, please take them to quarters below."

Jenkins hesitated, perhaps questioning the authority of Swailes. He had just seen us minister to a fallen captain, and now he was being ordered to put the helpers in chains. The rest of the crew seemed unwilling to have another mutiny on their hands, and they drifted away up to the main deck, going about their duties as if nothing had happened. Swailes looked around to the dwindling crew and decided that it was better to rescind an order that would not be followed rather than to have an order ignored.

Kelley looked at Joseph and me and said, "I told you I would help if I could."

He left quickly to get to his post.

The *Intrepid* was closing in on Plymouth, and there was plenty to do before we got to port.

Chapter 13

Plymouth was a busy port, but was losing ground to the thriving port of London on the Thames. London was now where all the trade and growth was happening, and the city had grown immensely over the past twenty years. London was by now a city of nearly 200,000 souls, and it continued to grow. People in abject poverty were signing on as indentured servants to ships going to America. Shipments were coming regularly from America, the Far East, Africa, and Italy, and the city was sprawling outward into the countryside. Plymouth, on the other hand, was a port on the wane, beautiful in its own way, but already a symbol of the changing times.

Departures of people from Plymouth to the New World seemed to epitomize the excitement of places other than Plymouth. In a few days, the *Mayflower* would be departing Plymouth for the New World carrying religious pilgrims to freedoms now no longer found in England. Political and religious foment, formulated in London, could be felt in Plymouth. It was to Plymouth that people gathered to flee the oppression of the crown in London. The destination, America, would receive these pilgrims and give them the chance to start a literal New World.

A lookout in the lighthouse high above the port spotted a ragged ship several miles out at sea heading home for rest from a difficult voyage. He had been alerted by Alvin Toll that such a ship could be coming in the next few days, and that he should be notified immediately of the first sighting of it. The *Intrepid* was heading into Plymouth.

Toll ordered that a sloop be dispatched to meet the *Intrepid* to let her know that Plymouth would not accept her. The *Intrepid* was labeled as a ship with plague, and, if she could not prove otherwise, she would be denied entry. Several royal dragoons were sent with a crew of eight sailors to intercept the *Intrepid* and to inform her of the situation. Toll also ordered the shore batteries to prepare to fire at the *Intrepid* should she try to gain entry to the port without permission.

Aboard the *Intrepid*, the exhausted crew was exhilarated upon seeing the welcome sight of port. Food and water were depleted, and port was to be reached with no time to spare. They expected no reception upon arrival, but when people became aware of the exploits of this voyage, there would be adulation, women, wine, and rewards. They were more than ready for all of those benefits.

Mr. North was still quite dreamy from his ordeal, and he was in no shape to command the ship. This task fell to Swailes, who led a crew wary of his command in the final leg of the journey. Shepherd and I were tending to Mr. North, ensuring that he got regular, ample doses of tincture of opium mixed in brandy or rum to aid his sleep and recovery.

Swailes met the boat loaded with dragoons and sailors by hailing them, "Come to meet the heroes, have ya?"

David Marks, sergeant of the dragoons, grimly replied, "I am here to order you to return to sea, or the shore batteries will commence firing upon your ship."

Swailes was stunned at this retort. Marks continued, "Your ship has the plague aboard and will be denied entry into the port of Plymouth."

Swailes screamed at the dragoons, "There is no plague on this ship! We shall proceed into port; your guns be damned!"

Mr. Marks had no need to argue with the doomed vessel, and he turned away, ordering his small crew to return to Plymouth. By now, word was spreading through the *Intrepid* that they were being denied entry into Plymouth. Anger and disbelief were mixed among the crew, but none had the presence of mind to think beyond fighting their way into port. Swailes, fool that he was, seemed unable to take control of the crew. He merely fed off the raw emotions being displayed by his men, and was caught up in the plan to blast his way into Plymouth.

I looked at Joseph Shepherd and Mr. Kelley and asked their thoughts. Joseph Shepherd suggested that we try to reason with Swailes, offering ideas that had not come quickly to his simple mind.

"As the ship's surgeon, I can offer to attest to the health of the crew," I said. "Producing a few healthy sailors free of disease might convince a reasonable person that we have no plague. We can offer to be quarantined offshore as long as they provide fresh food and water for a week or two."

Shepherd agreed with the idea, but his agreement was probably not enough to convince Swailes of the good sense of the plan.

It appeared that Alvin Toll had no interest in such an idea either, or he would have suggested it to begin with. There seemed to be other reasons why this ship was being denied entry to Plymouth of which we were unaware. Meanwhile, the mood on the *Intrepid* was turning very ugly. Desperate men were ready to plunge ahead into Plymouth to challenge the threat of force that Toll had promised. The crew began to prepare the last of the shot and powder for battle against Plymouth. This crew was now in the grip of fear, coupled with lack of leadership. They had tasted the blood of battle on the sea, and now that seemed to be the only course they trusted.

Swailes ordered the sails to be fully raised, and the *Intrepid* sailed for Plymouth.

Chapter 14

William Bradford was studying his Bible before settling down for the night to sleep. Bradford was the leader of the Puritan separatists who were preparing for a trip to the New World. Bradford had been reading the book of Exodus, chapter 3, verses 11-12. There he read a conversation between God and Moses at the burning bush. God had told Moses to lead His people out of bondage in Egypt. Moses replied, "Who am I, that I should go to Pharaoh and bring the Israelites out of Egypt?"

And God replied, "I will be with you…"

Bradford was feeling very much like Moses this night. He had taken on the responsibility of leading a group of religious separatists, known as Pilgrims, to the New World. He was to be the religious leader on a ship called the *Mayflower*, which would be departing in the next few weeks for America.

"Who am I," he thought, "to be leading a group of believers across the world? Has God prepared me for such a duty?"

Then he read the twelfth verse of chapter 3 in Exodus, "I will be with you…"

"Surely," thought Bradford, "that is the only way I can lead people to a foreign land which promises freedom."

Bradford had been told by his friend and mentor, John Ward, that he was the man for the job, the man God had appointed to the task. Now his friend was in the tower of London, a prisoner of King James for his religious beliefs.

While Bradford pondered these ideas, he heard a commotion in the street below. A town crier was warning people that a renegade English ship, the *Intrepid*, was heading for Plymouth, and that ships in the harbor were at risk. Bradford's thoughts were for the *Mayflower*, which was the vessel to take his people to the Promised Land.

People began to scramble down to the harbor. Men with flintlocks were clambering out of their houses. Young men with torches were seen coming out of taverns, and women were closing the shutters on their seaside houses. In the distance, the silhouette of a ship could be seen against a large full moon still hovering near the horizon in the late evening. William Bradford sensed that he was to do something – to begin his mission from God, somehow – to help avert this coming confrontation.

Bradford made his way through now congested streets toward the port authority building on the docks. There he encountered a seething Alvin Toll. Toll's round jowly face was beet red, contrasting with his white breech coat and white collar. He was short of breath from the short trip across the way from the tavern where he had been drinking and boasting that the damned ship *Intrepid* had better not test his shore batteries. Now that the test might actually take place, Toll seemed as much frightened as angry. As much as he would boast about his shore batteries, they had not been fired in years, and never in anger.

Toll blustered orders to a ragged crew of dockworkers who would now double as grenadiers. Toll ordered them to secure powder and shot from the armory. The small company of dragoons of the King's Army was placed around the docks at various points. It was apparent that Toll had no idea how to defend against the attack of one lonely fighting ship – a crippled one at that.

In the midst of this emerging chaos, William Bradford approached Alvin Toll with an idea – an idea so very fresh in Bradford's mind because he just that moment had come up with it.

"What do you want?" inquired Toll of Bradford.

"May I propose an idea to you, Commander Toll?" asked Bradford. Bradford's disarming friendliness, his tone of voice, and his deferential reference to Toll as "Commander" seemed to soften Toll to hear out Bradford.

"Go on," said Toll in a restrained tone of voice.

"Commander," he said, "I am William Bradford. I will be sailing out in a few weeks on the Mayflower with my company of God's people for America. It struck me that the men on the *Intrepid* may need to be heard, their story checked out. From what I have heard, they deny that there is any plague aboard the ship. Perhaps we need to verify that first hand. I offer to go to the ship to check out their situation. If there is any evidence of plague on that ship, I will stay on the *Intrepid* with the crew. May God be with me in that event. However, if there is no evidence of plague, I will notify those who row me out to the ship, and we can allow them entry to port in due time."

Toll retorted quickly.

"Mr. Bradford, I have it on good authority that the *Intrepid* is a renegade ship, under the control of a mutinous crew. They have set their good captain Braden adrift, and he only survives by the grace of God Almighty. This ship is not just taken by the black plague, they have the plague of mutiny and murder as well!"

Bradford seemed unshaken.

"Commander Toll," he continued, "I have reason to believe that God has prepared me for such an encounter. We have nothing to lose by sending a party out there to talk with them. We just gain the possibility that there will be no innocent blood shed if we try. If we fail, better that one man die than many. Besides, we could gain more time for a peaceful solution if we try to meet with them. As it stands now, there could be a blood bath."

Toll considered Bradford's brave, if foolhardy, offer. Toll could send another small crew to meet once again with the *Intrepid*. There would be great danger for such a mission, but it would buy Toll more time to plan a defense of Plymouth. Frankly, he had considered the possibility that the *Intrepid* would try to come into port violently. Marks and his dragoons had suggested that Swailes and the renegade crew might do anything, including blasting their way into port. Indeed, now that such a scenario was playing out, he was caught with too much bluster, and not enough firepower.

"Mr. Bradford," said Toll, "if you can get other volunteers to go with you, you may try. I believe that we can send a few of His Majesty's sailors to accompany you, but you will be without military support on your mission."

"Commander Toll," replied Bradford, "this is not a military mission. It is a mission of mercy and peace."

Alvin Toll was not a religious man, nor did he have much respect for religious people. His brief encounter with William Bradford, however, had touched him in a way to which he was unaccustomed. Bradford's simple faith, coupled with tremendous courage, was an amazing thing to Toll. He was hoping that Bradford would succeed, but he was more inclined to believe that the time bought by this foolish diversion would allow him to get some help, and to shore up his defense plans.

"I shall leave as soon as you can get me that crew of sailors to get out to the *Intrepid*," said Bradford. "I have another member of my company who will go with me. James Mullins is a young man of great faith and courage. He is also a physician, and he will be able to determine the health of the crew. I do not even need to ask him, and I know his answer. He will come with me anywhere."

It was nearly 2 a.m. by the time that the crew was assembled and a rowboat secured for the trip. The *Intrepid* was now within a half mile of port, and no gunfire had been exchanged. It was apparently Mr. Swailes' plan to continue his advance toward Plymouth, and call the bluff of Alvin Toll. Evidently, the *Intrepid* would not fire unless fired upon. The water was very calm, and with the full moon rising higher in the sky, the night was well lit. A handful of inquisitive townspeople bearing torches gave a farewell to the crew in the tiny boat heading out of port. The scene was quite beautiful, yet there was tension in the air.

The plan was to have William Bradford and James Mullins approach the *Intrepid* and ask for a meeting. If they were invited aboard the ship, they would ask to inspect the *Intrepid* for signs of plague among the crew. If they found signs of plague, they would signal to the crew in the small boat. The signal would be to jettison two rocks over the port side, one after another. The crew would then turn and head back to port without Bradford and Mullins. If there were no sign of plague, there would be one rock tossed over the starboard side. The absence of plague would be the good news needed for the *Intrepid* to safely gain entry to Plymouth. Bradford and Mullins assumed that if plague were on board, they would be held hostage, and indeed would have been exposed to it anyway, and their lives were in serious jeopardy. They chose to take this chance to secure peace.

The boat quickly covered the half-mile out to the *Intrepid*. As they pulled closer to the ship, crewman John Cates yelled to Mr. Swailes, "They've sent a boat – eight crew and two others. They do not appear to have weapons."

Swailes called to Cates, "Find out what they want!"

"We come in peace," yelled Bradford. His voice carried well in the still night, and the words seemed to calm Cates. "May we board to speak with you?"

Swailes was now with Cates, and the boat was right beside the *Intrepid*. Swailes responded, "No weapons. We check out whoever comes on board first. You will be covered by my sailors with guns the whole time you are here."

"We agree," said Bradford. "Only Dr. Mullins and I will be boarding."

A rope was lowered to the small craft, and Bradford and Mullins climbed up with some difficulty. The *Intrepid* crew ended up hauling the two aboard. Bradford spoke directly to Mr. Swailes.

"Sir, we have requested to come aboard to determine if there is any sign of plague on this ship. If Dr. Mullins finds any sign, and he must be given access to every crewman here, you will be denied entry to Plymouth."

"I agree to that," said Mr. Swailes.

Bradford and Mullins were stunned by the immediate compliance, and Swailes' respectful tone of voice. Swailes and the crew were tired, hungry, and ready to come home. Swailes also believed that there was no plague to be found on board, so he felt that he had nothing to lose. There were, however, other secrets, which may not be so easy to overcome. Those secrets should not keep them from coming into port, but they could be a problem later. But that was later.

Mr. North was coming back around from his shoulder injury. He, of course, had felt very little pain since our regimen of brandy, laced with tincture of opium. I had secured a fair amount of this substance from a merchant who had been to China. He told me of the qualities of the compound, but that many people smoked opium all day, staying in a kind of stupor much of the time. I found that, given the proper dosage, it had wonderful sedating qualities, although the aftereffects could be troublesome. I used it only with great caution. I must admit that I was not extremely careful when dosing Mr. North, and at times, I am certain that he received enough to restrain a man twice his size.

"Dr. Greene," whispered Mr. North from his haze, "what time is it?"

"Mr. North," I replied, "you might want to ask what *day* it is, not what hour."

North in his confusion did not follow that little humor. He truly did not know what day it was, nor where we were, nor our rather strange

61

circumstance of being within a thousand yards of port, but not allowed to enter. His shoulder was healing, but it was, I am sure, still quite painful. It was back in place, not broken, and he had more of his range of motion now available. We would need to back him down from his sedation, and reintroduce him to reality. That would cause another bit of a problem since Mr. Swailes had taken to leading the ship. Mr. North's odd behavior the prior few days, and his violent temper, had alerted even the simplest of crew members that he was capable of harm. Their only real concern was now to get home, and perhaps to relay to their family and friends a great adventure. Leadership of a ship coming home was not a great concern now.

As Mr. Bradford and Dr. Mullins walked around the ship, they saw some of the ravages of pirate battles and storms. Below deck was a complete disaster, with swirling water, rotting food, fouled powder, and splinters of the main mast floating about. We had become accustomed to the odor on the ship, but Bradford and Mullins nearly retched several times from the smell. The crew was told to comply with medical examination from Dr. Mullins.

Dr. Mullins sought me out after Mr. Kelley directed him to me as the ship's physician. Mullins told me of the plan, and I was relieved to hear that, somehow, reason seemed to prevail in this chaos we had been living in.

I spoke again to Mr. North.

"Captain North," I began deferentially, "the crew will be given medical examinations by a doctor from Plymouth to determine if we can land there. They believe that there is plague on this ship, and if that is found in any crew member, we will be forced to remain at sea. I am asking of you that you order me to be part of the medical examination on your ship as your ship surgeon."

I guided Mr. North in his order to Mr. Swailes. I made sure that Mr. Kelley was nearby when I brought North to see Mr. Swailes to give the order. Mr. North actually sounded plausible in his order to Swailes to have me assist Mullins and Bradford. Swailes agreed, since he did not want trouble in front of a crewmember, and in front of our visitors.

I now had the opportunity to get the aid and attention we desperately needed from Mr. Bradford, and Dr. Mullins.

Chapter 15

William Harvey reached London and received a warm welcome from King James. Harvey enjoyed great respect and honor from the court, and seemed to know every person of influence in London. His arrival seemed to set off a round of balls and social gatherings, which attracted lords and ladies from all around the kingdom. Harvey explained to people at these gatherings his latest adventure on the *Elizabeth*, as well as his exciting discoveries about the body. Harvey was convinced that the heart played a major part in the flow of blood in the body. He had done dissections of human bodies, and had seen little valves in the veins, which appeared to restrict the flow of blood to one direction. The arteries also had valves, which forced blood away from the heart.

Harvey also knew that knowledge was only part of science. Scientists also need to have patrons who support them in their endeavors financially. He was learning the fine art of money politics, as well as social and practical politics. Being in the king's court was a fine way to advance science, he reasoned.

Edwin Carr had also come to London, invited by Lord Kensington, who had bought a thousand shares of the British East India Company. Kensington was very fond of Edwin Carr, and very protective of him as well. After all, Captain Carr would continually bring home good cargoes on the *Elizabeth*, giving the British East India Company vast returns on their investment. Carr was a great asset, one to be protected. Lord Kensington had just secured a bonus for Captain Carr, and he treated Carr like a son, although there was not more than ten years of age difference between them.

Edwin Carr also had the asset of dashing good looks, a fine sense of grace and humor, and a way with people. He was indeed an asset to have as a business partner.

As Carr was talking to Lord Kensington, he was regaling him about the latest voyage from Padua, Tuscany, the Greek islands, and the return trip to England. He told the story of Captain Braden's rescue at sea, and the mutiny on the *Intrepid*. Kensington was fascinated with the adventure stories, but also somewhat upset about the plight of a British navy captain. After all, it was the growing power of the British navy that afforded the protection for the British East India Company's maritime commerce. A weak or corrupt navy meant trouble for profits. That would not do!

"Captain Edwin Carr!" called an attractive woman walking briskly to offer her hand to Carr.

"Lady Kensington," said Carr softly, "so good to see you again."

Lady Anne Kensington was the somewhat recent bride of Lord Andrew Kensington. Prior to the marriage, she had been the Kensington's mistress for several years. Lady Kensington was twelve years younger than her husband, and had been a friend of Carr long before she met Kensington. It was ironic that Anne Kensington now carried the title "Lady," for when she was Anne Fox, she had acted very little like a lady. Carr remembered the stories about Anne Fox and the way that she had acted when serving his sailing friends at the Pier's End Pub. She had met Andrew Kensington at a reception given by Jacob Carr. Jacob moved in circles that included the highest and lowest of society, where the common ground was money or the chance to acquire it. Jacob Carr had friends who were dockworkers, and friends who lent money to kings. Anne Fox had grown up in the neighborhoods of East London, near the Carrs' home, and while not childhood friends, they were linked by the poverty of the underclass.

Lord Kensington had been attracted to Anne from the moment he met her through Jacob Carr. It was not long before Anne was seeing Kensington every week, and sharing both his bed and some of his fortune. Upon the death of Kensington's wife, Alice, Kensington married Anne. He did this partly to satisfy his partners at the East India Company, and partly because Anne Fox would have nothing less than marriage and the title she had coveted since she was a girl.

"Captain Carr," she continued, grabbing Carr by the arm, "I want to introduce you to some of my new friends."

Carr was amused that she insisted on calling him "Captain Carr," when in other settings she did not hesitate to call him Eddy, or "Bunky," a nickname that had some rather coarse origins known only to a few of Carr's intimates.

"You don't want to introduce him as much as show him off!" chided Lord Kensington. "Show him off, then, he really is a prize," he called out.

Lady Anne barely looked back at her husband, enthralled with the man at her arm. Indeed, she would show him off, and she would enjoy the evening.

As Edwin Carr and Lady Kensington whisked off to other guests, Andrew Kensington began doing some business. He circulated among the guests, discussing the current political concerns. There were a number of new faces in this gathering, and Kensington inquired of some of these new guests about their business, their family, their estates. He found that King James had opened the door very widely to peerage. There were numerous new barons, baronets, dukes, and other titled gentry, all admitted to the social elite for the price of a title. If new titles needed to be created, so be it. This was a crown with very little available money, mostly due to James' refusal to convene Parliament. No Parliament meant no revenue from new taxes, so the resourceful king found new means of prying money from the landed wealth. He also found that these newly minted gentlemen and ladies cared little for their benefactor. Most found him to be weak, lacking in courage, and hopelessly out of touch with the people he ruled. Rumors also circulated about his fondness for young men, yet there was a strange ennui regarding the king personally. They cared little for James I, King of England, but they cared a great deal about the burgeoning economy and the potential wealth that colonies could generate. There were the very rich and the very poor. While the very poor far outnumbered the very rich, wealth had a way of keeping power away from the wretched masses in the cities.

Politics was for those who had passion for governance. Business was the passion of Lord Kensington, and he cared only for those who shared his passion, or those who could help his passion to flourish. Kensington found some kindred spirits who were interested in the tobacco trade just beginning in the colonies. More acres needed to be planted in the rich Virginia soil to increase the amount of tobacco available for export to England. Englishmen were just beginning to acquire a taste for the tobacco now being shipped to England, and Kensington was willing to bet that such a taste would mean merely the start of a valuable product. King James believed that tobacco was unhealthy, and did not promote the sale of the product. Kensington knew that there was money to be made, and that he did not necessarily need the support of a king to get rich. Yes, he would like the King's support, but he was determined to find greater wealth no matter what.

Kensington's attention turned to the entrance of some important guests who were just being introduced.

"The honorable Captain William Braden, accompanied by the Royal Court Physician Sir William Harvey!"

The crowd was gracious in its reception of these late-arriving guests. Many had heard the story, which had been abuzz earlier in the evening, about the rescue of Captain Braden, the mutiny on the *Intrepid*, and the reports of that renegade ship still at sea, possibly trying to enter Plymouth.

William Harvey was already well known in these circles as a brilliant scientist. While many failed to understand the import of his research, they knew of his prominence in the court of King James. Harvey was also well liked by those who met him, and his reputation was growing.

Kensington made his way to Captain Braden to hear firsthand of his ordeal. Braden looked frail, and every bit of his nearly sixty years of age. Kensington, at fifty-one, felt much younger in Braden's presence, and he gave the deference to the old warrior that befitted the age difference and the respect for military service as well. As Kensington spoke to Braden, Dr. Harvey approached them with another physician friend.

"Captain Braden," began Harvey, "my apologies for interrupting your conversation with this gentleman, but I do want you to speak with Dr. Jenner about your experience on the *Intrepid*. I have told Dr. Jenner that a Dr.

Shepherd treated you in a most unusual way for the plague. Do you mind telling Dr. Jenner about it?"

Kensington chimed in, "By all means, Captain Braden, please tell us of your experiences on the *Intrepid*. I am most interested in the state of our Royal Navy and your ghastly treatment on board your own ship."

Braden sighed, reluctant to speak once again of what felt to him like such a failure. Losing your ship, no matter what transpired, was a failure to a navy man. Nevertheless, Braden told in some detail the story of how he became ill, how Joseph Shepherd had given him moldy bread, had anointed him with oil, and prayed over him. Dr. Jenner seemed very compassionate toward the old captain, and listened out of respect. He thanked Braden for relaying the story, excused himself from the conversation, and returned to his wife, who was waiting for him near the wine porter.

William Harvey was anxious to meet Joseph Shepherd. Harvey's greatest gift, aside from his ability to charm people with his wit and savvy manner, was his willingness to embrace new ideas. Harvey was a true scientist, desiring to advance medicine, and willing to look beyond currently accepted beliefs.

Harvey was intrigued by the idea that Braden was cured by this odd assortment of prayer, oil, and moldy bread. He was not willing to see a miraculous healing, but he was open to see medical science at work. Perhaps there was something about the bread. Maybe Shepherd had applied some other medicines, which Braden, in his delirium, had forgotten. Harvey decided that he would find Joseph Shepherd to discover more of this fantastic story. If nothing else, he would meet an interesting person. Dr. Jenner, on the other hand, dismissed the story of healing as a nice tale from a poor old man. Lord Kensington, seeing Harvey's interest, decided that he too could be interested in pursuing this story. One never knew but that a man as well connected as William Harvey might be worth the investment of time.

Harvey glanced toward Lord Kensington and asked if he could arrange travel to Plymouth when the *Intrepid* arrived in port.

"I am at your command, Dr. Harvey," answered Kensington with an exaggerated bow.

Chapter 16

William Bradford and Dr. Mullins were told that Joseph Shepherd and I were to accompany them on the rounds of the ship, and we were to be available to answer questions about the physical health of the crew. Mr. Swailes would also accompany us as acting commander of the *Intrepid*. Mr. North, recovering well from his shoulder injury (and more slowly from the opium treatment that we had liberally administered), was able to sit up in sickbay, but he was not clear on any recent details of the trip, and he remained below deck.

"Dr. Greene," began James Mullins, "I expect that you will be totally honest with me about the condition of the crew. I realize that you have much to gain by withholding information about the health of the crew, but you are said to be an honorable physician and a man of integrity, so I will proceed on that assumption."

I wanted to feign indignance at his remarks, but the fact was I probably would have shaded the truth a bit to allow entrance into port – I am not above it – but I also believed that plague was not active on the ship. For all I knew, the symptoms we had seen were not truly those of the dreaded plague. What I did know is that for weeks we had seen no sick sailors, and that we were no threat to the port of Plymouth.

"Yes," I replied to Dr. Mullins, "I am a man of integrity, sworn to uphold my oath to medicine as well as to the crown of England. I can tell you that we have treated no sailor for signs of the plague for over three weeks. Those symptoms we did see may or may not have been the plague."

Bradford and Mullins looked at one another and Bradford said, "If that is so, then why did you put your captain Braden adrift to die in the ocean? It is only by the grace of God that he was rescued by the *Elizabeth*. He lived to tell of the treatment he received from this crew."

Shepherd and I were completely shocked at this statement, but no more than Mr. Swailes, who blanched whiter than his shirt at the pronouncement.

"Those two told us he was dying of plague!" Swailes managed to stammer out. Always the coward and now the fool, Swailes had, in his effort to save himself, shaken the credibility of the only people on board who could help get the *Intrepid* safely into port. Shepherd spoke through the haze of confusion, which was gathering around this conversation.

"The simple truth," said Shepherd, "is that Captain Braden, ill, but recovering, was forced off the ship by Mr. North. You will find no more signs of sickness on this ship, at least no more physical sickness."

Swailes was beaten, and he knew it. To refute the truth now would doom the *Intrepid* to more wandering outside of Plymouth. Further, his earlier outburst only served to strengthen the observation that he was a fool, a liar, and part of a rebellion that cast Braden off the ship.

William Bradford could see the truth, but he ordered that we proceed with an examination of the crew. Upon finding no signs of illness, the *Intrepid* would be led into port by the crew that had brought Mullins and Bradford out to the *Intrepid*.

Mr. Kelley, who stayed close to Shepherd and me during the visit from Bradford and Mullins, interjected a word of caution to Bradford.

"Sir," said Kelley, "I think that you might have Swailes here and Mr. North put in irons. They was the ones who put Captain Braden out to sea."

Swailes reached for his sword and unsheathed it quickly. He was about to slash Kelley when a pistol shot rang out from the cabin. The ball from the pistol hit Swailes in the back of his head, just at the base of his skull, and a mist of blood sprayed out around his entire head. I believe that he was dead before he hit the deck. He crumpled where he stood, and the sword flew into the air as he fell.

Bradford and Mullins were aghast at the sight of the murder. Mr. Kelley seemed undisturbed by the violence, while other crewmembers scuttled out of sight. I bent down to check on Swailes, knowing that he was dead. I never saw an exit wound, so I assumed that the projectile had coursed around his brain, killing him quickly. He was spared the hangman's noose by the quick justice of a nervous crewman.

"He is dead," I pronounced.

"Who fired that shot?" asked Bradford.

"Could have been a lot of men," ventured Kelley. The casual response to death and the complacent attitude about who had killed a man shocked the visitors. I believed that it was the natural consequence of a ship that had lost discipline, and where desperate young men, exposed to battle, simply acted upon their emotions.

"Where is the captain?" asked William Bradford.

"Mr. North is below deck, recovering from an injury," I stated.

"This is the same man that ordered Captain Braden overboard?" asked Bradford.

"Yes," I replied. "Dr. Shepherd and I will take you to him."

"I was not aware that there were two physicians on the *Intrepid*," said Bradford.

"I am not this ship's physician," said Shepherd. "I am only assisting the very capable Dr. Greene."

"I notice too that you call your captain Mr. North, so you do not afford him the same deference as you do Dr. Shepherd."

"He is not my captain," I said softly, letting Bradford take that how he wished. We went below deck while Kelley and two others covered Swailes with a sheet and carried him to the aft of the *Intrepid*.

We encountered North as he remained in a pleasant haze. He had probably heard the gunshot and the commotion, yet he had hardly stirred from his bed. Bradford introduced himself and Dr. Mullins, and he explained what they were about to do.

"Mr. North," I began, "we believe that in a short time, after the men are examined, that we will be allowed entry into Plymouth."

"Yes," North said, "we should land at Plymouth."

"We will proceed then with the examinations," said Dr. Mullins.

"Yes, proceed," we seemed to say in unison.

The examinations went smoothly. Mullins, Shepherd, and I gave essentially a cursory examination, consisting of visual examination, looking for the presence of buboes, performing palpation of glands under the arm and groin, and determining the presence or absence of fever. All of the men, including the two that had previously shown symptoms of the disease, heartily denied ever having felt the least bit sick in the past three months.

I noted that Mr. North had been acting a bit more suspiciously the past several hours, but I attributed that to his removal from the medications that I had been administering. However, as we came to North to discuss the plans for entry into port, he became very aroused in his anger, and he began to speak to no one in particular, saying that he would have no disloyal crew members on his ship, and that he would sail triumphantly into Plymouth with "two other men, if they are the only ones I find loyal!"

"Captain North," said William Bradford after the examinations were complete, "we shall return to port and advise the authorities that we find no presence of illness on the ship. You will be given permission, I'm sure, to enter port in the next day or two."

"Fine," said North. "We shall proceed when you signal us, but I will find the crew that is loyal to me." Then he barked to the crew around him, "Anyone who wants to leave my command had better do it now, or I swear I will hang the mutineers from the mast!"

He glared at the startled crew that was starting to gather around.

"You, Mr. James, are you loyal to me?"

David James, one of the young crewmen on his first voyage, turned red, then stammered his loyalty to his captain. Others muttered their fealty to their captain, then scrambled to posts around the ship.

Mr. Kelley then stood up and said to North, "If you want me to leave, I will."

Kelley was quite matter of fact in his demeanor, without a trace of fear, or even anger.

"Yes, Mr. Kelley, I want you to leave," hissed North.

At seeing this I was sure that Mr. North was completely losing his grip on reality. Surely he knew that Mr. Kelley, Shepherd, and I would tell the truth about what had happened to Captain Braden. Yet in his state of mind, he could only posture, bark orders, and intimidate those who would be intimidated.

"You all leave then. Dr. Greene, Kelley, Shepherd, and anyone else who cannot follow my command!"

I quickly took Joseph Shepherd by the arm and escorted him to Bradford and Mullins who stood nearby. Mr. Kelley joined us as we clambered overboard to the waiting small boat.

"The signal for permission to enter Plymouth shall be three blue flags flown from the mast of the *Mayflower*," said Bradford. With that news, Bradford and Mullins joined us in the boat to depart for Plymouth. Our voyage had come to its long-awaited conclusion.

Word would quickly spread from Plymouth to London about the *Intrepid* and the possible plague on board, Captain Braden's amazing rescue by the *Elizabeth*, and the problem of the *Intrepid*'s entry into port. People were also abuzz in Plymouth about the venture made by Mullins and Bradford to the *Intrepid*. As our small boat approached Plymouth, it was getting close to noon. We were exhausted from our ordeal, and William Bradford offered to have us spend the next day with him and Dr. Mullins. He would afford us a warm bed, good food, and delightful companionship. These were things that I had so missed on the *Intrepid* for the past three months.

Bradford went to Alvin Toll immediately to apprise him of our findings. Toll realized at once that the ship was deemed to be clear of disease by our presence in port. William Bradford spoke to Toll in a cheerful tone.

"Mr. Toll," he said, "we have found no evidence of plague aboard the *Intrepid*, and we believe that it is safe for her to enter Plymouth. We must also tell you, however, that we found Captain North to be quite mad, and possibly guilty of mutiny."

Toll seemed to relish the idea of such an adventure. "I will have North arrested the moment the ship docks!" he said.

"My part in this is over, Mr. Toll," said Bradford. "I told North that we would fly three blue flags from the *Mayflower* to indicate permission to enter Plymouth."

"Thank you, Mr. Bradford," said Toll. "I will arrange for the signal to be displayed."

Bradford left Toll's office, feeling that he had taken a step in leadership. His lesson from Exodus seemed to have been fulfilled in his life. He was able to lead, to have courage, to have wisdom, but all only if he submitted to God's will and provision in his life. It was a lesson he would utilize to great advantage for the rest of his life.

Toll busied himself with preparations to receive the *Intrepid*. He believed that there would be a struggle with North upon entry, but that his cordon of troops would be able to handle that. Bradford and Mullins had also shared with Toll that North's hold on the crew was tenuous, and that North's madness was probably wreaking havoc on the crew. Toll thought it best to make sure that his arrangements were complete, so he ordered that all of the available troops were to report for duty on the dock immediately. He then ordered the flags to be flown from the *Mayflower* so that the *Intrepid* could begin her journey into Plymouth.

Within the next several hours, preparations for receiving the *Intrepid* were proceeding at a busy pace. Unfortunately, on board the *Intrepid*, things were also becoming very busy. North, becoming increasingly irrational, ordered his crew to prepare the cannons for use. His thinking was totally consumed with suspicion about everyone around him. He now believed that the *Intrepid* would be denied entry into Plymouth because of a bad report from Bradford.

When North trained his eyepiece toward Plymouth, he saw the three blue flags fluttering from the *Mayflower*, but he also saw troops scurrying into position near the dock, and he saw cannon balls being loaded into piles near the shore batteries. North was now convinced that he would need to fight his way into port. Moreover, he believed that the *Intrepid* was perfectly capable of taking the port in a battle. His men were battle-hardened. The soldiers in Plymouth were mostly men too unreliable for service to the King in other, more important places.

North ordered the *Intrepid*'s crew to prepare for battle. The men scrambled to their posts, many more dazed than excited for battle. Many wondered how they could be preparing for a fight coming into their home port. North tried to rally them, standing on the bow of the ship, sword drawn, shouting orders. North ordered the *Intrepid* to come about and to prepare to fire a broadside at Plymouth.

Tensions were growing in Plymouth as the *Intrepid* drew closer to shore. Alvin Toll raised his spyglass to see the activity on board the *Intrepid*. His first glimpse of the *Intrepid* was of Mr. North, standing on the deck, wildly waving his sword and shouting something to the crew. Toll saw that the *Intrepid* was slowly turning to starboard, exposing her bristling array of cannon to Plymouth. Toll screamed an order to his aide, "Prepare to fire the shore batteries at once!"

The aide hurried down the steps of the tower and ran toward the bewildered soldiers standing near the cannons looking out to sea.

"Prepare to fire!" he shouted. The men looked at one another, then several began to laugh.

"Fire at our own ship?" they laughed. "You fire the cannons if you want, we're not."

At that they laughed some more, but the aide cut them off, "You fire those cannons, or I will kill you where you stand!"

He brandished his gleaming sword at the sergeant in charge and swore oaths at him. Suddenly, the *Intrepid*'s guns cut loose and iron balls smashed into the tower, dislodging some stones, and knocking out part of the tower's wall.

The soldiers hurried to load the cannons while another volley from the Intrepid slammed into a nearby ship, the *Majesty*. Splinters from the *Majesty*'s deck flew into the air as the soldiers hit the ground.

"Up, you cowards," screamed Toll's aide, "and defend this port!"

Mr. North looked pleased at the destruction he was raining on Plymouth. He could see the people on shore running for their lives. He could only imagine what they were saying and thinking as the *Intrepid* prepared to unleash another volley. He had not noticed Mr. Dooley approaching behind him. As he turned to ask Dooley to check on the powder supply, Dooley walked directly up to North. North looked him square in the eye and said, "Didn't you hear me, man? I told you to check on…"

Before he finished the sentence, Dooley had plunged a dagger deep into his chest. North reeled as blood spurted onto Dooley and onto the deck. North attempted to remove the dagger, but his strength was gone before he could budge it. He fell heavily to the deck, bleeding profusely.

"The killing ends with you, North!" Dooley screamed. He turned and walked back toward the stunned sailors. "The killing is over, the killing is over," he kept repeating.

As several crew went to check on North, they seemed to know that he was already dead. Dooley's dagger had probably hit North in the heart, and he died quickly. Dooley kept walking around the ship screaming, "The killing is over." The crew had indeed quit firing its cannons. The killing was over.

The soldiers on shore never did fire their cannons. As they scrambled to load and prepare to fire, Toll saw that the *Intrepid* was no longer in position to fire. She looked sad and beaten as she drifted toward the shore on the tide. Masts splintered, mainsail tattered, the real *Intrepid* was now coming into view. She was no longer a fighting ship. The *Intrepid* was a sad hulk drifting home after too much violence.

On board the *Intrepid*, several of the crew had finally taken charge and decided to raise a white flag of surrender. Toll ordered a boat full of soldiers to meet the *Intrepid* and bring her in. It was only after the white flag was hoisted from the *Intrepid* that the boat shoved off to its mission. What a bizarre scene – an English warship surrendering itself to an English port.

Mr. Dooley, still ranting, said, "I killed Swailes, I killed North, the killing is over, the killing is over."

Chapter 17

As the *Intrepid* was being sailed into port, Shepherd and I were having a conversation with William Bradford and James Mullins.

"Such a shame about the *Intrepid*. What really happened on that voyage?" asked Bradford.

I began to try to explain to Bradford what had happened on board the *Intrepid*, but I realized that I had no explanation for the strange tale of the *Intrepid*. How does one begin to tell of treachery, disease, battle, deceit, natural disasters, and, in the end, destruction?

"The ship lost its purpose," said Shepherd. "The grab for power overcame the natural purpose of the ship. In the end, ambition, glory, and pride caused this disaster."

"Could a good leader have prevented this?" asked Bradford.

"Yes, a courageous leader could have kept the focus," said Shepherd. "A leader who knows his mission can lead people past disaster into promise."

"Like Moses?" asked Bradford.

"Yes, like Moses," said Shepherd.

"I have been reading about Moses," said Bradford. "He led his people through the perils of the desert, selfless in his desire to get them to the Promised Land."

"Yes," said Shepherd, "that is true, but his goal was not the Promised Land; his goal was to do the will of God."

Bradford reflected on that statement for a while. He had been thinking a great deal about his own ability to lead his people to the Promised Land of America. He wondered how he could govern his people and lead them on a ship across an ocean. He desperately wanted to be a good leader, and he needed to do more than simply get them safely to America. He must care about their souls as well as their bodies. He must help them to true freedom in every sense, not just religious freedom from King James' tyranny.

Shepherd continued, "People need something to reach for, not just run away from. You will never succeed if you simply escape the tyranny of King James. You must build a land of freedom for your people."

"I know that I must lead in that way," said Bradford, "and I want to establish a place where people are free to worship God without the King deciding the religion of the land."

"Yes," said Shepherd, "and the people need to govern themselves. Government is good in that it allows people freedom to serve God and man. In the book of Romans, Paul tells the Christians that government is established to preserve the peace so that people can worship and serve freely. People who govern themselves can only do so properly if they have a higher goal in mind. Look at the *Intrepid*. Pride and ambition are the sins which destroyed the ship. If people are dedicated to serve the Lord God, they will be able to govern themselves in peace, and God will prosper them."

"We must have a document that proclaims these ideas," said Bradford. "We must make a compact which lays out these ideals which will serve as our basis of governance and order in America."

"May God bless you in that endeavor," said Shepherd.

Dr. Mullins was near tears as he listened to this discussion. He had, for years, struggled with his own convictions about personal and religious freedom. The upcoming trip to America would be his vindication of beliefs, as well as a chance to have a new start in life. His life had been broken by the execution of his brother because of his outspoken religious beliefs. Mullins had sworn to live a life worthy of his brother's legacy, and to pass on to his children the need to stand up for convictions. He was already teaching his ten-year-old son to stand true to his beliefs. The trip to America would be a challenge for his young family, but he relished the chance to give his family a better life than his parents had experienced. In fact, his decision to become a physician was part of his idea to care for others as his life mission.

I too was quite taken with the conversation between Shepherd and Bradford. These were fascinating ideas being discussed, and I was enjoying the session immensely.

"Be sure to bring cannon and powder," I said. "Not everyone has such lofty ideals."

Shepherd laughed, "Dr. Greene must always insert the other side of the equation. Leave the guns for King James, Mr. Bradford. You concentrate on leading your people to your King, not just away from the king of England."

Chapter 18

Lord Kensington and William Harvey set off for Plymouth when word reached London that the *Intrepid* had arrived in port. The story had already taken on a life of its own, embellished by the reports of Alvin Toll. Toll had been spreading the news that he had saved Plymouth from the rogue ship *Intrepid*. Toll's story was that the shore batteries under his command had hit the *Intrepid*, split her mast, and forced the crew into surrender. The buzz from the story had been getting a good deal of attention in southern England, and even King James had heard a few variants of the story.

Kensington had left his wife behind in London where she and Edwin Carr were renewing their old friendship. Kensington seemed to care little that there was also some talk about the balls and gatherings they were attending together, and that Lady Kensington seemed to have reverted to her "pre-lady" days. Lord Kensington was putting his attention to the business to be done in Plymouth. He also seemed to have an interest in the approaching departure of the *Mayflower* for America. Kensington believed that there might be a way to secure some trade connections with the trip. He would visit William Bradford to discuss such thoughts. Harvey was only interested in talking to Shepherd and me about the medical aspects of the *Intrepid's* voyage.

Shepherd and I were about to say farewell to William Bradford and James Mullins as the *Mayflower* was ready to depart. Lord Kensington and William Harvey met us as we were heading out to the busy *Mayflower*. I was thrilled to meet Harvey, who I had come to believe was a genius of growing proportion.

"Dr. Greene?" greeted Harvey as he jumped out of his carriage to meet us.

I quickly introduced Harvey to Joseph Shepherd. I was amazed that they embraced on the spot in a spontaneous recognition of one another, though they had never met before that moment. Lord Kensington also seemed astounded at the sight, but he quickly recovered, and introduced himself to me. It somehow seemed that the two brilliant men in the group had gravitated to one another, leaving Kensington and me to recede into the shadows together. Our mundane conversation quickly led to expedient matters of the *Mayflower's* departure, and Kensington's desire to meet William Bradford. I told Kensington that I would arrange a brief meeting with Bradford if he so desired. Meanwhile, Shepherd and Harvey were already discussing new and fascinating medical ideas.

"Dr. Harvey, I know that you have had the benefit of studying with some of the masters on the Continent," said Shepherd. "What is the most fascinating thing that you have discovered in your travels?"

Harvey replied that his study of human cadavers had led him to speculate on the role of blood in the body. Harvey stated that he believed that blood circulated through the body, pumped by the heart and conveyed by the veins throughout the entire body. While the exact process was not yet clear, Harvey could see the implications of radical changes in medical thought if this theory were true.

As usual, Shepherd had ideas of his own on the matter. As was also usual, Shepherd had both clinical and philosophical ideas on the blood. Shepherd began to explain to Harvey that the Bible indicated that the life of the body is in the blood, citing Leviticus 17:11. From this, Shepherd had, by intuition, agreed with Harvey that the life of the body is nourished in every organ by a fresh supply of circulating blood. Shepherd continued that he had seen healthy people become ill after having touched the blood of a sick person. Shepherd also said that he had seen people who were sick being bled by physicians as a treatment, and that he was appalled by the practice. Yet many physicians persisted in the practice, despite limited results. Shepherd said that he was amazed that so many physicians would persist in a practice that did not yield good results. Harvey nodded in agreement. Harvey too was concerned that medical practice was carrying on treatments that could not be proven to be effective.

"Dr. Shepherd, I have heard that you are a man of faith, and that spiritual ideas seem to dominate your treatment methods, yet you defend scientific principles. How do you explain this paradox?" asked Harvey.

"Well, Dr. Harvey, I see no conflict between faith and science," said Shepherd. "The same Creator who formed the earth put those very scientific principles in place. There is no conflict there. A man's body can be healed in very predictable, scientifically explainable ways, yet the cure may be the forgiveness of his sins and the cleansing of his conscience. That's what Jesus said in the book of Luke: 'Is it easier to say 'Get up and walk,' or, 'Your sins are forgiven?' Both messages are healing."

Harvey and Shepherd continued discussing such ideas as Lord Kensington and I were boarding the *Mayflower*. While their minds were contemplating higher ideals, Kensington and I were thinking more along the lines of business and treasure in the New World.

"Lord Kensington," I asked, "what is your interest in the voyage of the *Mayflower*?"

"My interest is to start more tobacco planting in the New World. I would like Mr. Bradford to consider raising tobacco once his colony is established. The money from tobacco may be the real salvation of his religious journey," sniffed Kensington.

76

"They are not bound for Virginia," I stated. "I do not know if tobacco grows in all parts of the New World."

Kensington seemed to have little interest in my comments about the climate in the New World. In fact, it appeared that he knew surprisingly little about America at all. I was stunned at this apparent ignorance. A man who made his wealth on commerce through trade and sailing ships around the world should be more attuned to such matters, I thought to myself. Lord Kensington was more one-dimensional than I had imagined. His world was money.

Lord Kensington was looking for ways to grow tobacco outside of the control of Virginia. King James had restricted the importation as well as the growing of tobacco. Kensington hoped that finding other places in the New World would allow for ways around the royal restrictions. Tobacco grown outside of Virginia, controlled by Kensington, and imported to England, could bring great wealth. He knew also that men like Jacob Carr could help to arrange such deliveries. What Kensington needed was a connection in America. Perhaps William Bradford would see the value of marrying his mission with a way to finance it.

As we reached the *Mayflower*, there was a buzz of activity and excitement all around the port. William Bradford was buried in the flurry of details in preparation for departure. As we approached Bradford, he was cordial to me. As I tried to introduce Lord Kensington to him, Bradford was suddenly cool and distracted. Kensington pressed to discuss his idea of tobacco farming with Bradford. He quickly explained his idea to Bradford, and pointed out the economic benefits that tobacco could bring to the new settlement. Bradford heard Kensington out for a few minutes, then interrupted, "My Lord Kensington, I thank you for your interest in our wellbeing, but I cannot commit to growing anything but food for my people. We are not interested in commerce; we are interested in freedom. We cannot be distracted from our mission. Now I really must be about my business."

With that, Bradford was off to oversee the loading of salt fish, fresh water, and other provisions. Lord Kensington was angry, but he managed to hide it from those around him. He was very good at this. However, anyone who knew him also knew that his anger, while hidden, would someday come to expression. Lord Kensington was always amazed at people who turned their back on making money. He simply could not understand them.

Harvey and Shepherd were still engrossed in their conversation, which now had wandered to such topics as poverty, nutrition, and the divine right of kings. Harvey was fascinated by Joseph Shepherd, and he invited Shepherd to return to London with him.

"I beg you to come with me," said Harvey. "Have you ever been to London?"

Shepherd replied that he had not been to London, but he had done a good bit of traveling around the world, and Shepherd agreed that London would be a fascinating destination. Shepherd also stated that he had no immediate plans, and that he would accompany Harvey to London.

"Good. Then it's agreed; we shall leave tomorrow," said a smiling Harvey. "I shall introduce you to King James."

Shepherd thanked Harvey, and then he approached me.

"Dr. Greene," began Shepherd, "would you please accompany me to London? The good Dr. Harvey has invited me, but I will not go unless you come also."

I thought about the offer, and I realized that I had made no provision whatsoever for my next plans. My medical practice had virtually disappeared after the death of my wife three years earlier. I had begun to drink more heavily than I cared to admit, I had left my practice, and I had entered into the service of the Royal Navy. I too was running from my past, much like many of the sailors on the *Intrepid*. I had supposed that I would go on to sail on the next voyage of one of the Royal Navy vessels, but I had not given much thought to that even though I had no real source of income secured.

"Yes, I will come with you," I said. I could not believe that those words had come from my mouth so quickly and comfortably. There just seemed to be something about Joseph Shepherd that drew me to where he was, and I agreed to follow him, having no plans, but having also, strangely, no fears.

Harvey knew that Kensington had been listening to the conversation that was rapidly expanding to larger plans. He seemed to see some unease in Kensington.

"Lord Kensington," said Harvey, "I fear that I have prevailed upon your good nature to invite these men back to London with us."

Kensington looked unfazed by the prospect.

"As you wish, Dr. Harvey," said Kensington. "I would think that we could put these two men to work profitably for the East India Company."

I looked at Shepherd, amazed at my good fortune. Perhaps I would have plans after all, even if they were not of my own making. Perhaps those were the best plans to have.

Chapter 19

The trip to London was pleasant, if uneventful compared to our recent adventures. Harvey and Shepherd were cementing a friendship based upon intellect and mutual respect. Harvey, the renowned physician to the court of King James, was drawn to Joseph Shepherd, a physician, philosopher, scientist, theologian, and world traveler. As they discussed the concept of the circulation of the blood in the human body, Shepherd seemed to speak with the authority of a scholar. Harvey began to write as they spoke. I have seldom seen such animated conversation. My medical training seemed insignificant compared to their lofty discussions. I satisfied myself listening to their discourse. Kensington, bored by the conversations, alternately slept or read through reports he had collected from voyages of East India Company ships. He was particularly interested in the tobacco crops growing in Virginia, and he was planning to find other areas in the world where this miracle crop might grow.

We arrived in London on the evening of the 5th of September, 1620. We disembarked from our carriage at Lord Kensington's estate in West London. We were greeted by a group of servants who quickly scooped our bags from the carriage. We were led into the entry room, where we found Lady Kensington and Edwin Carr laughing over a bottle of Madeira.

"Andrew!" greeted Anne Kensington. "I see you have brought guests."

"Yes," he replied, "I see that you have kept yours with you."

"Edwin Carr is not a guest here," said Anne. "He lives here." She giggled a drunken little giggle. Andrew had seen this many times before.

"I shall have the servants prepare a feast," said Anne.

"Spare them the trouble," said Lord Kensington. "We will do well with brandy and some eel pie."

"Just the brandy will be fine with me," I retorted. "I am ready to go to bed and get some real sleep for a change."

Shepherd, Harvey, and I sipped some brandy, talked with Edwin Carr about his voyage, which had been strangely intertwined with ours, and retired for a restful night's sleep.

I suspected that Lord and Lady Kensington's night was not as peaceful as ours. Raised voices could be heard throughout the spacious house as the Kensingtons fought over her latest new friend who would share the house. Edwin Carr was not the first man to have spent time under Lord Kensington's roof, and this was not especially a secret in London social circles. Lord

Kensington's anger at his wife seemed less about her lover than about the increasingly brazen manner in which she flaunted such affairs. Whereas in the past she had been somewhat more discreet about such liaisons, she now seemed almost excited to bring such affairs to his attention. For his part, Lord Kensington seemed resigned to her behavior, but embarrassed by her disregard for whatever was left of his public image. Indeed, Lord Kensington had never been lacking for female companionship either, but Anne's insistence upon equal consideration for outside lovers rankled him to no end.

Harvey and Shepherd were anxious to get back to Harvey's office and laboratory. I was simply anxious to get on to a new adventure – something to distract me from my growing sense that my life was increasingly without direction or meaning. I had to admit that seeing Harvey and Shepherd's animated medical discussions both shamed me and sparked a renewed interest in my need for continued education in these advanced ideas.

Shepherd, ever the gentleman, invited me to accompany them to Harvey's laboratory the next day. I accepted the invitation. We embarked the next morning by carriage to London Square. I was struck by the busy streets, the sounds of street vendors hawking their wares, and the smells that emanated from the alleys. The stench of human waste, the entrails of animals that had been discarded by butchers, and the rotting fish dumped by vendors after the day's sales were completed came together in my nostrils. Indeed, having spent the last few months at sea aboard the *Intrepid* had almost inured me to such smells, but I was struck nonetheless.

The colors of the cloth for sale by some merchants caught my eye, and the sound of languages foreign to me all turned my head in this fascinating city. Perhaps the excitement of London could renew my spirit.

Shepherd too was drinking in this mixture of sounds, smells, and color, but he seemed troubled by the street urchins who pounced on us for money at each step. They knew the territory, and they knew that we were visitors – perhaps by our continual gawking at each new sound. These children were dressed in rags, mostly. They seemed to have renewed energy each time they saw a new mark. Shepherd was drawn to them, and he quickly dispensed what few coins he had to the first children who approached him.

"Best not to do that," cautioned Harvey. "They will never leave you alone. Worse, you'll be marked as one with money, and you will be dragged into the nearest alley as soon as you're not alert."

"I will take that chance," said Shepherd. "These children must live a terrible life."

"It is the life of this city," said Harvey. "They survive somehow."

We spent several hours touring Harvey's office and laboratory. There were the usual specimens, skeletons, chemical solutions, books, and other academic papers. However, I was fascinated by the odd-looking tube of metal and glass sitting prominently near the window. I asked Harvey about it, and he seemed proud to discuss it.

"That is my magnification scope," he said. "With it, I can see minute parts of cells in the body. For example, I can see that in the blood there seem to be bodies of various shapes and sizes. I am looking forward to having Professor Janssen build me a better scope when I see him in Holland next year."

Harvey offered to let me look through the end of the scope. I looked at a drop of water, and I could see small bodies wiggling in the drop. The water itself seemed to teem with life, unseen by anyone else. I felt the awe of discovery wash over me as I pondered a new world that I had never before conceived of. I believed that I was in the presence of something sacred, yet somehow very mundane. It was, after all, a simple drop of water, yet it seemed to be the very microcosm of a new world of discovery and hope.

That evening, Kensington took us to the Boar's Head Tavern, where we drank some fine ale and ate a hearty stew. The food, while heavy and filling, was not the main attraction of the pub. The people who were in the place were a lively mixture of merchants, sailors, and even the occasional member of Parliament. Women who were looking for business seemed to know exactly which men to approach. There was no shortage of takers for what they were selling. Smoke filled the air, as that new fad seemed to be becoming widespread. At first, I choked on the smells in the air. Gradually, I became accustomed to it, and, eventually, enticed by it. Kensington pointed to this room and explained to us his desire to capitalize on the habit.

"These people are paying a lot of money for tobacco, and I see more and more converts to it," he said. "I believe that we can dedicate a fleet of ships to its import from America. I would like you and Dr. Shepherd to help me in that venture."

Shepherd answered Kensington quickly. "I see many better uses for shipping than to import tobacco," he said. "There are some interesting food products which I believe will improve the health of the people of England. Tobacco is not one of them."

Kensington replied, "Dr. Shepherd, I am not in the health business, I am in the business of making money."

"Yes, that is true," replied Shepherd, "but I am in the business of making people healthy. Therefore, you will need to find someone else for this venture."

"So be it," said Kensington. "If you do not wish to make money, you have no need of me, it seems. Making money is what I do best."

"Is it what you live for?" asked Shepherd.

"I suppose it is," said Kensington. It seemed that Kensington had never considered that there was any other reason to live, so he was puzzled by Shepherd's question. I felt a bit awkward at this exchange. Lord Kensington was, after all, our host, and we were all faring quite nicely from his ability to make money. I was hoping that Kensington did not believe that Shepherd spoke for me also in his thinking. I was in need of a living, and if Lord Kensington saw fit to employ me in his business, I would not turn him down.

"I believe it is time to go home, gentlemen," said Kensington. "Would you like to spend another night at my home?"

Harvey responded that he would be happy to have Shepherd and me stay with him in his quarters for the next few days until we had better plans. Shepherd agreed to stay with Harvey, but I felt that perhaps the time had come for me to be thinking about a future with Kensington's offer.

"I would be most honored to take your offer," I said to Kensington. Kensington seemed pleased. I believed that he wanted someone else to come home with him rather than to face Anne alone. I could be a good distraction for him.

As we got up to go, we heard a great commotion from the next room. Shouts and cursing filled the air, followed by the crash of a table and breaking glass. A scream pierced above all the din. At that moment, a bloody man came running out to the innkeeper.

"There's a man been stabbed in the belly in there," he said. At that, he fled the pub. He was followed quickly by several other men. Shepherd and I went to the next room to see if we could help the victim.

We came upon a scene of chaos. A man lay on the ground in a growing pool of blood. Blood was pouring from his stomach area, and he was moaning and writhing in pain. We approached him, and he looked at us wide-eyed and frightened. I quickly grabbed a cloth from a nearby table and held it to his stomach. He was not a very stout fellow, so I tied the cloth around him to try to staunch the blood flow. We had to put several layers of cloth on the wound as each layer became soaked with blood. It became clear that he would quickly bleed to death if we could not control his bleeding.

"Bring him to my office," said Harvey. "I will try to save him by suturing the wound."

We bound the cloths around the man as tightly as we dared, and there seemed to be some success in slowing the flow of blood. However, without treatment, I felt that he would be dead within the hour, if not sooner. We carried him in a large cloth, and began to take him out of the pub. Just then, Lord Kensington cried out, "Good God, that is Jacob Carr!"

Carr looked up at him and smiled weakly.

"I am at your service," he said.

The trip to Harvey's office took almost twenty minutes, and Carr was starting to lose consciousness. We carried him up to Harvey's office and placed him on a table. Harvey seemed confident, even in this, by my estimation, hopeless situation.

"We need to tie him down to the table," said Harvey.

We quickly secured some straps and began to tie him down. By now, Carr offered little resistance, being only barely conscious.

"We must open the wound further, find the vessels which are severed, and tie them off. I pray that there is not too much internal damage," said Harvey. As we took off layers of bandages, we saw that he was still bleeding, but with much less force. "Indeed," said Harvey, "his blood volume is so depleted that there is evidently little pressure left."

Harvey opened the wound so that he could reach inside to the bleeding vessels. We had threaded a needle with catgut, and Harvey proceeded to tie off the bleeding vessels. He closed the wound quickly to minimize the suffering of the awakening Carr.

"I believe that he will survive if he can avoid the fevers which often accompany such wounds," said Harvey. Shepherd and I concurred that he could survive the wound, but perhaps not the complications that often presented in these situations.

"We must take him to a hospital," I suggested. "The Franciscans care for the poor and the sick in a small hospital next to the monastery."

We allowed Carr to rest for a while as we discussed our plans. Lord Kensington had gone to the constable to gather townspeople to pursue the assailants of Jacob Carr. We had no illusion that the assailants would be brought to justice. Indeed, Jacob Carr had so many connections with violent men, it would be hard to track them down.

Kensington returned as we were loading Carr on to the wagon.

"What are you doing with Jacob Carr?" he asked. Kensington seemed surprised that Carr had survived.

"We are taking him to the Franciscans so that they can provide medical care while he recovers," I said.

Kensington said, "They may be too full with street people, beggars, and lunatics. However, I will see if I can arrange transport to the Franciscan mission," Kensington said.

Carr was a frightful sight indeed. Matted blood covered his hairy chest and stomach. His trousers were soaked with blood. Bandages covered the ends of catgut sutures, which protruded from his closed wound. Carr was moaning now and asking for a drink. He looked like one of the casualties of the battlefield that I had seen in years past.

Kensington had secured a hearse from the mortuary for the trip to his manor. What irony that a hearse afforded the softest ride for a man in distress!

Shepherd was curious about the Franciscans and the work at the mission. Shepherd asked if I would show him the monastery, so I agreed to take him there. It had been some years since I had ventured to that part of London, or seen the monastery, so I too had some curiosity about the place.

We arrived at the monastery just before dawn. Some of the friars were beginning to make breakfast for those who were in their care. As we walked through the piles of clothing slumped on the floor, we came to realize that some of these "piles" were children, curled up in a little ball to stay warm. An early autumn chill added to the misery of the damp, dark surroundings. The friars were coaxing a fire back to life in the hearth, and a large kettle was taking its place on the rack above the fire. Some of the figures on the floor started to rouse, and it was only then that we saw eyes staring out from under the rags.

Many of the men had been there for some time. There were those who were sick and had come there to die. Some were just those who had no other shelter, and had begged the friars to provide for them. In all, it was a sad and miserable lot, and were it not for the Franciscans' charity they would be under bridges, on the street, or dead already.

I noticed that Joseph Shepherd was very silent. He took in these sights without comment, but his sadness and displeasure were evident. He seemed indignant that these people were relegated to such a state.

After a long silence, Shepherd said, "Dr. Greene, I believe that I will stay here and offer my services for a while."

"You cannot be serious!" I said. "Lord Kensington has offered us a position with the East India Company. That is an opportunity that we can hardly ignore."

Shepherd looked at me as if I had not heard him.

"Dr. Greene," he said, "this too is an opportunity."

Chapter 20

People seemed to be naturally attracted to Joseph Shepherd. His compassion was evident in his exchanges with people who were hurting, diseased, or broken in some way. Yet he had the capacity, and the tendency, to be ferociously honest. With someone like Kensington or the notorious seaman North, Shepherd would not fail to point out the error of their ways, and he did not much care about the consequences of it. I was not sure if he were simply fearless, or perhaps a bit of a lunatic. His wisdom and insight of knowing how to read people were uncanny. I knew that I needed to be around him to learn more of such things. I was always a cynic, seeing the worst in people, or perhaps just expecting the worst. Nonetheless, people never let me down in my expectations – they always seemed to live down to them.

I left Shepherd to return to the Kensington manor, and I told him that I would return to see him the next day. Shepherd nodded, but he seemed to be disappointed that I had chosen to go with Lord Kensington. Shepherd remained with the friars and planned to minister to those children who were sick and dying. I admired his compassion, but I questioned his decision. The opportunity to have a position with the East India Company seemed too good to turn down.

The ride to the Kensington Manor was uneventful. Upon arrival, I was met by Edwin Carr. Evidently, Kensington had seemed to relish giving him the news that his brother had been stabbed at the pub. Edwin pointed out that Kensington was a man of small compassion, and an even smaller sense of civility. Carr was not surprised.

"I cannot tell you how often that fool gets in fights!" he said.

"His injuries are very serious," I noted. I continued, "We left him at the Franciscan monastery, and the friars are attending to him."

"Well," said Carr, "I hope that being around the good men of God will do him some good."

Anne Kensington appeared as Carr was speaking. She was wearing a wine-stained gown, and had evidently consumed a good bit more than she had managed to spill on herself. Kensington turned to me and said, "To think that I married her and gave her a title! And Edwin Carr, a man who I loved and promoted, is no better than her. There is simply no one I can trust anymore." Kensington had a strange sense of resignation in his voice. He had started his sentence in anger, and he finished it in a trailing and sad voice. "Let us leave these two together and go back to London."

With that, he picked up his hat, grabbed me by the arm, and led me out of the Manor. I did not mind the decision. I had no interest in seeing the sad tale unfolding in front of me. I also did not like the prospect of seeing a future business partner like Edwin Carr treating Kensington in this way. For that matter, I was a bit worried that I may be out of the business before I even got into it. I had not even been officially hired by the East India Company yet, and I already began to have doubts about the sour side of the business. Kensington was rapidly changing his mood once again. He seemed invigorated with new ideas, and he wanted to share them with me at a pub. We proceeded to make the trip back to London, only this time Kensington was talking constantly about new business ideas. He would find another captain to sail for him, and he would concentrate upon trade with the New World. Tobacco would be his main import, and he would introduce it to Africa on a scale never before seen. Tobacco for slaves would be the plan. He would send a fleet of ships to the New World and begin the tobacco business there in earnest. When sufficient crops were established, he would export the tobacco to England, where he would have no shortage of customers in the pubs and markets. He would make huge profits, to be used to purchase African slaves for export to America, making another fortune in that. Those slaves would be sent to America to work the tobacco fields under the direction of colonists who would be tied to the East India Company. He was actually planning a huge enterprise as we rode to London. There seemed to be an eerie calm about him as he spoke. While I was not the canniest business man, even I could see the potential profits to be made in this venture.

We arrived in London just in time for supper. By now, Kensington was feeling very good about himself. He had launched into a creative business venture in order to cleanse his mind of the pain he had experienced in his own home. Indeed, business seemed to be this man's salvation.

"Let me buy you a fine dinner to celebrate our new business plan!" he exclaimed.

"What part do I have in the plan?" I asked. I had heard nothing about my involvement in the plan, and I did not have anything particularly helpful to offer it in any case.

"My dear Dr. Greene, you may be the only man I can trust anymore," he said loudly. "You may have any part in it that you choose. You are an educated man, a doctor, surely there is a place in this for you!"

I did not know whether to be excited about this or apprehensive. It could just be the ramblings of a vengeful man. It could have just been his creative mind bubbling with ideas to entertain himself (and perhaps me too). Or, this could be the chance of a lifetime to get in on a moneymaking plan for the ages.

The next morning, after we had eaten (and drunk) of England's finest fare, I decided to go to the friary hospital to check on my friend Shepherd. The day dawned with an absolute glow. The mid-September morning was clear and crisp. The Inn we had secured for the night was of the highest quality, and its new straw mattresses and down pillows offered us a good night's sleep. I decided to take an early morning walk through London to visit the friary. Once again I was struck by the squalor of the streets and the smells of the alleys. Beggars, thieves, and prostitutes had been out late the night before, working the neighborhoods for their livelihood. The early morning stirrings were led by the fishmongers and vegetable sellers. Fish were usually sold by late morning to the wise shoppers who grabbed them fresh before the sun worked its havoc on them. The smell of fresh bread from the bakeries stirred my hunger, even though I had eaten quite enough just hours before. Nonetheless, the smell of fresh bread can do wonders on the senses. I bought several loaves of bread, and I purchased a dozen fresh cod to take to the friary. I knew that food there was always welcome, and I wanted to celebrate what could be a new business life for me.

As I entered the mission, Joseph Shepherd was busy tending to several children who were coughing loudly.

"Joseph," I called, "I bring you breakfast!"

"Dr. Greene!" he called. "We will be happy to eat that breakfast."

Indeed, as soon as I came closer, I was surrounded by children, who all could walk. The smell of fresh bread had excited them as well, and I was set upon by the hungry patients. Joseph patiently waited until the bread had been parceled out, and he brought the fish to the kitchen area where he deftly filleted the cod, laid them on some glowing coals, and served up a breakfast feast to the patients, residents, and friars. I was struck that these dozen cod and the loaves of bread were able to serve the gathering of people. Yet, everyone seemed satisfied after the meal was consumed.

Just two days before, Harvey had persuaded the Franciscans to take in Jacob Carr for further care. Harvey had escorted Carr back into the care of the larger community that the Franciscans had to offer. He further wanted to remove himself from Anne Kensington and Edwin Carr.

I began to ask Joseph about his plans. He had alluded to the idea of staying at the mission to serve the poor and the sick who regularly populated the place.

"Joseph," I said, "you are a very talented physician, an educated man. Do you plan to stay here and tend to these few sick people, or will you take on a larger task, worthy of your talent?"

Joseph mused at this statement.

"Is there a higher calling than caring for these people?" he asked.

"Well, yes, I believe so," I replied. "You can stay here and serve dozens, or you can take Dr. Harvey's offer to meet the King of England. Perhaps the King will give you a mission to serve people in the entire country!"

We had received the invitation from Dr. Harvey, but we had not yet been able to secure a time to meet King James. I felt that the least I could do would be to see to it that Shepherd got the opportunity to meet the King. I decided to encourage such a meeting again, and I would ask my new associate, Andrew Kensington, to arrange for Dr. Harvey and Joseph Shepherd to meet with the King. Adventures this large were now starting to seem like possibilities again to me.

Chapter 21

William Bradford was busy making final arrangements to set sail on the *Mayflower*. He seemed to have a new resolve, and more confidence after having discussed his mission with Joseph Shepherd. He was aware that this mission was much larger than himself, and that all he could do was to prepare as best he knew how, and to pray as hard as he knew how. With that, he was ready.

Alvin Toll was encouraging Bradford to leave as soon as possible, because he was fearful that the people of Plymouth were getting restless with so many people of controversy still in his port. Toll was ever mindful of the mood of people, and the political implications of his every move. Having these religious zealots out of his port would certainly not hurt.

On September 16th, at 5:30 A.M., Bradford and the *Mayflower* pushed out of Plymouth and slipped into the ocean. It was at that exact moment that William Harvey was awakened out of a deep sleep, having experienced a dream of staggering proportions.

Harvey dreamt that a small sailing vessel was coursing through a labyrinth of tubes. The vessel went round and round in an endless journey, always arriving at the same place. It would pass through cliffs and canyons, valleys, narrow openings, sometimes quickly, and at other times slowed to a crawl, but always moving. Always the vessel returned to the same place after the journey, only to begin the trip once again. It was only when the liquid that the vessel sailed upon turned a bright red that Harvey woke with a start. He realized that the liquid was blood, and the vessel was flowing through the human body. The tubes were veins and arteries, and the landscape was the inner workings of the human organs.

Harvey had been up the night before, reading and checking through his latest papers, and talking about them late into the night with Joseph Shepherd. He realized that this revelation confirmed his beliefs about the circulation of the blood. He had reasoned that certain blood vessels had the job of carrying the blood away from the heart, which pumped the blood at the regular pace of its beat. Other vessels, which had tiny valves to direct the course of the flow only one way, carried the blood back to the heart for the return journey. His work with the magnification scope had revealed these little valves, but he could not understand the function until this moment. Harvey had conjectured over the years, as early as 1616, that his theory of the circulation of the blood in the body was a superior explanation of blood movement and function than the traditional theory by the ancient philosopher-physician

Galen. Yet he had been somewhat circumspect about how he shared his beliefs, and the audiences who might receive the ideas. Now he was convinced that he had been given a definitive revelation about the theory.

Harvey immediately began to make notes on his dream, and to write out more of his beliefs on the circulation system. He couldn't wait to share this information with Shepherd. Shepherd seemed to be much more willing than other men of learning to discuss this issue in such an open and creative manner. In fact, it was Shepherd who told Harvey to not restrain his thinking to the conventional medical thought of the day. Shepherd seemed to think that Harvey was on to something extraordinary, and he encouraged Harvey to be bold in his theories.

"Joseph," Harvey called to a sleeping Shepherd. "I just had the most extraordinary dream!"

Shepherd turned over out of his sleep and said, "Is it about the circulation of the blood?"

"Well, yes," Harvey stammered. "How could you possibly know that?"

"I simply made a guess," Shepherd said. "You were up late last evening talking about it, and the fact that you woke me to share the dream just made sense. You have talked of little else for the past two days. Are you now convinced of your theory?"

"Yes, I am," replied Harvey confidently.

"We are indeed fearfully and wonderfully made by our heavenly Father," said Shepherd.

"This is indeed a great day," said Harvey. "Today we shall be honored to meet King James."

Shepherd was glad to be able to meet King James, but not especially excited. Shepherd wanted to ask the King if he knew of the extent of the plight of the poor and sick who populated the streets of London.

"Dr. Greene, I trust that you have prepared to meet with the King," said Harvey.

"Well, yes, I suppose I have," I ventured. Actually, I did not know what I would say to the King. There was so much to say, and yet so little. I could talk for hours of our adventure on the *Intrepid*, but I did not know if he would really care to hear our tale of woe. It certainly affected the kingdom very little, I should think. Perhaps the damage to an expensive ship of the battle line would bother him, and perhaps he would have thought little about it. I was more interested in extending whatever business career I might have by aligning with Andrew Kensington, and discussing the burgeoning trade with the New World. I had not discussed the plan with Shepherd, because I was certain that he would not endorse it. Too bad, because there was money to be made in it, I was sure.

Upon our arrival at the Court of King James, we were met by Robert Carr, one of the King's gentlemen. Robert, cousin of Edwin and Jacob Carr, was one of the King's favorites, and often spent the night as his gentleman chamberlain. Robert was cordial and welcoming to us.

"Perhaps your visit is well-timed," he told Harvey upon greeting him. "The King seems to have taken ill for the past few days, and he looks quite pale and weak."

"Then we shall be glad to tend to him," said Harvey. "In fact, the King will be graced with three physicians, for Dr. Greene and Dr. Shepherd are my new traveling companions."

I noted that Harvey too had now recognized the medical talent of my friend Shepherd. Indeed, I was coming to believe that Shepherd had access to more healing power than both Harvey and me.

Upon coming into the King's chambers, I was struck by the beauty of the palace. Simple in many ways, the halls were lined with portraits of James and his Scottish ancestors. Signs of the burgeoning trade of the Kingdom included tapestries from India, silks from China, and books from Persia. The smells of cloves and cardamom wafted from the kitchen, where various pies were cooling.

We were greeted by George Villiers, Duke of Buckingham, who was attending to the King. The King was in his bed, weak from this unknown bout of illness that had caused him to quickly lose his strength and vigor.

"You may sit," said the King.

We took seats around the walls of the spacious room. Light was streaming in from the windows on two sides of the room, brightening an otherwise gloomy setting. The Duke of Buckingham took the lead in asking Dr. Harvey to diagnose the King's malady. Harvey went up to the King, asking permission to begin his examination. The King quickly assented, and Harvey began to feel the King's head for fever, and to palpate under his arms and around his neck.

Dr. Harvey made notes as he continued the examination. He asked the King and Mr. Villiers about how long the symptoms had been persisting, and they indicated that there had been a gradual weakening. The King's appetite had been diminishing over the past few weeks, along with his energy. During the absence of Dr. Harvey, the King had been attended by a physician, a Dr. Jones from the Royal Society, Villiers noted casually.

"What treatment did he begin with His Majesty?" Harvey asked.

"I believe that he treated my lord with some herbs, and he bled him several times when the King suffered from fever," replied Villiers.

"Herbs?" asked Harvey.

Villiers, somewhat proud of his memory and attentiveness, replied, "Yes, milk thistle made into a tea."

"Nothing else?" queried Harvey.

"No," said Villiers.

Harvey looked over at Shepherd and me – a look that asked us for our input without directly asking us. I started to defer to Shepherd as had become my new, albeit somewhat disconcerting habit, but Shepherd prodded me to answer. In truth, I had become good at recognizing possible side effects from herbal medicines, and I suggested that milk thistle could cause some problems with the bowels, possibly diarrhea, which could, over a period of time, weaken the patient. Harvey asked the delicate question about the King's bowel habits, and Villiers did not flinch. He responded affirmatively, that the King had experienced diarrhea recently, actually a "bloody flux," he called it. Feeling more confident, I then suggested that Dr. Jones may have been concerned about the King's liver. I knew that milk thistle was used often to treat liver problems. Harvey and Shepherd concurred, and suggested that the treatment may have been appropriate, but that the bleeding concerned them. Why would Dr. Jones bleed him? Villiers picked up on our conversation and stated that the King had a fever, and that Dr. Jones felt that bleeding would help. Indeed, the King felt some relief after the bleedings, but he also then felt weaker.

Shepherd then spoke up. "Dr. Harvey, may I suggest that we use some of your new equipment?"

"Yes, what did you have in mind?" Harvey asked.

"I think that your magnifying scope may be of some help," he replied. I certainly had no idea what Shepherd was talking about, but I had learned from being around him that it was usually a good idea to follow his lead. Harvey too seemed to respond without question to Shepherd's idea, so we simply asked how he would like to proceed.

Shepherd said, "This will involve all of us."

Now I was really very curious, but I also had a sense of excitement. All of us were involved in the medical care of the King of England. Selfishly, I was looking for some of the reflected glory that might come with helping the King in a medical problem. Shepherd laid out his plan for us as we left the room. He began to explain that we would require a sample of blood from all of us – Shepherd, Harvey, me, as well as the King. He would then look at the blood in the scope that Hans Jannsen had built for Harvey. Shepherd believed that we would be able to see differences in our blood and that of the King. He reasoned that there was a problem in the blood of the King. Indeed, Dr. Jones had determined that the King had a liver problem. Shepherd believed that if the liver were the problem, the blood would be affected. Indeed, perhaps the blood itself was the problem, causing the liver problems.

Harvey and I looked at one another with expressions that stated our disbelief, shock, and even the allowance that Shepherd could be a genius. Villiers, now a bit suspicious, took on his role of regal protector. He was following us as we left the room, and overheard some discussion about blood samples.

92

"Gentlemen," he began, "I believe that the King cannot stand another bloodletting. You physicians are just short of charlatans, I do declare!"

Shepherd interrupted, "My dear Duke of Buckingham, I appreciate your concern and protection of your King. You are to be commended for your diligence and care of His Highness. I am not suggesting another bloodletting. In fact, that is the very last thing that should be done. We will only require a small amount of blood from him. Actually, if you would like to participate, all of us will be submitting a small amount of our blood for the procedure I want to try. You may help by giving some of your blood as well."

Villiers was taken aback by such a suggestion, but he did not discount the idea immediately.

Shepherd had once again showed his ability to engage people to a higher cause. He continued to amaze me, but I was not prepared for what was soon going to happen.

Chapter 22

Harvey returned to the King's chambers and explained to His Majesty the need to draw blood, but not nearly the amount normally taken in a therapeutic bloodletting. In fact, Shepherd had suggested that only the smallest amount of blood would be needed; a small vial would do. Harvey found some acceptable vials, washed them out, and found stoppers to contain the sample of blood to be taken. Shepherd had suggested that they be carefully labeled, with each of our samples of blood well marked on the vial. Harvey brought out a fresh lancet from his bag in the palace dispensary. He always kept medical supplies available just in case he would need to treat the King, or perhaps one of the courtiers from time to time. Harvey made a small incision on the King's fingertip, and proceeded to repeat the procedure with each of us. Villiers then insisted that he too give a sample of blood, and Harvey gladly obliged him.

We left the palace in the most expectant of moods. I was initially disappointed that I was unable to really speak with the King of England, and that our trip became no more than a medical visit. On the other hand, I could not shake the idea that we were participating in the most extraordinary scientific experiment that one could conceive of. While all of this was swirling in my head, I did not notice that a man was fairly running out to catch up with us. As we turned, we heard the puffing breath coming from an aging man anxious to catch us before we left the palace. He was, I guessed, about sixty years old, in fair shape for a man of his age. He had a ruddy complexion, sharpened by a graying beard. He had a distinguished look, and it was clear that he was a man of some prominence, based upon his clothing.

"Stop a moment, I beg you," he stammered out. Clearly, he was now quite short of breath, so we stopped to ask him of his need for us. "I have heard that you are planning an experiment of some kind," he gasped.

Harvey went over to him immediately. "Francis!" he shouted. "How did you know that we were pursuing an experiment?"

"Villiers told me," he replied, now starting to regain his breath and his decorum.

"Gentlemen," Harvey said to Shepherd and me, "I would like you to meet Sir Francis Bacon, the honorable Lord Chancellor of England!"

I had of course heard of Bacon, a brilliant scientist, artist, and writer. I had not expected to meet him as he was running to catch me and my friends! Shepherd as usual was gracious, but nonplussed at meeting him.

"Dr. Bacon," he began, "I am quite honored to meet you. I have read many of your works, and I am especially taken with *The New Atlantis*. We must talk about that sometime."

Bacon seemed appreciative, but was clearly more interested in discussing our mission.

"Gentlemen," he began, "your experiment with blood: I want to know more about it."

"Well, so do I!" I laughed. At that Shepherd laughed out loud.

"Come," he said, "let us all see what is in the offing."

We went to a carriage that Villiers had procured for us, and we proceeded to Harvey's office. Bacon was animated now as the discussion turned to science. Clearly that was his love. He began to talk about the need for certain controls in our model, even though he had no idea of what the experiment was. Shepherd was nodding in agreement, and then he began to tell all of us what he was looking for.

Shepherd began, "Gentlemen, I believe that we may discover some important things about blood today. Dr. Harvey has put forth the beautiful theory that blood circulates throughout the body, pumped by the heart, nourishing and sustaining all vital organs – our very lives, indeed, in the process. I believe that blood also carries vapors, airs, as you call them, to all of our organs as well. As we inhale air, there is a reason why we are built to need it refreshed so many times a minute. Did you ever consider this?"

I had to admit that something as elementary as breathing was something that we all take for granted. Just as we must eat, we must breathe. It was obvious, but, at the same time, inexplicable. Shepherd went on.

"Blood is the courier of all nourishment to all parts of the body. There are chemical processes that none of us understand that must take place within our body every moment. Could one ever doubt that we are fearfully and wonderfully made?"

Well, I wouldn't doubt that, but I also did not understand these chemical processes of which Shepherd spoke. Shepherd went on.

"There must be 'couriers' in the blood which transport vital elements to the whole body. It only makes sense to me that, if we can get a close look at the structure of the blood, we may be able to determine how this life force works. In the book of Leviticus, it is written that the source of life is in the blood. I intend to show that to be true."

Francis Bacon was beside himself. His facile mind seemed stimulated by such discussion. He said that he was anxious to be part of any research that used the scientific method to which he was so dedicated.

"Well, you may participate fully, Chancellor," said Shepherd. "You may give a sample of blood, then help us to examine our samples. My hypothesis is that our blood will differ from that of the King. His deteriorating health may be indicated by changes in his blood. That, at least, is the theory that I wish to test."

Villiers had suggested that the King's royal blood was obviously different than that of commoners such as the small group being tested. But Harvey and Shepherd had dismissed that comment out of hand without even mentioning it to Villiers. People cannot hear truth until they are ready to hear it.

Bacon was delighted with such deeply intuitive thinking. "What will you be looking for?" asked Bacon.

"If my theory is correct, there are small couriers of some type in the blood itself. These couriers carry nutrients to all the organs in the body, and, somehow, convey the very air that we breathe to these organs as well."

Hearing this, Bacon, Harvey, and I were amazed at the ideas presented, and we were ready to get on with the experiment.

We returned to Harvey's office, and proceeded to unpack the small samples of blood that had been drawn. He noted the names on the side of each vial. He took out the sample of the King's blood, and placed a drop on a small plate of glass under the Jannsen scope. We all took turns looking at the sample, noticing indeed that Shepherd had been correct. There were small disc shaped "boats" coursing through the sample. There were other shaped items as well, some of which looked similar, but without the little indentations of the more numerous bodies that we saw.

We then took turns placing samples of our own blood under the magnification scope, and found some minor differences in ours. However, we all agreed that the King's blood sample contained far fewer of one type of body than ours. We concluded that this was indeed a bodily process that either produced the sickness, or was the evidence of it.

Shepherd had an idea that perhaps the King's diet was the culprit. He had not had a good appetite, according to Villiers, and perhaps nutrition played a part in forming these "blood bodies" that the King seemed to lack. The King's appetite had been diminished, according to Villiers, so perhaps he had not been getting some vital nutrient.

"Give him some calves' liver," I suggested.

"Why do you suggest that?" asked Bacon. I was about to answer, trying to sound like there was some good medical idea behind it, but then, perhaps influenced by Shepherd, simply told the truth.

"I really do not know," I said. "It just seems to me that about the bloodiest thing I have eaten lately was calves' liver. If he needs more blood that would be a good way to get it in him!"

Bacon laughed, as did Harvey. Shepherd however pondered the idea, and said that it just might help. We all agreed that, if he would eat anything, it would be helpful. Eating calves' liver probably could not hurt.

We went back to the palace the next day with our somewhat odd prescription. Villiers listened, and then he told the cook to prepare a supper laden with calves' liver and fresh greens. We were invited to stay and eat, but we each had other things to be about. We did not want to intrude on the King, who was ailing and needed privacy and rest.

Harvey was eager to continue his studies on circulation work, and was planning to write up his findings for the Royal Society. Shepherd was interested in going back to the Franciscan hospital to work with the poor and dying. I was ready to get back to Andrew Kensington to see where I would fit in his moneymaking schemes. None of us was ready for, or aware of, the adventure that awaited us.

Chapter 23

It had been over four months now (it now being January, 1621) since we parted company after leaving the palace and our little medical experiment with King James was completed. Harvey stayed on at the palace for a while to see to the treatment of the King. He wrote to me that the King slowly but steadily improved after his diet began to include higher amounts of calves' liver and greens. He drew blood from the King several times to satisfy his curiosity about the changes he anticipated in the amount of little bodies he saw in the sample. He wrote that there appeared to be many more of the odd-shaped saucers he identified in his own blood. He included this in his report to the Royal Society, but that was overshadowed by the entire concept of blood flow throughout the body. Harvey wrote that he had been in contact with Shepherd, who was staying at the Franciscan hospital, and that he had shared the results with Shepherd.

It was at the hospital that Shepherd, who was caring for all the sick and homeless, also was treating Jacob Carr. Carr was almost completely recovered from the grievous stab wound he had sustained at the pub. Somehow, he had managed to escape the fevers that so often accompanied such penetrating wounds. I could not help thinking that Shepherd's care was responsible for this. Perhaps he had used another of his odd treatments on Carr, or perhaps Carr was just cheating death once again as he was wont to do. Shepherd had also written to me that Jacob was making some changes in his behavior, and that he had been staying away from the old thieves and brigands that he had usually associated with.

"That alone should keep him healthier," I wrote back to Shepherd.

I, on the other hand, was not faring as well. I had taken Kensington's offer to stay at his home. Edwin Carr had moved out, perhaps to appease Kensington, or perhaps because Anne tired of his company. The Kensingtons seemed to have mended their relationship at any rate, so my stay with them was not unpleasant. Being in the company of these two, while somewhat exciting due to their social contacts and entertaining, was also once again fueling my desire for gin. Kensington had access to the delightful curse due to his Dutch trading contacts. I began a regular routine of drinking "Dutch Courage" every night – then every day and night. I feared that I might just end up as a patient of Shepherd at the Franciscan hospital like one of the homeless derelicts who frequented the place. Then again, maybe being in his care would have been just what I needed.

Drinking together with the Kensingtons, however, gave me plenty of time to plan with Andrew about his business plans for trading routes. He had been refining it since we first discussed it months ago. It was what he called a "trading triangle." The plan looked like this:

The first leg of the triangle now would be from London to a port in West Africa, on which his ships would carry supplies for sale and trade, such as copper, cloth, trinkets, slave beads, guns, and ammunition. When the ship arrived, its cargo would be sold or bartered for slaves. Kensington suggested that slaves could be tightly packed like any other cargo to maximize profits.

On the next leg, ships would make the second journey, the "middle passage," from Africa to the New World. Once the slave ship reached the New World, enslaved survivors would be sold in the Caribbean or the Americas.

The ships would then be prepared for return voyage by being thoroughly cleaned, drained, and loaded with export goods for the third leg to their home port. From the West Indies the main export cargoes were sugar, rum, and molasses; from Virginia, commodities would be tobacco and hemp. The ship would then return to London to complete the triangle.

In my haze, this plan looked both profitable and somewhat unsettling. I did not have the same compunctions that Shepherd had about slavery, but I was not sure that I wanted to be an active part of it. On the other hand, it certainly looked profitable, and I was not in a position, nor frame of mind, to turn down a lucrative plan.

Kensington was busy getting investors lined up for his new venture, as well as pursuing Edwin Carr to captain the first voyage. He had reconciled with Carr, and indeed Carr seemed repentant for his behavior with Anne. Perhaps that was because Anne tired of him, or because he saw how this caused so many problems with his business relationship with Kensington.

He also was interested in securing a crew that could depart as early as June, 1621. One of my jobs would be to examine crew and slaves as medical officer. Kensington assured me that I would not need to spend the rest of my life on ships. He said that he would pay me well, and that with money I saved on a few voyages I could buy in as a partner in the venture, and I could then do as I pleased in England, or wherever I decided to live. It was not my desire to get right back on a ship after my experiences on the *Intrepid*. However, three, maybe four voyages would be enough for me to get the money to invest in the operation, and then I could live a gentry man's life out in the country. I finally had what looked like a plan for my life.

I was not looking forward to telling Shepherd of my plan, but I felt the need to do so. He had become as good a friend as I had ever had. Certainly, we had shared some experiences that draw men closer together than many men ever have.

I ventured to London to see Shepherd at the Franciscan hospital. Upon greeting him, I was shocked to see that his hair and beard had grown longer.

He was starting to look like the people whom he served! He appeared somewhat haggard, and thinner than I recalled. His dark brown eyes still had a depth and a sparkle to them, but there was a sadness too, I was sure. As I approached him, I saw Jacob Carr walking up to me as well. Carr smiled (another unusual mark), and I managed a smile myself. Never trusting of Carr, I was wary of every emotion he might display, figuring that my money purse might be missing if I did not keep my hand on it.

"Dr. Greene," he began, "I want to thank you for what you did that night to save my sorry carcass from bleeding to death!"

"I was only a small part of how you got saved that night, Jacob," I said weakly.

"Well," he said, "my life is different now than it was then, and I just want to thank you for being a part of what happened."

I was now getting very uneasy with the way that this conversation was going. Jacob Carr was a brutish lout of a man, and this gentle talk was bound to be a way to part me from my money, I was sure. Shepherd intervened.

"My good friend Dr. Greene, it is so good to see you! Tell me, what brings you here?"

"Well," I haltingly began, "I wanted to let you know that I have accepted Andrew Kensington's offer to be part of his new trading venture."

"Tell me about it," urged Shepherd.

I began to blanch a bit, fearful of being judged by a man whom I cared for and trusted.

"I will be sailing on some routes on the Atlantic trading cargoes between England, Africa, and the New World," I said.

Immediately, Shepherd knew what I was up to. He simply looked at me and said, "Luke," the first time he had ever been so familiar with me, using my given name, "I trust that you have given good consideration to this, and that it will be good for you." With that, he took me by the arm, and said, "Come, let me show you around the place. You will be surprised with the changes we have made here."

I was shocked at the response, then relieved that he did not look down on me, or shame me for a decision that must have been odious to him. This man amazed me every time I encountered him!

Shepherd and Carr showed me a group of young street children who were bringing in some wood for the fire. They looked much cleaner than the children I had seen there months before. They had on clothing that was in reasonably good repair, and there was not a stench pouring forth from the place. Rows of straw mats held men who appeared to be patients of the place, but they actually looked presentable. There was a sense of peace and calm in this bastion of pain and sorrow that defied my understanding.

"How did you make these changes?" I asked.

Shepherd and Carr seemed not to notice the question, and they busied themselves with greeting the patients and encouraging the children who were busy raking straw, preparing food, and tidying up after a night of lodging the street people.

"Joseph," I asked again, "how did you make these changes here?"

Shepherd turned and said, "I did nothing, really. I simply challenged people to love one another. We also gave people the dignity of helping one another, having a mission larger than themselves."

"Yes," I said, "that is a wonderful thing, but how did you get money to buy food, clothing, bandages, and all the other supplies that you have here now?"

"Dr. Greene," he said, reverting back to a more formal, almost pedantic tone, "you must stop acting as if God cannot provide when we ask Him for help."

"All right," I said, "how did God provide this?"

Shepherd replied, "Jacob Carr has some resources, and he knows many people here. His help was invaluable in getting this hospital what it needed."

"You mean Jacob Carr helped to provide this hospital with his own money?"

I was too shocked for words.

"Yes," Shepherd replied, "he has been most generous."

I knew that Carr had made a bit of a fortune with all of his dealings, thieving, extortion, skimming, and conniving. The idea of him giving it away was more than I could imagine. However, it was true. Jacob Carr had given of his own money, ill-gotten though it was, to help these street urchins, paupers, and lunatics who frequented this hospital.

After looking around the hospital, I went to Joseph Shepherd, and wished him the best in his endeavors. I told him that I would return after my first voyage to see how he was doing in his work. I was amazed at what they had accomplished. The Franciscan friars were busy looking after their regular guests, and things seemed to be very peaceful. However, not everyone was so happy with the situation. As I walked through the streets, I noticed that the street hawkers and professional thieves were not happy that their legion of willing, hungry, and ragged children was not available to do their bidding and stealing.

As evening approached, I hailed a hansom cab to take me to the Olde Cheshire Cheese pub. I had frequented this pub in earlier days, and I had decided that I deserved a good night's drinking. Indeed, I reasoned that nearly every night, but tonight there was a mix of excitement, loneliness, and uncertainty that lurked as my dark companion. Perhaps some beer and perchance a woman would give me some cheer to expel the unknown that awaited me.

I arrived at the pub at around 7 p.m., and I was hungry and thirsty. I quickly downed a pint of ale, followed by a delicious stew. I was surrounded by rough men and easy women who were eyeing their marks for the evening. I was bound not to be one of them, but I did want some company, and the women were friendly.

"Lonely, are ya?" asked a woman who had spied me from across the room.

"Is it that obvious?" I mused aloud.

She smiled and said, "I'm Margaret, and I can make sure that you don't spend the night alone."

"Margaret," I said, "I would like someone to talk to, but I do not need for them to spend the night."

"We'll see," she said, and she proceeded to sit next to me. She was an attractive woman, probably around my age, and free of the pocked face that one was accustomed to oftentimes. She had red hair flowing in curls down her back. Her gown showed a rather small bosom, but it was low enough to show that she was interested in displaying what she had. Her manner was straightforward but not harsh. She seemed to be a veteran of making men feel wanted and comfortable, and so she began with me.

"What brings you here?" she asked.

"I simply want to have a good time tonight," I said.

"I can show you that!" she said.

"Margaret," I said, "If I wanted to take you to bed, you would follow me right now, wouldn't you?"

"Maybe I would," she said.

"I will buy you drinks, and we can talk, and maybe at the end of the night we can decide that," I countered.

"Fair enough," she said. Under her breath I thought I heard her say with some disgust, "I get a talker!"

It's not that I did not want to lay with her – I had done that before with other women. I was just feeling a need to talk with someone, even if they did not care so much about me or what I needed to say.

"Honey, if you just want to talk, I can listen to you. I'm just not used to a man who would rather talk to me than have me spend the night. If you don't think I'm pretty enough…"

"Wait," I interrupted her. "I didn't say you weren't pretty. Besides, you're just trying to work me here, aren't you?"

She smiled at my candor, and said, "You might just be fun to talk to."

I told her about my experiences of the past year – about the *Intrepid*, Shepherd's amazing medical techniques, Harvey's ideas about the blood, meeting King James and treating his illness (something I should not have done, and would not have were I completely sober), and, finally, about my new adventure with Kensington that was about to unfold. She was increasingly fascinated by the stories, and before I knew it midnight was approaching. I was starting to get tired, and I was ending my story when I mentioned Jacob Carr. She stopped me when I mentioned his name.

"Jacob Carr?" she said.

"Yes, Jacob Carr. Do you know him?"

"Honey, I've known him dozens of times," she said. "Roughest, vilest man I've ever met!"

"Yes," I said, "up until a few hours ago I would have said the same thing. What I saw of him today was a different man."

"I don't believe it!" Margaret said emphatically.

"You don't have to if you don't want to, but if you want to see it, come with me tomorrow, and you can meet both Joseph Shepherd as well as Carr," I offered.

"I just think I will," Margaret said. "Come on, spend the night with me and we can go in the morning," she offered.

"I hope you take no offense, but I will get a room by myself tonight, and I will meet you here tomorrow morning at nine o'clock. Prepare to be surprised!"

Chapter 24

Margaret decided to accompany me to the hospital mission to see Joseph and Jacob Carr. I was beginning to like Margaret's simple, earthy ways, and she was certainly not unattractive. Her profession notwithstanding, she was an interesting woman, and certainly brighter than she let on. Women of her standing were never encouraged to express any deep thoughts – maybe that would break the mood, who knows. At any rate, I was interested in getting to know her a little better and to perhaps help let her innate savvy and intelligence grow. Meeting Joseph Shepherd indeed had that effect on people.

As we approached the hospital, Jacob Carr spotted Margaret, and immediately moved toward her. He broke into a smile and moved to embrace her. Margaret was a bit taken aback, but she was very good at making men feel welcome, especially old, loyal customers, whether or not she really felt anything at all, or even if she were repulsed by them. She laughed and exchanged the embrace of Jacob. Somehow I sensed that this was not a lustful gesture, for there was a warmth and innocence to it that made it seem simply like a kind and welcoming gesture. Margaret seemed to feel this as well, and she smiled at Jacob as he took her by the hand to introduce her to his new friend Joseph Shepherd.

Shepherd smiled at her as Carr introduced her as "an old friend." I felt the need to explain why I brought her to the hospital, but Carr was already on that.

"Dr. Greene helped to save my life, Margaret, and so indeed has Joseph," he said. "I suspect that Dr. Greene has been shocked by the changes in my life, and he wants to let you see who is responsible for that."

I could not have expressed that any better than Carr. He evidently had been learning a great deal from Joseph, and his demeanor and insightfulness were truly transformed.

Joseph certainly knew Margaret's background, but he could not have been more accepting of her, showing her around the surroundings, which by now had improved immensely since I first saw the place. Margaret seemed drawn to some of the children who looked up at her with eyes of pain, and many with eyes bereft of any human emotion. As she walked further, I saw tears roll down her own eyes, which she now averted from most of the people around her.

Joseph broke the growing silence. "We have much left to do here," he said. I was saddened to hear that, even though I knew that he seemed drawn to this godforsaken place. I was not drawn to this place, and I knew that my time with Shepherd was growing short. I did have compassion for these people, and I was starting to see that it was not a waste of time to help these people, even though many were going to die shortly. I was hoping to begin a new venture in my life, and I really wanted to share it somehow with Shepherd. Yet, a plan that involved the slave trade was clearly something he would never do. I was shocked out of my little reverie by Shepherd's next statement.

"My dear Luke, I think I have been called to leave this place."

"But you just said that there is much left to do here!" I said.

"Yes, there is a great deal left to do here, but Jacob has indicated that he is planning to join the Franciscans, and use the rest of his fortune to help this hospital. He will take the vows of poverty, chastity, and obedience, and live the life of a monk. Jacob Carr has found his life's work here."

I was stunned to the core. Jacob Carr was going to be a monk? Jacob Carr was giving up all his wealth for these people? Jacob Carr was taking a vow of chastity, poverty, and obedience? Shepherd saw my expression, and simply said, "We should rejoice when someone finds the reason for their life. You know the Scripture says that 'with God, all things are possible.' This simply is another example of that truth."

Hearing this made me think harder about my own life. My decision about my next life adventure was simply that – what adventure could I take and make a fortune at the same time. I thought that was what life was about. Seeing that Jacob Carr would make such a drastic decision, based upon a call of God in his life, somehow made me feel very small. Very small indeed!

Margaret too was stunned by this remark of Shepherd. Jacob Carr then broke in.

"Joseph is right in all that he said. I felt a strange sensation as I recovered from my wound here at this hospital. I was cared for by people who probably knew that I had been a thief, a murderer, a drunkard, and a womanizer of the worst sort."

Margaret winced as he continued.

"Yet they cared for me, nursed me to health, and showed compassion to others like me. My mother had taught Edwin and me that God loves people through other people. I did not understand that until I received that kind of love, at a time when I was close to death. It touched my soul in a way that I cannot explain, other than that I knew that I must live differently from that time on. So I have discussed this with Joseph, and I have decided to stay here as he moves on with God's call in his life."

"Joseph," I blurted, "what is that call for you? Where are you going?"

"I have been talking with Dr. Harvey quite a bit lately, and he has an interest in returning to Italy to do more study on the blood circulation theory. While we are both quite convinced of the rightness of this theory, we want to discuss it with others. Harvey is concerned that this break with Galen's teachings will be met with resistance. He wants reassurance of its validity. Sir

Francis Bacon has been so encouraged that he may travel with us. Our little experiment with King James's blood so fascinated him that he would like more interactions with us and the science community in Italy. However, Bacon told me that there are charges against him of accepting bribes while in office as chancellor. Nonetheless, he said that his friend Ben Jonson may be persuaded to travel with us."

"May I join you?" I asked. Surely I did not just say that, I thought. That was not even my voice, was it? Nonetheless, I must have said it, because Shepherd quickly replied.

"I have been counting on that," he said, almost matter- of- factly.

Margaret looked downcast. She had actually connected at some depth with men who accepted her not for her body but for her entire being. I wanted to think that she may even have had some interest in me. I certainly wanted to know her better, but I felt that strange sensation that Carr must have felt. I needed to follow a different path in my life, and, somehow, life with Kensington and the British East India Company was not that path. Margaret would be left behind, but not forever. My new adventure was just beginning.

Chapter 25

Three weeks later we were on our way to Padua, Italy. We had been able to get passage on a ship that Edwin Carr was sailing to Venice. Our group consisted of Shepherd and me, William Harvey, Ben Jonson, and Herbert Wesley, a Nonconformist leader who was a friend of William Bradford. Bradford had spoken highly of Shepherd just before he sailed with the Mayflower several months ago. Wesley was increasingly disillusioned with King James's weak and vacillating religious sentiments, and he favored the unrestricted expression of religious thought and practice. Wesley had also become acquainted with Bacon and Jonson many years ago when he had been arrested for statements that James felt were too critical of his taxing efforts. Bacon had intervened simply because he believed that someone should not be arrested for the expression of ideas. Bacon later befriended Wesley because he liked Wesley's fiercely independent spirit. Bacon had finally declined the invitation to go on the trip due to legal and health problems. He and all of our travelers were disappointed, but we were understanding of his situation.

I was a little apprehensive about approaching Kensington to tell him that I would not be participating in his East India Company plans, at least not right away. He surprised me with his response. He had told me that I could reconsider my plans after a trip with Edwin Carr on a trading voyage. He had assured me that I would enjoy the journey, on which I could bring along my companions, and that he would assume all the costs associated with the trip. I then realized that the real reason for such generosity was the group with which I was going. William Harvey and Ben Jonson were leading thinkers of the day. Jonson was very well connected with King James as the leading masque writer of the court. Both Jonson and Harvey had the ear of the king. This did not hurt Kensington's relationship with the crown, nor did his boast that he was funding a scientific research voyage to Italy. Further, it gave me some good feeling that I was ostensibly the reason for his generosity, that I had offered something of value to this journey. Kensington figured that my gratitude would bring me back to his plans. He wanted me as part of his circle, and he expected that my "spiritual leanings" would quickly be exhausted.

The voyage itself was peaceful, and very enjoyable. Carr was a superb sailing man, and his mastery of the ship and crew contrasted with the chaos of my most recent voyage. More importantly, the conversations with Shepherd and Wesley were completely fascinating. All these men were well read, and the discussions about Galileo, Boyle, and Copernicus, and Janssen, among other great thinkers, were inspiring. Wesley was more engaged and connected with scholarship than I could ever have imagined. A voracious reader with unrestrained curiosity, he sought out new ideas at every opportunity. He was describing a meeting with Isaac Beeckman, whom he had met just last year in Utrecht. Beeckman seemed enamored with the ideas of a young man named Renee Descartes. Descartes, he suggested, will "turn the earth upside down" someday with his amazing mind and his willingness to question everything. Bacon had suggested before the trip that we make every effort to meet with him, right after we met with Galileo in Padua.

"We plan to meet with Galileo?" I asked.

"Yes," said Jonson. "I have been in correspondence with him for several years. We have become friendly, due to our common friend Bacon, and I have concern about him and his troubles with the Church."

"Troubles with Papists!" countered Wesley. "Surely the Pope should stay on matters of faith, not the pursuit of science," Wesley said with some evident rancor. Bacon would have agreed heartily, and Harvey smiled at the thought of how Bacon might have weighed in on such a thought. This idea of scientific thought independent of spiritual underpinnings was a growing cause of unrest with the intelligentsia of Europe. Few openly questioned the Church's authority for fear of excommunication, or even an interdict on a city. Yet, the last century of religious questioning had resulted in an openness of mind in areas beyond matters of faith. It was a dangerous time, and a very exciting time for those who were willing to explore truth unbound from religious constraints. Yet most people still believed that such "truth-seeking" was merely a tool of the devil to entice man into another "Garden of Eden" pursuit of human pride.

When I could tear myself away from these discussions, I spent a little time with Edwin Carr. I was curious about his relationship with Lord Kensington, as well as his reaction to his brother's remarkable conversion. Edwin was essentially a rugged, worldly man, plenty bright, but uninterested in spiritual things. He was honest in his business dealings, highly competent as a sailor, and very forthright in expressing himself. At the same time, having an open affair with his business partner's wife seemed to me contradictory to his good sense and moral sensibilities. Carr laughed when I gently brought up the subject of Anne.

"Are you worried about Anne, me, or Kensington?" he asked.

"I suppose that I am simply curious about it, and perhaps it is completely none of my business," I said.

"You are right, Dr. Greene, it is none of your business!" he laughed. "However, I will tell you about it," he said quite amiably. "Lord Kensington has become impotent, and he does not want many people to know that, of course. Anne would not live her life without passion, and Kensington does not care much for her at this point anyway. My presence is almost reassuring to him. Anne enjoys my company, and I enjoy hers. I try not to be too intrusive or frequent in my visits, and I am a nice diversion from their fighting. The fact that Kensington has allowed you and Shepherd to know of this arrangement did strike me as unusual at first, but I came to realize that he really does seem to like you. Shepherd frightens him a bit, I must say, but he likes you. Nonetheless, I have decided to keep some distance from Anne. I see the pain it causes Andrew, and I see that Anne is using me like Andrew uses people. I suppose we all use people for our own needs."

I could certainly see Carr's point, and saw that, indeed, that was the nature of people. Yet I saw in Shepherd, and those who were influenced by him, a change of heart. I saw Jacob Carr, Margaret, and even me, changing due to his presence in our lives.

I was reassured by this conversation. Kensington would be a nice option for me should I change my mind about this new journey, and friends like him, who are well connected with the Crown, never can hurt. His moral compass notwithstanding, Edwin Carr was a fellow I could appreciate and trust.

Our arrival at Venice was magnificent. The beauty of the city was breathtaking. We wound our way through a series of islands as we approached the harbor. Commerce was king in this wealthy city, but art and music flourished as well. Ships crowded the harbor, laden with tea, silk, spices, cotton, wine, and fine glassware. The harbor was a beehive of activity as dockworkers unloaded the ships, and merchants were bidding for the sales of some of the goods not already under contract. Street vendors, garbed in colorful cloaks of red, purple, yellow, and green, lined the Venice-Padua road, and the smells of bread, fish, perfume, and rotting garbage somehow blended together to make a distinctive aroma. Carr disembarked from the ship, smiled, and said, "Smells like Venice always smells!"

The sights and smells were intoxicating to me, and I wanted to spend some time just experiencing the city. Jonson and Harvey, however, more widely travelled than I, were simply interested in getting to Padua to meet with Galileo. Harvey seemed interested in discussing his thoughts on the circulation of the blood. Shepherd was interested in supporting Galileo in his growing troubles with the Church regarding his defense of the Copernican theory of a heliocentric system of the known universe. However, Shepherd was strangely quiet in his anticipation of meeting with Galileo. While he respected and admired him, Shepherd seemed to be intimidated by no one, and he moved with ease among the brightest lights of the scientific and royal circles of the age.

On the ride to Padua, Wesley engaged Shepherd in a conversation about the Church. Wesley's disdain for Papal authority, and the Church's intrusive role in scientific matters, was increasingly evident. His stridence and vigor in damning the Church seemed to interfere with his normal reasoned thinking, and Shepherd, ever the one to speak the truth, confronted Wesley on this. Harvey, always savvy and measured in his responses, smiled discretely as Wesley became flushed and defensive.

"My dear Wesley," continued Shepherd, "do you think that the Creator of the universe can only be explained or approached in terms of blind faith?"

"What do you mean?" asked Wesley.

"I mean," explained Shepherd, "that the Creator manifests himself in His creation as well as in the heart of man. Faith and science are not antithetical, but rather complementary. There must be congruence in all truth. Scientific thought and the pursuit of knowledge through the most rigorous experimentation does not preclude that God is the author of the creation. Just because we learn that the earth orbits the sun, or that blood circulates through the body pumped by the heart, or that the moon is the cause of tides on earth, or that atoms are the building blocks of all matter, it only confirms the incredible mind and power of the Creator. It does not mean that we can or should separate Him from His creation."

Shepherd had just expounded on some of the most controversial and latest thought being discussed in the world. His articulation of these theories seemed to have the conviction of knowledge, not mere speculation. I was struck by this statement, but Harvey was moved beyond words. It was as if Shepherd had not only read his mind, but he had put into words the very things he wanted to express to Galileo. This was going to be a very interesting meeting in the next day or two.

Chapter 26

John Ward had been freed from the Tower of London on Christmas Day, 1620. He had long been an irritant of King James, and there were those who still believed that Ward was one of the men who was part of the plot engendered by Guy Fawkes in 1606 to blow up the King in a spectacular fashion. This, of course, was nonsense, since Ward was one of the dissenters who neither embraced the Catholic Church nor the Church of England. He was a Pietist who believed in the "sola scriptura" movement, fueled, interestingly, by King James' effort at having the Bible translated into a common parlance. Now an old man of 66, Ward was not seen as a threat anymore, and King James felt that releasing him might generate some good will for his sagging reputation. Ward looked the part of an insane man, with long white hair and beard, and wide, dark eyes that seemed to penetrate to the soul. He continued to fiercely preach for faith to be separated from affairs of state, and he did not care how much he irritated the powers that be. In fact, he seemed to rather enjoy such conflicts, feeling that he could bring the wrath of God upon the evil mix of the state determining the faith matters that were highly individual in nature. A man's personal faith was just that – personal. The King had no business in that, and, for heaven's sake, a King had no special authority from God for his position. Indeed, the leader should be the servant of those governed. Didn't Jesus say that he came to serve, and not be served? Was a king better than Jesus? God forbid such arrogance!

King James believed that allowing Ward to be seen by his followers would burst the bubble of the image they had of him as a spiritual leader. His wild appearance, angry outbursts, and continued appeal to Scripture would be seen as the ravings they were. Kings were, without doubt, anointed by God.

James, however, was wrong in his belief about John Ward. Ward was, despite his wild appearance and behavior, a formidable force among people who were hungry for some hope. John Ward had no idea that the King wanted to use him for his own purposes. Ward was convinced that his King, the God he served, wanted him for heavenly work, and therefore it made perfect sense to him that God had arranged for his release.

Soon after his release, Lord Kensington saw a bit of an opportunity. Kensington was increasingly convinced that his plan for a triangular trade route that included tobacco and slaves could only flourish if King James was at least open to the import of tobacco. James had not shown any indication of that, and Kensington never liked to hedge his bets. He always wanted a sure thing. Therefore, he might benefit from the presence of the insane Ward. Kensington could offer a solution to the King.

In order to solve a problem for the King, Kensington first had to create one. So Kensington arranged to give Ward a platform for his wild ideas, have people begin to respond to them, then offer the King a solution in order to curry his favor. If Ward stirred up enough dissent and anger, Kensington could find a way to permanently silence Ward. He would have no problem removing Ward if that might help the King. Kensington decided to see where this plan might lead.

Kensington was well connected to people who had grievances against the King. He had been involved with the mysterious stable fire last year that allowed some mischief in London. Now he would stir things up a little more to see what the level of unrest was in London against the King.

Kensington summoned Oliver Craft to his home and asked about the mood of his mob of London rabble these days. Craft was puzzled.

"My people are always angry and frightened," he said, as if this were a patently obvious statement. The street people of London were poor, addled by gin, desperate, and always ready for someone to lead them in an adventure against authority. It was the boredom and desperation of generational poverty, as well as the effect of a willingness to cling on to anyone or anything that could give some hope of a future. Yes, Craft could lead them wherever Kensington wanted. So, what did he want?

Kensington laid out his idea. John Ward was someone who might appeal to people who were so desperate that they could only look to God for a solution. John Ward had the ability to appeal to people's deep spiritual need. That also might mean that they would reject James' "divine right" ideas. A little chaos, like in the Guy Fawkes days, might just be the best thing for his plans right now.

"Understand?" asked Kensington.

"Not completely," said Craft. "But if you want angry people to gather to hear John Ward, I can do that real easy."

"Yes," said Kensington, "that is what I want."

Ward was excited when Craft told him that he could arrange for a group of people to hear him talk about his ideas. The plan called for people to gather at the Wool Guild Hall the next Tuesday night. Craft had the dockworkers and guild members in his network of disaffected people. Indeed, the dockworkers and guild members were much better off than the townspeople who had no real source of income, but they had connections through a benevolence system that had been established many years ago. Kensington had seen the possible benefits of organizing poor and hopeless people, and had not really cared for the fact that the benevolence actually helped to sustain people in hard times. The church had long ago been in the

112

business of giving aid to poor people. It was Kensington who saw the added "benefit" of using that help to put people on the side of the benefactor.

John Ward was in rare form as he spoke to the assembled crowd that night. He implored people to turn to Jesus alone as their savior and King. The Church of England, King James, or any other human intermediary was not only unnecessary but might even be of the devil if it separated people from attending to personal faith. Faith alone was the way to God, and that only through the atonement of Jesus.

There seemed to be a stirring among people that night. Hope in the future was tied not to the institutions that had let them down, but to a saving knowledge of Jesus. He could be trusted, while man or manmade institutions could not. People began to weep and cry to God for salvation, confessing sins publicly to anyone or everyone within earshot. This was not what Craft was expecting, but he would wait and see what came of it. Perhaps anger would follow later after this ecstatic expression.

The next day, Craft reported to Kensington what had transpired the night before.

"I am not looking for peace!" Kensington retorted. "This is what happened?" he asked.

"Yes," replied Craft. "Not everyone responded, though. Some simply left, the same as they came," he said, hoping to alleviate some of Kensington's anger.

Upset that his approach did not give the desired results, Kensington decided to manufacture the anger on his own. Kensington asked Craft to arrange another meeting for Ward, but this time Craft was to salt the crowd with people who were to ensure that the message of hope became a message of hate and desperation.

Ward's next meeting was larger than Craft expected. Word had spread that there was to be another meeting the next Tuesday at the Guild Hall, and those who had responded with a heartfelt conversion were joined by others who were there because they were told that there would be discussion of a new royal tax to be imposed upon wool, and that cotton was to be allowed to be imported from Egypt.

The mood was tense as people assembled with very different expectations. As John Ward went before the crowd, he was completely unaware of the machinations of Craft. He was simply thankful that God had provided such an audience to which he could preach! It soon became apparent that people were restless as he spoke only of Scripture, faith in Jesus, and salvation in Jesus alone. Soon, some of the dockworkers began to ask about wool taxes and cotton imports. Ward was struck by such comments, and he responded angrily to people who would disrupt a holy time. That was all it took for Craft's crowd plants to start shouting epithets at those who were questioning Ward. That seemed to have been the cue for a number of the dissenters to bring out clubs, and quickly order broke down.

Soon there were several bloody heads that had been cracked open according to Craft's plans. Chaos emerged as men began to punch one another, screams of pain punctuated the air, and order broke down completely as John Ward looked on in horror.

"What has happened?" he asked plaintively to no one in particular. Within moments, Ward began to see what was happening. He realized that this burgeoning riot must be stopped immediately. He breathed a quick prayer, and suddenly got the idea that he should begin singing. His voice was strong as he began the words of Luther's stirring hymn "A Mighty Fortress Is Our God." Others began to see what he was doing, and they joined him as loudly as they could. It began to swell in the crowd, and by the second verse more people were singing than swinging at one another.

Craft's thugs continued to yell at people, and brandished clubs. However, even Craft's dullards realized that hitting someone with a club while they are singing a hymn does not make it appear that the crowd is responding to political rhetoric. It looks like a staged riot, which indeed is what it was.

Pretty soon things got calmer, and Ward led the group in another hymn. Craft's bruisers slipped away from the rest of the crowd, and Ward resumed his time of teaching. The disturbance seemed to energize the crowd in an amazing way, as people started to claim that the presence of God was in that place. Ward led the crowd in prayer, and, after two hours of preaching, he dismissed the crowd to go home and tell others of the events of the evening. He believed that God had released him from prison for just this purpose!

Chapter 27

As we approached Padua, I was excited to meet Galileo. Jonson, a close friend of Bacon, was telling us of Galileo's problems with the Catholic Church. He knew that Galileo was certain that scientific thought should not be hindered by the Church's heavy-handed squelching of new ideas. Yet his fear and respect of the Church's position as God's institution on earth compelled him to acquiesce to the Church's demands to recant his ideas. Descartes, Jonson said, was in much the same position, but was more willing to publish his ideas and allow others to make the decision about where the truth may lie. Further, Descartes, despite his questioning of the Church, was with the Catholic army fighting in Bohemia against Protestant forces in the escalating war that was ravaging parts of the continent. Ferdinand II, the Holy Roman Emperor, was in the process of forcibly converting Protestant Bohemia and Austria to Catholicism. The Catholic Church, despite withering criticism and growing skepticism from leading intellectuals, was reasserting itself on the Continent as the power it had been for hundreds of years. Now the power was from military strength, and not the moral and spiritual strength that had once marked its rise as a cultural civilizing force.

Shepherd was saddened by the affairs of the time. He believed that God had called him to assert the truth of God's intervention in the life of man – that God was pleased with His children at peace with one another, and that love of creation and of his fellow man was the highest worship that one could attain to. Sadly, many did not understand this, and most believed that he was a naïve idealist. At worst, he was seen as subverting the natural way of things. Common belief was that power was to be wielded by the King and the Church on behalf of a population that was too ignorant or too sinful to approach a holy God. The idea that people would fight a war in the name of God was appalling to him.

Upon meeting Galileo, I was impressed with his superior intellect. Harvey, Jonson, and Shepherd once again dominated conversation with him, and there seemed to be a common, if unstated understanding that someday, science and religion would be able to transcend petty battles for control of the minds of people. I was coming to see that God valued truth more than control, and that if He wanted to connect with His people He did not need the Church, Kings, or even scientists. He needed humility from those who were seeking that truth.

Galileo seemed tired. He was enchanted with Harvey and his theories about the circulation of blood in the body, yet he seemed to have grasped that intuitively as a truth long before Shepherd and Harvey went in depth about the idea. Shepherd's acceptance of Galileo both as a Christian and as a scientist seemed to hearten Galileo. He had never encountered someone who felt so at ease in both worlds. It reminded him, he said, of a young man he had met not long ago – a man by the name of Rene Descartes. Galileo urged us to head on to Prague, the place where he had last heard that Descartes was staying. The revolt in Bohemia still raged, and the travel might not be entirely secure, but Galileo assured us that a visit to the University at Prague and an opportunity to meet with Descartes would be worth the travel. Galileo also asked us to give his regards to Bacon, with whom he had recently corresponded. Galileo showed concern for Bacon, telling us that perhaps Bacon was in more peril in England than we would be if we headed to Bohemia. Harvey looked concerned.

"Bacon is in serious trouble?" he asked.

We knew of some problems that Bacon had, but Bacon had been dismissive of the gravity of the charges against him.

"Yes, I have known for some time that there are those in London who would bring him to ruin," Galileo replied. "He is being accused falsely of bribery. Anyone who dares resist conventional thought does so at his own peril," said Galileo resignedly.

All the men agreed with this sad comment. It was true, it seemed. Only those who knew how to work with and around kings, or wealth, seemed to be able to thrive in these dangerous times.

We were invited to go to the University of Padua, where Harvey was to provide a series of lectures on his theories of the circulation of the blood. Harvey invited Shepherd to lecture with him specifically about the experiment he had done on the blood of King James. The King was not mentioned as the subject of the experiment, partly out of courtesy to him, partly because few would believe the circumstances present that allowed us to perform such an experiment, and partly because of fear of reprisal from courtiers who might have lost their positions (or their life) for allowing such a practice. Whether any of these scenarios would have applied made less difference than the fact that the science of the experiment may have been lost because of whom it was performed upon.

Our two weeks at the University were stimulating, and we were met with warmth and enthusiasm by the scholars there. Mostly I suspected that this was because of Harvey, but Shepherd was captivating in his continued weaving of faith and science in ways few could confute and many could not grasp. I suspected that two weeks was long enough for people to hear these new ideas, since new ideas often can generate more heat than light. While most were fascinated and appreciative, there were those who were restless, and even angry that such ideas could stand so boldly in the face of accepted concepts of ancient learning.

116

It was Galileo who suggested that we move on to meet Descartes. He had received word through friends in Prague that Descartes was disillusioned with the war, and he was ready to leave for France. Descartes had indicated his desire to go to Rome to meet with the Pope. He hoped to be there in late January, 1621. Galileo had another reason to visit Rome. He had a desire to meet one more time with Pope Paul V to make his peace with him, despite all the turmoil that had taken place and the crushing restrictions that the Pope had imposed upon his science. I felt that this was prompted by Shepherd's talks with Galileo, and the growing influence Shepherd had on his views of science and religion as part of a unified theology.

Galileo's plans to meet Paul V were thwarted by the Pope's death on January 28th.We decided that we would move on to Rome, wait for the new Pope to be elected, and see if a new Pope might have different reactions to the changing times in science.

Chapter 28

Rome was more (or less) than I expected. We found Rome to be a place of squalor and degradation. While knowing that Rome was the seat of the power of the Catholic Church, I knew it also held the distinction of being the destination of artists and poets, sculptors and scholars. Yet it seemed to bring out the worst in these creative people. Drinking and excesses of every type seemed to be prevalent wherever we looked. I was simply a bit surprised, but Shepherd seemed to be not only shocked but enraged by this desecration of a supposedly holy city. I had no illusions about "holy" because I expected the worst in people. That Rome was a place of hypocrisy and debauchery did not disrupt my world. Shepherd seemed deeply wounded somehow.

We travelled to Rome expecting to meet Descartes at some point, but more interested in meeting the new Pope. It turned out to be Gregory XV. He was already sixty-seven years old and evidently was seen merely as a caretaker. We wondered how this might affect Galileo, who was in a running battle with the Church regarding his theories on physics, mathematics, and scientific theory. Shepherd was reassuring to Galileo about his beliefs that science and faith were not antithetical. The Church, however, was far from reassuring on this, and was indeed dogmatic on choices to be made – faith in the literal words of the Bible on the matter of how the world worked was the only acceptable path.

On the way to the Vatican and its splendor was the path of human misery in the streets. Children in rags, vendors barking about their wares, and roaming lost souls seemed to mark a very odd seat of Christian life. If Rome were the capitol of Christendom, the world may be in real trouble, I thought. Then again, I knew for a fact that the world was in trouble. I had seen it firsthand as I dealt with some of the dregs of society in England.

Galileo had decided to meet with the new Pope, Gregory XV, to discuss his ideas once again, with the hope that he could pronounce his science without being excommunicated. He had been very careful over the past several years to not upset the Church directly, although his writings could be seen by some as a thinly veiled screen for his true beliefs. Directly confronting the Church was still too risky for him.

I was amazed that I could venture in the company of Harvey and Galileo – men who were known in Europe as scholars and thinkers of the first degree. Wesley was a theologian of the first rank, but too controversial for most in the established church. His disdain for the Catholic Church was palpable, yet he remained in our party because of his respect of Joseph

Shepherd. The fact that he would venture to Rome with us was a testimony of that respect – and perhaps a function of his enormous curiosity.

I continued to write letters back to Andrew Kensington to apprise him of our travels and the contacts we would make for his business ideas. Trade and tobacco potentials always kept his interest.

On March 11, 1621, Galileo was given an audience with the new Pope, Gregory XV. I was amazed at the splendor of the Vatican. The Sistine Chapel, St. Peter's Square, the stately basilicas ornate with paintings and sculptures, were truly beautiful. The wealth contrasted with the poverty all around was simply a fact of life for people in the city. Shepherd, however, was increasingly disturbed by it.

Galileo was summoned before the Pope while we were politely detained in a small café outside of the holy grounds. Shepherd, Harvey, and Wesley talked animatedly over a meal of fresh fish, cheeses, hearty bread, and wine.

"I cannot see why Galileo must recant his findings," started Harvey.

"Not all people are as open as you, my friend," said Shepherd. "These things take time for people to absorb and understand."

"Time!" exclaimed Harvey. "How many years has this poor man been trying to please this group of theologians about things beyond their understanding?"

"I am less inclined to be upset about their ignorance than their arrogance," stated Shepherd. "Does the church not read the book of Amos, or the hundreds of references in the Bible about caring for the poor? Where is the justice?"

The conversation continued for nearly two hours as we waited for Galileo. Finally, upon his return to us at our lodgings, he shared with us his frustrations about the meeting with the Pope and his advisors. It was clear that Galileo was not successful in his meeting, and he simply wanted to leave Rome. He spoke little of the specific discussion, perhaps for fear that this was beyond his rights, and partly due to his immense sadness and pain, which did not allow for much expansion on the stifling papal response.

As we prepared to leave, we came upon some beggars who were covered with sores and layers of filth. The sight was not uncommon in this city, or any large city in Europe. Shepherd however stopped to give them some coins to help relieve them of a bit of their suffering. He then stooped very close to them and seemed to whisper something to one of them. The man began to weep, then laugh. Soon the other two men began to smile and nod as we walked on. I suspected that they were laughing at the fool who had just given them money for their miserable begging. I challenged Joseph on this.

"Joseph, haven't you learned anything about giving away money to beggars? Those men take you for a fool even as you give them money," I said with disgust. "What did you say to them?"

"Well, with that response that you just gave, I am not sure you would understand what I told them," he said.

I pressed him. "Now I am even more curious; what did you say?"

"I told them that money was not the answer to their problems," said Shepherd. "I told them that they need healing of the soul first, then healing of the body."

Wesley nodded in agreement. Harvey seemed to feel the answer was profound. I felt bewildered and somewhat ashamed. Once again, Shepherd was unafraid of what people thought of him and pursued an ultimate truth. For all I knew, they were on the way to healing. But my skeptical self reminded me – they were just beggars looking for some money.

Descartes did not meet us as we had hoped. This trip to Rome seemed to be a complete failure. I did get to experience the splendor (and squalor) of the capital of Christendom as part of my life journey. However, I was ready to get back to England and start my business life with the East India Company. The call to go on an adventure with Shepherd had seemed like an exhilaration. Now it seemed beyond my station in life. He was simply too far above my inadequate makeup.

In Rome, two beggars were walking toward a well-dressed visitor who appeared to be a priest. Perhaps he had stayed there after the papal election, but the beggars only cared that maybe he would be an easy mark like the man they had encountered yesterday. One turned to the other and said, "It looks like the sores on my feet are gone." The other agreed that the ugly marks they had been covered in yesterday seemed to be gone.

Part II July, 1621 – America

Chapter 29

Andrew Kensington had not succeeded in his attempt to foment trouble for the king. Oliver Craft's clumsy thugs had been unable to disrupt John Ward's religious revivals, and in fact had added to their success.

Kensington however was on to other things. He was busy making plans to implement his scheme of New World trade of slaves and tobacco. Upon Edwin Carr's return he would approach him about the plan. The East India Company was becoming aware of the possibilities of huge profits to be made from the trade of tobacco largely through Kensington's efforts.

Our sea journey from Rome had been mercifully uneventful. Upon our arrival in London, Shepherd immediately went to visit the Franciscan hospital, which Jacob Carr was organizing into a place of healing for many sick and destitute people of the street.

I went to visit Kensington, and I found him in a foul mood. He was desperate to begin his trade route plan, and decided that with or without royal approval he would proceed. He told me that a "Mr. Kelley" had inquired of him as to the whereabouts of Dr. Greene and Dr. Shepherd, whom he had sailed with on the *Intrepid* last year. Kelley was looking for help in getting back on a ship, though he was "damaged goods," as he put it, having been wounded in the service of England while in a fight with pirates. He limped slightly on his damaged right leg, and now was unable to find any kind of work. Worse, he was under suspicion for inciting mutiny, and he was staying away from old sea mates and any royal military people. Yet he had told Kensington of Shepherd and me, stating that he had never met finer men, and if there was a way to get aboard an East India ship, he would want Greene and Shepherd aboard.

I was pleased to hear that Kelley was still around, and that he had said such good things about me. This seemed to solidify for Kensington that I would be on his ship to Virginia when it sailed in the next three months. It looked to me like my near future was already planned for me, especially when I had not really had my own ideas on the subject. My only real plan had been to follow Joseph Shepherd on his quests. I thought that this might be an opportunity to engage Shepherd on a quest with me.

I also knew that Shepherd would be loath to become involved with Kensington's ventures, especially since it would involve slave trading as part of the arrangement.

"Lord Kensington," I began. "So good of you to have such faith in me in being part of your business enterprise."

Kensington interrupted me at that point. "Dr. Greene, I will be direct with you. I have been told that the King seems to feel very kindly disposed to you and Shepherd for some reason, and if I can invoke your names in the discussion of a royally commissioned trip to Virginia, I plan to do just that."

Kensington must have been referring to our visit to King James, and our odd experiment with his poor health. I was certain that no one else knew of this, and likely the details would never be known, but the King knew, and that was all that mattered.

Kensington had the ability to make a request seem like a direct order that could not be disobeyed except with the most dire yet subtle consequences. On the other hand, I had just heard that King James was kindly disposed to me. Had I just been dreaming this, or did my future just get much brighter?

I was snapped out of my reverie when Kensington said, "You need to convince your friend Shepherd to go on this voyage with you. I am prepared to pay whatever it may reasonably take to make this happen."

"Lord Kensington," I said, "Joseph Shepherd will not go on this voyage no matter what you may want to pay him. He is deeply opposed to slavery, and anything that is involved with it will crush the idea with him."

"Well, Dr. Greene," he sniffed, "your job just became more difficult, but you need to make this happen."

I was convinced that he was simply using his arrogance, intimidation, and nefarious implication to force me to do something that he really had no control over. I really had nothing to fear from him, but the idea of going to America, and doing it under the protection and blessing of the King, was too heady for me to dismiss. Somehow, if I could convince Joseph that our trip was purely scientific, and that he could bring along some of his philosophers, scientists, theologians as guests, he might be willing to come along.

"What an opportunity!" I would say to him. He could see firsthand a New World, one that he had already influenced through his lengthy discussions with William Bradford last year. I knew he would be excited to have some influence on the spiritual growth of these people in America. Perhaps the reason for the trip could be explained as a fact-finding, scientific voyage. Indeed, that would be true, at least to some extent. If Kensington could be persuaded that the plan for slavery as part of the trade arrangement could be at least shelved for now, maybe this would work.

I met Joseph Shepherd at the Franciscan hospital mission, where he seemed to be completely in his element, encouraging friars, teaching the children, who were increasing in number daily, and ministering to the medical needs of patients. Jacob Carr also seemed to be very content with his life, especially now that Margaret had decided to stay and help also. Carr's fortune, larger than even I had expected it to be, seemed to be a large source of the funding now for the mission. The friars were amazed at the turn of financial events, and Joseph simply said to them that "God provides."

"Joseph," I said, "you have really done some fine work here!" Almost immediately I caught myself, because I knew his response would be something like, "God did this, not me," so I added quickly before he could answer, "And I know this is God's work, but He surely picked a fine servant to make it happen!"

Shepherd smiled. "You're learning!" he said. "Are you ready to join us?"

"Actually," I said haltingly, "I am asking you to join me on a trip to America." I held my breath, pleading to someone that he would not immediately cut me off and dismiss the idea out of hand. If I had a chance to talk to him, maybe I could at least get him to consider it.

"A trip to America!" he said. "I have been thinking about that."

I am sure that my eyes widened and my jaw dropped. "Is that true?" I stammered.

"Yes," he said. "Just two days ago I received a letter from William Bradford. He is now governor of the settlement, which they have named Plymouth after their home port in England. He told me of the incredible hardships they have faced there. Great illness and famine are their torments. He also told of native people there, and most have been helpful to his group. In fact, without their knowledge of the land, how to grow crops, deal with weather, et cetera, all might have perished. As it is, nearly half have died. He also told me of the vast beauty he has seen: lush forests, abundant game, and, importantly, freedom to worship as they see fit."

I was trying to soak this all in. The fact that nearly half of his people had died in less than one year did not sound very enticing to me. "This *is what piqued Joseph's interest?*" I thought.

"Joseph," I said, "I came to ask you to accompany me on a scientific trip to America, not to go die there!"

Shepherd laughed. "Every adventure has that possibility, Luke, but that is not my plan either!"

We both laughed, and that eased the moment. We then began to discuss the idea further. I explained that Kensington had arranged for a scientific trip to determine how crops may grow in America. Of course, Shepherd knew that this included tobacco. I felt that I could venture that much, but I certainly could not even hint at his idea of a slave trade as part of the plan.

Shepherd countered with his own reasons. As a scientist and medical man, he was fascinated by the potential of finding new medicines and cures for disease, since there were certainly whole new plants and herbals that could possibly fight disease. He reasoned that people displaced from one part of the world to another were exposed to a whole host of new diseases that their bodies could not fight off. He used the word "immunity" to explain how some people were able to avoid getting ill while others around them did. He also observed that people who had developed cowpox never ended up getting smallpox. He had witnessed this, and it gave him the idea that somehow our bodies could "fight off" getting smallpox.

Once again, his ideas were beyond my grasp, but he did make a very convincing case, even if it were simple coincidence. Shepherd was not one to put much faith in coincidence. He wanted a logical, scientific explanation of the world around him, and he was willing to be ridiculed for his ideas if need be.

"So, you may be willing to become part of this trip?" I asked. "Kensington told me that you could bring along other men of science in whatever field you desired. He also feels that King James would be most honored if you were to go."

I had saved that little bit for last. It was not entirely accurate, but there was truth in the statement somewhere.

"Luke," Shepherd began as he looked directly at me and into my eyes, "I do not want any part of the slave trade, nor the tobacco trade, and I am certain that Andrew Kensington has both in mind. Is that true?"

I was completely disarmed at this, and I said, "Yes, both are true. He wants to grow tobacco, and as part of that plan, he wants to import slaves to do the work of growing the crops."

There, I had said it. As I spoke it a sense of shame came over me. Not because I was ashamed of being part of the slave trade (although I felt that to be at the very least a disagreeable institution), but because I was deceiving a very decent and honorable man – a man with whom I had endured pain, danger, fear, joy, and every human emotion. What kind of a person would deceive a close friend?

"Luke," said Shepherd, "I would love to go to America with you, but not as part of Andrew Kensington's plan. I hope you understand that."

"I do," I replied. "I do."

Chapter 30

John Ward was amazed at the following he was starting to gather. His simple message of salvation by faith seemed to resonate with people. Among the people attracted to this message were Herbert Wesley, who had been away with us on the trip to the Continent, and Henry Adams. Wesley was smitten with the simple theological message, but Henry Adams was touched by the sense of freedom and independence that stirred in his restless spirit. Adams could never understand why religion needed to be tied to the governing of the country. Religious wars were, to him, completely illogical, and an affront to his spiritual as well as moral senses. Consequently, he became convinced that he wanted to move his growing young family to America. There was a growing number of people who decided that the adventure of crossing the sea to America was both an adventure and an opportunity. Land there was said to be so plentiful, forests so lush, animals so exotic, and freedom so intoxicating, that the risks were believed to be well worth the effort. Dangers were discussed, but as with all enticing ideas, the emotion of the calling seemed to outweigh the logic of the risks. He was also convinced that his wife Edith would be as excited and taken with the idea as he. She was a hardy, strong woman (who would eventually bear him nine children), and she could manage anything, including a trip to the New World of freedom and opportunity.

Wesley met Adams one evening at a gathering where Ward was preaching. They struck up a conversation about Ward's message that evening.

"I like the message that Ward gives these people," said Wesley. "He tells the truth no matter what the Church of England tries to force on him."

"It's not the Church of England that is the problem," countered Adams. "The King simply wants central control, and he can control people with religion. The real problem is with a King who wants us to believe that God has anointed only him as the leader of a country. I value the freedom to believe more than I value the belief itself, I think," continued Adams. "Kings only want more power and control, and if religion gives that to them, they will use it."

Wesley pondered what Adams said, but he could not agree.

"Faith is all that we have and all that we need!" Wesley said somewhat firmly. "Don't be confusing worldly power with faith. But keep in mind that Paul said in the book of Romans that God anoints Kings to rule, and we should be subject to that authority."

"I suppose you would then say that the Pope in Rome is an authority, appointed by God whom we must obey," Adams countered, knowing that this would likely raise the temperature of the conversation.

"I most certainly would not!" Wesley shot back. "The Pope is the head of the anti-Christ Babylon – a perversion of God's plan. Scripture is the only authority in matters of faith. Kings are earthly authority whom we are required to obey."

Adams smiled at Wesley and said, "Friend, let us agree that God is in authority, and man needs to follow his conscience in responding to Him."

Wesley was disarmed by Adams' smile, and he agreed that arguing was not productive here, especially with someone he had just met.

"You remind me some of a friend of mine with whom I journeyed last year – a man named Joseph Shepherd."

Adams looked surprised. "I remind you of Joseph Shepherd?" he said. "I hear that he consorts with the scoundrel Jacob Carr. Andrew Kensington told me that Shepherd cannot be trusted."

"So you consort with Andrew Kensington?" replied Wesley. "Kensington is the one you need to hide your purse from, not Joseph Shepherd!"

"It seems that we cannot agree on anything!" Adams said, again with a smile.

"Perhaps not," said Wesley, as he tried to suppress a smile of his own. "Shepherd is an interesting man. He can be challenging, I will give you that, but he is bright, fair, and caring. He will make you angry and troubled, and at the same time give you hope and encouragement. I have never met anyone quite like him. So, rather than judge Joseph Shepherd without knowing him, would you like to meet him?"

"Yes, I think that is a fine idea. Let's agree on that," said Adams.

"Meet me tomorrow at the Franciscan mission on Market Street," said Wesley.

"I know the place," said Adams. "I will meet you there about mid-morning."

Wesley and Adams met at the Franciscan mission the next day, and Wesley introduced Adams to Shepherd. They exchanged pleasantries, then Wesley got right to the point.

"I think my new friend, Mr. Adams, has the wrong idea about you," Wesley said to Shepherd. "He has heard that you consort with Jacob Carr, and that anyone who has dealings with Carr has dealt with the devil himself."

Shepherd looked at Adams and said, "Is that what you believe?"

Adams looked back at Shepherd and said, "I know of Jacob Carr, and he is of the vilest sort. Two years ago he and his unholy mob broke into my cousin's shop, stole all of his wine, gin and brandy, and all the gold coins from his money drawer, then cracked his skull with a truncheon. They left him for

126

dead, and he might have died if it were not for my wife Edith who was coming by the shop the next morning. She bound his wounds, brought him to our home, and we slowly nursed him back to health. To this day, he is blind in one eye, has headaches and dizziness, and has fits from time to time where he falls down drooling and clawing the air with his fists drawn up. He cannot work, and we care for him as he tries to do a little work in our garden. So yes, Jacob Carr might be of the devil himself. If you want to be around such a man, perhaps you too are misguided, or foolish, or evil."

Shepherd did not respond for a long while. "You and your family have suffered a great loss and a great injustice," Shepherd said. "In what way can I be of help to you?"

Adams replied, "You owe me nothing, sir, but Jacob Carr should be hanged."

"So, you would be pleased to see Jacob Carr hanged?" he asked.

"Yes I would," said Adams.

"But that would not restore your cousin, now would it," said Shepherd.

"No, it would not," said Adams, "but it would be justice."

"Perhaps it would be justice, but does justice restore or does it simply punish?" asked Shepherd. "If there is a chance for restoration, would you choose that over punishment?"

"Perhaps I would. I don't know," said Adams, "but I cannot speak for my cousin Albert. He is the one wronged here the most."

"Yes, that is true," said Shepherd, "and perhaps there is a chance to begin that journey right now. Jacob, can you come out here to meet Mr. Adams?" Shepherd asked.

Carr walked out of the mission and approached the gathering of men. Adams, shocked, eyed him warily and moved toward him. Shepherd stepped in and said to Carr, "Jacob, this is Mr. Adams, and he has told me about the harm you did to him and his family."

Carr was solemn as he said to Shepherd, "I have wronged so many people in my life, I am ashamed to say that I do not know this man, or his family member, or specifically what I did to them. I can say that I humbly ask for forgiveness. If you will be so kind as to tell me my crime, I will do my best to make restitution to this man and his family."

Adams was not sure how to respond, but his anger was still not dissipated. "You beat my cousin Albert Adams nearly to death, and you stole almost the entirety of his shop. You robbed him of not just his goods, but his livelihood and his dignity. He is physically damaged, and he cannot care for himself. What you have stolen from him cannot be restored."

"I ask your forgiveness even though I do not deserve it," said Carr. "I will restore the value of what I have stolen, and I will give you a pension for your cousin for the rest of his life. I know that this does not restore his body or his mind, but it is all that I can offer, and I offer it in the hope that you may

127

find some peace in it." Carr finished and bowed his head to Adams. He then turned and walked slowly away, allowing Adams time to absorb this act of repentance.

Shepherd said to Adams, "It is now up to you if you would like to accept this offer, or if you would like to take Mr. Carr to the sheriff to have him thrown into gaol."

Herbert Wesley stood silent as he watched this dramatic event unfold. He believed that he had just witnessed an act of faith that was an experience of what the Bible prescribed. It was faith in action right before his eyes.

"I will need to think about this," said Adams.

"Yes," said Shepherd, "we all need to think about this."

Chapter 31

I began to think about King James' part in the expedition to America. Kensington had said that King James was kindly disposed toward Shepherd and me, and he wanted to use our influence with the King to help finance the journey. Imagine that!

If that were the case, we could bypass Kensington, appeal to the King, perhaps with Harvey, to form our own scientific mission. I was actually considering giving up the lucrative benefits offered by Kensington to spend more of my life with Joseph Shepherd. More and more I was feeling that whatever journey I was to take next, I wanted it to be with Shepherd. Going to America would be a wonderful (albeit dangerous) and exciting venture. Shepherd would respond favorably if he knew there were to be benefits for people, especially if he could exercise his scientific mind. He would love to bring some of his new friends along if they were up for the adventure.

I went to the Franciscan mission the following day and found Shepherd busily tending to some new arrivals.

"Joseph," I hailed to him warmly, "I have an idea for us."

"Another idea for the trip to America?" he said smiling.

"Well, in fact it is," I said. "Let me hear it," he said.

I proceeded to explain my idea about approaching Harvey and King James about a trip to America. The primary reason for some of us was for the adventure, as well as the scientific benefits. For the King, however, there needed to be some military, political, or economic value. So we needed to find out how we could approach the King in those areas. There are risks to such endeavors, not the least of which might be how we would alienate Andrew Kensington, stealing the expedition out from under him. However, the potential rewards were just too great to pass up.

Henry Adams was increasingly torn about moving his family to America. He believed strongly in the freedom principles that drove many adventurers to leave England for America, but he felt that he had a responsibility to care for his cousin Albert. Henry Adams had told his cousin about his encounter with Jacob Carr at the Franciscan mission. Albert was strangely quiet as Henry spoke.

"I have upset you, Cousin Albert. I am so sorry," said Henry.

"No, that is not the case, Henry. You and Edith have been so kind and helpful for me these past two years, and I do not want to be a hindrance to you any longer," he said.

"Nonsense!" said Henry. "That is what families do for one another. You would have done the same for me."

"That is what I have been thinking about, Henry. I want to do the same for you and your family," said Albert.

"What do you mean?" said Henry.

"I mean that I am leaving your kind family to free you to go to America. I cannot live with myself if you stay in England only to provide for my care. I am leaving tomorrow. Please do not try to stop me."

Henry was completely dumbstruck. "You cannot survive without help and care. You surely know that."

Albert seemed wounded by this remark, true as it may have been.

"I did not mean to hurt you, Albert, but truth is truth."

"I need some time to myself, Henry. Please indulge me that," said Albert.

"Yes, of course," said Henry.

Albert took off for the The Bard tavern to drink a pint of ale and think about his next move. He had been considering for some time how to free Henry and his family from the burden of caring for him. He had no other family, his wife having died just before he was robbed and beaten. He had a son who had died at birth, and a daughter who had perished with smallpox as a child. His parents had died in a fire when he was seventeen years old. He had been fiercely independent as a youth, starting his business when he was twenty-two, and finding a way to survive by guile and a flair for business. Now he faced another life challenge, and he was sure not to let his disability get in the way of his cousin's dreams.

As he walked in the dusk down to the tavern, he was deep in thought. Suddenly he had another of his fits. He fell to the ground with a grimace, grasping wildly at the air. He bit his tongue deeply, and blood started to pour from the side of his mouth. He was lying helpless on the ground, unable to even call out for help. Even if he had, it was not likely to result in real help, as three people on their way to the tavern simply stepped over him.

"Helpless sot!" one of them called out. Another said to his friend, "Another victim of demon gin!" as he laughed at Albert's helpless body beneath him.

The fit subsided finally, but Albert was unable to get up. He was completely exhausted, bleeding and unable to speak intelligibly. As he lay in despair, a stranger came up to him.

"Friend, it looks like you need help," he said.

Albert could not speak, but he simply nodded. Then a look of terror came upon him. The man standing over him was Jacob Carr.

It turned out that it was not as difficult as I might have imagined persuading the King about financing the trip. It turned out that the Dorchester Company, which was a trading company poised to exploit New World wealth, was looking for added support for their venture in establishing a new settlement at Cape Ann near Plymouth. We would become part of that expedition, and we would be given a royal charter to "explore the American coast, begin a settlement, determine which crops can best be grown, find new medicinal plants and herbs which can benefit the people of the realm, and provide for the health of people who have travelled to America."

Shepherd and I and our new travelling companion, Henry Adams, began talking about our upcoming trip.

"Tell me again how you decided to make this trip with a young family, Adams," I said. Shepherd had told me earlier about Adams and his disabled cousin, and I wanted to know why he had decided to risk his own family, as well as how he had provided for his cousin.

"My family, and generations beyond mine, will live free of royal abuse of authority, and free of religious oppression. As for my cousin Albert, that is an interesting story. I sometimes think that this was somehow an affirmation from God about my decision."

"Why is that? I asked.

"Albert was caught with another of his fits last week and he was left on the street until, of all people, along came Jacob Carr. Apparently, Carr has taken to searching the streets, especially near taverns in the evening, looking for people who might be in trouble. That evening, it was Albert. He picked Albert up from the street and carried him to the Franciscan mission. Then, weeping, he asked Albert's forgiveness, and he pledged to take care of him at the mission for as long as he needs care. I am still stunned at both God's provision for Albert, as well as the miracle of Jacob Carr's conversion. Albert says that we are now free, all of us, to pursue our own calling. Funny thing, but Jacob Carr says he is now free also."

Chapter 32

It had taken months for the trip to be organized, but we were growing in our excitement about it. When Sean Kelley had heard of our plans, he jumped at the opportunity to come along. He had not been able to find any steady work due to his bad leg, and he needed a way to survive. His wife had left him for another sailor she met when he was on the *Intrepid*. He was more than ready to leave England for a new start in life. Kelley was grateful for the opportunity to work and to be reunited with old friends. He was, indeed, a friend of the first rate.

We sailed out of London on a bright August morning in 1623. The sun was rising slowly and brilliantly as we tacked toward the Channel on our way to the Atlantic from the Thames. Our crew of twenty-two men was captained by the aging Captain William Braden. He seemed to be completely recovered from his last dangerous voyage. This was a veteran crew, unlike the ill-fated lot who manned the *Intrepid*. The *Merriweather* was not a new ship, but she had only five or six voyages under her belt. Loaded with barrels and casks of provisions for our new settlement at Cape Ann, as well as some refreshed supplies for Plymouth, we felt well stocked. Further, Shepherd had asked Harvey for help with medical supplies, and we had a veritable hospital on the ship, including Harvey's latest medical equipment, graciously given to us for the trip to America. Shepherd had made the case that the New World offered a potential supply of new medicinal plants and herbs that could benefit both England and America if properly developed and tested. He had heard of the dreadful diseases that had decimated Plymouth in the past two years, and he was firm in his resolve to make America a healthy place for people seeking a new way of life. He had also heard of the native people of America, savages really, but Shepherd never called them that. He felt that they could benefit from the scientific advances we had seen in England also.

"Captain Braden," I said as I walked into his cabin, "how has your health been since our last adventure?"

I was once again named ship's physician, so I felt that I had reason, even the duty, to open our dialogue in this way.

"Dr. Greene," he said, "I cannot tell you when I have felt better than I do at this moment!"

I smiled at him. "That is certainly good for a passenger to hear from his ship's captain!"

We both had a good laugh as we went into a reverie of our last voyage together. Both of us could have died on that voyage, and we were both close to it, although in different ways. We talked about some of the old crew as Kelley joined us in our casual discussion.

"Whatever happened to old Dooley?" I asked.

Kelley joined in, "Dooley is in Bethlam Asylum. He seems almost sane these days, I think, but when you are in a place like that, nobody seems sane," he said matter-of-factly. "When he killed Swailes and North, I thought that to be the sanest thing a man could do. The judge in the case as much as said that when he sent Dooley to Bethlam instead of hanging him. I was on trial then too, for mutiny on a Royal ship. Old Dooley said that there were only about three or four people on the ship who were not insane, and he named Braden, Greene, me, and Shepherd as the ones who saved the ship. I think Dooley did too, but when he told the judge that the angels and the demons were fighting in his head all the time, and that he heard God talk to him sometimes, the judge thought it would be easier to just put him in Bethlam than to hang him. It was easier to just put that whole thing of the *Intrepid* away by saying that a madman had killed some of the crew. No one cares now what really happened on that ship, so we are all better off now. I got off charges mostly because Dooley was the one who the judge says was out of control. Nobody told of my 'incident' with Mr. Kent. For that I am grateful. Truth is, that whole ship was out of control!"

We came away from that conversation sad for Dooley, but glad it was behind us. In fact, had it not been for the *Intrepid* disaster, I would not be where I am today. I felt very fortunate.

The days melted away for me in reading, and discussions with Shepherd, Kelley, Braden, and Adams. As I looked out over the port side one day, I saw a spout of water rise out of the sea, followed by hundreds of jumping dolphins. What a sight! I thought. Tacking to deal with the prevailing "Westerlies," we had drifted much farther south than intended, and we were experiencing some warmer water and weather. Braden seemed unconcerned, and we became accustomed to the hot days, and enjoyed the evening light shows of "falling stars."

Shepherd told me that Galileo had told him of these "falling stars" a few years ago while we were in Italy. Galileo did not think them to be stars, but likely some heavenly bodies that raced through space in a predictable way, since he could plot their appearance year after year. In fact, this is part of why he had said that the earth too was a wanderer through space around the sun. Mathematics could predict these patterns, but the Church seemed too threatened to consider these ideas. Shepherd was saddened by this, not really angered like some of the great minds of the day. Truly, I felt that Shepherd was one of the great minds of the day.

Shepherd spent time with Henry Adams on the voyage, discussing his politics, religion, and views of farming science. Adams was an independent sort who seemed to embody a nonconformist, perhaps contrarian worldview.

133

Fiercely independent, he was convinced that America could become a new chance for the English people. Shepherd and Adams talked a great deal about the Dutch philosopher Hugo Grotius, who seemed to have the idea that natural laws did not contradict God's laws since God was the author of all, including natural law. He believed that the rule of law should govern any human disputes, and that men should be free to establish governments that represented this natural approach to human coexistence. The idea that a sort of "social contract" should exist between those who govern and those governed was a very radical kind of thought. This flew in the face of the arbitrary type of ruling that existed all over the civilized world. It certainly refuted the Divine Right of Kings, which was the hallmark of monarchy. If such thinking could somehow be implemented in America, the world indeed would be turned upside down!

Captain Braden told us that we were making great progress. This, I believe, was due to the favorable winds and his savvy tacking maneuvers. At this rate we would be in America in the next two weeks, a swift six-week journey. What a start to our adventure. It seemed to bode well for our brave group of travelers.

As Braden had predicted, in the next ten days we began to see signs of land. Gulls began to be sighted almost daily. Passengers grew restless as we neared land. Anticipation and wonder ruled the day. The Dorchester Company had designated a leader for the new community at Cape Ann. His job would be to establish the settlement, and to make a relationship with the native people to help with favorable deals for trading goods, as well as learning about this new place from them. This leader was John Levine, a very cunning, no-nonsense man whose job it was to not only make a settlement but to make money for his investors at the Dorchester Company. He was generally respected by most in the company of travelers, but their goals differed from his somewhat. Most had come wanting a new start in a new world. Levine wanted to make money for his employers. In order to do that, he had to make sure the settlement was successful. The tradeoff seemed to be fair and understood.

We landed on September 26th, and we immediately held a service of thanksgiving for the providence God had given to the voyage. Not one death, not even significant illness, despite the privation of a treacherous ocean voyage in the most challenging of circumstances. Levine was unfolding his plans for building structures that would sustain us through a winter that we anticipated might be as difficult as that faced by the Plymouth group. We had, he reckoned, about six to eight weeks before we could expect cold temperatures, perhaps snow, and even blizzards of some type, as William Bradford had discussed in his pamphlets published in 1622.

We had provisions for the winter on board the *Merriweather*, and in the spring we would plant the seeds that we brought along. We hoped also to learn of new crops to plant, including tobacco, which was of particular interest to Levine, though not a prominent incentive for the trip. Levine had his own ideas about the role of tobacco, but no one was sure that it would grow as well in a cooler climate like Plymouth settlement as it did in the relative warmth of the Virginia area. Immediately, he assigned several men to scout the area for game so that we could begin to get some meat for the winter. Bradford had talked about how American native people had smoked meat to preserve it. The country teemed with deer, beaver, turkey, fish in freshwater rivers, otters, and a host of other creatures that could be hunted. Surely, food should not be a problem.

Chapter 33

Andrew Kensington was still seething about the voyage to America that was taken away from him. He had done all the work on arranging to have his voyage underwritten by the East India Company. Shepherd, Harvey, and I had gone over his head and called in the favor from King James, who made our voyage possible by having us added on to the Cape Ann settlement voyage, which had both economic and now scientific purposes. Kensington's plan for a tobacco, slave, rum triangle as part of his financial empire's beginnings would have to wait for another investor, or for the East India Company to endorse it – something they had not yet been persuaded to do. We had convinced the King and the Dorchester Company that a settlement and a medical/scientific voyage would be more beneficial in the long run for England, especially as an increasing colonization of America held out huge potential as a new market for goods and a raw material bonanza.

King James was not fond of tobacco as a crop, and that seemed to help sway our argument as well. Besides, it was becoming increasingly clear that the country that could populate the new American settlements with the most people would have an advantage over the others – the Dutch, Spaniards, and French. Finally, though Kensington was not aware, King James had wearied of Kensington's poor reputation, and the King did not want any more connection with him than necessary.

Kensington decided that his revenge would come in several ways. First, he would put together another company to finance his plan for trade to America. The London & Western Trading Company thus came to be. He had contacts all over Europe, and he had already discussed his plans with a number of financiers. He had, of course, many contacts also in the shipping world, and it did not take him long to put this plan together, even without royal help or protection. Further, he came to believe that King James' power was weakening, and he was going to continue to hasten that weakness with other mischief as he could.

His other revenge would be more personal. He would hurt Joseph Shepherd and me in any ways that he could. As for me, he would simply find ways to ensure, through his shipping contacts, that I would never again find employment on a ship as a ship's physician. Whatever reputation I may have had would be ruined, or at least downgraded, if Kensington could have any say in it.

For Shepherd, it would be more sinister.

Late one evening, Oliver Craft and James Bidwell walked around the Franciscan mission asking if they could locate an old friend who, the morning before, had come up missing after a night of drinking. One of the senior friars bid them to come in from the crisp evening and warm themselves by the fire as he tried to locate a newcomer from that day. There had been several, since the weather was turning cold in the evenings and nights, and the drinking always seemed to increase.

They were alone in a receiving room used to house overnight transients, and since it was still early in the evening, there were no occupants. Bidwell followed after the old friar, engaging him in conversation, and Craft took that opportunity to throw a flagon of oil into the fire. He trailed out a line of oil into a pile of rags, which he had soaked with the oil, and soon flames were snaking through the room. Craft then followed where Bidwell and the friar had gone into the main great room of the mission. In the room he saw some children playing innocently in a corner. Some people began drifting into the room from their meager supper to prepare for the evening prayers and Bible story.

Craft caught up to Bidwell and the friar and said, "I found old Jack Merton just outside the mission. We can be leaving now."

With that Craft and Bidwell thanked the friar and hastily made their exit.

They had expected only to make some mischief for now. Had they wanted to burn down the mission, they would have done things differently. However, they did not know that the friars had just laid in a supply of brandy and had placed it in the receiving room until they could later bring it into the kitchen. The brandy, in wooden crates, caught fire quickly, and fire accelerated wildly into the adjoining room.

One of the children smelled smoke and instinctively yelled "Fire!" Some friars came running to find smoke and fire pouring into the great room. As Bidwell and Craft were walking down an adjacent alley, they saw the glow of a growing fire – something well beyond what they expected. The walk turned into a trot, then a full run as they slipped into the darkening evening.

At the mission, chaos prevailed. Screaming children began to run. Some ran right into the receiving room, thinking it to be the fastest exit. Alarms rang out and townspeople began to organize into the well-known procedure for putting out fires. The residents of the mission began to run in all directions. Jacob Carr ran down the steps from his room and began to lead the children and the sickest residents out of a safe exit in the building's rear. He then thought about Albert Adams. Albert had just had another of his fits, and he was fast asleep in the hospital ward. Carr grabbed a blanket from the storage area and soaked it in water. He threw the blanket over himself and went back into the hospital ward. Patients who could walk were shuffling to the exit he pointed out to them. He saw one patient, an elderly man who was paralyzed,

137

screaming for help. Fire was his worst nightmare, and it was happening right now to him. Carr grabbed the man up and slung him over his shoulder with a quick heave. He moved toward the exit, laid the man safely out of the way, and went back in. By now, smoke was enveloping the building. It was hard to see, and the smoke began to choke Carr. He went back into the ward, and he saw Albert writhing on the ground in another fit. The noise, smoke, and confusion must have set off another of those dreadful episodes.

Carr reached down and tried to lift Albert, who was simply dead weight. With fire now closing in, and the smoke choking and blinding him, Carr decided to drag Albert out of the building. Carr saw flames lapping at his blanket, and he felt immense heat under it. The water had turned to steam and it was scalding Carr as he dragged Albert to safety.

Once outside, he asked if all had made it to safety. Margaret and Sister Clarice of the Order of the Poor Clares were tending to some children who had been burned. Many others were choking with smoke inhalation. Jacob went to douse his blanket once again for a return trip into the Mission.

"No!" screamed Margaret. "You cannot go back in there."

Jacob ignored her pleas. He knew that there were other people still trapped in the inferno that was rapidly becoming no longer a mission but now crumbling rubble. He soaked the blanket in fresh water and went back in the building. The crowd comprising a bucket brigade was now concentrating on nearby buildings. They had learned that, at a certain point of a fire, saving the burning building was no longer the goal, but containment of the fire to prevent it from spreading through the city.

Carr could barely see now inside the building that he had reentered. He went to the hospital ward, believing that they were the most vulnerable at this point. He heard, somehow, the high-pitched wail of a baby. He remembered that they had taken in an abandoned child just last week, a baby boy who had been left in the chapel, wrapped in a ragged blanket with a note that was nearly illegible that simply said, "SAVE ME."

Carr made his way to the sound of the baby and scooped the boy up. He took off his blanket, wrapped the boy inside and stumbled his way to an exit. He dropped to the ground as he passed off the child to Margaret. Margaret screamed in terror.

"He is on fire!" she screamed. A man with a bucket threw the full contents on Jacob, and he smoldered as the flames went out.

Had he not passed out at that point, he would be screaming in pain as the crowd saw his burning flesh cling to the bits of clothing that remained on him. Two friars lifted him gently and moved him away from a gawking crowd. They were sickened as they smelled the burnt flesh of his back and legs. Other friars gathered around him and began to pray for his soul.

The mission continued to burn for another hour, but buildings nearby had been saved. Jacob Carr would not be saved.

Chapter 34

London was stirred by the remarkable tragedy at the Franciscan mission. Word quickly spread about the heroics of Jacob Carr in saving three people from the fire. There had been a growing awareness of the ways that the mission had expanded its role in caring for people, especially with the hospital, which took in the sickest and poorest in London.

Kensington was outraged. Not so much because of the horrendous loss, but because it had been done in such a clumsy and reckless manner. A little fire in part of the building to disrupt and send a message was one thing, but being possibly tied to deaths and destruction of a "poorhouse" would not be good for him or his new business.

Bidwell and Craft met with Robert "Red" Locker just outside the city, near a little hideaway they used to meet secretly, drink, and occasionally take a woman. Bidwell was shaken as he talked with Locker. Locker was a gruff, angry man who simply took care of what his boss, Andrew Kensington, told him to take care of. Fiercely loyal to Kensington, he would make sure that Kensington would not be tied to this disastrous crime, no matter what it took.

"Did anybody see you other than that old friar?" Locker asked.

"Maybe some kids in that great room," said Bidwell. "But I don't think they was really lookin' at us," he said hesitantly.

"The one we need to worry about is that old friar," Craft said matter-of-factly.

"I'll take care of him," said Locker. "Now, you two scum need to get out of here."

"Where do we go?" they asked.

"Lord Kensington is putting you two on a ship next week headed to America. You will be deckhands on the trip, then when you get to America, you are on your own. You are lucky that he didn't tell me to just kill you right now."

Bidwell was chilled to the bone as he heard this. He knew that such things could, and had, happened before, so he indeed did feel lucky. Craft on the other hand was not as grateful.

"We was just doing what he wanted us to do, now he wants to send us to a strange land to let us rot!" he said.

"You are too stupid to even know what you did wrong," countered Locker. "If you don't want the deal just let me know now."

Craft was silent, recognizing that resisting this deal would indeed be fatal.

"Just tell us where to meet the ship," said Craft in a resigned tone.

"You'll stay here until next week," said Locker. "We will send someone for you."

Margaret was devastated in her grief over the loss of Jacob Carr. She had, of course, known him for several years, but in the past year she came to know the new Jacob Carr – a man transformed. He was kind, loving, selfless, and dedicated to his new mission in life. He and Margaret had cared for the poorest of London's rabble together, and, in the process, fell deeply in love. Margaret did not know where to turn. The Franciscan mission was gone, and people who were cared for there seemed to vanish back into the streets of London. The friars, demoralized, decided to return to their home province in Ypres, France. The atmosphere in France was much more welcoming than England, and they saw that, perhaps, God was calling them back to a more receptive land, even though all would agree that God had worked through them to serve the people of London. That time was now apparently past, and they voted to return to Ypres.

Margaret felt responsible for Albert Adams. Jacob had lost his life saving Albert and that little baby from the fire. Margaret decided that she would give a legacy to Jacob by providing for Albert and that baby. How she would do that, she did not know, but she felt deeply that this was her mission now. Margaret had prevailed upon an old friend from the Boar's Head Pub to provide a place to stay for her, Albert, and the baby, now renamed Jacob. She had heard that there was a ship leaving for America in the next few weeks. She decided that, since many people were deciding that a new start in America was possible, she would do just that, despite the tremendous challenges it posed. She also had no idea how this trip could possibly happen, but she trusted that God did, so she prayed a simple prayer: "God, if you want me to go to America, and if you want me to take care of Albert and Jacob, please find a way for me."

Edwin Carr sought out Margaret. He knew that she loved his late brother, and he felt that he needed to speak with her. She had been the last person to talk with him, and he really did not know much about his brother after his conversion. He wanted to know.

Friar Theodore, the elder friar who had brought Craft and Bidwell into the Mission, was preparing to move the Franciscans to Ypres in the next few weeks. He went to the Boar's Head and inquired about Margaret, Albert, and Jacob. He was directed to the home of Emma Stone. Emma seemed to be the person whom everyone knew. She was aware of people, places, and things that others had no idea about.

"If you want to know, ask Emma," seemed to be the wisdom among people of London's East side.

"Sure, I know where Margaret is," said Emma. "Staying at Mother Rose's. She takes in the girls when they get old or tired or sick. Margaret is a fine young woman, and I don't care what people says! I just directed Edwin Carr there. Do you know him?"

Friar Theodore began to weep. "I knew his brother, Jacob. I would love to see him."

"Well, hurry along!" said Emma, "and you'll see them both."

Friar Theodore headed to Mother Rose's place. As he was walking up the alley to her door he was accosted by a red-haired man. Locker walked quickly behind the old friar, took out a knife and jabbed it into Theodore's back. Friar Theodore stumbled and fell down quickly – so quickly that his feet tangled with Locker, and Locker fell heavily on top of him. Just then, Edwin Carr turned a corner and saw the scene. The old Friar was moaning, with blood oozing from his back. Locker scrambled to his feet, intent upon raining a death blow on the old friar. Carr picked up a loose cobblestone and hurled it at the attacker. He at least wanted to distract the attacker until he could get closer to intervene. In fact, the stone caught Locker on his shoulder and he screamed in pain. By now Carr was at Locker, and he jumped straight at him. Locker was stunned by the stone and in obvious pain. He was no match for the enraged Edwin Carr. Carr punched him in the wounded shoulder to knock him down. He then made quick work of him with a kick to the face, then a kick to his mid-section, and a final kick to his head. Locker was not moving after the final kick.

Carr moved to the wounded friar. He had been fortunate that the stab in his back was high and to his upper right back. While it was indeed painful and bloody, it was not fatal. Given the old man's age, however, it was serious. Carr took him to Mother Rose's house, where he met Mother Rose, Margaret, Albert, and little Jacob. Mother Rose knew what to do. She had dressed much worse wounds in her day, and she had seen plenty of street fights.

"I will care for the friar," she said. "I know you want to talk with Margaret," she said to Edwin Carr.

Margaret talked at length to Edwin about his remarkable brother, his selfless acts of heroism, and finally of her love for him. Edwin was moved, and he sat silent for a long while. He felt guilt over not knowing his changed brother. His only memories were of the man people knew as a schemer and thug. While Edwin never saw much of the criminal traits of Jacob – he did not want to see them – he also felt cheated out of knowing this wonderful person his brother had become. He finally spoke.

"Margaret," he said, "I am sailing for America in the next two weeks. I am sure this is probably a shock for you, but I would like to take you, Albert, and little Jacob on that trip. I can make all the arrangements. It would be a new start for you."

Margaret was stunned. She quickly composed herself and said simply, "I accept your kind offer."

She then asked Albert Adams about this large decision. Albert was alert this day, having one of his good days where he had some energy. He smiled at Margaret and said simply, "There is a verse from the book of Ruth which states, 'Whither thou goest, I go also.'"

Chapter 35

"Red" Locker never came back for Craft and Bidwell. After two weeks, they left the hideaway and melted into the countryside. Some said that they went to Scotland, others said that they died fighting as mercenaries in Denmark.

The cause of the fire at the Franciscan Mission was never solved, but there was always a great deal of discussion and plenty of rumors about who had done this vile deed. The Franciscans moved to Ypres and did not have a presence in England for many years.

The *Courageous* left for America on May 8, 1624 under the command of Captain Edwin Carr. The ship was primarily one of emigration. The movement was growing, and passage to America was much more popular and marginally safer than it had ever been. Not that it was truly safe, but people had more faith in the voyages, and ships returning from America carried people with amazing stories of adventure, even wealth. The *Courageous* was headed for the Cape Ann settlement. Margaret was aboard the ship, amazed that her prayer had been answered in such a clear and dramatic manner. She was still grieving Jacob Carr's death, but she found some comfort being in the presence of his brother. She talked with him at length about Jacob, and also about her new mission in life. At any rate, she would have that new life in a new world, and she was beyond excited to start it.

The Cape Ann settlement had experienced the usual problems of disease, storms, crop failures, and problems with native people. However, there seemed to be a sense of hope there. Shepherd and I had made some remarkable discoveries with native plants. The American Elm tree, we discovered, could produce a concoction from parts of the brewed inner bark that would help in soothing coughs and would help those who had bleeding disorders. This was most helpful for women who were bleeding after childbirth. This was a common complication of birth, but we had real success in reducing the rate of such deaths.

The native people had showed us how to tap maple trees for their sap. Upon exposure to prolonged cooking to reduce it, the product was a wonderful syrup that had a delightful taste – sweeter than sugar produced from the canes in the West Indies.

Sassafras trees had leaves and roots that had great medicinal effect in healing sores and also in numbing pain when used on the skin. Its natural oils were aromatic, and, brewed as a tea, were a fine calmative agent.

We began to harvest these herbs, roots, and medicinal products, and the Dorchester Company was happy to see that there was a market back in England for these as medicines. Shepherd was content in this pursuit. He had made a place for himself in the settlement, and he enjoyed teaching children and native people who came to appreciate his care for them.

Not everyone, however, was able to communicate with the native people. Most of the settlement was interested in learning from the native people how to subdue the land. The native people just wanted to live in harmony with the land, but there was no profit in that. The Dorchester Company needed to make this settlement profitable. Shepherd was an exception, and he was not always appreciated for his differing views. Some thought he was a fool, some others felt that he saw himself as better than others. Almost all saw that he was exceptional, but people are often intimidated by such people, so he lived in the odd tension of brilliant healer, man of wisdom, and isolated eccentric.

The *Courageous* touched the shores near Cape Ann on July 4, 1624. The weary crew and passengers had a reasonably safe and routine voyage, but no voyage across the sea to America was completely safe. They had lost three passengers to death. A woman who gave birth prematurely to a baby girl at about five months of gestation died after hemorrhaging that could not be stopped. The child perished after about one hour of life. Another of the passengers, after a night of drinking in the hold of the ship (unbeknownst to others on the ship), died when he went up to the top deck and fell into the ocean. One of the crew saw him fall, but the standard order was that ships did not turn around for such occurrences. People who could not follow the rules earned their fate. This man was no exception.

We met the *Courageous* as she anchored in the harbor. Men in the settlement worked alongside the crew to unload the precious cargo, which included tea, beer, salted cod, and ammunition for muskets. We also took possession of two cannon and powder and shot. While we had not encountered any hostile natives, we wanted the comfort of these weapons for our defense. We also never knew if the Dutch, the Spanish, or the French might develop a hunger for the land that we were painstakingly developing.

I saw Margaret disembark from the small boat sent out to meet the *Courageous* in harbor. I was stunned to see that she had made the journey, and I found myself quite excited to see her again. I had not thought that I would ever see her again. She had been there, along with Jacob Carr, to see Shepherd and me off for our journey. Shepherd had given his blessing to Margaret and Jacob to ensure that things went smoothly at the mission as he left. While it was the Franciscan mission, Shepherd and Carr had been very instrumental in transforming the place into an important hospital and care center for the poor of London. Shepherd's vision and leadership and Carr's money worked wonders in that regard.

144

Margaret saw me and immediately ran to me with tears in her eyes. She threw herself into my arms, something I was not expecting, but which was very welcome.

"Luke," she began, "I have so much to tell you, and so much heartache!"

At that moment I saw Henry Adams running up to another craft which held his cousin Albert. They too embraced and wept. Edwin Carr was with Albert, helping him to steady himself to become accustomed to land after the voyage. Albert was somewhat unsteady, and Carr was very helpful and solicitous of his wellbeing. Shepherd came up to Margaret and me and embraced the weeping Margaret.

We went back to our quarters at the settlement. Spartan and small as they were, we were as comfortable as we could reasonably expect. Edwin Carr, Shepherd, Henry Adams, Albert Adams, Margaret, and I sat with flagons of ale, and we heard the story Margaret had to tell. Shepherd was visibly upset upon hearing of the death of Jacob Carr and the loss of the Franciscan mission. She talked about Jacob's bravery in saving people from the mission, including little Jacob, renamed after his rescuer.

Friar Theodore had described the two men he met with that fateful evening of the fire, and some said it sounded like Oliver Craft. Craft had disappeared, and that added to the speculation. Further, Craft was a known associate of Andrew Kensington, as was "Red" Locker. The fact that Locker was now dead, found in an alley near Mother Rose's dwelling, added to the speculation that there was a connection between Kensington, Locker, and Craft.

Each of us was moved in different ways by this report. Edwin Carr stayed silent as Margaret talked about the demise of "Red" Locker and the disappearance of Craft and Bidwell. I began to think about how close I had come to getting into business with Andrew Kensington, and about what wrath could come upon those who parted ways with him. Margaret was still grieving a lost love, and Shepherd was pained by the loss of a friend as well as the loss of a vision.

Shepherd brought the discussion around to what would happen from here. We agreed that we were each in America for a different reason, but that this land offered something amazing and special. It offered a chance at a new start, a chance to form this place into a place where freedom of religion and freedom from royal oppression may be really possible; finally, it was a place where we had no past, and we were not judged by it. For Margaret this seemed especially pleasing, but it was good for me also. I might be able to determine why I was even alive, and that is something I had been avoiding by simply pursuing the next enticing thing I found. This could be a very special place for all of us.

Chapter 36

Margaret was quite solicitous of little Jacob and loved the little boy – probably more because she could continue to say, "Jacob, I love you." Little Jacob had a number of women who bustled about him. Children were in short supply at this settlement, and the chance to care for the child gave an outlet for care and nurture in an environment that challenged those virtues daily.

Margaret Brennan (she received the name Brennan from her brief marriage to Ian Brennan, an Irish sailor she met when she was young), was a changed woman. She had been a prostitute, and had even propositioned me at the Boar's Head Pub years before. While she had never been of the very rough sort of harlot I had encountered, she was worldly wise and cunning. Yet her transformation at the Franciscan mission with Carr and Shepherd had been complete. She had great compassion for people, and she had a disarming smile. While she was certainly physically attractive enough, it was her spirit that showed her real beauty. I know that I had been attracted to her from the start.

Joseph Shepherd had been communicating with the native people and was beginning to learn some of their strange language. He seemed more interested in learning their tongue than teaching them English. Part of our mission was to be able to communicate well with these people, begin some trade with them, and learn to exploit this wealth of natural resources all around us.

John Levine was always telling Shepherd to teach the "savages" English and not spend much time on the foolish gibberish they spoke.

"Mr. Levine," Shepherd would say, "how do you expect me to teach them English if I do not know their tongue? Besides, I think we can earn respect from them if we attempt to learn their ways, not just expect that our ways are superior on the face of it. There is much to be learned from these people, but also about them. For example, they have told me that they are known as Algonquin people, and their language is virtually the same name, Algonquian. There are numerous tribes of Algonquin, and not all are alike"

"Yes, Mr. Shepherd, I see you want to be around those savages. Just do not turn into one of them someday. Remember who you are and what your mission is," said Levine.

Levine would usually just shake his head and puzzle over Shepherd's way of seeing and treating people.

Shepherd also started treating sick natives in our little hospital, incorporating both our practices, as well as some of the native medicine. Shepherd believed that this diversity of learning only enhanced medical practices in general, and he kept an open mind to some things that appeared to be foolishness to most of us.

We also noticed that many of these native people, these Algonquins, were becoming sick since we arrived, with illnesses that they said they had never seen before we came. In fact, this was causing increasing tension in our connections with the natives. Shepherd believed that we had brought with us some type of illnesses that we carried somehow but were not affected by for some reason. This gave credence to his theory, having seen how cowpox made people immune from smallpox, that exposure to some illnesses was then preventive of others. He had also read of how in some ancient battles invaders had tossed blankets that had been on people dying of the plague into the camp of the enemy. The enemy then succumbed to the plague. Clearly some unseen body, perhaps like we had seen through the glass from Janssen, was responsible for these illnesses. We noted how he had often washed his hands after seeing each patient, and would wear a cloth over his nose and mouth that he had rinsed in vinegar when he was visiting the sickest people. The natives watched this in amusement, feeling this was an English practice – foolish to them just as some of their practices were to us. I watched him with an open mind. I had seen how effective his work was both on the *Intrepid* and throughout our travels. I was convinced that if Joseph Shepherd said something was a wise practice, I would likely never dispute him.

One day, Mr. Kelley was out with several other men hunting for game. It was now late August, and they had decided to go out early in the morning to avoid the heat of the day. It did not take long to spot a large white-tailed deer buck drinking at a stream. Mr. Kelley leveled his musket and fired at the deer. His shot sailed over the buck as the buck dipped down to drink. They quickly heard a scream from the brush just behind the deer. Just then, one of the Algonquin natives, hunting in the same area, staggered out to the stream, blood streaming from his thigh. Kelley ran to the wounded native, unsure how to proceed, but knowing he must help somehow. As Kelley proceeded toward the hunter, the other Algonquin hunters showed themselves from the surrounding bushes. Kelley froze, and then realized that they were going to come after him. Surrounded, and having no useable weapon other than a hunting knife, he threw his hands into the air in surrender. The Algonquin hunters grabbed Kelley, and then turned to help their fallen brother. The wounded Algonquin quickly explained to his fellow hunters what had happened.

The little group proceeded to take their wounded brother and Kelley back to their village. As they lay the wounded man they called Achak down, he was bleeding profusely. The other hunters had bound his leg at the site of the wound, but it appeared that Achak was losing his battle for life. He was pale, nearly gray, and losing consciousness. Kelley tried to gesture that he knew how to help Achak. Kelley recalled that his fellow sailors aboard the *Intrepid* told him how Joseph Shepherd had bound a cord tightly above the site

147

of his bleeding wound, and that it had stopped the bleeding immediately. Kelley had a leather strap around his shoulder holding his bag of lead shot for his musket. He grabbed the pouch and made a "cutting" gesture to explain that he wanted them to cut off the strap of the pouch. One of the women standing by, whom they called Chepi, directed the men to cut the strap Kelley had offered. Kelley, grateful for her understanding, smiled at her and motioned that the strap should be tied around the upper thigh of Achak. He did this by demonstrating on his own leg.

Chepi directed the men to do as Kelley had said. Kelley moved closer to Achak and began to work with the men helping Achak. He tightened the strap and Achak screamed out in pain. Kelley kept working, expecting that he would be stopped in his efforts to help Achak, but Chepi intervened and allowed Kelley to keep working on Achak. The bleeding stopped, and Achak calmed a bit. He was near unconsciousness, but he asked for water. He drank the cool water offered to him just out of the nearby stream. As he drank more, he was revived just a bit and seemed somewhat more comfortable.

Kelley was amazed that Chepi had allowed him to help. She had obvious power and influence in the camp, and, for some reason, knew to allow Kelley's benevolent actions to take place. Chepi came over to Kelley and spoke some words of halting English to him. She said something that sounded like the words, "Joseph Shepherd, friend, children, learn."

Women in the Algonquin culture seemed to have a great deal of influence – more so than our English women. Chepi seemed to be revered as a kind of mystic. She was a beautiful woman, with coal black hair, high cheekbones, and piercing eyes.

Kelley began to see that Chepi was aware of children who were being taught by Joseph Shepherd. Chepi was also part of the group that met with Shepherd, and she had learned some English. More importantly, she had learned to have some trust in the English settlers. This willingness to trust may have been what saved Achak's life, as well as Kelley's. Kelley repeated the words Chepi had used and said, "Your children learn from our friend Joseph Shepherd."

Chepi smiled broadly when she heard this. She had made language contact and was understood by Kelley!

They continued this halting conversation with some English words and mostly with gestures and smiles. Chepi told the others to prepare food for Kelley and to treat him as a friend. Many of the Algonquin, however, were angry over this intrusion. Here was an English settler who had shot their brother while he was poaching on their sacred hunting ground, and they fed him!

Word spread through the camp about what was happening, and the elders decided to meet to discuss it. There was division about what to do with Kelley. On the one hand, he was stealing their food by hunting their traditional land. Further, he had harmed a brother in the process. On the other hand, they feared starting trouble with the English. They saw that the English had powerful weapons, including large guns on wheels that had just come off an arriving ship. Further, Kelley had tried to help Achak, and indeed, Achak was still alive, but was also in danger of dying.

Kelley had explained to Chepi that Joseph Shepherd and I were doctors (healers and elders in her understanding) who had powerful medicine. We had saved his life when he had been severely wounded, and his doctor friends could help Achak. Chepi entered into the elders' meeting boldly and explained what Kelley told her. She was strangely powerful and persuasive, and they seemed to be willing to listen as she pleaded her case.

"The English can help Achak, and we must allow them to do this."

Chepi, Kelley, and three members of the Algonquin tribe went to the English settlement. Upon arrival, Mr. Kelley explained what had happened, and talked of the urgency to help Achak. Shepherd and I asked if we could go to the Algonquin camp, but Levine was skeptical.

"We cannot get involved in this native business!" Levine said.

"Mr. Levine," I said, "we are already quite involved in this! Mr. Kelley has wounded that man, and we are bound to help him. If we do not, he may die, and so may our mission here!"

Shepherd was not interested in waiting for Levine's response.

"We are going to the Algonquin camp," he said. He went out to gather medical supplies as he grabbed my arm, ensuring that I would follow him. Levine went pale with rage, but said nothing. He then made a point of authorizing our trip to the camp with a direct order to have two others accompany Shepherd and me to the camp.

Upon our arrival at the Algonquin camp we saw Achak. Clearly in pain, and his lower leg white and cold with the cord firmly cutting off blood flow, we saw that we needed to remove the lead ball, if it were still present, and close the wound as quickly as possible. It was now late afternoon, so poor Achak had been suffering for the better part of the day.

When we saw what Kelley had done to save his life, we were overcome with gratitude for Kelley's courage and quick thinking. The way had been smoothed for us by Chepi to have essentially free reign in treating Achak. Once again, Shepherd took the lead in calming the patient, giving him some rum and speaking in a very calm, soothing voice. I was again amazed that language seemed to not be a barrier, and I heard some words that I did not understand, which I assumed to be Algonquin. Achak relaxed deeply, and I began to probe the wound with my fingers to see if I could feel the lead ball I presumed to be there. I could not determine from this cursory examination the presence of the ball, so I told Shepherd I needed to probe with the knife. I hated the thought of this, but it needed to be done. Shepherd gave me the nod to proceed. I pulled out the scalpel and cut away some muscle as Shepherd

149

soothed Achak. Soon I came upon the ball and grabbed it out with forceps. I saw the artery that had been ruptured by the projectile, and I sewed it back together with catgut. As I had seen Shepherd do, I washed the surgery field with rum, and Achak winced briefly. I sewed his leg back together with a few stitches, and we released the leather cord that Kelley had affixed earlier. Within a few seconds the lower leg got a return of color and warmth. Achak was breathing more calmly and deeply, and he drifted off to sleep. It looked like we were successful in helping Achak.

The elders nodded to us and pointed to some tea made from the root of the sassafras tree. We sat with them and enjoyed the tea as they showed us gratitude and friendliness for helping Achak. Chepi especially seemed to favor Mr. Kelley, whom she viewed evidently as the hero of the day – ironic since it was his error that caused the entire problem.

The Algonquin camp was not all in agreement with the friendly attitude toward the English. At the time, we were not aware of the French agents who had been meeting with native people all the way from Lake Champlain to points south and east. There was a growing tension both in Europe and now in America between France and England. There were rich resources to be exploited, and the nation that did that best stood to gain handsomely in trade. Spain already was draining loads of gold and silver from America in the south and from the Caribbean area. The Portuguese were exploiting South America, and the Dutch were beginning to see trade in the area just south of Cape Ann. There was a much larger picture than we had the ability to see, but we would be in the middle of the contest nonetheless.

Chapter 37

I had been spending more time with Margaret and little Jacob. I saw Margaret's attention and caring for little Jacob, and I was drawn to that compassion and selfless giving that is intrinsic in parental love. Indeed, she was the mother to this child, even though she had not given him birth. She had given him life.

Albert Adams seemed to draw new life also in America. He was now living again with his cousin Henry and Henry's family, but he seemed better able to care for himself, and he could do some work in the settlement community. Captain Braden, now somewhat stricken with ailments such as rheumatism and a slight palsy, came to enjoy the company that Albert gave to him. They were becoming friends who increasingly counted on one another. Braden's sailing days were over it seemed, and he contented himself with advising on the defense of the settlement. He advised on the building of walls and positioning of the cannon. He, with the experience of having fought in England's wars with Spain, was respected for his military insight.

Tension had grown between the Algonquin people and Mr. Levine. Levine was convinced that the French were going to use the Algonquin to ally with them and squeeze out our little foothold in America. There had been raids in other parts of America on English settlements, often by native people who were aroused against the English. Levine was sure that such an ambush would eventually happen to us. Levine's response was to build up defenses and make our settlement a costly target if attacked. This also led to increasing tension between Shepherd and Levine. Shepherd's conciliatory approach to the Algonquin seemed to offend Levine.

"Show them our strength," he would often say. "They see our kindness as weakness. They will only respect us if we are strong and defiant."

Levine saw the Algonquin people as childlike and naïve. Indeed, the general feeling of the French, Dutch, and especially the Spanish, was that the civilized Europeans were here to educate these native savages into the modern world, and to Christianize them away from their primitive religious practices. Levine would want to accomplish this by brute force. Shepherd wanted to show them God's love by ministering to them and by understanding them. Ironically, in this stance, Shepherd was the one misunderstood, I felt.

Trouble began the day Achak died. In the first week after our surgery, Achak improved well. He began to get up and walk, albeit with a noticeable limp. But it looked like he was on his way to a nearly full recovery. One day in the second week of his recovery, he complained of difficulty breathing. He began to cough and wheeze and soon was coughing up blood. Later that evening, he died.

Several of the elders were incensed that this had happened with no apparent cause other than the strange treatment that the English doctors had given to him. Some felt that the wood spirits were angry that the hunting ground had been violated by intruders, and that Achak's death was their revenge. All agreed that Achak would still be alive if the English were not on their tribal lands.

The French trappers who had befriended the tribe for a few years fueled the fire of English intrusion as the cause of trouble in the land. The French trappers reminded the Algonquin that they too cherished the land, and were not building settlements. The English, they said, did not respect the tribal lands and were out to destroy the life that they knew.

As tensions grew, the French decided to make them worse. One night several French traders and trappers dressed in Algonquin garb, painted their faces and arms, and snuck into our settlement. They let out whoops and cries, set fire to our drying crops in the field, and killed two horses. They were seen (and I am sure that they wanted to be seen) running away into the night. Several of our men on guard chased after them, but they did not seem too interested in following them far into the woods. They did not want a full-scale confrontation with the whole Algonquin camp.

Levine was livid, but he saw this as an opportunity to move against the Algonquin in force. He planned to bide his time, gather support from other English settlements, and make a full assault on the Algonquin.

Joseph Shepherd was distraught. He was making progress, he believed, in making a real connection with this native people. He had been teaching them English using the King James Bible. Just yesterday he had read to them Psalm 19 with the help of Chepi, who was learning English remarkably well with the help of Mr. Kelley, who seemed to love to spend time with her. He liked this Psalm because he felt that it helped transcend language. God showed Himself to people all over the world through His creation. He said that language is not a barrier when using the language of creation and beauty. The "language of nature" appealed to the Algonquin, and they seemed to appreciate that there were some common bonds between the English and themselves as odd, but as basic, as that they were all under God's creative hand. The God they understood was possibly the same one Shepherd discussed.

Psalm19
1The heavens declare the glory of God; and the firmament sheweth his handywork.
² Day unto day uttereth speech, and night unto night sheweth knowledge.

152

^{3} *There is no speech nor language, where their voice is not heard.*

^{4} *Their line is gone out through all the earth, and their words to the end of the world. In them hath he set a tabernacle for the sun,*

^{5} *Which is as a bridegroom coming out of his chamber, and rejoiceth as a strong man to run a race.*

^{6} *His going forth is from the end of the heaven, and his circuit unto the ends of it: and there is nothing hid from the heat thereof.*

^{7} *The law of the LORD is perfect, converting the soul: the testimony of the LORD is sure, making wise the simple.*

^{8} *The statutes of the LORD are right, rejoicing the heart: the commandment of the LORD is pure, enlightening the eyes.*

^{9} *The fear of the LORD is clean, enduring forever: the judgments of the LORD are true and righteous altogether.*

^{10} *More to be desired are they than gold, yea, than much fine gold: sweeter also than honey and the honeycomb.*

^{11} *Moreover by them is thy servant warned: and in keeping of them there is great reward.*

^{12} *Who can understand his errors? cleanse thou me from secret faults.*

^{13} *Keep back thy servant also from presumptuous sins; let them not have dominion over me: then shall I be upright, and I shall be innocent from the great transgression.*

^{14} *Let the words of my mouth, and the meditation of my heart, be acceptable in thy sight, O LORD, my strength, and my redeemer.*

As Shepherd thought about the possible slaughter that might be about to take place, he determined to do what he could do to stop it. Typical of Shepherd, he went directly to the person with whom he had disagreement. He went to see Mr. Levine.

"Mr. Levine, a word with you?" he asked politely.

"Yes, Shepherd, what is it?" asked Levine.

"We hear plans of attack on the Algonquin people. Is that true?" Shepherd asked.

"I have been talking with other settlement leaders about our defense, yes. It is my responsibility to provide for our security!" Levine said smugly.

"I agree with that, Mr. Levine, and I truly am thankful for your attention in caring for us," said Shepherd. "However, I do not believe that provoking a battle with the Algonquin will provide the security you desire," he said simply. "I also do not believe that the Algonquin are our enemies. I believe that we all know that the attack last week was not the Algonquin hunters."

This was becoming common wisdom among many settlers, but Levine had dismissed that talk as simply a way to cover the cowardice of those who did not want conflict.

"I understand that you want no part of battle, Dr. Shepherd, and I do not require that you participate. You are of much more value as a physician to help those who may be wounded – and I do not mean aiding the enemy," he said coldly. This was, of course, a reminder to Shepherd that he had acted against Levine's wishes in helping Achak.

"In fact," Levine added, "your so-called help of Achak may have caused this problem. Those natives think you killed him with your odd medicine. You and Greene…"

Shepherd interrupted Levine, "Mr. Levine, Dr. Greene and I saved Achak's life. His later death was something no one could have prevented. I do not believe that the Algonquin blame us for his death. I do believe that there are people who want war and people who want peace," he said.

"We will not agree on this, Dr. Shepherd," Levine concluded, and he dismissed Shepherd from his quarters.

Shepherd came to me and told me of the meeting with Levine. "Good Dr. Shepherd," I said, "you are such an honest and direct man, and I admire you for it. However, in dealing with men like Levine you must fight the way he fights. I have been thinking about this as well. I think we should visit Captain Braden."

Shepherd and I went to Braden's quarters, where we found Captain Braden and Albert Adams laughing over an incident that had happened days ago with little Jacob Carr.

"Yes, the women were actually arguing over who should give the child a bath!" Albert said laughing.

"Aye, the women in camp need someone to mother," said Braden, "and soon it will probably be you and me!" he laughed.

"Good afternoon, gentlemen. May we intrude?" I said warmly. Indeed, I loved my visits to Albert Adams and James Braden, two men who had broken bodies, who had learned to accept their limitations, and indeed even joke about them.

"Come in!" hailed Braden. "Join us for some tea."

"Thank you," I said. "Dr. Shepherd and I have something to discuss with you."

My tone was now more somber, and Braden picked up on that.

"Trouble, my boy?" he asked.

"Yes, I am afraid so," I said. "Shepherd and I are concerned about the plans to fight with the Algonquin."

Braden seemed a little surprised.

154

"I was not aware of a planned attack," said Braden. "I have talked to Mr. Levine about our defenses here and what we need to do to improve them since the attack, but I was not aware that he was really planning an attack."

"We assumed that you were part of his 'war council,'" I said.

"I know he has spoken to other settlement leaders, but he has not asked me to participate in that," said Braden with some hurt in his voice.

"As I suspected," said Shepherd, "Levine goes off on his own to plan for the community. We may as well be back in England if we want one man making all of our decisions for us."

"Captain Braden," I said, "people here love and respect you as a commander, captain, and military man. You are trusted. I think you need to talk with Mr. Levine about this idea of an attack on the Algonquin. It will not only cost lives, it may jeopardize our whole settlement."

Braden was buoyed by this sentiment. He sometimes wondered if he were simply not considered to be a doddering old man. Even he had been shaken about his own ability to lead after the disaster on the *Intrepid*.

"Please speak to Levine," I urged. "We will help with some of the other details."

Shepherd looked at me but said nothing. He did not know what I meant, but I would fill him in later on what I intended.

"Albert, we need your help also," I said.

Albert looked up, surprised. "My help?" he asked. "What could I possibly offer?"

"You shall see," I said.

155

Chapter 38

Captain Braden planned to visit Mr. Levine as soon as possible to confront him on plans being made without the advice of his "military advisor."

"Give us two days before you visit him," I asked.

"Time is of the essence, isn't it?" asked Braden.

"Yes, it is," I said, "but we just need some time to set the stage a bit."

"Alright. If there are any men I trust here, it is you and Shepherd," said the aging Captain.

"Don't forget Albert!" I winked at him.

"Of course, my friend Albert!" smiled Braden.

I told Shepherd of my plan for the "action of the people," as he and Henry Adams had often discussed. I was simply reflecting upon how people can exercise power when they believe that they have none. Shepherd and Adams loved to discuss governance and the ideas of Hugo Grotius. Grotius was terribly radical, I felt. However, the practical idea of engaging people to change a particular situation appealed to me. I began to meet with people very casually at our little gathering place, which was part tavern, meeting hall, church gathering place, and lecture hall. I found no trouble "coming across" the people I wanted to speak with there. Edwin Carr and Henry Adams were there to pick up mail that had been delivered from Plymouth. I mentioned to them my concern that there was a plan afoot for attacking the Algonquin. Once again I found that they had some vague idea of Levine talking about the need for the increased defense of our settlement. However, the idea of a full, coordinated attack on the Algonquin was never really discussed. I grew a little more restive as I talked about how our dear Captain had not been apprised of a "military" decision that affected our camp. Edwin Carr told me, however, that about twenty men, several of whom had been crew on the *Courageous* and *Merryweather*, were well aware of some "military action," and they were doing some training near Gloucester. I suggested that we might want to alert others in the settlement about our "concerns."

Meanwhile, I asked Albert to stop by some of the women who seemed to always be near Margaret and little Jacob. The women seemed protective of Albert and his handicaps, and they always gave him sympathy and a caring ear if he should come by. Albert went to Margaret's house and saw three women with her, putting a new little outfit on Jacob that one of them had sewn. Albert innocently said to the women, "I wonder if you kind ladies could tear up some strips of cloth to make bandages."

"What could you possibly mean, Albert?" they asked.

"Dr. Shepherd and Dr. Greene told me to ask you for the favor of making bandages for the men who will likely be wounded when we attack the Algonquin," he said matter-of-factly.

The women were shocked, just as I had hoped. They went forth with their concerns to their homes, and before two days were gone the stories of the women and the concerns from Adams, Carr, and several other men had burst forth like steam from a kettle.

Captain Braden met with Levine to register his concern, and Levine was patronizing to him.

"Dear Captain Braden," he began, "your role is that of defense advisor of the settlement. Frankly, I simply asked you to do that out of courtesy to your age and your skills as a Captain. I would never ask you to be involved in an active attack."

"So you *do* plan an attack on the Algonquin," he said.

"None of your concern!" Levine said sharply. With that he dismissed Captain Braden.

"I will give you my last piece of advice, Mr. Levine," said Braden. "It is a fool who takes only his own counsel. You, Mr. Levine, are the worst kind of fool – one who does not know he is one!"

By the next evening, Henry Adams had met with several other men and asked for the word to be spread about that there would be a settlement meeting. He planned to challenge not only Levine's decision about attack, but about where governance came from. We had been chartered by the Dorchester Company, and we were subject to their decisions. Henry Adams and others were ready to ask for a council of men who would be elected by the community to decide how the growing settlement would be governed.

Levine, seeing that the unrest would only grow if he did not put an end to it, came to the meeting, where he addressed the men assembled. He began, "My only concern and charge is for the safety of this settlement. Therefore, I have commissioned a band of men to defend our settlement from the attacks of the Algonquin warriors. You have seen the damage, and if we do not punish them they will continue to attack us until they wipe us from this place. I further believe that the actions of Joseph Shepherd have hurt us. He has, by his rash and provocative behavior, put us into harm's way! I also must tell you that this assembly is unlawful, as it is not condoned by the Dorchester Company to whom we have sworn allegiance."

Almost on cue, a band of nearly fifty men marched outside the building. They were armed with muskets, and marched in a line similar to the English Royal Guard. I nearly laughed at the incongruity of the ragged dress of these men who were trying to emulate the Royal Guard. Then I realized that laughing would not be a good response to this intended show of force.

Henry Adams was incensed and demanded that the settlement not be subjected to this demeaning show of force and humiliation.

"By God, we are free men, and we will not be cowed by your arrogance!" said Adams.

"Then perhaps a rope would be more to your liking!" taunted Levine. He was relishing his authority now, and many present were frightened. Others were considering the legal standing they had to defy the Dorchester Company to whom they had indeed pledged allegiance and service in exchange for the opportunity to come to America and make a new life.

Joseph Shepherd spoke up.

"Gentlemen," he began, "we are indeed subject to the authority of Mr. Levine, the duly authorized head of our settlement. My only request is that we try to settle this issue with the Algonquin in a peaceful and forthright way, not by military force and killing. Mr. Levine, am I allowed this opportunity to go to the Algonquin camp and try to settle this peacefully?"

"You would go to the enemy to propose peace with them?" questioned Edwin Carr.

"Mr. Carr, I go not to our enemies, but to people who want war no more than almost all assembled here," he said.

A great swell of, "Hear, hear!" went up from the crowd. Shepherd had managed to acknowledge the authority of Levine while at the same time offering a peaceful solution.

"By all means, Levine, let this man try to reason with the Algonquin. We have nothing to lose!" said Captain Braden.

A swell of, "Aye! Aye!" rose up from the assembled group.

"We lose nothing but the most important military tactic," shouted Levine, "the element of surprise!"

"This is not war," I inserted. "We are here in an attempt to live in this new country without the tyranny of kings and individuals exerting their own power over others! Let Shepherd try. God knows he has the best chance of averting bloodshed!"

Once again the men assembled shouted in approval. Levine, once again trying to save face, said, "I will authorize Dr. Shepherd to approach the Algonquin, but should he fail to secure from them an apology, a promise to never again intrude on our land, and restoration of loss from their attack, we will surely seek retribution!"

"I will go with him," said Mr. Kelley. "I owe my life to this man, and I will follow him to the Algonquin camp to help however I can!"

"I will also," I heard myself say. "I will go to the Algonquin camp with Shepherd and Kelley."

"Very well," said Levine, "it is settled. You may go in the morning, and may God go with you."

"He is already there," whispered Shepherd with a discreet smile. "He is already there."

We left the next morning to head to the Algonquin camp. We were strangely at peace with our mission. Shepherd had said that he had prayed about the trip, and he felt comfort from that. I trusted my fellow travelers, and I trusted in that. Kelley and Shepherd were warriors in their own special ways, and I took strength and comfort from that. Somehow, I believed that our mission would succeed.

We set off early in the morning on a beautiful day. A little crispness had entered the air, but the sunrise was invigorating as we left for the Algonquin camp. It was well less than a few hours' journey to reach the camp, and we discussed our approach to the Algonquin. Kelley believed that most of the Algonquin did not blame Shepherd and me for the death of Achak. He also was assured by Chepi that she did not believe that the Algonquin had been involved in the raid on Cape Ann. She believed that the French were behind the raid, and pointed out that had the Algonquin done a raid, it would not have been as sloppy and noisy as the raid that happened. Further, she said that the Algonquin wanted more of the muskets that the English had, and that a raid would have included the theft of firearms. But most of all, she did not think that the elders were interested in raiding the English. While many wanted the English to leave, they would not do such a clumsy and provocative thing.

Shepherd too believed that the Algonquin people were not prone to such actions unprovoked. Yes, Achak had died, but even many of the elders said that the spirits take whom they will, and not because of someone else's actions, but because they simply do what they want. Shepherd had been trying to expose them to a God who loved them and cared about them, not an arbitrary being who punishes at will.

As we reached the camp, Kelley spoke in what of their language he had learned from Chepi. He asked if we could meet with the elders, and if Chepi could be present to help interpret. We were ushered into the camp with little commotion, almost as if we were expected. We explained that the raid on Cape Ann had been very disturbing, and that some in the settlement believed that it was the Algonquin people, but most did not. However, to avoid trouble, the leader of Cape Ann was requesting restitution and a promise for peace in the future. We did not mention a formal apology, believing that restitution would take care of that.

Some of the elders began to stir, and we realized that there was something more than we had realized taking place. Two of the elders were visibly upset, and a little argument broke out among them. Indeed, some of the Algonquin warriors had been a part of the raid, spurred on by the French, who had given them plenty of whiskey the night of the raid. These elders were embarrassed by this participation, and had hoped that the issue was over and forgotten. Now, there had to be some decision as to how this would be resolved.

159

There was a lengthy discussion among the elders that at times became quite animated. Some seemed to favor making the restitution and promising to live in peace. However, a few others seemed to want to use this as an opportunity to rid their land of the intruding English. They felt that, if any group had to be tolerated in this land, it should be the French, who seemed more interested in trapping, hunting, and living off the land. They seemed to be better neighbors than the English they had experienced so far.

The discussion ended abruptly when one of the elders stood up and motioned us out of the meeting area. Chepi told us that the elders had decided to fight the English if they were attacked. They would not make restitution for something they had not stolen, and they would not make a promise they could not keep. Two elders seemed to dissent, but they were overruled. If the English attacked, there would be a battle.

Chepi told us we had better leave quickly, since we did not know when the English might attack. Joseph believed that Levine had given a time of reprieve, and he would not attack until we returned with a decision from the Algonquin. I wanted to leave as soon as possible, since I did not trust Levine, and I wanted no part of the potential battle. Kelley wanted to stay at least one more night to spend some time with Chepi. It became obvious to me that Kelley and Chepi were more than friends, and that their relationship could become a problem. However, at this point, that was not our biggest problem.

Levine indeed had been planning to attack the Algonquin regardless of our peace mission. He seemed to believe that with Shepherd and me out of the way and not causing trouble, he could act with impunity. In fact, as it turned out, he had put Henry Adams in irons for rebellion, and he had confined Captain Braden to his quarters. Braden seemed to be a broken man, and he submitted to this humiliation without much quarrel.

Levine had marched his band of about fifty well-armed men through the night, and, at first light, they attacked the Algonquin camp. The Algonquin were surprised, and it looked like it might be a complete rout. A line of musket fire had been set around the entire eastern edge of the camp and, upon the signal of his pistol, the line opened fire. The roar sent a wave of fear through the camp, and lead balls were ripping through their birch bark structures. The second wave of musket men then fired quickly while the first group reloaded. Chaos was surging through the camp.

As the rest of the camp was roused, the Algonquin made a fierce charge directly at the source of the musket fire. They were met with another murderous volley of fire from the line at the east edge of the camp. Then from the north of the camp a roar of cannon fire signaled a deadly rain of grapeshot. Screams were heard from inside the thin birch bark wigwams. The women and children under the cover of these wigwams were exposed to the killing shot of the cannon. There was a stream of Algonquin now heading west from the camp into the surrounding woods. The Algonquin warriors regrouped and fired a volley of arrows in the direction of the cannon. Then they fired a few volleys in the direction of the musket fire. Then, inexplicably, they headed west in the direction of those retreating from the camp. In a matter of minutes, the entire camp was empty; the only things left were tattered wigwams, some wounded Algonquin, and the smoke of untended fires. The rout was complete.

Shepherd, Kelley, and I had run in the one direction that was not involved in the hostile action – we had headed south. There was no reason for this other than that we felt we needed distance from both the Algonquin and the English. The Algonquin, we thought, might blame us for being part of treachery – making them think we were negotiating while actually lulling them to sleep. The English obviously had betrayed *our* trust, and had made us the fools. We were certain that Levine planned all along to hang us out and possibly kill us in the battle. Either way, we felt alone in a now very hostile land.

Levine and his men headed cautiously into the deserted camp, inspecting the site of their great victory. As they came upon wounded Algonquin, they cut their throats. They had no desire for prisoners, and the medical people from the camp were gone now. I was sure that the plan all along was to simply destroy the camp and kill everyone in sight. It was a disgusting, horrifying scene.

Levine's men plundered what they felt was worth keeping, such as some dried meat, axes, knives, and some French muskets. The attack had been so much of a surprise that the Algonquin had no time to even get to this stock of firearms. Levine and his other leaders called the band of men together, formed them into a marching unit, and headed back to Cape Ann.

As they trudged through the woods back to Cape Ann the mood was bright and cheery. They had suffered no casualties, had routed the "enemy," and they were feeling confident – indeed arrogant. About a mile from the Algonquin camp, they heard a scream from one of the men in the rear of the line. Pretty soon there was screaming all up and down the line as arrows filled the air on both sides of the line. Fear gripped the men as unseen death came upon them from seemingly every direction. As fear gave way to chaos, the men began to run in all directions, but there was no safe place. It dawned on Levine that his men had been surrounded by the Algonquin, who had doubled back from their "retreat" and set up an elaborate ambush. They had filtered back toward Cape Ann from the north, even further north than the cannon emplacement had been.

Levine tried to rally his band, but they had scattered into the woods, and few made it very far before being knifed or hatcheted to death. Levine was captured as a prize to be admired. His fate was now completely in the hands of the Algonquin whose people he had recently butchered.

Chapter 39

Andrew Kensington was enjoying success with his trade routes in Africa, England, and Virginia. He had worked with tobacco growers in the Jamestown area of Virginia, which seemed to be beneficial for the crop. Kensington had been one of the earliest known importers of black slaves from the west coast of Africa, and he was considered to be the expert on how to negotiate with tribal leaders in Africa who were slaveholders themselves. He seemed to understand the concept of tribal allegiance, whereas his other trading counterparts seemed to understand only business and government ideas of trade. Kensington would laugh at the disdain some of his fellow traders had for the slave business. He knew that there were plenty of willing partners in Africa to supply slave labor in exchange for goods like guns, tobacco, gunpowder, and fine rum. Indeed, tribal leaders were hungry for these items, and slaves were easy to acquire through the constant tribal warfare that wracked Africa.

He seldom thought now about Edwin Carr, Shepherd, and me. Although his wife, Anne, did still correspond with Edwin Carr, Kensington made it a point not to care about that. He was making more money than he had ever made, and he had made a lot of money in the past. He was enjoying the wealth and power that these trade routes were providing him.

Anne was persistent with Andrew Kensington about a trip to America, ever since Edwin Carr had begun writing about his vivid and alluring experiences in America. Edwin had described the beauty of the forests that covered the land, and the breathtaking views of the rolling hills, abundant game, etc. However, it was description of the freedom he felt of starting a new life that struck Anne. She was terribly bored in her current situation. Andrew was gone most of the time, but that did not really bother her – she was bored of him as well. What she felt was more than boredom – it was emptiness. She was attracted to the idea of being with Edwin again, and he did make her laugh, but the stirring in her was even more than that. She was an ambitious woman who had made her way through the social ranks of London by marrying well and by flirting and entertaining people. She needed a new challenge. Indeed, she had made some powerful friends in King James' court, and had established some business dealings of her own. But her restless spirit trumped such ventures. She was very moody, impetuous, and prone to seek adventure. When she settled on an idea, she seldom let it go.

As much as Andrew Kensington wanted to distance Anne, he also knew that she was an asset to him in London society and with her own business connections. There were many men who did business with him because Anne first flirted with them and made them feel special. She could put them at ease with her coarse humor, or she could charm their wives with demure social graces when she had to. Still trim and attractive in her forties, she had a presence in a social gathering. Andrew did not want to lose that, even if they had no real marriage anymore.

Andrew consented, finally, to her request to go with him to America. He was planning a trip to Jamestown, Virginia to look at some land there to expand its tobacco growing potential. He had been encouraged to do this by his partners in the London & Western Trading Company. They departed London aboard the *Conquest*, a compact but sturdy vessel that had shown her ability to travel stormy seas with little damage and reasonable speed. Among the passengers was Herbert Wesley, who had felt the call to preach in America. He had seen John Ward's profound influence as he preached, and Wesley felt the "calling" to bring salvation to America, especially to the savages he had heard about who did not know the true God.

The passage to Virginia was mercifully benign, at least at the start. About two-thirds of the way across the Atlantic, they saw signs of a tremendous storm heading toward them. The Captain of the *Conquest* decided to head for a course to the north of where the storm seemed headed. The closer the *Conquest* came to the brewing clouds, the more ominous they became. Captain Phillip Monroe of the *Conquest* continued his northern course and began a more extreme northern route to avoid trouble. The ship took some damage as winds like they had never seen ripped into them. Most of the passengers, who lacked any sea experience, were ghastly ill much of the time on board. Significant damage to the sails caused the journey to be prolonged, and violent seas caused damage in the hold where the foodstuffs were stored. They were now on a voyage that was weeks longer than planned and hopelessly off course, with less sail power than needed to do correction. It was then that Captain Monroe made the decision to head straight for land and the nearest port he could find. The weary and ill passengers, including Kensington, could not disagree with the Captain's decision. It was now about survival.

Nine weeks after their departure from London, the bedraggled *Conquest* made it to Gloucester, the small fishing settlement in Massachusetts. While they were hundreds of miles north of the Jamestown destination, they were at least safely on shore.

Anne was excited to see the land that Edwin Carr had described, and simply happy to be alive at that point.

Any spot on land was appealing to Anne after the dangerous trip on a foul-smelling ship. She breathed in and smelled the salty sea air. She could not wait to explore the area and experience some refreshment in her life.

"I have no idea what we do from here," said Kensington. "However, this is your home for perhaps the next several months. I hope you do not get as bored with it as you get bored with me," he sniffed.

Anne ignored this jibe with her usual disdain for him.

"It looks like this land will hold my interest longer than you do," she said matter-of-factly.

"Of course," said Kensington, "of course."

Kensington began to whirl with ideas about how he might exploit this part of the New World. It certainly was different from Virginia, and it did not look like land that would grow tobacco, but he believed that he could find a way to expand his fortune, even in this foul place. Maybe his misfortune could somehow be used to enhance his monetary fortune!

Chapter 40

The Algonquin had been surprisingly restrained in their treatment of Levine, but he did endure some torture on a regular basis. Perhaps they did not want him to die immediately for his crimes and desired to prolong his suffering. They routinely bound his hands behind his back with leather thongs and made him run a gauntlet naked between lines of women whose husbands had died in the attack on the camp. This was meant to be humiliating to him, and satisfying for the women, who swung thorny bramble branches at him, pelted him with stones, and hurled feces at him.

The Algonquin seemed to want to keep him alive for some time, not letting him know the date when they would kill him. The waiting was indeed a terrible torture, and he began to go insane. He screamed in the night, tried to run from imaginary assailants, and he eventually begged them to kill him. His wish would be granted sometime, but he did not know when. His misery was horrific.

Shepherd, Kelley, and I had been hiding with the help of Chepi, who had found us easily outside the camp. She told us of the fate of Mr. Levine, and I felt no sympathy for the fool who had engineered his own demise, as well as the deaths of an untold number of men. We heard from Chepi that not all the men had perished in the attack, and some had made it back to Cape Ann. We planned to return to Cape Ann with Chepi's help, but she kept putting us off, suggesting that she could provide food for us as we hid out, and that it was too dangerous to return to Cape Ann. She confided to us that the Algonquin might soon go to Cape Ann and wipe out the rest of the settlement, but none of us could be sure if that was their plan.

Finally, we found out why Chepi was reluctant to help us escape back to Cape Ann. She was pregnant with Kelley's child. It was now apparent that we would be welcome neither in the Algonquin camp nor at Cape Ann. Chepi broke down in tears as she told us the news. She did not know what to do or where to turn. We pledged to her and to Kelley that we would not leave them, and both were immensely relieved. However, we did not have any better plan than to keep travelling in this foreign land, and live off that land. Chepi was something of an expert in this, and we counted on that knowledge of hers to survive.

Chepi decided to make one more secret trip to the Algonquin camp to secure some needed supplies. Horses, food, some guns and ammunition, and some blankets were what we were hoping to secure from the trip. Risky as it was, it was necessary.

165

We set out in the middle of the night with a faint moon giving scant light. Chepi knew the area completely, and we followed her as she crept in the woods surrounding the camp. She knew where all the supplies were, and she had a way with horses. We were making good, unnoticed progress as we slipped into the camp. She found a supply of dried, smoked fish and some parched corn that she stuffed into a sack. We moved along the edge of the camp and found a small cache of muskets and lead shot just where she had thought it would be. We moved on to the corral where several horses lazily munched on dried grass. Chepi spoke softly to the horses to calm them as Kelley and I slipped a rope around the necks of two of them. We were ready to make a clean escape when one of the horses got very skittish and let out a loud protest. The others picked this up, and soon there was an awful commotion that roused the camp. Just then, Shepherd walked into the middle of the camp, picked up a large stick, and stirred the embers of a smoldering fire. The fire kicked up, and attention was drawn immediately to his presence in the glow of a growing blaze. Numerous warriors ran to him with raised spears. He walked toward them slowly, reassuring them of his benign intentions with his limited Algonquian language. Two men seized him amid the shouts of the now roused camp. We knew what he was doing, and we were both humbled and grateful for this selfless act. Chepi urged us on, but Kelley and I hesitated. We could not leave Shepherd in the camp to die!

We decided to wait and see what would happen. We had withdrawn to a safe vantage point, but we felt uneasy, ashamed, to be safe at his expense. Shepherd spoke to the group haltingly.

"Brothers," he said, "I mean you no harm. Mr. Kelley, Dr. Greene had I no part in the terrible attack on this camp, and I ask that you grant me safe passage from camp. We ask forgiveness on behalf of the English, and mercy on your prisoner, Mr. Levine."

Chepi was interpreting for us as Shepherd talked.

"Mercy!" I thought, "I would kill the bastard myself if I had the chance!"

It slowly dawned on me that the Algonquin understood this message from Shepherd. I was sure that he had not learned that much of the language, yet they seemed to follow every word. Chepi too seemed surprised at his fluency, but she was intent on following the events unfolding before us.

Shepherd continued to speak, now more softly, and he drew something on the ground with a stick as several gathered around him. There was no turmoil, no conflict, and soon one of the elders addressed the crowd.

"My family," he said, "Joseph Shepherd has been a friend to us. He tried to save Achak, but the spirits took him from us. He has tried to keep peace, and he has tried to learn our ways. He has talked with our children about a Great Spirit who loves all people, English and Algonquin. He shows us by his action the Great Spirit he speaks of. We will let him go in peace."

166

"And what of Levine?" asked Shepherd.

"He has murdered our people without cause," said the elder. "He deserves to die."

"Then I ask that you do it quickly. No man deserves to undergo torture such as he endures."

Chepi nudged me, and we realized that the goodwill Shepherd had earned over the past year had bought us freedom. We also realized that the elder was aware of our foray into the camp, and he was going to look the other way. Shepherd would be free, and we would accept the unspoken gift of freedom given to us on his account. Chepi would be spared the shame of carrying Kelley's child in her camp.

We met up with Joseph Shepherd outside the Algonquin camp. Chepi was in tears as she realized that she would no longer be with her people. Mr. Kelley told us that he would stay with Chepi, and that we were free to pursue our own course. Shepherd and I quickly decided that we would not leave them. We discussed a return to Cape Ann, and we recognized the risks involved. We spent the rest of the night in fitful sleep, trying to decide what to do. Finally, Shepherd said that he believed that we should go back to Cape Ann. We had friends there who would understand. Levine and his tyranny were gone, but we did face uncertainty in our return. Would they believe our story of efforts to avert the bloodshed? Was the settlement taken over by military rule? We decided to return and find out.

As we set out early the next morning for Cape Ann, the elders quickly executed justice upon Levine with a spear to his heart. His suffering was now over, but he left behind a legacy of pain and death. Shepherd said he forgave him. Kelley, Chepi, and I were not so gracious, but we realized that our hate would not serve us well. We could not waste any more of our energy on Levine. We needed some healing in our own souls.

Chapter 41

We returned to Cape Ann to find a broken place. Henry Adams had been released from his chains, and he was trying to organize and encourage in a demoralizing situation. There had been a loss of forty-one men to death or desertion in the face of battle. Four of the men who had been wounded were in some stage of recovery, but we feared at least two would likely not survive. Women who had lost men were distraught. Many talked of leaving America to return to England. Margaret, little Jacob, and Albert met us with complete joy. Our fears about being blamed or suspected of treachery were unfounded – or perhaps the people were too weary to pursue any kind of retribution or blame.

Margaret rushed up to me and hugged me tightly, weeping and laughing. I saw, for perhaps the first time, that she cared deeply for me. I was overjoyed, but restrained. Henry and Albert Adams asked to meet with us to hear of our story and our version of the battle that had taken place.

Chepi wondered how she might be accepted at Cape Ann. Kelley was very protective of her, and she did not leave his side. Her pregnancy was not evident yet, and she wore a loose gown-like tunic that covered her almost completely. At some point the situation needed to be addressed, but not now. Mr. Kelley made it very clear that Chepi had been loyal to the English, and had served as a faithful interpreter during negotiations. Loyalty to Kelley from the settlement ensured that Chepi would be safe at Cape Ann. He told Henry Adams and some other leaders that he planned to have Chepi as his wife. Some in the camp may have been surprised, even offended, but Shepherd's testimony, as well as mine, affirmed that Chepi was a loyal and needed member of our settlement now.

"Captain Braden, Edwin Carr, and I were set against the attack," said Henry Adams. "I was shackled, Captain Braden confined to quarters with Albert assigned to minister to his needs, and Edwin Carr was placed in provisional charge of the settlement since he refused to be part of the attack. Levine thought Edwin to be competent to be in charge while at the same time disappointed that he refused to enter the battle. Edwin chose a wise course of offering to be part of leading the camp while avoiding the misled attack."

Henry Adams reached out to Joseph Shepherd immediately for help and guidance in organizing leadership of the settlement. Edwin Carr was in agreement with asking for wisdom in how to proceed. The settlement was in a tenuous situation. Fear of Algonquin reprisal was rampant. The settlement, now comprising about 250 people, was in jeopardy of collapsing.

Shepherd had some clear ideas of how governance should take place. He had discussed these ideas countless times, whether it was with William Bradford, Henry Adams, or Edwin Carr. He was enamored with the idea that self-governance was in the best interest of people. He knew that, people being inherently flawed, there would be flaws in such a government, yet he also believed that shared ownership of the governing process was ennobling for people. He trusted that with proper checks on power such a system could work.

Soon Carr, Adams, and Shepherd were putting in place a plan for government for Cape Ann that responded to the needs of those governed, not just the desires of the Dorchester Company. They held an election for a council of seven governors, with the man getting the most votes becoming Chief Governor. This man would report to the Dorchester Company, but would also be held responsible for securing the rights and needs of the people of Cape Ann.

Henry Adams received the most votes for the Council of Governors, so he became Chief Governor of Cape Ann. When he convened the Council of Governors, he first brought up the idea of defense of Cape Ann. It had now been almost a month since the battle with the Algonquin. We had been surprised that they had not come to our camp to wipe us out in retaliation for Levine's attack. Shepherd told the Governors that he believed that the Algonquin were not a warlike people, but that our biggest threat was from the French – either through a pact with the Algonquin, or directly from them. Many of the Algonquin elders began to figure out that trouble only began when the French started the problems with us. Those elders had been successful in persuading the rest that the Algonquin would only be puppets of the French if they went along with the French desires. Besides, who had died in the battle with the English? It was not the French, but Algonquin who had died! The Algonquin knew that they had inflicted a dreadful loss on the English, and perhaps that would be lesson enough.

In fact, that was the very thinking of the elders, as we later found out. At the time, however, we could not discount a threat from the Algonquin as well as from the French. We were very vulnerable. It was for this reason that the Council decided to dismantle the camp and move south from Cape Ann. We would move down to Gloucester, where another small settlement that was mostly dedicated to fishing was starting to show signs of thriving. Besides, we had understood that the soil down there was better than the rocky soil of our area, and that crops would grow much better there.

We dismantled some of buildings and packed them on wagons to transport them on the short trip south to Gloucester. We had heard that the *Conquest* had recently arrived at Gloucester after having been rerouted because of the terrible weather she had encountered in the crossing. Repairs on the *Conquest* would take some time, and there were no trained shipwrights available to help refit her. In the meantime, those passengers bound for Jamestown were now in Gloucester, biding their time.

Word came to Gloucester that the Cape Ann settlement was packed and moving south to Gloucester. Leaders at Gloucester were afraid that the Cape Ann settlement would bring trouble since they had attacked the Algonquin. Gloucester was a small fishing village that wanted no harm from the natives they called Indians. Nonetheless, they were mostly ready to welcome their English brothers. There was some strength in numbers, and Gloucester was struggling to establish itself as a viable settlement. They were successful in fishing, and they actually were exporting some salted fish back to England.

Anne Kensington could hardly believe her luck. Edwin Carr was coming to her after all. While he had been rather coy about her obvious affections toward him, she hoped that time and distance had rekindled some romantic feelings in him for her. She knew that she could hardly stand to stay with Andrew much longer, even though it was in her financial best interest to do so.

Our group from Cape Ann arrived in June, 1624. Anne Kensington sought out Edwin Carr, and they exchanged a warm embrace. Andrew Kensington saw Shepherd and me and greeted us as if we were old friends. His ability to demonstrate warmth while nurturing rage was remarkable indeed.

"How have your adventures been here in America?" he asked us.

"We have indeed had adventure," I said. "How did you end up in Gloucester?" I asked.

"That is a long story," said Kensington, "but it matters not. Anne and I will be going to Jamestown as soon as we can get passage there. And your plans?" he asked.

I had been considering that very question. I was becoming convinced that there might be a life here for me with Margaret.

Shepherd seemed to want to stay, because he told me that he was very disturbed by the way these Indian people were being decimated by disease. Our part of this trip was to be scientific and medical in nature, and what better way to fulfill that mission than by trying to stop the devastation of disease that felled these Indian people? Chepi had told us that her people were not sick with the strange illnesses that beset them now until the English came and interacted with them. Many of the Algonquin believed that the Great Spirit was disturbed by the presence of foreigners, and the Spirit stirred up strange and fearsome diseases that killed them. Shepherd saw patterns in these diseases, and he saw that many English were not affected by the diseases that were running through the Algonquin camps. Smallpox, bloody flux diarrhea, debilitating coughs, and a host of other ailments were felling these native people.

Shepherd's suspicions seemed verified that, somehow, we English had brought these illnesses to America, and that, for some reason, we were immune to these diseases. He said that we acted as "hosts" for these illnesses, but we were usually unaffected by them. "Why was this?" we pondered. Shepherd continued to work on this problem in earnest as the death toll mounted for the Algonquin. He made meticulous notes that he kept diligently. He was truly a man of science, I believed.

I was uneasy with Kensington – he had been much too friendly, and I did not trust him. Edwin Carr was used to such behavior.

"You just need to keep your hands in your pockets while you talk with him so he does not steal your purse!" he laughed.

Despite his outward casual acceptance of Kensington, Carr was deeply suspicious of Kensington's part in the mission fire that had killed his brother. At the same time, Kensington was unaware of who had been responsible for the death of "Red" Locker. Lady Anne's presence simply added to the unease that was always present. Kensington and Carr were locked into an odd tension of suspicion, yet both tried to maintain the outside appearance that all was well. Both knew it was not.

The Cape Ann settlement melded into Gloucester rather seamlessly. The Dorchester Company was losing hope that the settlement had any economic benefit. Perhaps a successful fishing port might turn things around. In the meantime, Andrew Kensington was working on having his London & Western Trading Company buy out the interests of the Cape Ann expedition from the Dorchester Company. If he was going to be in America, and he was involved in this venture, he wanted to be in charge of it.

As the weeks unfolded, and an unusually cold fall came creeping in, living conditions became harsher. Fishing was now dangerous and difficult as storms and even ice appeared in the bay. The chief source of food was now game killed or trapped, and that brought inevitable interaction with the Algonquin hunters. The Gloucester camp was now more fortified with cannon, wooden walls, and a militia of about seventy armed men.

Chepi began to show her pregnancy, and it could no longer be concealed. Kelley announced to the weekly assembly that Chepi was pregnant, and that he was the father of the child. Chepi did not really get along well with the women in the settlement, and she received no support from them. Herbert Wesley, who held the weekly church services, was confronted with a problem. How could he not condemn the obvious sin that had beset the camp? What should be done to deal with this? Sin in the camp unpunished would surely be visited upon the entire camp. Wesley recalled the sin of Achan at Ai from Joshua chapter 7. Because of Achan's sin, the entire Israelite camp was defeated in battle. The sin of one man had caused havoc and judgment. Better that this be punished by the leaders in the camp than by God's fearful wrath upon them all. Chepi must be punished, he believed.

He convened the Governor's Council, which now included Gloucester leaders also. He explained to them the need to act on this sin. Andrew Kensington had insinuated himself into the Governor's Council by virtue of his financial holdings in the community. It would soon be a matter of law that the London & Western Trading Company would own the rights to the charter of the settlement. Kensington was not yet chief governor, but that would happen as soon as official word came from London that Dorchester had concluded the contract sale to his London and Western company. Now he did not have complete control, but he had great influence.

Henry Adams and Edwin Carr still seemed to have a coalition of control on the council, but the animosity was growing. Kensington, true to form, seemed to thrive on the chaos of tension and hostility. It was in that atmosphere that he could manipulate those who had less of a stomach for conflict. He was in his element.

"Mr. Wesley," Kensington said as they met privately to discuss the situation, "I agree that you must act decisively in this matter as spiritual leader of our settlement. I was moved by your sermon from Joshua 7 yesterday, and we must remove sin from the camp!"

Kensington's newfound interest in religion was his entrée to exert his influence. It was very clear that Joseph Shepherd, Edwin Carr, Margaret Brennan, Captain Braden, Henry Adams, Albert Adams, and I were supportive of Chepi and Mr. Kelley. We represented the faction that bristled against his attempt at control, and Chepi's situation had now brought the uneasy truce to a head.

While Kensington was calling for judgment and Chepi's expulsion from the settlement, Shepherd was calling for ways that we could help resolve the situation.

"What Chepi and Kelley need now is help, not punishment," he said.

Margaret and I had discussed that approach also, and we believed that Chepi's unborn child should not be punished for the actions of his or her parents. For his part, Sean Kelley was ready to fight for the protection of his child, but the wrath of many of those in the settlement seemed to rest on Chepi. She was the outsider, the savage, perhaps even a witch who had seduced Kelley. Many, especially the women, noted that she seemed to have a strange hold on people, a mystical air that influenced others unnaturally. Chepi did have a transcendent quality about her, but it was certainly not like the magic charms of a witch. Such talk always baffled me, but a large number of the settlement were convinced that Satan worked evil through such women, and that they must be executed. Chepi's mystical sexual behavior had seduced Kelley, and he could hardly be blamed for succumbing, they reasoned.

Kensington demanded that this be settled with a trial, and he pressed the council of governors to convene such a trial.

"English law demands it!" he thundered.

172

While several members of the council were reluctant to convene a trial, they rationalized that a trial would be a fair way to get facts out in the open and allow the accused to have their say in front of the entire community. They thought it best to let God judge through a trial, and not by sending a disaster to the community.

A "grand jury" of six men was convened to review charges against Chepi. The formal charges were:

"Fornication with a man, and seduction of that man by the wiles and mystical powers of a witch under the power of Satan; worship of idols and unknown gods which are in conflict with the worship of the One True God; stirring of conflict and war which threatens the tranquility of the Cape Ann and Gloucester settlements."

The last charge added to the list of charges was championed by Kensington himself. That charge was one that could result in the execution of Chepi, and that raised the level of the trial far beyond what was originally proposed. Now Chepi might be on trial for her life.

Chapter 42

The trial began with Herbert Wesley presiding. The trial was an odd combination of English law and theological court. The rules of the trial seemed to evolve as the trial progressed. What was clear was that Chepi would be allowed to speak on her own behalf, and that there would be an official "accuser" functioning as the "prosecutor." The jury consisted of six men (different from the "grand jury"), chosen by the Council of Governors.

Sean Kelley was beside himself with anger and fear. He was convinced that this "trial" was a complete sham designed to humiliate Chepi and to vicariously punish the Algonquin by persecuting Chepi. He had pleaded to go on trial with Chepi, but Herbert Wesley had reminded him that no charges had been brought against him, only against Chepi. While he had transgressed the moral law by fornicating with Chepi, it had not been adultery since neither was married. No one present was aware that Kelley had been married, and probably still was legally married, to the woman who had left him for another man. The grand jury had spoken, and a trial must proceed. Further, since the charges against Chepi were serious, she would be put into gaol, with settlement matrons ordered to minister to her needs during confinement.

Margaret Brennan stepped forward to ask that she be given the task of caring for Chepi. Since no other women had volunteered, Margaret was assigned to be her caretaker. Both Chepi and Kelley were much relieved about this, since Margaret was about the only woman with the care and compassion Chepi so needed at that point.

The trial began with Herbert Wesley appointing Leviticus Martin as prosecutor. Martin was a former barrister who had left his law practice in London after hearing John Ward's preaching. He felt compelled to come to America with his wife after they lost two small children to smallpox. His wife, Annette, was so distraught after their deaths that Leviticus believed that she might die of failure to eat, or that she might simply take her own life directly. The only thing that may have saved her life was the two sons who survived, boys of thirteen and fifteen years of age. He was a fair man, but prone to very strict religious justice, and a very literal interpretation of the Bible.

Chepi had no representation, and Herbert Wesley felt that she needed a proper defense. He brought this up just after he appointed Leviticus Martin as prosecutor. Immediately, Joseph Shepherd stepped forward and asked if he could be appointed as her counsel.

"Do you have any experience as legal counsel?" asked Wesley.

"I do not, Mr. Wesley," Shepherd said, "but I believe in Chepi and her innocence in this matter. So, while I do not have training, I have a strong commitment to her defense."

Wesley asked Chepi if she wanted to have Shepherd as her counsel, and she responded a definite, "Yes, I do!"

"Mr. Martin, have you any objections to Mr. Shepherd acting as her defense?" he asked.

"I do not," Martin said simply.

"Very well then, let us proceed," he said.

The charges were read formally to Chepi and the jury. Wesley proceeded to tell the jury of the possible consequences. If Chepi were to be convicted of any of the charges, she could face, at the least, banishment from the settlement. If, however, she were to be convicted of the third charge, she could be hanged. She could possibly be burned to death if she were convicted of having the Satanic influence of being a witch. Being possessed by demons often resulted in having the body completely eliminated by burning.

A chill came over the place as both jurists and spectators recognized, in this more formal setting, the possible grisly outcome. I wondered what would happen if, by some miracle, she were to be acquitted. Banishment might as well happen, since she no longer had a place in the settlement. Even if found innocent, she would carry a life sentence, I believed.

Leviticus Martin proceeded to address the jury.

"Gentlemen of the jury, I bring to you today the case of a woman whose behavior has caused this settlement great grief and danger. As a result, at least indirectly, she has caused the death of forty-three men, lost to the Algonquin savages in battle. Further, she has seduced one of our men, albeit a morally weak one, into fornication, which has resulted in her pregnancy. Indeed, as we see in Holy Scripture, a woman caught in adultery was to be stoned to death. Her lascivious behavior has caught up with her, just as Achan's behavior at Ai did to him, and, indeed, the entire Israelite camp. Can we let that go unpunished? Can we risk God's wrath if we do not punish her? It is indisputable that she has fornicated with Mr. Kelley – she carries his child. It is indisputable that she does not worship the One True God – she is a heathen who worships woods sprites, and a 'Great Spirit' she talks of. Her seduction of Mr. Kelley led to the incident which provoked this entire problem – the death of one her own kind – a man named Achak. Even her own people, I am told, believe that she possesses a spirit of deception, a spirit that causes men to have little control of themselves in her presence. I am told that she has this power even over her own people. Gentlemen of the jury, we are confronted with the presence of evil here, and I beg you not to look directly into her eyes lest you fall prey to her wiles and powers!"

A little gasp came from the jury and from some of the women in the spectator gallery. Such powers, they believed, were indeed the work of Satan, and, heaven forbid, such power might be at work in our very own midst!

Martin proceeded, satisfied that he had made an impression on the jury. He still had some courtroom flair, and he seemed pleased that he had a chance to use it again.

"Gentlemen of the jury," he began again, "I cannot emphasize enough the danger we face here. Not just from the Algonquin heathen, but from the very powers of Satan. I will proceed to ask for a finding of guilt on all charges and a swift execution of the sentence of death by burning! We must consider the safety of our settlement. An influence such as this foul woman will corrupt our men and expose our children to danger! You must find her guilty, and, in so doing, you will please God and keep safe your settlement!"

With that he sat and looked toward Wesley.

Wesley asked him, "Have you concluded, Mr. Martin?"

"Yes, I have," Martin said.

"Mr. Shepherd, would you like to make an opening statement?"

"Yes, I would," Shepherd said, and he approached the jury box. "Gentlemen of the jury, I beg your indulgence, as I have neither the eloquence nor the expertise of Mr. Martin. I do have a belief in the defendant, Chepi. I will call her by name, and I encourage you to do the same. She is a woman, a human being, carrying a child in her womb. She has no more supernatural powers than you, although Mr. Martin would have you believe that she can make you do things you do not want to do, and that her influence comes from demons in her. Mr. Martin calls on Scripture to have you find this woman guilty like the adulteress in John 7:53. In that case, Jesus simply asked those without sin to cast the first stone. However, his larger intent was to point out to them that they simply used the law to their benefit and to suit their own needs. Those people brought Jesus into that situation to trap him, much like Mr. Martin has set a trap for you. Jesus knew that they had not followed the law, since the witnesses were to cast the first stone, and because the man caught in the act was not similarly prosecuted. And what, I ask you, did Jesus do after confronting the crowd in this attempt to pervert law? He told the woman to go and sin no more. They were ashamed, and each went away chastised. I suggest that if you want to proceed in a strictly legal manner, you charge Mr. Kelley as well."

The jury members looked at one another with surprise. Was Mr. Shepherd going to ask for indictment of his friend to save Chepi? Shepherd seemed to read their mind.

"Gentlemen, I asked for an indictment of Mr. Kelley knowing that it will never be brought. This charge has been trumped up to prosecute Chepi and the Algonquin people – to have flesh for flesh in retribution. Besides, Mr. Kelley would relish the opportunity to step into this trial if it could save Chepi.

176

Doesn't the Scripture also say that there is no greater love than to give your life for a friend? Indeed, Mr. Kelley would give his life for Chepi. I say that shows great love, not seduction and blind following. So, I will proceed in the defense of Chepi, as long as the jury and all present know that this trial is a sham, produced for no other reason than to exact vengeance on someone who actually tried to prevent the entire unfortunate incident!

"As for Chepi's beliefs, I ask the jury to consider the reasons for many of you for coming to America. That was for religious freedom – freedom to worship as you choose. Does this not apply to the people who were here before we came? Some of you came to preach the gospel to the native people here – certainly a right and good thing to do. Mr. Wesley, you are one who came for that very reason. I suggest to you that the Apostle Paul recognized that people at Mars Hill were worshipping the 'Unknown God' to whom they had built a temple. He commended them for their search of God, and he purposed to show them the One True God by virtue of his willingness to listen to them and share with them about faith in Jesus as the only way to God. I ask you, are you doing the same with the Algonquin people? Have you shown them kindness and understanding, or have you come only to exploit them and their land? How can they ever come to know the God you worship if you behave in such a way? Is that the God they would be inclined to worship?"

Shepherd sat, yielding to Mr. Martin as Martin stood before the court.

"Mr. Shepherd," he began with some condescension, "I would not be so presumptuous as to question a valid grand jury indictment, whatever you may think. English law has, thankfully, followed us to America, and we are bound to follow it. If you want a separate indictment on Mr. Kelley, I will be most happy to bring charges against him as well, which a grand jury can ponder. Meanwhile, let us proceed with this trial, and with due haste."

Mr. Wesley asked them to proceed with witnesses, and he asked Mr. Martin to call his first witness.

"I would like to call Mr. Andrew Kensington to the stand," said Martin.

Mr. Wesley asked Kensington to swear before God and the assembly that he would tell the truth, and Kensington affirmed that he would.

"Mr. Kensington," Martin began, "have you testimony that will corroborate the charge that this defendant has the power of seduction, and mystical powers that emanate from occult practices and beliefs?"

"I do," said Kensington.

"Please proceed, Mr. Kensington," said Martin.

"I have begun to have some business dealing with some traders in the area to discuss the shipment of beaver pelts to markets in England. One of these men, a French fur trapper, told me that he was well acquainted with this woman on trial, and he has seen firsthand her ability to influence the minds of men – to have them do things they would not normally do. She has this power

177

over men of her own tribe, as well as men who are not of the savage type of mind."

"And what did this trapper say about the defendant?" asked Martin.

"At the risk of being indelicate with women present here, she seduced him to have relations with her, and on more than one occasion," he concluded.

Several women gasped at this type of testimony.

Mr. Martin interjected, "I apologize for this lewd atmosphere, but we must get at the truth. Go on, Mr. Kensington."

"This man, Charles Asante, related this to me as I told him of our problems here at Gloucester. He told me this because he fears this woman, and he said that he and his fellow trappers want her to be executed. They fear that her presence may cause conflict with the French and Algonquin, perhaps like we have experienced with the Algonquin because of her," he said.

"That is all, thank you, Mr. Kensington."

"Your witness, Mr. Shepherd," said Herbert Wesley.

"Mr. Kensington," began Shepherd, "did you just tell the truth there?" he asked bluntly.

Kensington rose out of his seat in a rage.

"How dare you accuse me of lying!" he sputtered.

"I simply asked if you told the truth," Shepherd said softly. "A simple 'yes' would have sufficed, Mr. Kensington, but you seemed to take rather extreme offense at this question."

Kensington glared at Shepherd.

"My honor was questioned!" Kensington retorted.

"Indeed, Mr. Kensington, I can hardly believe that this was the first time your honor was called into question," Shepherd said.

"This is an outrage!" screamed Kensington.

"Mr. Shepherd, you seem to be badgering this witness; please proceed in a more dignified manner," said Wesley.

"I beg your pardon, Mr. Wesley, Mr. Martin, gentlemen of the jury. I am simply seeking the truth, and I have merely asked the witness the simplest question about it. I observed a slight twitch in Mr. Kensington's eye when he testified. I also saw him drumming his fingers when questioned. He also showed some flushing on his neck as he spoke earlier about Charles Asante. In my medical practice I have noted these physical signs to be often present when someone is not telling the truth. That is why I asked if he were telling the truth so that I could verify if these findings were present again. Indeed, his response seemed far beyond the question I asked," said Shepherd.

"As to questions about his honor, he is an experienced businessman who has had dealings with some people of questionable repute, such as slave traders, port workers who have some past problems with the law, and some associates who were not the most trusted of men. Surely I am not the first to imply that he has questions about his honor."

Kensington was now burning with rage. He had indeed acted out of character. He always had a way of keeping that simmering rage under the surface, and then using it against people at a more opportune time. He had been baited and then trapped. He hated Shepherd, and he hated himself for this foolish response.

He composed himself and gave a slight chuckle.

"No, Mr. Shepherd is right; I have been questioned about my honor before, as has every savvy businessman who knows how to make a shrewd deal. Accusations are often made without any facts to back them up!" he smiled.

"I certainly agree, Mr. Kensington. Just like in this case against Chepi, wouldn't you agree?" smiled Shepherd, on to his game.

Kensington's face darkened, then he quickly recovered. "No, Mr. Shepherd, not like in this case," he replied.

"Now, Mr. Kensington, why is Mr. Asante not here to testify?" asked Shepherd.

"He fears too much involvement with the English settlements. There have been tensions between French and English in America, and he fears that he cannot risk coming here for a trial that does not really concern him," replied Kensington.

"So you believe Mr. Asante's word on this?" asked Shepherd.

"Of course. He has no reason to lie," said Kensington.

"Perhaps that is true, perhaps not," said Shepherd. "Is it possible that Mr. Asante wants to please you for the sake of business, and would say what you want him to say? Who knows, perhaps there is no 'Mr. Asante.'"

Kensington caught himself this time and simply smiled at Shepherd. He made no response to this bait from Shepherd. Mr. Martin rescued him.

"Mr. Shepherd, I object to your treatment of this witness! You have continued to speculate about his testimony and to denigrate his character. You ought to be ashamed!"

In fact, there was a Mr. Asante, and he did hear of Chepi's great influence in the Algonquin camp from some of the hunters he had dealings with. But he had never met her, and he would never even be able to identify her. This testimony was indeed a sham, and Shepherd had suspected it. His only hope was to expose Kensington, and trip him up as best he could.

Kensington's motives were becoming clear. First, he still held a grudge against Shepherd and me, as well as Edwin Carr. He wanted our influence in the settlement gone, or at least diminished. Further, he was starting to see some value in having a presence in both Virginia and Massachusetts. Here, he could develop the fishing trade, beaver pelts, as well as boat building. In Virginia he could ship tobacco, import slaves, and use his own boats to conduct business. He could do business more or less as he pleased, and he did not need or particularly want interference from natives like the Algonquin.

179

Trouble with the French might even work to his advantage in the future, but for now, they would make good allies and trading partners. Asante and his people knew this too, and were happy to work with Kensington.

"Do you have other witnesses. Mr. Martin?" asked Wesley.

"I do not," he said. "I think that the facts, as well as the corroborating testimony of Mr. Asante through Mr. Kensington are more than enough to make the case that this woman is a seducing witch of the lowest estate. Besides, I fear that if she is allowed to have this child, the child itself, conceived in such circumstances, may bring untold harm to us!"

"Are you asking for the death penalty for this woman?" asked Wesley.

"Yes, I am," said Martin. "Her behavior clearly warrants it, and I fear the wrath of God should we not carry out this justice."

"Mr. Shepherd, do you have any more witnesses?" asked Wesley.

"Yes, I do," replied Shepherd. "I would like to call Mr. Martin."

Leviticus Martin was stunned, as was the entire assembly in the hall.

"Excuse me, Mr. Shepherd, perhaps you are confused with the legal procedures here," said Wesley. "Mr. Martin, as Prosecutor, cannot be called upon in defense of the defendant."

"Yes, I understand that, Mr. Wesley. I am calling him not to defend her, but to defend himself," he said.

"Defend himself?" asked Wesley. "Do you understand the legal system at all, Mr. Shepherd? Your behavior here today is most puzzling and disturbing."

"I appreciate your questions, Mr. Wesley, but I believe that I need to understand better why Mr. Martin is so intent upon asking for the death penalty. The only way that I can get at the information is to ask him to testify."

"You understand that Mr. Martin will be considered a hostile witness, do you not?" asked Wesley.

"Yes, I do, sir," said Shepherd.

"Very well, Mr. Martin, you understand that you are under oath," said Wesley.

"Yes, of course," said Martin.

"Proceed," said Wesley.

"Mr. Martin, are you aware of the genealogy of Jesus, the one found in the book of Matthew?" asked Shepherd.

"Of course!" said Martin. "But please do not ask me to recite it," he smiled. For the first time, the jury laughed.

Shepherd smiled, "I will not ask that, Mr. Martin, but I do want to know if you know who the mother of Perez and Zerah was?"

"Well, not right at this moment," blushed Martin.

"That is understandable, Mr. Martin," said Shepherd, "there are a number of names there! The mother who is in the genealogy of our Savior Jesus is Tamar. Are you familiar with her story?"

180

"Not right at the moment, but I know I have read of it," Martin countered.

"I am certain of it, Mr. Martin. However, I will help you recall that Tamar conceived these twins as a result of an act of prostitution with her father-in-law Judah. Do you recall that?"

Leviticus Martin blushed some more and said, "Is this necessary, Mr. Shepherd? This lewdness mentioned today should not be spoken in the presence of women."

"Mr. Martin, if the Author of Scripture saw fit to include this, I think we need to honor the Word of God, would you agree?"

"Yes, of course," he said, trailing off.

"Mr. Martin, are you familiar with who is listed as the mother of Salmon, who was the father of Boaz who was the father of Obed, who begot Jesse, the father of King David?"

"Again, I am sure that I would know when you tell me," said Leviticus Martin, now becoming exasperated.

"It is Rahab, known as the harlot, the woman who delivered Jericho to the Israelites."

"Yes, of course, I know the story," he said.

"Mr. Martin, do you know of Bathsheba, the woman who David seduced, the wife of Uriah the Hittite?" Shepherd asked.

"Yes, again, I know the story, Mr. Shepherd. Are you trying to discredit me because I do not have the same familiarity of the Bible as you?" he asked.

"Oh no, not by any means, Mr. Martin, I am trying to discredit you because you do not know the spirit of the Word of God. I believe that you know the stories, but you fail to grasp the spirit beneath the stories," said Shepherd.

"Whatever are you saying, Shepherd?" said Mr. Martin, now clearly unnerved by the line of questioning.

Shepherd responded, "The story of Jesus and his lineage is filled with people of low estate, sinners, liars, even murderers – in other words, plain people who Jesus came to redeem."

"What has this to do with the defendant, Mr. Shepherd? Why did you say you were questioning me, so that I could defend myself? From what am I defending myself?" Martin asked.

"You had proposed that Chepi receive the death penalty, partly because she is carrying a child. You speculate that this child could do grievous harm to the settlement, and therefore, we should kill Chepi and the baby on that chance. What if some jury had been convened to judge Rahab, or Tamar, or Bathsheba? Would that have been good? What if some jury had decided that your mother should die because…"

"Stop this I say, stop!" cried Martin. He burst from the witness chair and left the room.

I do not know to this day if Joseph Shepherd knew that Leviticus Martin's mother was a prostitute – I rather doubt it – but that caused the jury to deliberate more deeply than they might have earlier in the day. Martin's and Kensington's behavior had shown them to be out of control of their usual legal, clear thinking, and displaying emotional responses. Shepherd pointed this out in his closing argument, absent Leviticus Martin, who did not return to the courtroom.

Shepherd in his closing argument made it clear that Chepi and Kelley had acted in a reckless way, a sinful way, but that God was the judge of that, not this jury. Chepi had done nothing to threaten the settlement, and in fact she had likely averted further harm to the camp by her positive actions toward the English, much like Rahab had done for the Israelites. Rahab's reward was to be included in the Israelite camp, and indeed, she had an important role in the line of Jesus.

"Can we display the same grace to Chepi?" he asked.

The jury deliberated for less than one hour. Chepi was found not guilty of being a witch, and further was acquitted on the harsher charge of treason. Chepi was found not guilty, but that did not mean that she was found to be innocent. She faced judgment from most people because of her behavior with Sean Kelley, and she was not generally accepted by those in the settlement, especially the women. She faced isolation and rejection. Her trial was not completely over, but she had been spared.

Chapter 43

Margaret and I were becoming closer. I was attracted to her compassion and care for little Jacob, who was now toddling about the settlement and making himself both a nuisance and a lovable little scamp. Margaret also was about the only woman who reached out to Chepi. Margaret worked on getting better at the Algonquian language while teaching English to Chepi. She still managed to look in on Albert Adams, but he seemed to be finding a place of service by helping Captain Braden, who was really starting to fail physically. Albert moved in with Captain Braden to care for him on a regular basis, and Margaret made sure that both were getting along, especially in the cold of winter.

Margaret and I found time to be together, and soon I realized that my attraction to her was shared by Edwin Carr. Margaret was discreet about how she handled this attention, but it became apparent that she would need to make a choice. I believed that at least some of her attraction to Edwin Carr was based upon her desire to have some kind of connection with her beloved Jacob, whose death she still mourned. I needed to know if Edwin felt that way also, or if his intention was to simply comfort Margaret. I doubted that, wished for that, but I probably knew better.

Anne Kensington had her own desires about Edwin Carr. She had never really given up on him despite Carr's decision to break off their mostly physical relationship some years before. Anne and Andrew Kensington were now again in some major arguments over her time with Edwin Carr, her growing disaffection with the American weather, the loss of the comforts of London, and her growing sense of emptiness that a trip to America had not solved. Her mood had changed again, and she wanted another change in her life.

One day, Anne decided to pick a fight with Andrew. She was bored, and conflict seemed to be the only thing that gave her energy anymore.

"Andrew," she began, "are we going to stay in Gloucester forever?"

"We have been here barely six months," he said, "and you are restless already."

"You promised that America would be a place where there would be adventure and eventually greater wealth," she said. "I see neither so far."

Andrew looked at her blankly.

"I have an idea," he said. "Why don't you and Edwin sail back to London together? I have business that I need to have conducted there, and Edwin, despite his increasing distaste for me, has some obligations for the

Dorchester Company, or rather the London & Western Company now. Whether he wants to work for me or not, he will do it because he needs me. Besides, that is what you want – to be with him. Here is your opportunity."

"Is that what Edwin wants?" she asked.

"I do not know, Anne. Why don't you ask him?" he said.

The lines had been drawn, and both Kensingtons had played out their part in it. Andrew, having had his fill of Anne, had dismissed her back to London. Anne, now without other good options, decided to approach Edwin to see if there was a chance for them again. She approached Edwin that evening with the proposal that Andrew had suggested. Edwin mused at the suggestion.

"Andrew has his way, doesn't he?" said Carr. "In one step he rids himself of both of us – me because he knows I must fulfill my contract with the company, you because, well, I think he detests you."

Anne looked stricken. She had hoped for a bit more positive response from Edwin.

"Do you want me with you when you return to London?" she asked.

"You will be a welcome guest on the ship," he said. "There is no future for us together, Anne."

"Is that because you love Margaret Brennan?" she asked.

"I think I may love Margaret Brennan," Carr said, "but Luke Greene loves her more, I believe. He is prepared to marry her and spend his life with her. I am not prepared to do that. Besides, I cannot live my life in my brother Jacob's shadow, and I believe that he may always be in her heart somehow. I cannot be reminded of that. Loving her at a distance may be best for all. I can let her go to Luke Greene, and I will be satisfied that she is cared for. Good Dr. Greene will provide for her and little Jacob. Perhaps I will be 'Uncle Edwin,' and that will suit me fine."

"And what of me?" asked Anne.

"You will be fine in London, Anne. Andrew will support you in a fine style, and you will be free to have the romances that you seem to desire," said Edwin.

"You don't love me?" she asked in a plaintive voice.

"I do like your energy and fire, Anne. You have strong determination and passion. Your fire runs hot, but usually a banked fire can be counted on more for heat and consistent warmth," he said. "I won't satisfy you, and I doubt any man can. You need more than I have the energy to provide," he concluded.

Anne was a bit wounded and confused. She would once again start over in her life. This time it would be back in London, but alone. Edwin Carr saw the trip as a relief. Rather than curse Kensington, he chose to see this as a way that perhaps God was doing something for him that he could not do for himself. He would fulfill his contract with Kensington, and then decide where his life would go. He oddly felt free for the first time in a while. He was going

184

back to sea, and that was something he knew well. He could then be free of Andrew Kensington.

I called upon Edwin Carr shortly after he had met with Anne Kensington, and he told me of their meeting. I was elated to hear his decision about Margaret, and he was most gracious in giving a blessing to Margaret and me. It affirmed to me that others saw my love for Margaret, and he knew before I did that I should marry her. Of course, I would ask her to marry me!

Chapter 44

The first case of smallpox in the Algonquin camp was a very disturbing sight. Kitchi was a young hunter who was known to be reckless and violent. He hated the white people who were invading his land, and he did not distinguish between French and English. All of them were a threat to his life and that of his people, and he took it upon himself to be an avenging force. He was not joined in this hate by most of the Algonquin, who had come to enjoy the gifts that the French trappers gave them. Guns, knives, metal tools, and glass ornaments were valued by the Algonquin. The guns were useful in the wars that the Algonquin periodically waged with neighboring tribes.

Kitchi would head out at night on his own and use his superior stalking skills to sneak up on unsuspecting French trappers. Once near the camp, he would wait to pick off the poor soul who had to leave the campfire to go into the woods to relieve himself. Kitchi would wrap his hand over the mouth of the victim as he was standing to urinate, or squatting. He would then quickly slice his throat, severing the vocal chords so quickly that the dying man could not even let out a squeal. The man would bleed to death in silence in the woods. It would not be until morning that the rest of the camp would find the corpse of their countryman covered in blood. This had a chilling effect on the trappers, needless to say.

One day Kitchi broke out in small bumps all over his body. Within two weeks Kitchi was covered with the bumps and had a fever. Days later he was dead. Several of those who ministered to him also developed the bumps, and most also died. Smallpox had visited the Algonquin camp, and it began its devastation. It had been unknown to these people until we came from Europe. It would prove to be devastating to them.

Unbeknownst to the Gloucester settlement, Shepherd had made periodic visits to the Algonquin camp. He told the Algonquin that he wanted to continue to learn their language and to give them medical help. His original intent in coming to America was for medical and scientific research, and, despite the setback of Cape Ann, he was determined to fulfill his mission. He had not included me in these trips because he felt that he might be exposing me to danger, so he began these trips shortly after we moved to Gloucester. He only told me after he discovered that smallpox had been visited upon the Algonquin. Now he felt he needed help to minister to them. He also theorized that both he and I, and likely many others in the Gloucester camp, had an immunity to smallpox due to prior exposure. Certainly Leviticus Martin, he believed, was immune, since his two children had died of the disease, and he and his wife had survived.

One day, Shepherd came to me with a look of grief on his face.

"Luke," he said, "I need to ask you a favor."

"Of course, Joseph, how can I help?" I asked.

"The Algonquin camp is stricken with smallpox. I need to help them, and I need another physician to help me. Will you come with me?" he asked.

I was taken aback by the question.

"Joseph, aren't you afraid of getting smallpox?" I asked.

"I have been exposed in the past, as I suppose you have been also as a physician," he said calmly.

"Yes, I suppose so," I said, "but there is always a chance of getting the disease."

"I don't really think that there is a great chance of that, Luke," he said. "Yes, it could happen, but we are physicians, committed to care for the health of people. Those are some of the risks we face in our service. Besides, remember my theory that exposure to smallpox can result in future immunity. In fact, that is what I want to try. I had seen once, while I was in Byzantium, a man who had deliberately infected people with a dose of small pox by scratching their arms with some of the powdered dried scabs from healed smallpox pustules. These people got somewhat ill, but when they recovered, they did not get smallpox. Recall also that those milk maidens who were stricken with cowpox, a close relative, I believe, of smallpox, never came down with smallpox. I believe that this helps to confirm my theory," Shepherd concluded.

I had to agree that risks are part of our profession, and this was, partly at least, a scientific journey. I hesitantly agreed to accompany him to the Algonquin camp. Shepherd had been going to the camp more than anyone knew. He had originally risked the journey soon after we arrived at Gloucester. He had thought it best to keep this mission quiet, and perhaps his goodwill was part of the reason that there had never been any reprisals from the Algonquin after the massacre months ago.

We arrived at the Algonquin camp to find much illness and disarray. The oldest and youngest in the camp had succumbed most quickly to the disease. There were a fair number who had survived the illness, but whose faces showed the disfiguring pockmarks of this dreaded plague. Shepherd went to work discussing his plan with the elders about trying the procedure he had seen used in Byzantium. He had become reasonably proficient in Algonquian, and the elders seemed to have some understanding of what he planned to do.

We proceeded to prepare the odd concoction of smallpox scabs – we dried them and ground them to a fine powder. We mixed this with the lard rendered from wild pigs that had been slaughtered for meat. With this "paste," we planned to make small scratches on the upper arm and apply the paste. We

187

did not know what the outcome might be, but Shepherd believed that this would prove his theory of what he called "inoculation."

There was just one more problem. Shepherd believed that we could not ask the Algonquin to undergo this procedure unless we were first willing to have it performed on ourselves. They could not be expected to trust that we were acting in their best interest unless we would be willing to expose ourselves to it.

At first I was stunned that he would expose himself to this possible death sentence. When I realized he meant that both of us should submit to it, I was outraged that he would ask me to do this. Quickly I realized that such a gesture was consistent with Shepherd's character, but not mine. The fact that he asked me to do this meant that he believed that it *was* in my character, and I just did not see it yet.

While I had no idea about this odd procedure, I knew Shepherd and I trusted him. I agreed to have this done to me. We would "inoculate" one another in front of several of the elders. We would stay in the Algonquin camp several days after we had done this so that they could see what was happening with our health. Further, if we were to somehow develop the full disease, we could not risk exposing the people at Gloucester. We told the elders of our plan, and that we would return in several days to actually start the inoculation process.

Upon our return to Gloucester we told Chepi and Kelley of our plan. Chepi by now was nearly ready to deliver her baby. Shepherd had decided not to take Chepi with him on his visits to the Algonquin camp, since he did not want to expose her to smallpox. I included Margaret in this secret discussion also. I wanted her to be aware of my intentions. I was not certain that we would return from the Algonquin camp, and I needed to have her with me at this time.

Sean Kelley asked us how we planned to explain our week-long, perhaps longer, absence from Gloucester. Before we could answer, Kelley said, "I will tell people that you two are doing some scientific experiments on plants to find medicinal remedies."

"That sounds good, Kelley," I said. "You are always the quick-thinking one!"

Stocked with a supply of provisions, we headed off again to the Algonquin camp to begin a scientific experiment. I wished it were as simple as gathering plants! Upon reaching the Algonquin camp, Shepherd explained what we were going to do. We prepared the dried, powdered scabs, mixed them in with some fresh lard and made a fine paste with it. Shepherd prepared my arm with his usual meticulous care. I had learned that he believed very strongly in what he called a "clean field." He washed my upper arm, then he applied rum to a cloth and wiped a spot on my arm where he intended to make some scratches with his scalpel. He let it dry, made a few scratches just on the

188

surface, and applied the paste. He covered it with a cloth, then asked me to do the same with him.

The Algonquin leaders watched in amazement at this experiment. They knew that we were taking a risk, and that we were doing this in an effort to help save people at the Algonquin camp. It took only a few minutes to do this, but now the waiting began. What would happen with us?

Chapter 45

Back at Gloucester, Chepi went into labor about two weeks before her due date. Kelley fetched the midwives to help with the delivery. He was very worried about this turn of events. Her pregnancy had been very uneventful, and she had been healthy. Shepherd and I had hoped to be available to tend to Chepi if we were needed, but the midwives typically took care of all the births and the women who delivered. Margaret helped in the delivery, having gained experience at the Franciscan mission.

Chepi delivered a healthy baby girl, and she was named Kimi. Chepi had chosen this name because in Algonquin it means "secret." Indeed, this little girl's life had been born of secrets.

During that week also, Edwin Carr, Anne Kensington, and a cargo of salted fish, medicinal herbs, beaver pelts, and some fine timber, headed toward London on the *Conquest*, now repaired. Andrew Kensington was pleased that this voyage was taking place. It represented his freedom from Anne, his power over Edwin Carr, the start of trade of specialty goods from Gloucester to London, and an example of how his new shipbuilding plans could refit a ship. If he could not yet fully implement his tobacco-for-slaves trade plan, this would do until he could make that work. He had also sent Edwin Carr to transact some business with the King's ministers regarding trade with America. He hoped that this successful voyage would pay dividends with the King.

Two weeks passed in the Algonquin camp, and we waited for symptoms. Shepherd was meticulous in taking notes of anything that we experienced. I noticed that glands under my inoculated arm swelled, which produced some minor pain. I had a slight fever for about two days, and I felt tired. By the end of the two weeks, I felt quite normal. Shepherd had not experienced any symptoms, yet he was not surprised by this. He had believed that he had been exposed to cowpox in the past, and he decided that he already had immunity. My minor symptoms were good news to him as well. He believed that I had developed a slight reaction, as he had hoped, which would make me immune from smallpox in the future.

Shepherd approached the elders about inoculating the Algonquin camp, and they agreed. Any Algonquin willing to have the procedure done would come to Shepherd and me, and we would inoculate them.

Despite our success, only seven men and three women came forward. We prepared the ingredients of our paste to be applied, and we followed the exact procedure we had used upon ourselves. We were very deliberate and obvious in making sure that the elders saw us prepare the paste and apply it exactly as we had done to ourselves.

We told the elders that we needed to get back to Gloucester, but that we would return later the next week to check on our inoculated group. We left early the next morning, confident that we had averted a disaster in the Algonquin camp. Upon our return to Gloucester, we were greeted with the news of Kimi's birth. Chepi still did not benefit from the acceptance of other women, but the presence of a newborn baby did make for a bit of a truce. I was delighted to connect with Margaret again, and I told her of the adventure at the Algonquin camp and the apparent success of Shepherd's inoculations.

Margaret told me of the birth of Kimi, and the miracle of birth that she was blessed to see again. Little Jacob was growing, Margaret believed, to look like his namesake, even though Jacob Carr was not his father. As Margaret described how little Jacob would grow to be a wonderful man like Jacob, I was somewhat uneasy.

"What troubles you, Luke?" Margaret asked.

"I see how little Jacob pleases you," I began. "I am certain that he will become a fine man under your care," I continued.

"Then why are you troubled?" she asked.

"I think that no man may ever be able to take Jacob Carr's place in your heart," I said, "but I have hoped that perhaps I could be a part of your life also. I think I may have loved you ever since I met you at the pub that evening years ago. Since then, I have come to admire your loving concern for others, your tender care of little Jacob, your understanding and kindness to Chepi, your amazing faith which seems to sustain you…"

Margaret had tears on her cheeks as she stopped me.

"Luke, don't you know I love you also?" she asked. "I have seen your desire to pursue good, to use your gifts to help others, and mostly, I have seen that you love me. A woman like me who has such a past…" She trailed off. We embraced, and I asked her to marry me. She said yes.

Upon our return to the Algonquin camp, we were shocked to see that nine of our ten "patients" were showing significant symptoms of smallpox. We were, of course, deeply concerned and fearful that some may be indeed dying. We had told the elders to isolate the ten volunteers from the rest of the camp, but they had failed to enforce this. Consequently, when people became sick, family members took them in to tend to them. Once again, we were now looking at the potential of another round of smallpox ravaging the camp.

We met with the elders to discuss this latest crisis. The group of elders was divided in the way that they saw us. Some were pragmatic, and thought that the illness was being visited upon them by the gods for some reason. They did not seem to hold us responsible for the illness. Others, however, had a much darker view. They believed that we had made an elaborate show of our inoculation, but that it had been a trick to spread the illness in their camp. They had heard of stories about other people from "across the water" who had deliberately spread disease in native camps to decimate the population in order to steal the land. Some contended that we knew what the outcome would be from the start. This was refuted by those who held us blameless by the fact that we had returned to the camp. Had we known that the smallpox would be caused by our actions, why would we return?

They argued among themselves for some time. Shepherd asked if we could try to treat the victims of smallpox. He pleaded with them that we only wanted to help those who were sick. Matwau, the spokesman for the elders, made it clear to us that we were to leave as soon as possible. He could not ensure our safety if we stayed. It was only because we had some defenders in that council that we were not taken prisoner or killed outright.

We left quickly after hearing this from Matwau. It would be disrespectful to try to argue his directive to us. We were defeated, and we suspected that one or two of our "patients" were going to die. Our largest fear was that smallpox might indeed devastate the Algonquin camp. We really did not know what other devastation could happen, but we would soon find out.

Chapter 46

We returned to Gloucester, where life was picking up after a long, hard winter. Spring brought some crisp mornings, but milder afternoons made planting almost a joy. A new food was brought back to our camp by Chepi. Chepi told us of a tuber that had been grown by her people since it was brought to them perhaps twenty years earlier by some travelers who claimed to have been in the far western area of the land. At that time, the Algonquin had been experiencing one of the frequent famines that would be brought on by changes in animal migration, weather, illness, and wars. The tuber, which they began to plant, was called "patata." The tuber grew well, seemed to be a hardy plant, and it had no insect predators. It was versatile, and could be prepared in many ways. It even seemed to keep well if stored in cool, dry places. This food was filling as well, and after the initial success they decided to try to continue to grow it. They also decided to keep it as secret as possible, believing that the Great Spirit had sent those travelers to them to avert starvation in the camp. Knowledge like this was a great survival advantage, and it was kept highly secret. The fact that Chepi had smuggled out some patata and shared the information with strangers (if that were to be discovered) would probably seal her fate. She could then no longer return to her native family. She would now be part of the English world. She and her daughter, Kimi, indeed had shown the name to be well conferred.

One secret that was not kept was the fact that Shepherd and I had visited the Algonquin camp. I suppose that such a thing can never be kept secret; few things of significance can. Perhaps aging and ailing Captain Braden had become aware and in his confusion had let it slip. Perhaps Albert Adams, never one to miss a chance to gossip, had put together the facts about our extended absences from the settlement. I could not imagine that Margaret would divulge this secret, certainly not intentionally. Had we mentioned something to Leviticus Martin as we inquired of him about the death of his children and his likely smallpox immunity according to Shepherd's theory? Had he inferred something? We do not know to this day, but it became generally known that we had gone to the Algonquin camp. The fact that there had been some possible benefits from our visits, such as the acquisition of the patata, allowed people to simply ignore the trips and enjoy some benefit. We never knew.

It had been nearly three weeks since we had left the Algonquin camp. Two of the nine "patients" had indeed died of smallpox, causing a great deal of fear and anger among the camp. Some of the younger warriors took it upon themselves to seek revenge upon the English who had brought death to their camp, now twice. A group of probably ten to fifteen warriors made their way into our camp at night. Sneaking up on the guards, who had built a small fire to ward off the evening chill, they seized the watchmen and slit their throats before they could yell out a warning. They then grabbed torches from near the fire, lit them, and began to throw them into whatever dwellings they could reach. As soon as people were roused by the shout of "Fire!" the warriors cut them down with a hail of arrows. Chaos ruled the camp as men found their muskets and began to return fire toward the nearly invisible warriors. The night began to glow as fires started to rage out of control. People could not risk getting to the well to get enough water to quench the fires. The warriors gradually began to be silhouetted by the very fires they started, and musket fire began to have some effect, with at least three warriors felled by lead shot. Having done the damage they had hoped to produce, the Algonquin raiding party melted into the night, gone for good. What they left behind was devastation. Fires raged as women screamed for their children, and men organized an effort to put out the fires. By dawn, we could see the remains of our settlement. Stores of food had been destroyed, and dwellings were reduced to ash. Six men were killed by arrows, and the two watchmen had died from slit throats. One woman died protecting her two young children, huddling over them in a burning log building.

Rage and fear ruled the settlement. We had lost several dwellings and much of the town meeting hall, as it had come to be known. The Governor's Council met later in the day to determine our course of action. Andrew Kensington was beside himself with rage. He demanded that Joseph Shepherd and I be hauled up for charges and a trial. He was convinced that our trips to the Algonquin camp was the cause of the disaster. He was, in fact, correct in that thinking. His intentions were not justice, however. They were revenge. He had resented us for a long time, and this was a chance for him to get rid of us as well as exercise his power. Others on the Council were inclined to agree with him about our culpability. However, all this became a moot point when Shepherd, upon hearing of the clamor, simply came forward and took full responsibility for the venture.

"I believe that you are correct in your assessment, Lord Kensington," Shepherd said. "I went to the Algonquin camp to help them overcome the smallpox outbreak there. I believed that it was the right thing to do. In fact, I still do, even though the results were so unfortunate. I failed them, and I have exposed Gloucester to this danger."

Kensington raged at him, "You decided to help these savages at the risk of bringing smallpox to Gloucester? You risked yourself and us for those animals, those killers?"

Shepherd stood silent before Kensington, interrupting only to contest Kensington's contention that the Algonquin were less than human beings.

194

Kensington finally finished, having done what he intended to do – to cast Shepherd in the light of a madman who was dangerous to Gloucester.

"I say that we burn him at the stake, just like Anna Moore died protecting her children – burned to death!"

"Greene also ought to die. He was every bit as guilty as Shepherd," added Marcus Turner.

I froze at that statement. I had never had any ill dealings with Turner, but he seemed to want equal justice, if justice were to be the intent here.

Shepherd spoke up clearly and firmly at this point and said, "If you decide that my death is warranted for this tragedy, then so be it, and I will go to the stake. Do not take the life of Dr. Greene, who went with me only because I begged him to do so as a physician. As you know, we have sworn an oath to help patients regardless of circumstances, even at our own personal risk. Dr. Greene was simply following a sacred oath he had sworn. How can you penalize him for upholding his sworn duty?"

"That applies to civilized human beings, Shepherd," said Kensington, "not these brutal savages!"

"Were we not also brutal to the Algonquin?" asked Shepherd.

This aroused a loud stir in the Council.

"We simply responded to the Algonquin attack on us!" several shouted.

"Yes, and the means which we used were not done with proper motives nor means. You were deceived into that attack, and many of you know that to be true," Shepherd said. Before they could answer, Shepherd posed a question to them. "The child Kimi, daughter of Chepi and Sean Kelley, is she human, or is she a wild beast?"

There was a moment of silence, then Kensington responded, "Bastard child that she is, perhaps she is half human because of her English father."

"Have you ever seen an instance where a human being was bred with an animal and produced offspring?" Shepherd asked.

"Such talk is crude, vulgar, and pointless," ventured Kensington. "Shepherd is guilty, and so is Greene. I submit to this Council that we quickly execute them for the sake of justice, and as a message to the Algonquin that we tolerate no murderous attacks!"

Feeling emboldened, and also that I had nothing to lose, I stated, "The murder of innocent men sends no message, but simply proves the point that we are indeed the real savages here. If we mete out punishment for merciful acts, may God help our souls!"

Word quickly spread through Gloucester about the deliberations of the Governor's Council. They had not followed the standard English law procedure of finding a bill of indictment before convening a hearing. Henry Adams quickly remedied this by asking for such a bill from a hastily called and empaneled grand jury. However, as members of the community were called upon to serve, great dissension shook Gloucester. There seemed to be a tremendous divide among the people about the whole matter. The divide was becoming clearer, and there was talk of a group of people who were willing to leave the settlement and either relocate or even return to England. Life was hard in America, and the idea of putting up with the danger of Indian attack, on top of hunger and disease was becoming too much for some. It had been an adventure of a lifetime, but people wanted that lifetime to last longer than what America seemed to promise.

Others believed that moving away from the Algonquin, perhaps to a new area of the land, was preferable to trying to stay in this hostile place. Much had already been lost at Gloucester. Was there enough to stay for? There were no guarantees anywhere in America, but the people attracted to come to America were those who wanted a new start. They were restless, and they wanted challenges in a new place. Perhaps another part of Massachusetts would prove satisfying for that need of new challenges.

There rose a clamor, not for a grand jury, but for a town meeting. This practice was becoming popular, and people liked the idea of a voice in governance. The Council agreed to a full Town Meeting on the matter, Kensington being unable to stop that approach. Perhaps a Town Meeting would serve his purposes just as well.

Henry Adams was presiding for the Governor's Council and called the meeting to order. Broader topics were to be discussed at the meeting, not just a decision for a bill of indictment. Adams called upon people to speak their mind on the matter, and he reserved the right to keep them on topic and to monitor their time for speaking. This somewhat broad range of powers had been conferred upon him by the Council, partly to maintain good order and partly due to the respect he had gained in the past months in leading the Council.

A line of people took turns standing to say their piece about the situation at hand. To my surprise, there were a fair number of people who were not willing to cast all the blame for our problems upon Shepherd and me. However, the presence of Chepi and Kelley and their infant daughter Kimi seemed to evoke some outrage that had always simmered. Now people gave vent to those feelings, and many saw a solution of sending them to the Algonquin camp as banishment – as if somehow that would undo the tensions boiling up.

People's reactions to Shepherd were typically strong and divided. There seemed to be anger toward the very core of his character – his sense of justice and compassion. I had always puzzled over this. I was drawn to his desire for the welfare of others, even at his own expense, yet others seemed to feel themselves judged in comparison to his strong beliefs and intolerance of wrongdoing. They saw him as arrogant, perhaps. I knew him and knew that there could be nothing farther from the truth. People often do not want truth, however; they want their own views supported.

Nearly at the end of the line of people, and as tensions seemed to be mounting to consider a bill of indictment simply to have a way to come to a just solution, aging Captain Braden came forward on the arm of his friend Albert Adams. They slowly moved forward to be heard. Albert, ever since his injuries, rarely spoke before a group of people. His command of language was not what it once was, and he believed that he could hardly express himself well any longer. Braden, now nearly feeble in all respects, had very little strength to spare.

"May I address the group?" asked Braden softly.

"Yes, of course, Captain Braden," said Adams.

"I have known Joseph Shepherd and Luke Greene since our voyage on the *Intrepid* some five years ago. I do not know what transpired at the Algonquin camp, nor really do any one of you here who try to sit in judgment of them. What I do know is that I was dying on the *Intrepid*, and because of the efforts of these men, and the grace of God, I am still alive today. Perhaps the result of their efforts did not turn out as they or anyone wanted, but their efforts were right. Just like on the *Intrepid*, their efforts saved me from plague, even though the actions of others nearly resulted in my death. Can we judge them simply because other people misunderstood their efforts, just like on the *Intrepid*?"

Albert then haltingly spoke.

"I was taken in by the Franciscan mission in London. They helped me. Jacob Carr, the man who beat me, later took care of me, and he died saving me. I forgave him. A lot of people helped me because Joseph Shepherd helped them…"

Albert began to cry and could not continue. Braden helped Albert to a seat, and silence ruled the meeting. Margaret silently wept as she buried her head in her hands, likely recalling that awful night of the fire. Then I saw Henry Adams with a tear running down his face. He could not speak for a brief moment, then finally he asked that we take a recess.

Kensington watched the Town Meeting turn to a place he did not expect. He could no longer hope for a bill of indictment. There was still division in the Gloucester settlement, and now he had an inspiration. He could use this moment to offer a solution and get his business needs met at the same time. He had been considering the idea for a little while, but now was the time to offer it to an emotional and vulnerable community.

After a short recess, Kensington asked if he could speak. Adams acknowledged Kensington, and he began calmly and almost reverently, "People of Gloucester, I think we have seen today that we are divided on this and several matters. I would like to withdraw my request for a bill of indictment on Shepherd and Greene. I still find that their reckless actions have

197

put us into a very vulnerable position – a place we can no longer sustain. I propose that we each make a decision where we will go. Some may want to stay here in Gloucester and face the risks of that. Others have discussed a return to England, while others have talked of moving to a different place here in Massachusetts.

"I have an offer of another opportunity, in Virginia, which was my original plan. I have a company which now has not only funding but a promise of a royal charter from the Crown in Virginia. I will begin our shipping and exporting business there with the charter and protection of the King. Those who follow me there may truly find the wealth that America offers!"

In fact, just the year before, the King had indeed revoked the charter of the Virginia Company and made Virginia a Crown colony, under royal direction. Edwin Carr's mission had been at least two-fold. His successful return voyage to England had been the proof of what Kensington had been promising the King – potential profits from enterprises that were not tobacco-driven alone. Shipbuilding and ship repair, lumber, pelts, medicines, and a variety of goods could bring wealth to England, like Spain had been able to do. Kensington likely downplayed that slavery, tobacco, and perhaps rum were to be the profit leaders of the enterprise. However, Kensington showed amazing flexibility and a genius for making money. King James was desperate for money, and Kensington could be a moneymaker. That seemed to transcend the King's distaste for the tobacco trade. Kensington knew how to make things work.

The crowd stirred at this turn of events. Many found relief – they no longer had to decide on punishment, they had to decide on their future! We could not know the next level of danger we faced from the Algonquin, but it seemed very real and imminent to some. Already we had faced near devastation at their hands. People were restless and ready for a change. Kensington gave some people that opportunity with his offer.

Henry Adams concluded the Town Meeting with the charge that people decide what they wanted to do. The question would be how the settlement would divide. There were some clear lines of division, with some wanting to continue at Gloucester, a group seeming ready to move with Kensington to Jamestown, and another group ready to move on simply to start anew.

I knew that Kensington's offer did not include Shepherd and me, and we, of course, would not choose that anyway. Shepherd and I needed to discuss what our next steps might be, but first I wanted to speak with Margaret to see her reaction. I was relieved, excited, and fearful all at the same time. Margaret had been thinking about what this meant for both of us. We had decided to marry, so whatever decision we made, it would be as one. Little Jacob, now nearly four years old, would once again be facing a new world, as would we all.

Chapter 47

Margaret and I seemed to be of the same mind almost immediately. We wanted to start fresh. Her thoughts immediately turned to Chepi, Kimi, and Kelley. Where might they turn now? Chepi would not be able to return to her people, and Margaret felt that they would need help with little Kimi. If we could gather a good-sized group, we could venture to the place of our choosing in this exciting yet formidable land. We needed people with certain skills also – fishing, farming, hunting, building – all critical for survival. We also needed men who could bear arms to defend a new settlement. There would be competition for such people if there were the splits in thinking that we believed existed. Kensington could offer the prospect of wealth with his Crown connections and business plans. Some would be swayed by this enticement, but Shepherd pointed out that if we were to meet with people about coming to a new venture with us, we would only want people who shared a commitment to the same goals. If wealth were the only inducement, they would become disaffected when wealth did not come as quickly as they hoped. He quoted from Ecclesiastes, "He that loveth silver shall not be satisfied with silver; nor he that loveth abundance with increase: this is also vanity." We would look for people who valued independence, self-reliance, freedom of faith, and a desire to build a community that could be good for future generations. We would need people committed to vision for the future, not immediate wealth.

We met and listed those we believed would join us in these beliefs. Certainly Kelley, Chepi, and Kimi; Leviticus Martin and his family; Albert Adams and Captain Braden, knowing that they brought limited skills and would require some care; Henry Adams and his family; Herbert Wesley; Thomas Hancock and his family; Thomas Gerry and his family. These were people we believed were of the same mind. Surely there were others, and we decided to meet with these people, propose our ideas, and ask for help in direction.

Our meeting went well with this group as we explained our desire for a new community not ruled by greed and power but with shared determination of governance, faith as a cornerstone of that governance, and a desire to build for future generations. We left with a plan to find those who shared our beliefs and to invite them to join us.

It was now nearly August, and we decided that we could wait for the crops to be harvested before we left. The patata plants that Chepi had brought seemed to be doing exceedingly well, and we looked for a large harvest. Chepi told us that the patata might well be ready to harvest in about two weeks, so we decided to gather our share of the harvest and depart within two weeks. Chepi also said that she did not believe that the Algonquin were likely to attack. She did not give specific reasons for this, but we surmised that she still had some type of contact with her people. She had not shared her belief very widely, because she thought that if people sensed that she still had some contact with her people, her life and that of Kelley and Kimi might be in trouble.

Kensington was gathering his own group to head for Jamestown, and he was promising both wealth and power for those who followed him. Indeed, the prospects for his group seemed favored financially, and we could offer no such promises. By the first week of August, we could determine who would be going where. Kensington had nearly one hundred people, many of them the most able soldiers and men without families.

There was a group, of perhaps seventy people, who decided to stay at Gloucester. These were fishermen and their families who saw that Gloucester could sustain them with fish, even if crops were to fail. The cod catch was amazing at times, and there seemed to be a real future for exporting salt cod to not only England, but to the West Indies, where it was used to feed the growing slave population who worked in the sugar cane fields. They either discounted the Algonquin threat, or, willing to fight the Algonquin, disregarded it completely.

Finally, our group numbered around sixty people. What we lacked in military strength, we believed we made up in strength of will and principle. Shepherd spent a great deal of time with Henry Adams, Thomas Hancock, and Thomas Gerry – men who showed passion and ability to shape a new type of government in America. Excitement was building in that group as time grew closer to make the move to another part of the New World. Shepherd seemed confident that this group, led by principle, was going to impact the New World in a significant way. He shared that he had some personal stirrings that he needed to pray about, and we all assumed that this was just part of Shepherd's character and that he was excited to make a new journey.

Kensington and his group were preparing a ship to head south toward Jamestown. Henry Adams had negotiated an arrangement whereby his group could take passage on the ship to a point where Reverend William Blackstone had settled with his family in an area named "New England" by Captain John Smith some years earlier as he was exploring the area. Blackstone had corresponded with both Herbert Wesley and Adams since they had met at John Ward's meetings years before. Blackstone was an independent man, rugged and fierce in his desire to have religion untainted by the King, and by his desire for having liberty of thought as "ordained by God."

This seemed to be just the type of environment Adams and Shepherd were seeking. Blackstone spoke of the beauty of the area, "a hilly peninsula with a natural harbor." This is where our group would depart from the Kensington group and begin a new life.

Just before we were to depart, a ship arrived at Gloucester, the return of Edwin Carr on the *Conquest* from his trip on behalf of the London & Western Company. He carried another small group of people seeking relief from London's poverty, as well as some fresh provisions. There was also salt used as ballast for the voyage, then to be used for the fishermen to salt the cod catch, wine, beer, weapons, lead for ammunition, and other goods welcomed by the settlement. There was one more crate, which carried a valuable cargo – mail. Correspondence with England was difficult, but when letters arrived they were as precious as gold to us. Shepherd received letters from Galileo, Francis Bacon, William Bradford, and William Harvey.

Shepherd was delighted to hear from his friends and colleagues. He read of Galileo's increasing frustration with Rome and his need to conceal his truest scientific beliefs. He read about Bacon's legal troubles and his disgrace from Parliament and dismissal from public service. However, his letter from Harvey was most prized. Harvey wrote about his newest publication, which would define his studies on physiology and the circulation of the blood. In the letter, he begged Shepherd to return to England and work with him to finalize his book, *De Motu Cordis*. He related also that conditions in London were increasingly intolerable for the poor. Since the Franciscan mission burned down, there were few options for the poor, the sick, and the orphans, which it had served. Harvey indicated that he might be able to secure some support from the King for a new hospital and mission. Harvey, I knew, recognized that such an appeal might move Shepherd, even more than the thought of helping to advance medical science. Harvey also noted that some of the herbs and roots that we had sent back showed promise in helping to treat illness. Sassafras root, he noted, was becoming popular in teas and medical compounds.

Harvey concluded with an offer to provide housing and funds for Shepherd and me to return to England under a royal grant. Shepherd was clearly torn in how he now wanted to proceed. A return to England to work with Harvey, and the potential of having royal support for starting another mission, were very strong allures. I saw Shepherd's anguish the next day, and I approached him with an idea.

"Joseph," I began, "we have been through many things together, but perhaps it is time for you to part ways with me. Margaret and little Jacob and I have decided to stay in America. However, you have gifts and talents that need to be shared with men like Harvey, Galileo, and Descartes. Margaret and I will return to England to visit once we are established here. Please do not stay in America for my sake."

I realized at once how arrogant that may have sounded. Who was I to presume that I was the reason he wanted to stay in America. I immediately flushed with embarrassment.

"My dear Luke," smiled Shepherd, "you are a close and trusted friend, and my affection for you indeed is strong reason to stay in America, but I must follow my heavenly Father's wishes. I will go where He desires me to go.

"What is your decision, then, Joseph?" I asked.

He sighed and said, "I will pray about it, my friend, and I will let you know in a day or two. As you know, I have been feeling some unease about the move, and perhaps this is my answer to prayer."

I left feeling both relieved and sad at this discussion. Shepherd had influenced my life much more than I affected him, I reasoned, yet he gives me the grace of believing that I had been important in his life. I did however leave feeling resolved in my decision to make a new start in America with Margaret. I also believed that despite my promises to Shepherd, I might never see him again.

Preparations for leaving were now picking up. Shepherd had informed me a few days after our discussion that he planned to return to England. I somehow knew that he must do this, and I also knew that it was a very difficult decision for him. He promised to write regularly, which I knew he would do, as would I. I had also convinced myself that someday Margaret, little Jacob, and I would return to visit him in England.

Margaret and I decided that we were now married, and we declared this to our travelling group. We had asked Herbert Wesley to act as a church official to bless our marriage, and he had graciously done so, even though he said that he was not an ordained elder. Several other men and women made such a declaration before our departure, as we had decided that stable marriages would be an important part of the new community we hoped to establish.

Our departure in the fall of 1626 was filled with tension. I never did trust Andrew Kensington. It was not until the ship filled with travelers, headed to both Virginia and lower New England, harbored at a quaint little port. This port, which had been described by Reverend Blackstone, was to be our new home. Only after we successfully disembarked did I breathe a little easier.

An advance party had gone before us to set up some dwellings and to lay in a stock of salt fish so that we could winter over. The first order of business for the hunters was to hunt and trap enough game to last the winter, supplementing our supply of salt fish. Our blessing was that fish abounded, especially large cod. Oyster beds were so massive that we truly believed that they could never be exhausted. We could forage for wild berries and fruits, and we were convinced that we would not need to starve as long as we could live off this plentiful land. Chepi was a godsend in helping us to know the land, finding edible plants, lending her knowledge of game patterns, and methods of preserving food. Our lives settled into a routine of sorts. I continued to look for medicinal plants in this new territory, and I became more proficient dealing with the medical needs of our small group, which actually began to flourish as the months went on.

It was not long before Margaret became pregnant with our first child together. We were excited beyond words when little Anna was born. Life is both precious and fragile, especially in a primitive land where disease and violence seemed to abound. Yet we found delight in our growing community. The founding principles which we espoused seemed to be taking root. Adams, Hancock, and Gerry rose up as natural leaders, and we formed a governing body that reflected the will of the governed, and seemed to provide us with the peace to be able to go about our lives with freedom from want and freedom from oppression, both political and religious.

This contrasted with what was happening in Kensington's new settlement just outside of Jamestown in Virginia. We had heard reports of growing violence as Kensington imposed his financial will on people. Tobacco did indeed grow well in Virginia, and his plan of slave routes as part of a trading triangle with England, Africa, and Virginia took root. I rejoiced that we had made the decision to start our new life where we did.

Part III – Twenty Years Later, 1646

Many of the accounts in this section have been derived from notes and journals of the participants. I am deeply grateful to those people whose detailed and meticulous records, notes, and letters allowed me to chronicle much of the following activity of Joseph Shepherd, in this time when I was physically absent from my friend on his journey.

Chapter 48

Much had transpired over the years as my family grew. Anna was now over nineteen years old, and her older stepbrother, Jacob, was now a fine young man of twenty-five. He learned to love the sea, and he was sailing under the tutelage of his "uncle" Edwin. Edwin, now just over sixty years old, was still venerated as a sailing man. He had captained numerous trips between England and America, and was the most trusted captain on those routes.

Captain Braden had died over fifteen years ago when another bout of smallpox swept into our area, now known as Boston. Albert Adams was still living with Henry Adams and his family, having actually shown some progress in his seizure problems. Shepherd was keeping us apprised of medical advances on the Continent, and I suspected that these advances were actually his own ideas that he attributed to the "growing medical and scientific community" in Europe at the time. Shepherd had instructed Albert to get plenty of rest, and to take the powdered bacopa leaf that he had sent to us many years ago. Albert showed enough improvement that he was able to help take care of some of the children in the community while parents worked in the fields, fished, hunted, etc. In fact, it was in the care of Albert Adams that his nephew, John, met my little Anna. Lifelong childhood friends, they married in 1645, and made Margaret and me grandparents in 1646 with a son named John.

Chepi and Kelley had no more children, having lost two in childbirth. Chepi nearly succumbed with the last child she lost, but survived by, clearly, the grace of God. Kimi ran off with a French trapper when she was just over fifteen years old. Kelley, worried for her safety, tracked them down over a period of almost six months, almost losing his health over the ordeal. When he caught up with the trader, he saw that Kimi had been abused by him, and had miscarried a child herself. Beside himself with rage, Kelley engaged the much younger man in a fight. The details of this encounter have changed somewhat over the years, with the account of Kimi and Kelley differing just a little as to how the fight played out. There was no disagreement over the final result, which ended with the trader (Lehane, they called him) bleeding badly and with a bone protruding from his forearm, running as best he could into the woods. He was found some weeks later by some Algonquin warriors who finished what Kelley had started. Chepi had kept her contacts in the Algonquin community, and justice seemed to happen somehow when Chepi was in need.

Shepherd was a faithful writer, and we exchanged letters very regularly. His writings in fact were voluminous and detailed – the reason that I am able to convey many of his adventures. His journeys and his work always seemed to involve the leaders in Europe's scientific and political communities.

Upon his return in 1626, Shepherd had taken up Harvey's offer to live with him and also to assist him in his position as physician to the King, now Charles I. There Shepherd was in a position to mix with men like the Irishman Robert Boyle, whom Shepherd tutored for a while when Boyle and his father visited London. Shepherd discussed with Boyle the ideas about the expansion properties of gasses and how temperature and pressure affected the process. Shepherd wrote about our experiment with smallpox vaccination, and it was included in a publication of the Royal Society in 1639, although it was met with much criticism. It remained, however, as a topic that stayed in the discussion of the scientific community.

As part of the arrangement that Harvey had proposed, Shepherd helped Harvey write *De Motu Cordis*, which fully explained Harvey's theory of the circulation of blood in the human body.

Shepherd visited Galileo in Italy when Galileo was under house arrest for his controversial theories about the earth's orbit of the sun. Shepherd, while on the Continent, visited Blaise Pascal, with whom he had kept a lively conversation about religious as well as scientific matters. Pascal, a devout Jansenist, was insistent on the strictest definition of God's wrath toward those who do not follow the rigid, albeit confusing paths outlined by a God who was not easily pleased. Indeed, Pascal took to wearing an iron girdle with small spikes under his cloak so that he could, on occasion, press the girdle and produce pain, which reminded him of his sinful nature that needed to be suppressed and punished. Shepherd had explained that Jesus had taken care of such punishment, but Pascal was unmoved, preferring not to trust entirely in such provision, but trusting only that his own nature was almost beyond redemption.

Pascal believed that the Jesuits were almost heretical in their beliefs that man had great freedom in pursuing scientific knowledge, even if it may refute traditional church teachings. He saw Jesuits as libertines and pope-pleasers, having lost the rigid discipline he admired. Shepherd felt compassion toward Pascal, the tortured genius who had come up with mathematical theories that seemed to open a new door for predicting certain outcomes. Ironically, his work on producing a true vacuum was a puzzle and an enigma for traditional thinking, which held that vacuum states were antithetical to God's design. Shepherd merely took this as part of God's grand design that man could work at, but never completely explain. This was part of Shepherd's genius. He felt comfortable in ambiguity that led to more research on truth. He did not believe that God was so easily displaced by science, and he saw no inherent problems in both scientific knowledge and God's grand design. As long as one remembered who they were relative to God, one could pursue a life of exploration and questioning, which, of course, was no threat to almighty God.

He arrived in England just before his friend Francis Bacon died, and Shepherd told me that he was at his bedside as he passed into the next world.

He reestablished a hospital in London that served the poor, and he was able to engage William Harvey in this occasionally. Imagine having the best medical minds of the times (in my opinion) serving the poorest, most hopeless people in the realm. Shepherd had reminded me that such a thing should be the norm in a world that does not judge the worth of a person by their personal fortune.

As physician to King Charles with Harvey, Shepherd had access to great power. Yet Shepherd always believed that power only defined character.

"What does one do with power?" he said. "A man of character will help to give power to others, not save it for one's personal benefit."

Thus began a period of tension, and finally alienation from King Charles. Charles' belief that his position was directly given from God did not seem to bother Shepherd. As long as that power was used to benefit those he governed, Shepherd was satisfied and supportive. But Charles, arrogant, entitled, and lazy, seemed to only impose hardships on people, and his motive was to maintain his power as King. He failed to convene Parliament and took his own counsel. Shepherd had taken the brazen step to confront the king, in private, to be sure, but in direct terms. Charles, taken aback by Shepherd, was indignant, but he also did not take the step Shepherd expected – to remove him from the court.

The growing rift between Shepherd and King Charles led Harvey to advise Shepherd that his behavior toward the king was disrespectful and dangerous. Harvey, ever the political genius, knew how to curry favor as well as how to avoid trouble. It seemed that Shepherd had the disconcerting tendency to speak the truth, no matter whom it was directed toward.

"You are such a masterful physician," said Harvey. "Must you waste that gift by alienating others?"

"Have I alienated you?" asked Shepherd.

"No, my dear Shepherd, you have not. We have done great work together, and I am most appreciative of your contributions to my research and writing. But I fear for your wellbeing! Please be more discreet in your dealings with King Charles, especially in this perilous time. Men you are consorting with would bring down the Crown; then how could we have the stability and peace we need to continue our work?"

Shepherd was silent, then looked at Harvey. "My friend," he said, "we have done good things together, and I do not want to hurt you. However, I am bound by my conscience to speak out against tyranny and injustice. Such behavior often causes discomfort to people, and while I have no argument or disagreement with you, I fear that you too have been hurt by my actions. I ask your forgiveness for that. However, I find that I cannot much longer serve this king who has caused so much pain for so many in England."

"Just consider what I have said, Joseph," said Harvey, seeing that he would not convince Shepherd of anything that might go against his convictions. "Do not make any decisions in haste."

"William," said Shepherd, "I would like you to consider joining me in trying to move the heart of this king. We have influence as royal physicians. I am certain of that. Especially you. Are you willing to consider that?"

Harvey, silent himself now, said, "Perhaps."

The adventure that caused Shepherd to end his tenure in London began when he befriended Thomas Rainsborough. Rainsborough and Oliver Cromwell had seen in Shepherd a man who was strong in character, and who saw that people were suffering under the reign of King Charles. Along with Rainsborough, Shepherd helped start a group called the Levellers. Shepherd believed that through the use of pamphlets and petitions to reach the minds of people, they would be able to secure some share of power over their own lives. Indeed, Shepherd had seen the misery of poverty in London for many years. His hospital met the needs of people in the midst of poverty, but if he could help to prevent poverty, wouldn't that be a higher calling?

The Levellers met at the Garter Inn, wearing their distinctive symbols of a sprig of rosemary in their hats and a sea-green ribbon. The aims of this group appealed to Shepherd. They valued religious tolerance, popular sovereignty, and equality before the law. Shepherd saw in this how they valued the dignity of a man, and trusted that an individual was capable of reasonable rule, not needing the dominance of a king who claimed his only accountability was to God. Indeed, Shepherd believed that rulers were under the authority of God, and were placed in that position for the good of people. If this were to be abused, he believed that people had the right to remove an unjust ruler. He did not go as far as some, who believed that the king should be tried and possibly executed. That viewpoint was growing dangerously prevalent, he felt.

207

After one of their meetings at the Garter Inn, Shepherd was walking home in the dark London evening. There was a bit of a chill in the air, and he bundled his coat around him as he walked the few blocks toward home that he knew well. He was suddenly accosted from a dark alley by three men carrying torches.

"Dr. Shepherd?" one asked gruffly.

"Yes, who asks?" replied Shepherd.

"You don't need to know who asks!" replied the stranger.

"Looks like a sprig of rosemary in his hat" said another.

"The physician to the King has a sprig of rosemary in his hat! Can you imagine that?"

"That is high treason," said the third. "Let's take him!"

Chapter 49

Shepherd was whisked away down the alley from which the men had appeared. The men ducked into a stairwell that ran into a cellar. The cellar was connected to a tunnel that led into a maze under several buildings. The torches burned with soot that became choking in the confined spaces of the tunnel. The men had blindfolded Shepherd, and he was led gruffly by a rope that also bound his hands. The three men were moving quickly through the confusing tunnel, guided by an instinct developed over years of use and perfected through repetition, often in flight for their lives.

They finally reached a shabby door, and they pushed through it into a room lit just barely better than the tunnel. Shepherd, still blindfolded, was struck by the smell that offended his nose – burning flesh. Shepherd could hear muffled screams coming from the other side of the room, apparently from someone who was being tortured, but whose screams were almost silenced by a gag.

The men removed Shepherd's blindfold, ensuring that Shepherd could see what was happening to the poor devil in the corner of the room.

"That's what'll happen to you if you don't do what we tell you and answer our questions!" one of them threatened.

"This is what you brigands do to people?" asked Shepherd.

Immediately a hand came across Shepherd's face, knocking him off balance.

"Yes, we do this if we need to," said another. "You are one of the King's physicians and you take care of that filthy robber. Yet you call us brigands! Don't you know that he is the biggest robber in the land? He treats us like we have no rights or no power. He will soon find out!"

"And why are you telling this to me?" asked Shepherd.

"We want you to tell us who in the royal court is still professing loyalty to Charles Stuart, but might really be of a mind with us. We know that many in the court fear Charles and his soldiers, but have loyalty only through fear. We need to know who they are!" said the third member of the team.

"I do not know who that might be," said Shepherd, "but even if I did, I would certainly never tell you."

Another hand came across Shepherd's face, this time drawing blood from his nose.

"What about Harvey?" asked the third member. "Is he loyal to the King?"

"I can tell you this," said Shepherd, "If William Harvey professes loyalty to someone, he remains loyal."

"So he is on the Stuart side," said the third member.

"Well of course," said Shepherd. "He is the King's physician."

"You are a King's physician," said the questioner. "Are you loyal to him?"

"Yes, I am," said Shepherd, "even when I disagree with him."

"So you disagree with him?" asked the questioner, now surprised.

"Yes, I do disagree with him. Often, in fact."

"But you remain loyal to him," countered the interrogator.

"Yes," replied Shepherd.

"Does he remain loyal to you?"

"I suppose he does," said Shepherd. "I have never asked him," he smiled.

"Well, I wonder if he would pay a ransom for you?" mused the third member.

"I would think not," said Shepherd. "Kings do not bend to such rogue antics."

Once again the hand came across Shepherd's face, cutting his cheek.

"Be easy on this fellow; he may be worth some money," said a man from across the room.

"He just said the King will not pay for his ransom, you fool!" barked the rough-handed second member of the group.

"The king may not pay, but his friend Harvey might," said the third member, now warming to the idea of getting some money for his prize sitting before him.

Once they decided to keep Shepherd as a ransom prize, they agreed that they should try to keep him reasonably healthy and unharmed.

"Wash his wounds, and give him some rum," said the third member, whom they called "Whiteman."

Shepherd could see the wretched man being tortured far across the dimly lit room. His screams were still muffled by the gag, but he was weakening by now, and seemed to have little strength left. As the torturer was ready to apply the red-hot poker to the man's already seared arm, Shepherd screamed out, "If you continue to harm that man, you will never see a half-pence of ransom for me!"

Whiteman stopped the torture, incredulous at Shepherd's insolence. He then laughed, "Now how can you have any say in that?"

Shepherd quickly responded, "If you hope to get any money for me, the payer will need to know that I am alive and cared for reasonably. If you harm that man any further, I will surely tell the payer, whether it be Harvey, or anyone else, to not pay you a thing!"

"So, you would sign your own death warrant for that miserable wretch that you do not even know?" asked Whiteman.

"I suspect that you do not know him either, yet you torture him. People have dignity, and you have no reason nor right to torture him or anyone else," said Shepherd.

"We need information from him, and he is unwilling to give it to us. So, we torture him until he does. Some men just have more tolerance than others, but he will eventually give in," Whiteman said smugly. "Why do you care about him?"

"I see that I am talking with a fool," said Shepherd, "and what I say you could not understand no matter if I talked all night. Simply understand that if he is tortured, you will never even get a farthing for my release."

One of the men came over to slap Shepherd again, but Whiteman stopped him.

"Let him be," said Whiteman. "Let Craft go for a bit. Maybe he will be more talkative if we take his gag off," laughed Whiteman, trying to ease the humiliation of giving in to Shepherd's request. Others laughed uneasily also, wondering what was happening. Somehow this new prisoner seemed to be in charge, and it was quite confusing and disturbing.

The torture victim was Oliver Craft. He had a sordid history, and had not been heard from for many years, until he was caught helping a Royalist group in Scotland. He had been essentially running since the days of the mission fire. King Charles had been gathering support in Ireland, Scotland, and even in Holland as his support in Parliament eroded. He was getting increasingly desperate in trying to find arms, men, and money. To do this, he reached out to traditional foes and other Royalist sympathizers wherever he could. Oliver Craft, having no particular allegiance, simply followed schemes where he could get paid. Aging now, he was a pathetic sight. His arm was terribly inflamed and oozing blood and serum. He had lost his hair and his teeth over years of neglect and hard living. He wore rags and was gaunt from hunger. Truth be known, the band of brigands who were torturing him may have done better to simply offer him rum or gin for information. He likely had no real information for them anyway, but he was a convenient target of their bloodlust and revenge.

Shepherd heard the name Craft, and it brought back memories of twenty-some years ago. Was this Oliver Craft? Craft was a known thug at that time, and Shepherd had heard of Edwin Carr's discussion of "Red" Locker and his suspicion about Craft having some involvement in the mission fire.

While Shepherd was thinking of that distant past, Craft called over to Shepherd.

"Why did you do that?" he asked.

"No one should be treated as you were," said Shepherd simply. "Are you Oliver Craft?"

"Aye, that's me," said Craft. "You know me?" he asked.

"Yes, from many years ago, when I was first in London," said Shepherd.

"Then you know about me and my past," Craft said.

"I know stories of you, but I do not know you," said Shepherd.

"Well, them stories are probly true. I done some bad things in my life. That's why I wonder why you done that to save me," he said.

"As I said, no one deserves such treatment," said Shepherd.

"You are Joseph Shepherd, ain't you?"

"Yes, you know me?" asked Shepherd.

"You and William Harvey are the king's physicians, Royalists, I reckon. I don't care myself, but there are a lot of people who hate you, and I know that Charles Stuart is in trouble. How I get paid is by working for people who want trouble. That's what I done all my life," Craft said.

"Some people says that you and William Harvey are geniuses, but some says you two are insane," he laughed. "Which are ya, Shepherd?"

"What do you say I am?" asked Shepherd.

"I say I don't care which; I just know you saved my sorry arse, and that's all I know!" Craft laughed at this despite the obvious suffering he was undergoing from his burn pains.

Whiteman walked over to Craft and kicked him in the leg. "I can't get you to talk even when I burn you, and now you won't stop talking. You got something to say about who is paying you?"

"If I tell you who is paying me, I get killed by them. If I don't tell you, you probly kill me. I reckon I lose either way," said Craft.

"Well, you might be right about that," said Whiteman. "Truth is, I got you here, and I can kill you right now. If you tell me who pays you, that man may not catch you – at least not right away. You got a better chance telling me now, because I am losing my patience with you, no matter what Shepherd says."

"Look," said Craft, "my life is about done anyhow. Give me a good meal, a bottle of gin, and I will tell you who is paying me."

"Why didn't you do this two hours ago?" asked Whiteman.

"Like you says to Shepherd here, you get what you want sooner or later from a man. I give up. All I want is what I said – food and gin and a way out of here."

Whiteman smiled.

"Raymond, get this man some food and a bottle as soon as he tells us what we want to know. Now, Craft, who is the man paying you?"

"Who says it's a man?" he winked. "Could be a woman!"

"Well, is it a woman?" asked Whiteman, now getting irritated.

"Yes, it is a woman. Anne Kensington's her name. Meanest witch in London. Probly kill me, but I reckon that's my problem, not yours."

212

"Where is she now?" asked Whiteman.

"I don't know. I meet a man at the Boar's Head and he pays me. He tells me what I need to do, and I do it. I can't do it no more, anyhow. I'm too old and too sick now. I'm half dead already. I just want to get away now and live out what I got left in peace."

Whiteman left and went over to talk with Raymond in private, leaving Shepherd and Craft alone. Shepherd leaned over to Craft and said, "Do you mean it that you want to live the rest of your life in peace?"

"Yes," said Craft, "I just want to be left in peace now with what time I got left."

"If you want peace, speak the truth," said Shepherd. "Tell me if you had anything to do with the mission fire twenty years ago."

Craft lowered his head.

"I did," he said. "Me and Jim Bidwell done that. We didn't mean for it to happen like it did, but we did it. Worst thing I ever done, and I done some bad things. Probly ruined a life that was already bad. I think about that all the time. Preachers tell me I'm going to Hell for that. I reckon if there is a Hell, I'll find it even without that fire. But that fire haunts me. That is one thing I am really sorry for. Too late for that I reckon…"

Craft trailed off.

"It is never too late, Craft. God can forgive you for that," said Shepherd confidently. "Who put you up to that?"

"'Red' Locker was who paid us, but I'm sure that it was Andrew Kensington. Locker was just Kensington's man – least till he got killed. I don't know who killed him, but I got some ideas. I'm glad you think God can forgive me, Shepherd, but even if God does, other people don't," Craft said.

"Some do not, you're right, but I forgive you," said Shepherd.

Craft was taken aback by this quick response.

"You know what I done. It was the place you built up, and your friend Jacob Carr died in that fire. You lost so much in that fire. How can you forgive me?" asked Craft.

"I have been thinking about that fire for years also," said Shepherd. "I have had time to be angry and hurt, but I need to forgive to be free myself. I forgave the people who started that fire a long time ago. I just now had the chance to tell you."

Craft looked away from Shepherd as he heard his name called. Raymond had fetched a plate for Craft, and he carried with him a bottle of gin.

"We are going to follow you to the Boar's Head tomorrow, but it will be at a distance. You meet with the person who pays you, and then walk away from the tavern. That's all you need to do, and we are done with you. Now, if you want to tell us about other people who pay you, we can give you a bottle of gin every week, maybe food too. If we find that you are not dealing right with us, we'll just kill you. Do you understand?"

213

"I understand," said Craft, "but after I lead you to the Boar's Head, I am done with you and with all of this."

"You are never done in the work you do, Craft. Too many people want to kill you," laughed Whiteman.

"Shepherd, as for you, we want to contact William Harvey about some money to let you go. We are reasonable men, so £500 should be a good start," Whiteman said.

"No, you are most certainly not reasonable men," said Shepherd, "but that notwithstanding, Harvey will be unable to pay such a ransom."

"You are the king's physician. Charles Stuart should pay the money if he wants to keep his royal physician," said Whiteman.

"Sir," said Shepherd, "I am of no value to you if no one will pay for my ransom, and I refuse to ask my friends and colleagues or even the King of England for money for my release. If you plan to kill me, then do it and be done, but you will not profit from my capture."

"Perhaps I will do just that, Shepherd," said Whiteman.

Shepherd was held for several days, unwilling to contact Harvey or anyone else about ransom. Whiteman took it upon himself to send a message to William Harvey that he held Shepherd and expected £500 for his release.

Raymond had followed Craft to the Boar's Head, and the meeting seemed to go as planned. Craft met his contact while Raymond and his men waited outside in an alley. Craft lingered for just a while with the contact, then left the tavern. When the contact, a man named Crouch, left the tavern, he was confronted by Raymond and a small band of rebels. As they moved to grab Crouch, a mob of a dozen armed men converged upon Raymond and his group and overwhelmed them. One was shot in the face and perished immediately. Two others were clubbed down, and Raymond was thrown to the ground and bound. Oliver Craft appeared from the shadows and promptly kicked the downed Raymond square in his back, eliciting a scream from the stricken victim.

"You're a fool to trust a crook like me!" laughed Craft. "Now lead us back to your lair or I will kill you where you lie!" he screamed, the pent up rage of his torture now exploding from him. Raymond stood, shaking. He led them through the maze of buildings to the tunnel, and finally the rebel base.

Crouch took over, with several of his vicious band ready for a fight. Raymond led them to the door, and Crouch quickly kicked it in as his band overwhelmed those inside. Whiteman grabbed for his pistol, but he was clubbed to the ground before he could aim it. Shepherd watched in amazement as Craft came over to him.

"I figured that I owe this to you," he smiled as he got ready to slip out the door, glad to be away from the mess he had been in.

214

Shepherd still had on his sprig of rosemary that identified him as a Leveller. Crouch looked at Shepherd and said nothing. Then he said to Craft, "Take him with you. I am not going to travel with a Leveller. Just get him away from here like we talked about."

Chapter 50

Shepherd headed back to the King's court and found Harvey. He related his experiences and told Harvey that he had no interest in further royal intrigues, and it was time to do what he really wanted – he felt called to rebuild the mission. This is something that Harvey had alluded to in his letter to Shepherd that had been an enticement for Shepherd's return. The idea that the king might help to reestablish the mission was really more Harvey's hope than likely reality. Charles Stuart was more concerned with finding money for his own ventures than spending for the good of his people.

Shepherd was determined to establish a place for the wretched poor that he increasingly encountered. While he had made a great many friends in the natural philosophy community, he was unable to persuade them to support his efforts among the poor. Robert Boyle, the young man whom Shepherd had mentored, showed interest in the effort, and he was able to persuade his father, Richard Boyle, Earl of Cork, to contribute funds toward the building of a new mission. Shepherd also prevailed upon the Levellers to help in the cause, since it fit their belief in the dignity of the individual. However, the notion that poor people were simply living out the consequences of their sin and depravity was a strongly held belief. After all, people reasoned, Jesus himself had said that the "poor will always be with us." They were to be tolerated at best as one of those unfortunate inconveniences of life.

Shepherd found some friendly support from Amos Wesley, who shared the belief that one's faith should be displayed by how well we care for the needs of others. He shared Shepherd's belief that one could best love God by loving other people.

The mission began in a converted stable that had been involved in a fire over twenty years prior – one started by Jacob Carr. Shepherd thought this to be great redemption of Jacob Carr's name, and, in fact, named the mission the Jacob Carr Memorial Mission. With some work, the stable turned out to be suitable for the need. Thomas Browne was a willing partner of Shepherd who shared the belief that humanitarian interests were interests of God himself.

Once again, the genius of Shepherd was applied to medical science. He was curious and innovative in his approach, and, consequently, he was willing to try out methods and medicines that the general public would not tolerate. His patients, poor and desperate, accepted anything he tried. He began his practice of smallpox inoculations on a larger scale. He did surgeries with the use of diethyl ether, a distilled byproduct of ethanol and oil of vitriol. This put patients to sleep during the surgery – a major boon for both patient and surgeon. He used opium as a pain relief, harkening back to the days on the *Intrepid* when we medicated Mr. North after his injuries. He used his tourniquet to reduce the terrible bleeding that accompanied surgeries. He was fastidious about cleanliness, and he required that the area of surgery be cleaned after each surgery, a practice unheard of and ridiculed by others. He required that each patient be treated with care and dignity, believing that such treatment in itself was curative. He incorporated many of the herbs we had seen in America into treatment, relying on the shipments that I would regularly send to him.

People began to talk about the rate at which people were recovering in the Jacob Carr Memorial Mission. The established physicians of the time were quick to criticize the Mission, stating that such claims were outrageous, and that Shepherd was boasting of things he did not know. Yet, as casualties of the sporadic skirmishes of a civil war began to be treated at the Jacob Carr Mission, there was clearly a high rate of success, despite the fact that now only the most serious cases were being sent there.

Oliver Cromwell decided to visit the Carr Mission to see for himself whether this place was a real place of healing or a hokum of some kind. Cromwell had a very clear and narrow view of how God could work. Anything that fell outside his Old Testament viewpoint was likely to be condemned.

Cromwell asked to speak with Shepherd about the methods he used. As he was speaking, a young man and his father came in. They stated that they had come from Rome a few years ago. The father appeared to be in his late fifties, and he was weeping from time to time, speaking in a broken accent. They had been in England several years, but both struggled with the language. The young man was suffering from seizures, and they were crippling him to the point that he could not work. His father, a cobbler, was desperate for a cure for his son. No other physicians could give any relief or even hope.

The young man's father looked at Shepherd with a long gaze. He squinted through his wrinkled eyes at Shepherd, trying to place where he might have seen this man before. As Shepherd examined the young man, he asked if the man, Mario, had ever had a head injury. The father, Julius, said no, not that he had recalled. Mario was unsure, but allowed that everyone has hit their head at some time. Shepherd laughed.

"Indeed, they have," he stated.

Shepherd began to busy himself preparing a mug of water that he produced from a barrel of water brought in from nearby Epsom. The mineralized water seemed to have beneficial effects on seizures and some other maladies. Indeed, many people simply soaked in the natural springs found in Epsom, and claimed benefits to their health.

Then Julius cried out, "Joseph Shepherd! I am Julius Rosello. I met you in Rome many years ago."

Shepherd did not recall ever meeting the man.

"Yes!" said Julius. "You talked with me and my friend Marco. We were poor beggars in rags, sick and destitute. You told us that we needed not money, but healing for our souls, and you directed us to go to the priest after you prayed with us. The sores on my feet eventually went away, and later we were taken in by the priests. They taught me the trade of being a cobbler, and I was able to work. I married, had a son, and my wife died in childbirth with my second child, who also died. Mario and I came to England several years ago, and I found work as a cobbler. We are poor, but we survive. I thank God for you and how you healed me!"

"I am so pleased that you were healed, Julius," Shepherd said, "but it was not I that healed you. God does his work in you. I cannot heal, but I can help to connect you with the One who can!"

Cromwell watched this exchange and seemed taken aback. Cromwell already had deep suspicions about Shepherd, knowing that he had been physician to King Charles. Now he wondered if Shepherd might be using the powers of the Devil to heal. So many people had claimed that Shepherd spent much time alone and that his methods were, at best, unorthodox. Cromwell was suspicious as well as frightened a bit by Shepherd.

"I understand that your methods of treatment are somewhat unusual, Dr. Shepherd," said Cromwell.

"Perhaps by the standards of our current understanding," said Shepherd, "but I believe that in future years the things I do will be common practice."

"What arrogance!" said Cromwell. "You put yourself above the great minds of the age, and you say that years from now people will look upon you as the great mind and innovator?"

"I certainly did not say that, sir," said Shepherd. "I simply stated that these things will be commonplace, not that I am the innovator. Whatever I have, God has given me. My ideas are only because they are inspired by God, my Father and Lord."

"So," Cromwell proceeded, "you say that God has inspired you, given you special knowledge?"

"I don't know that it is special knowledge for me. I believe that God has given this to me to share with the world," replied Shepherd.

"You seem to speak about God in a very intimate way, like you have some special relationship with the Almighty," said Cromwell.

"It is the one we can all have with God. What he desires of us," said Shepherd.

"Are you with the Parliament, with the Royalists, the Levellers – to whom do you swear allegiance?" asked Cromwell.

"I have no particular allegiance to any of those groups, seeing both flaws and virtues in all of them," replied Shepherd.

218

"The day will come, and soon, when you must take a stand, Dr. Shepherd. You have influence, perhaps more than you realize, and you will need to lend that influence to a cause. I pray that you choose wisely," ended Cromwell. He bid Shepherd good day and left the Mission.

Shepherd pondered this uncomfortable conversation with Cromwell. People might expect him to choose sides, and he was not inclined to do so.

Chapter 51

Anne Kensington had continued to age well. She still had an air – a veneer – of grace and beauty. Her actions, however, belied such grace. She had been responsible for numerous rebel deaths as she clung to her royal backing. She had long been separated from Andrew Kensington, yet she maintained a business relationship with him after some years in London making friends the way she knew how.

Anne had been remarkably successful after finding herself alone in London some twenty years prior. She did what she did best – entertaining people of wealth and influence. She connected people to the trade in America, and soon persuaded Andrew that while they were no longer lovers, she could be of value to him in London securing contacts and trade partners. She counted as friends Cardinal Richlieu of France, and his protégé, Cardinal Mazarin. Mazarin, in fact, had a brief but torrid romance with Anne some years earlier, and Mazarin never completely let go of his passion for Anne. Mazarin was useful to Anne, and he gave her access to French trade companies, and exclusive rights to the fur trade, which brought in unimagined wealth to the Crown. The French people would never see the benefit of these profits, but the Kensingtons were deft in arranging alliances with French traders in America. Andrew had known that governmental allegiances were far overshadowed by economic ones.

Anne's mix of coquetry, charm, and lust for power and money allowed her to charm men, manipulate them, and often simply cheat them for her own means. Andrew had grown extremely wealthy in the slave and tobacco trade, and he made periodic trips back to London to ensure his Royalist connections. Anne had become a business partner, while no longer a lover of his. Kensington's health was now quite compromised, and many people believed that he was nearing his death. Speculation grew as to where his wealth might end up. Anne believed that she could still find a way to make much of it accrue to her. Since they had never been divorced, she had a claim to his estate. While Andrew had likely changed his will and excluded her, Anne was up for the fight in court. Indeed, her access to attorneys and the court system was now every bit as good as Andrew's, if not better. She was generally more feared than respected, and the fact that she was a woman with power made her even more of a target for her enemies.

Anne decided that she would meet with Andrew when he came to London. His latest trip back to Europe included a visit to France, where Anne had arranged for him to meet with Cardinal Mazarin to discuss an arms trade.

The French, winding down their involvement in the war that had consumed the Continent for nearly thirty years, were in need of weapons of quality. English gunsmiths were proficient in making musketry, but the French had trouble procuring these arms due to the distrust that existed between the governments. Anne Kensington was able to persuade Mazarin that she could arrange for shipments of muskets to the French through Gibraltar. Andrew Kensington had arranged to purchase one thousand fine flintlock muskets from Gibson & Sons Firearms. These newer weapons were shorter, lighter, and faster to load than previous models, and they were much sought after. Indeed, the English Crown forbade their export due to the superior design, and the fear of the potential that they would be used against England. The Kensingtons were not saddled with such concerns, and they found ready buyers in France. Upon Andrew's return from Versailles, and his finalizing the arms trade, Anne planned to meet with him to discuss his estate.

Andrew met Anne at her lavish home just outside of London.

"My, I have put you up in fine style all these years, have I not?" greeted Andrew as he saw Anne rise to meet him. Anne managed a gracious smile even as she nearly bit her tongue through. Andrew's "support" paled in comparison to her own business earnings, which allowed this estate. She had supported herself quite handsomely without Andrew's help. However, she had never declined the money he sent to her over the years, either.

"Andrew, how wonderful to see you after all this time," she gushed. "Has it been two years since I have seen you?"

"I don't know," he said gruffly. Andrew had seen Anne lay on the charm, and she was at it now with him. He knew her too well.

Anne was struggling to maintain her charm. This was partly due to how shocked she was to see the ghostly Andrew. He looked old, thin, and frail. His gray hair had mostly given way to baldness, and he had not bothered to wear his wig. He apparently did not care anymore how he appeared. His teeth were rotting, and he was difficult to look at now. Anne, only eleven years his junior, now looked young enough to be his granddaughter.

"Let's get to the business at hand," said Andrew. "You wanted to talk with me about the gun deal with Cardinal Mazarin. I suppose you want to know how much money you will make," he said matter-of-factly.

Anne, now no longer able or willing to keep up her façade, answered him directly.

"Yes, Andrew, I want to know how much money I will get on this deal. I also want to know the contents of your will. I expect that you have tried to cut me out of your inheritance."

Andrew smiled. He saw that he had gotten to her and that she gave up trying to charm him. The conversation would now be brutally direct.

"That is better," he said. "I have no intention of leaving you a farthing in my will, but I suspected, as you now tell me, that you already knew that."

221

Anne did not blink. She knew that he would respond this way.

"Well then, Andrew, I see that we have a bit of a problem. Do you really want people to know of your involvement in burning down the Franciscan mission? Or about how you arranged the murder of Red Locker?"

"I did not have Red Locker murdered and you know that!" he screamed. "In fact, I understand that your old lover, Edwin Carr, did that deed, without any help from me!"

"Very well," said Anne, "I suppose the murder of Jacob Carr and the destruction of a mission to help the poor will suffice to bring down enough public scorn on you."

Andrew peered at Anne with disdain.

"And if I get blamed for these things, do you think that you will come away unharmed?" he asked. "You lose the money from the deal with Mazarin, and some of our other ventures. You would also be implicated in these things as my wife."

"Andrew," said Anne with an innocent air, "women are delicate and do not get involved in such tawdry things. People will no more see me as part of your heinous crimes than they can see me as a woman capable of success. You yourself said that I live this way because of your largesse. Indeed, I have let it be known that you are the successful business man who keeps me as his younger London toy. People have no idea of how I do things or even what I do. I am just the Lady Kensington, kept woman of Lord Kensington, who treats his wife like a mistress. I am so mistreated!" she smiled coyly.

Lord Kensington replied, "You are clever; everyone knows that. However, there are people like Oliver Craft who know better, and they will be quick to tell their stories about you!"

Anne laughed.

"Yes, Andrew, Oliver Craft can tell stories about both of us, and who believes such a fool? Those who can tell stories on us are not believable, but people will believe me. I have been making friends in high places for many years while you were in America making your fortune. Who are your friends here in London?" she asked.

Andrew answered, "Your 'friends' do not care for you, they fear you."

"So be it," said Anne. "In fact, so much the better. They should fear me, but because they do, they will protect me if I need it."

Andrew pondered for a moment. Anne was not really serious, he reasoned. She was just negotiating. He almost kicked himself for getting caught up again in her games. "So, Lady Kensington, kept woman and helpless princess," Andrew mocked, "what is your offer?"

Anne smiled at this.

"Just like old times for a little while," she said. "We play the games and spar with one another. When we were a lot younger it was exciting to do this and we often ended up in bed after the battle. Those days are long gone, but it can still be fun matching wits with you!" she said lightly. Then the smile vanished, and she said, "My offer is this – one half of the estate, and I be named as a director in the London & Western Company."

Kensington was a canny negotiator himself, and he did not make any reply or reaction to this offer at first.

"Too much," he said. "If you want to be named as a director in London & Western, you must become a financial partner, risking some capital in the venture. No one plays for free," he said calmly.

Anne raised her eyebrow at this.

"I know very well that no one can benefit without risk," she said. "But as your wife, I will have your estate when you die and you know that. Changing your will does not stop me from taking it to the court."

"Yes, you do that, Anne, you do that. By the time the barristers take their cut of your fortune, you will have nothing left," replied Kensington.

At this point, Anne became weary of the argument that had at first been invigorating.

"Very well," she said. "We can discuss this tomorrow."

"If you want to keep discussing this tomorrow, I will do that," said Kensington, "but the answer will be the same. Try to blackmail me or steal my fortune in the courts when I die; I do not care. Your insolence and badgering have made up my mind. You will get none of my inheritance. We may negotiate your share of the arms deal, but that is money you have earned. So, do what you will, but I will not change my will back, nor will I give you a settlement."

With that, he left the room and returned to his carriage outside. He instructed the driver to take him back to his lodgings.

Anne was furious at the imperious old Kensington. Perhaps there was another way to deal with this old crook...

Chapter 52

Shepherd's letters over the years had been a constant source of joy and wonder to us. He was a faithful writer, obsessed with details, so I almost felt that I had been with him all those years. But I missed him, and I missed the adventures that we had as younger men. He had asked me to bring Margaret with me to visit him in London, and to see the mission, which again was flourishing. I had always declined, knowing that Margaret would not want to be away from our grandchild, and our daughter.

One day, Margaret said to me, "Luke, you have seemed restless, and I know that Joseph has invited you often to see him. Perhaps we should take his offer, and visit him and the mission. There are people we have not seen for over twenty years in England, and I know that you would love to see Joseph before you die. Of course I want to see him also, but I know how close you are to him. Would you like to take a trip back to England?"

I smiled at this and said, "Am I that close to death, dear?"

Margaret laughed and pinched my nose. "You may be if you get me angry!" she laughed.

Indeed, I had been restless, and I could not determine the cause nor the solution to that. I had done well in practicing medicine in America. That was perhaps in large part because I received the tutelage of one Dr. Joseph Shepherd, who kept me apprised of the latest medical happenings in Europe. His ideas on prevention of disease were remarkable. As always, he was meticulous about having a clean area for surgery, wound cleansing, and debridement, use of alcohol to clean wounds and equipment, and never using the same instrument on another patient without first cleansing it thoroughly. Other physicians scoffed at my practices, but my patients almost always had better outcomes than others, and I got a reputation as being, perhaps, the finest surgeon in New England. I was busy much of the time. However, I found time to lecture at Harvard College in medicine and biology.

Margaret continued, "I took the liberty of speaking with Jacob and Edwin last week after we had them over for supper. They are planning another trip to London next month on the *Queensgate*. She will be loaded with salt cod and pelts, mostly. There will be room for forty passengers. The best news is that several of our friends will be going on something of a governing mission – Thomas Hancock and Thomas Gerry will be representing the Massachusetts Bay Colony in discussions with the King about the stirrings of war in England and the effects on our colony. I know that the trip itself will be an adventure!"

I was struck by Margaret's excitement about the trip. I knew that taking a trip with her beloved Jacob was dear to her heart. But she also knew, better than I, that I needed to return to England at least once before I died. She also knew I needed to see Shepherd again. I knew that I could arrange to have my patients seen by the young physicians whom I was training. I could arrange my affairs for the trip back to England.

"I will be honored to escort my wife to England," I said.

"Of course!" she said.

Our trip to England was blessed with good winds and good weather. The trip east was always faster than the trip west, due to the wind patterns and the salutary effects of the warmer stream of currents, which aided a ship's passage immensely. The experienced captains like Edwin Carr were masters of finding and riding this "river of water in the ocean" and taking days off the length of the trip to England.

My talks with Hancock and Gerry were fascinating. Their beliefs about governance in the colony were at odds with King Charles and Parliament. While there were those in Parliament who were inclined to give some latitude to the governors in the colony, Charles was firmly against any such thinking. Gerry and Hancock knew that the trouble in England at this point was possibly beyond repair. Parliament was increasingly independent of the Crown, and Cromwell and the Roundheads were ready to once again go to war in the struggle for justice and religious freedom. Hancock and Gerry believed that while England was caught up in the thrall of civil war, Massachusetts might find itself free of meddling from mother England. Commerce was beginning to prosper, and the population was swelling with refugees from England's poverty and religious upheaval. America, they believed, was going to be a place of God's special calling and provision. As some of the preachers were saying in America, it was God's "beacon on the hill," a place of blessing and abundance especially prepared and set apart for those who sought unfettered worship of God and freedom. Some even likened America to the Promised Land, the destination prepared for God's chosen people on their journey away from an evil captivity in Egypt.

Upon our arrival in London we found a place vastly different from the one we had left over twenty years ago. Edwin Carr had arranged for us to stay with him and Jacob at his quarters at the Massachusetts Bay Company. After a day of rest from our journey, we arranged to go to the mission to see Shepherd. We had not had time to inform him that we were coming to visit, but I had been assured by him in previous letters that he had no travel plans due to his busy schedule at the mission. Our visit would be a happy surprise!

Margaret and I approached the mission early in the morning as breakfast was being prepared. Just like the first time I approached the mission, I was struck by the smells that met my nose. This time, however, there was not the stench of rotting food and diseased bodies. There was the smell of fresh bread baking in the kitchen. Shepherd insisted that the people who were served in the mission, when able, must serve others who were coming in. He believed that this allowed them to have the dignity of service to others – a factor in complete healing.

I walked into the door from a little alley just off Livery Street. Margaret told me to greet him alone at first. Edwin and Jacob stayed with her and showed her the area around the mission. I approached the kitchen area and saw a baker kneading dough to make another loaf of bread.

"Pardon me, sir, could you tell me where I might find Dr. Shepherd?" I asked.

The man turned, hands covered in sticky dough, and flour dusting his clothes. His beard was white flecked with flour, and he broke into a huge grin.

"Dr. Greene, are you here to help me bake bread?" he asked.

I rushed forward to embrace him, immediately becoming a dusty, sticky mess.

"Joseph," I said, "you are now a baker?"

"I am so blessed to see you, Luke!" he said. "You decided after all these years to visit me, but give me no warning! A man my age could drop dead with shock!" he said teasingly.

"Shepherd, you are no older than me. But as I think of it, my wife told me I need to see you before I die. We are aging, aren't we?" I replied.

"Yes," he said. "Let me finish this loaf of bread so that we can have a nice long visit before we pass away!"

"I will get Margaret, Jacob, and Edwin. I am certain that they are anxious to see you as well."

"Yes, please do that," he said. "This is a wonderful day!"

We sat for hours catching up on our years of separation. He told me of his abduction, his confrontation with Oliver Cromwell, his disaffection with King Charles, and the decisions that he, and many others, would soon need to make regarding allegiance to the Crown or Parliament.

I told him of our grandchild's latest development, my practice in medicine in America, and the successes I saw with his methods. Jacob, now a fine sailor and traveler in his own right, talked of world trade, and the slave trade, which was growing. While he and Edwin Carr had left the employ of the London & Western Trading Company for the Massachusetts Bay Company, they still ran into some interference from old Andrew Kensington and his unholy band of traders and thieves. Indeed, Jacob told of a trip just last year where he was sailing a ship bound for Virginia, then to the West Indies, which involved salt cod bound for the slaves in the Caribbean. This had become a rather large market for the slavers, who fed plantation slaves with the cheaper lots of salt cod that did not meet London standards. Kensington's people at London & Western did not like the price of the cod, which they had originally agreed to. When they declined full payment for the shipment, Jacob unloaded half the cargo of fish at Jamestown, and readied his ship to sail back to his Boston port with the other half. He had reasoned that Kensington's price was half of what he had promised. He said that "London & Western can deliver this cargo to the West Indies."

About one day's journey out heading home, his ship, the *Boston*, was overtaken by a schooner raider equipped with just four cannon. The fast, agile raider was built to prey upon unarmed trading ships – "a small pirate ship," Jacob called it. The little schooner fired upon the *Boston* twice, then moved in to make another firing run at the defenseless *Boston*.

"The schooner moved closer and closer, wanting to board us and seize my ship," Jacob continued. "I hoisted a white flag to surrender. I was hoping that this move would spare my ship damage as well as loss of life."

Shepherd was completely absorbed in this tale, and burst forth with a question before Jacob could finish.

"What happened next?" Shepherd blurted.

Jacob looked a bit sheepish as he answered.

"They honored my white flag, assuming that they had an easy cargo," said Jacob.

"So they seized your ship?" he asked.

"Well, they honored the white flag, but I did not," smiled Jacob. "As the schooner pulled up alongside us, three of my crew and I put our hands out to show we had no weapons. They pulled closer and told me to receive the extended ropes to bring the ships closer so that they could board. We stepped forward to receive our unwelcome visitors and help with the grappling hooks that they extended. Upon my word, my three officers and I fell to the deck, and fifteen of my crew fired a volley of musket fire into the crew of the schooner. Immediately upon firing, they were handed fifteen more loaded muskets, which were then again unloaded on the brigands. I left out the detail that I hire only the best marksmen I can find," he smiled. "The crew of the schooner was decimated by those volleys. If there were any left on board, they did not show themselves, for we heard no more sounds from that vessel. The "captain" – dirty pirate he was – was killed quickly by the first volley fired. We then towed the schooner back to Boston, where it has become part of our fleet."

"Another of Lord Kensington's schemes to rob, thieve, and destroy," I said. "I came close at one time to being a part of that awful group."

Margaret showed surprise.

"You were going to join his company?" she asked.

"Until I received a better offer from Dr. Shepherd, yes, I considered it. Don't you remember me discussing that with you at the Boar's Head when I first met you?" I asked.

She blushed.

"I try to forget about who I was then," she said softly.

227

"You were no different than me," I said.

"None of us needs to worry about our past," said Shepherd. "What is forgiven is gone, and we are all forgiven as we acknowledge our sins," he said.

Shepherd and I stayed at the Mission while the others went back to our quarters. I wanted to talk with him further about his plans, especially in light of the coming of another civil war, which we all knew was coming.

"On what side do you land?" I asked Shepherd.

"I take no sides," said Shepherd.

"You may not choose sides, Joseph, but they will choose you," I said. "You are a man of influence, a man of science, and a man of integrity. People will follow you, and the sides are going to chase you."

"Cromwell said something of the same sort," said Shepherd. "I am not sure I agree with that, however.

"Joseph," I interrupted, "you have written in medical and scientific journals, you have ministered to the King of England, met with leaders and travelled to many countries. You have more influence and power than you realize. Even now, Thomas Hancock and Thomas Gerry are meeting with King Charles, and they told me that you have had profound influence on them. They are trying to build a new future in America, and some believe that such ideas have been planted by you. William Bradford spoke of this a great deal in his Mayflower Compact writings. Henry Adams attributes to you his ideas of a democracy which can govern without the entangled mischief of the Crown. John Milton has written to Henry Adams in a letter just several months ago that you were an influence on him in his ideas of republicanism and governance by will of the people. I did not realize that you have been so naïve in your own influence," I concluded.

"If that is all true, I suppose that I am flattered, but influence is not my goal, unless it be for what God's will is," he said.

"Joseph, everyone who has an opinion on the governance of England and America believes that they are led by God, you know that. Someone must be right, but some must be wrong. I do think, my friend, that if you come down on some side in this conflict, I would wager that God is on your side!" I chuckled.

Shepherd laughed at this as well.

"Please do not wager on it, Luke," he said. "You never did very well in that area, as I recall!"

Chapter 53

I don't know if Shepherd would have ever decided on what position he could or should take in the growing likelihood of another civil war. He was close to William Harvey, who still had ties to the Crown, but he too was disinclined to ally with either faction. It was now April, 1648, and tensions were heightened between Parliament and the Crown. There were rumors of battles in Scotland between Scottish troops employed by King Charles to confront Cromwell's New Model Army.

I was with Shepherd the next morning after he had asked me to join him in seeing his patients for the day. One could never know who might come through the door next – a poor wretch who had a wasting disease, a stabbing victim from a tavern brawl, or a young waif whose intent was to beg money, or, as commonly happened, to try and steal money.

A wagon pulled up outside the mission with two soldiers from the New Model Army. The soldiers had apparently been ambushed by a roving gang who were followers of the Crown. Quite probably, they were from a group with which Shepherd was familiar – followers of Oliver Craft and the men he worked for.

One of the men was stabbed in the back, and while in pain, he was not likely to die from his wounds. The other man had been beaten with a club, and he was in much worse condition. His head was bloody, and his nose was broken and displaced. The grenadier in charge of the small cohort of soldiers who accompanied the injured men was intent on getting quick help for his fallen soldiers.

"Be quick now," he barked at Shepherd. "These men were hurt in the service of Parliament and the English people."

I took some offense at the insolence shown to my friend Shepherd. Having been in America for so many years, I was shocked that some lowly military man would so disrespect a physician. I certainly was not used to such treatment, and, in fact, had come to expect deference.

"See here, man," I said. "You are to speak with respect to people in authority. As a man of the military I would expect more from you."

The soldier was startled, and I suspected that he was trying to decide what to say.

"I beg your pardon, sir," he finally said. "I just want my men to be cared for."

"And they will be," I said.

Shepherd looked at me and smiled but said nothing. He was already assessing the situation with the new patients. After treating the men, Shepherd suggested that we watch both of them for a time at the mission, and he told the officer of the New Model Army of our plan. The officer, now much more compliant, thanked us for our work, and told us that he would pass on to Mr. Cromwell how helpful we had been.

"In the coming weeks," he said, "I suspect that you will be getting more of our men, but a lot more of the filthy Crown-followers!" he laughed.

"We are not looking for patients, and I detest the war that is looming," said Shepherd.

The officer then looked at Shepherd and said, "Who do you back?"

"It seems that is all people want to know," said Shepherd. "I back the policies that ensure peace and safety to people."

"Well then, you must be a follower of Cromwell!" the officer said.

"Yes, well, believe what you would like," said Shepherd as he turned to go back into the mission.

I spent the next several days with Shepherd at the mission, and he told me of his travel to visit Queen Christina of Sweden, and his eventual meeting with Rene Descartes.

"You would like Descartes," said Shepherd. "He is a man of faith, with clearly a first-rate mind for science. As such, he seems to be suspected by people of faith as well as men of science. Odd, isn't it, that one can be held in low regard by those who must have a clear choice of viewpoints?" he concluded.

I suspected that there was some self-revelation taking place in that statement. I had seen the same for Shepherd. His strong faith drew some people who wanted simple answers to hard questions. At the same time, his willingness to have scientific curiosity offended those same people.

His friend Descartes elevated the thinking of people. His belief in the power of the inquisitive natural mind put the power of the Church against him. Yet he was a deeply spiritual man. Shepherd saw this as another marker of God's plan to give man a searching mind, for at the end of that search through a complex and marvelously made world, surely man must find the Creator of it. Shepherd embraced science and believed that it was a clear sign of God's hand. How better to know the world and those in it than to follow the natural wonder of creation. Shepherd's search had taken him to the capitals of Europe, meeting with kings and queens, philosophers, writers, even popes. Yet he received his greatest satisfaction working with these poor people of London in this mission.

I was nearing my time to take Margaret to visit some old friends from my past. She knew little of my distant past, my first marriage, and the people whom I knew from my schooling. I was feeling that this was my last visit to England, now that America was home, and I needed to see some people before

I died. The rumblings of a mind starting to prepare for a next phase of life, I supposed.

Late one night, as I prepared to tell Shepherd of my plans, we were startled by the appearance of Charles Stuart, the King of England standing in our front door!

Shepherd addressed him, "My Lord, how can we be of service to you?"

Shepherd had probably repeated those words many times as Royal Physician with Harvey, so it came naturally in a most unnatural setting.

"It appears as if I am needing to flee for my life," he said, but he was eerily calm as he said those alarming words.

"Is it true?" asked Shepherd.

"Yes," replied the king, "I am told that Parliament has issued a writ ordering me to appear in that chamber. I have avoided receiving a copy of that writ, so it is just hearsay at this point. If I fail to appear, I could be taken into custody by Cromwell's soldiers. If that happens, I fear that harm may befall the Crown. Can you imagine?" he asked.

While I thought about the implications of this, Shepherd was much more aware of the danger to the king. He had been observing this slow deterioration of reverence for the Crown, which had now gotten to the place of utter contempt for many. There had been some rumors that Parliament would be taken over by the more radical types, and that, indeed, the king's welfare might be in jeopardy.

"May I seek refuge here until my quarters in Colchester Castle are ready?" he asked.

"Yes, your majesty," replied Shepherd quickly. "There is no official notice that you are under arrest, so I can offer asylum without legal repercussion, I believe."

Shepherd had not only eased the king's troubled mind, he afforded him the gesture of calling him by a name seldom used anymore – "your majesty." The tone of the country had become simpler in every way. Puritan thought and the Protestant influence in general had led to the desire to shed any deference to images of power and wealth. Catholic and papal authority was seen as unscriptural, as the Bible began to be read more by common people. French and Spanish monarchs who were under the influence of the Catholic realm were despised and feared. Charles Stuart was seen as at least friendly with Catholic thinking if not actually supportive. The reaction against privilege and wealth was becoming angry, even lethal. Charles Stuart was convinced of the divine right of kings, and he could not imagine why people were so ready to depose, maybe even kill him. Yet he knew that his life was likely in danger.

Shepherd took Charles around to the side entrance of the mission in the alley as the king's footmen unloaded a few trunks. On this journey, the king only carried the most basic needs, while much of the rest of his belongings were sent ahead to Colchester Castle. Actually, the king had misled us just a bit, as we later found out. Colchester Castle was perfectly ready for him to go directly there. His stop at the mission was to see if his entourage to the castle was being followed. If the supply train were captured, he would still be safe in the mission. He was accompanied by only three royal guards in order to keep the secret mission as simple as possible. Charles believed that he was relatively safe in the mission, since any leaks might disclose the trip to Colchester Castle, but not likely his stay at the mission.

I wondered how long we would be harboring the fugitive king. Once again, it appeared that Shepherd and I were in a very dangerous spot. Shepherd went about his business of tending to the sick, taking in weary and wounded souls from the street. King Charles of England had now become just our latest wounded and weary soul.

Chapter 54

Anne and Andrew Kensington had found a way to complete the deal with Cardinal Mazarin for the shipment of muskets to the French government. She and Andrew profited handsomely from the deal, even if some of the profits had to go to the men on the docks who loaded the guns, and the trade brokers who helped to label the crates as "scrap lead."

Anne was in no mood to be beaten by the old man, however, in the matter of his will. She felt entitled to half his estate for having put up with him and his arrogance and foul treatment for so many years. She also believed that King Charles owed something to her for all she had done to help defend the monarchy from the villainous rebels that Parliament now supported. Charles was in no position to recompense her now.

Her contacts within the king's court had told her of the king's recent flight for Colchester Castle. Her best source in the court told her the actual truth – that Charles would be at the Jacob Carr Mission for some time before the final trip to Colchester, as a way to get the rebels off his trail. Anne saw this as a unique opportunity that could resolve her problems. If her clever new plan worked, she could curry favor with the Parliament, gain revenge on Charles, and exact justice from Andrew Kensington. She just needed a little help and perhaps a lot of luck.

Malcolm Spencer was a Royalist sympathizer who was in the employ of Anne. Lately, he had been vacillating in his support for Charles, and had told Anne that he could see that the landscape was changing rapidly. She had asked him to invite Andrew to a secret meeting at the Jacob Carr Mission. The ruse was to lure Andrew to the mission as a "safe place to meet which no one would suspect," in order to discuss some sensitive matters about the Crown. Andrew Kensington was never loyal to any particular system of government, whether it be monarchy, republic, or some combination. What he did *not* want was anarchy. He needed stability of government so that his commercial activities could proceed. He would pay or bribe whomever he needed, and he did not care whose pocket it went into. As long as he could proceed without disturbance, he was willing to pay a certain price for the unfettered practices he enjoyed.

Spencer had sent Lord Kensington a letter through an intermediate asking him to meet at 10 p.m. at the Jacob Carr Mission on the evening of May 12th. The topic would be a discreet discussion of those men closest to King Charles and how they could be used to influence the King to abdicate the throne. Charles' eighteen-year-old son could be placed on the throne in his father's stead, and he would be much more pliable than his father.

Lord Kensington took the bait and decided to meet Malcolm Spencer at the mission. Kensington was intrigued by the idea of being a kingmaker. All his life he had done business with kings, financiers, bankers, even cardinals, but he had not been in the position of actually changing a regime. His desire to wield this power overcame any sense of danger that might be attached to it.

Near 10 p.m., Spencer arrived at the Mission and waited for Kensington. Shortly thereafter, Kensington arrived with a bodyguard. This was not unusual for Kensington, as he had advanced in years and felt increasingly vulnerable physically. Spencer noted the fact that Kensington was not alone, and while he was not surprised at this, he decided to feign anger and put Kensington on the defensive right away.

"Kensington, you fool! I told you to come alone," said Spencer.

"You did not say that, Mr. Spencer. I am accompanied these days by my guard. Besides, why should I trust you?" he asked.

"By calling this a secret meeting, one which requires the utmost discretion, you should have known to come alone!" said Spencer. "He is here now, so let it be. I must be certain that he can be trusted, however.'

"He has been my personal guard for over five years," said Kensington. "He can be trusted."

"Very well," said Spencer. "Keep your man here to be on guard for us, and come with me down the alley to the side entrance."

"Very well," said Kensington, and he instructed his man, Coleman, to stand guard as they walked toward the Mission.

"King Charles will be there to discuss some details about his escape. He will need our help to ensure that his son, Charles, will be named as his successor. Many of us believe that Parliament will accept this gesture in order to save the Monarchy, and also to avert another, bloodier, civil war," concluded Spencer.

Kensington looked at Spencer, incredulous.

"Are you saying that King Charles is here?" he said.

"Of course he is. I was quite sure you knew that," Spencer lied.

"And he is planning abdication on his own?" continued Kensington. "You led me to believe that he needed to be convinced of that idea."

"Things change, Andrew," said Spencer as he walked closer to the side entrance of the mission.

"Then why do you need me now?" asked Kensington.

"Money, connections in Holland where he is seeking asylum, and perhaps one of your merchant ships to give him cover as he travels," Spencer concluded.

Kensington was overwhelmed with the suddenness of this information.

"All those things will take me time," Kensington finally stammered.

Spencer smiled, happy that Kensington seemed to be in agreement with the plan, and said, "Of course, Andrew, but we do not have much time. Now let us speak with the King and discuss these things."

Spencer then lifted his lantern high above his head as if to see a bit further down the dark alley. As soon as the lantern was lifted, four men emerged from the shadows and grabbed Kensington. Another four men had already grabbed Coleman, gagged him, and dragged him into the bushes.

"What goes here?" demanded Kensington.

Spencer gave no answer, but said to the four hooded men who had Kensington," Here is the traitor who wants to help Charles Stuart escape. If you follow me, I will lead you to 'your king,'" he said, dripping sarcasm.

"That is why we came here," said the leader of the group. "We don't care much about this old man, but if he is part of the plot, we'll take him too," he said.

"Indeed he is!" said Spencer. "He was just telling me about his plan to spirit Charles out of the country to Holland in one of his merchant ships. Lady Anne Kensington can verify all of this if he ever makes it to a trial," said Spencer.

"Trials ain't what we are here for," said the hooded man. "We came for Charles Stuart, present King of England, but soon prisoner of the New Model Army."

Kensington by now was also gagged and bound as he feebly struggled against his captors. The soldiers banged on the door of the mission. It did not take too long for a response. People at the mission were used to late-night banging on the door from some wretch who needed food, shelter, or bandaging. Sister Clarice of the Order of the Poor Clares answered the door. The soldiers pushed through, knocking Clarice down in their haste to capture a king. She cried out, and this alerted others to come to her aid, but the soldiers leveled their muskets all around, and soon the other four soldiers joined them in the foyer of the mission.

"Just hand over Charles Stuart, and we will not bother anyone else in the mission," the Captain said.

Shepherd came down the stairs and asked the Captain what his business was at the mission.

"We have come to take Charles Stuart into our custody," he said.

Shepherd responded, "The King has asked for asylum here, and he is under our protection."

"You cannot protect him, sir," said the Captain. "I am ordered to bring Charles Stuart into custody to face trial before Parliament. I am under such orders from Mr. Oliver Cromwell, Protector of England and leader of the New Model Army. I am prepared to use force if I must." As he said that, the other seven soldiers raised their weapons and pointed toward Shepherd. "You will hand him over, or you will be the first to die here tonight," said the Captain.

I was ministering to Sister Clarice at the side of the foyer as this unfolded. Shepherd was determined.

"I cannot allow violation of this safe sanctuary. I have made a promise of protection for King Charles, and I am bound to honor it," he said.

Two of the soldiers cocked their muskets. The clicks sent chills through me as I anticipated an imminent murder of my dear friend.

"I will produce him for you!' I said.

The Captain looked over at me and said, with some relief, I believe, "Someone with sense in this building."

Shepherd shot a glance at me that signaled his disappointment.

"He is upstairs," I said, "but there are guards." As I said that, I realized that those guards were likely to be of no use to the king. If they were truly his guards, they would have engaged the soldiers before now, and maybe perished in his defense. But these guards did not have such loyalty. I wondered if they had already found a way out of the mission.

I led the soldiers up the stairs toward Charles' quarters. I pounded on the door, but there was no response. Indeed, there was no sound at all. I pounded again and heard nothing. The Captain, now impatient, hurled himself at the heavy door, but it did not budge. Finally, he ordered one of his men to shoot away the lock. He stepped close and blasted his musket at the lock, sending shards of wood and metal into the area around us. The noise was deafening and frightening. The door swung open to reveal no one present. The Captain looked at me angrily.

"Your little ruse will get you all in a great deal of trouble!" he screamed.

I was shocked that Charles was gone. I went down the stairs to see Shepherd, and I told him what had transpired upstairs. The soldiers were now spreading out around the mission, looking for a royal treasure that had just eluded them.

"Joseph," I said, "Charles is gone!"

"I know," he said calmly. "I saw a lantern at the edge of the Mission about ten minutes before they knocked down poor Sister Clarice at the side door. I alerted the guards and they whisked the king away down through the cellar and out a secret passageway. As you recall, this building was part of a stable that Jacob Carr tried to burn down years ago. He had told me that story and that his band of thieves used it as a clandestine hideaway for several years. They had built in a secret tunnel through the cellar. I think that there is hardly anyone left who knows about that passage now that Jacob is gone."

The New Model Army Captain came up to me and Shepherd and gruffly told us that we were under arrest for harboring a fugitive from justice.

I had unwittingly become a traitor to the state of England by enabling the king to escape. Shepherd and I were in deep trouble.

Unfortunately for Andrew Kensington, he was probably in worse trouble. The soldiers were in a foul mood after having "lost their prey." Capturing the King of England would have landed them great honors from Cromwell and Parliament. Now they faced possible discipline for failing in that attempt. They ungagged Kensington and demanded to know where the king had gotten off to. They thought that this was part of his scheme to spirit the king out of England to Holland, and they were none too pleased with him. Kensington was completely bewildered by the whole affair. He truly had no idea what had just transpired, but his protestations were discounted as further lies and cover-ups.

The soldiers began to slap the old man when he failed to answer their questions. He was now completely terrified, trembling from fear and from rage.

"Tie him to that tree over there," said one of the soldiers, "and we'll just flog him until he tells us what we want to know."

Kensington could hardly stand as they dragged him bound to the tree. They tied his hands so that he was hugging the tree, and they ripped off his shirt. One of the guards took a whip from his coach that he had used often on his poor horses when they failed to respond as he wished. At the first lash, Kensington screamed in pain. He knew that he could not withstand many more lashes like that.

"I know how he escaped!" said Kensington.

"Tell us now, or I will just have Roberts whip you to death!" screamed the soldier in charge of this grisly affair.

"Please, please," said Kensington. "I am an old and sick man. If you whip me more I am sure to die. I know how he must have escaped," he repeated. Roberts lowered the whip, as his superior motioned him to do.

"Tell us!" he said.

Kensington said, "I had no idea that the king was even here when I came tonight, but I think I know what has happened. I suspect that Shepherd and his cohorts smuggled him out through the secret passage off the cellar. Jacob Carr and I would meet there at times when this was a stable attached to a brewery. The brewery cellar survived a fire in the stables. Shepherd turned this into the Jacob Carr Mission after Carr himself died in a fire at the Franciscan mission many years ago. Shepherd must have known about the passage from Carr, with whom he became friendly after some kind of conversion that Carr had. He must have escaped in that way," Kensington concluded.

"Go into the mission and look for the cellar. Take Shepherd and his friend to show you. Torture them if you must. We will do what we need in order to capture our prize. We are not going back to Mr. Cromwell without Charles Stuart!"

Chapter 55

Shepherd and I were already bound by the time some of the other soldiers came to us in a very bad state of mind.

"These two know where Charles Stuart went. In fact, they enabled his escape," one said.

I squirmed at this accusation, knowing what might lie ahead. I had heard the screams of poor Kensington, and I suspected that it might be me screaming soon.

"Where is Charles Stuart?" asked the leader, a man we now knew was named Mullins.

"We do not know where he is," I said.

"But you do know how he left, and where that passage leads," said Mullins. "You must show us where that secret passage is!" he demanded.

I was now very uncomfortable, knowing that Shepherd would not give up any information, just for the sake of principle. Just then Shepherd spoke up.

"James Mullins?" he said to the leader.

"Yes," glared Mullins.

"Was your father Dr. James Mullins?" asked Shepherd further.

"Yes he was," said Mullins, now curious, but still skeptical.

"Did you and your father make the trip on the *Mayflower* as you had planned?" asked Shepherd.

"Yes, we did," said Mullins. "And how did you know my father?"

"He was a good man," said Shepherd. "He worked with Dr. Greene and me many years ago when we were on the ill-fated ship the *Intrepid*. He told us how your uncle died at the hands of tyranny, and that he was dedicated to standing for his convictions. He had also decided to pursue a medical life in order to help others. Is your father well?"

Mullins flushed and responded, "No, he is dead. Dead at the hand of that murderous traitor Charles Stuart!"

"I am so sorry to hear that," said Shepherd.

Mullins paused, then said, "You are Joseph Shepherd!"

"Of course! I knew that name was familiar. My father told me about his encounter with you and Dr. Greene several times. He related that he was touched by your ideas, as well as your courage. He took courage himself from your example, brief as that was. It came at a very important time in his life."

I now remembered the encounter with Mullins all those years ago as he had boarded the *Intrepid* in search of plague before it was allowed into Plymouth. I spoke up.

"It was your father who showed courage that day," I said. "He volunteered for a mission which put him directly into harm's way. Tell us how this terrible deed of your father's death happened."

Mullins told the other soldiers to wait outside as he took Shepherd and me to the kitchen to sit down. He seemed to be in no hurry now. Shepherd took the cue about the current situation and asked one of the Sisters to make some tea. We would sit and talk for a while.

Mullins began, "You see now why I want to pursue this criminal. My father was a good man, a kind man, a man of principle. He stood against Charles in his insatiable need to tax everything in the kingdom to raise money when he failed to convene Parliament to legally do so. He had my father hanged just three years ago. He had returned from America on a delegation to pursue more relief from taxes. Then he stayed on for a little longer in England when he was asked to run for a seat in Parliament. He did not win that election, but he was implicated during that election as having been treasonous to the Crown. We never were able to determine who arranged for his arrest, and how the charges were trumped up. My father was not one to be a political man, and I think he trusted people too quickly," concluded Mullins.

Shepherd addressed him.

"James," he began in a warm and familiar tone, "I know that your father was a good man who deserved much better than the treatment he received. You may also know that I served as an assistant to William Harvey as physician to the king. I have no real political position regarding Charles, but I did and do have the responsibility to honor my promise to harbor him in safety at this mission. I cannot reveal where he is – indeed, at this time I do not know. But I know that he did leave through a secret passage that exists in this building, as you have been told. I simply cannot lead you to the passage," he concluded.

"My men are searching all around the area," said Mullins. 'It would be helpful if you would help us to narrow the search. But I do understand your position of honoring a trust. I do need to arrest you two, but I will not inflict any harm upon you, for my father's sake. I will deliver you safely to Mr. Cromwell, and I will give you my word of honor about fair treatment."

"Thank you, James," said Shepherd. "We will go with you, but we must beg that no other person in the Mission be arrested or held culpable for this. It was my decision alone. Indeed, Dr. Greene had no part in the decision to harbor King Charles, nor was he even aware that he had escaped. He still does not know where the passage is, and he should be completely exonerated and allowed to go free."

"I respect your position, Dr. Shepherd, but I cannot decide that. That is for Mr. Cromwell or a jury to decide."

The other soldiers were getting restless outside as they now spread out to search for the missing monarch. Malcolm Spencer had told the soldiers that he would take responsibility for watching Andrew Kensington. Kensington's man, Coleman, bound and gagged in the bushes, was, apparently, slowly suffocating.

Kensington, now alone in the presence of Spencer, was starting to regain his senses from all that had happened that evening.

"You trapped me into this despicable plot, you scoundrel!" he hissed at Spencer.

"Treat me well, Lord Kensington. You are in no position to disrespect me," he said airily.

"Who put you up to this?" asked Kensington.

"Many people hate you, Lord Kensington. Perhaps you can pass the time deciding who hates you enough to plan for your demise. But as far as I am concerned, you simply had bad fortune – having New Model Army soldiers appear as you try to meet with the King you are so loyal to," he said.

"Spencer, we both know that this was a planned ambush. I did not even know that the king was here!" Kensington nearly shouted.

"Yes," said Spencer, "you keep saying that until people believe it – but they never will!" he laughed. "They never will."

The night passed with a fruitless search for Charles and his guards. In fact, they had never left the security of the passage itself and never appeared above ground. A large chamber opened up off the tunnel, and it was stocked with provisions for several days. Shepherd and I were incredibly fortunate that Mullins had treated us so well. He could have, indeed would have, tortured the information out of us had Shepherd not remembered him and his father. I know that I would have quickly given whatever information I knew (which I did, alas, not possess) under torture. Shepherd likely would not have given in quickly if at all. I was just grateful that Mullins showed mercy because of the legacy of his father's character. He had taken risk himself for this protective action toward us.

In the morning, we were packed off into a cart, bound but not gagged. The soldiers found poor Coleman dead in the bushes in the morning and simply dug a shallow grave near the mission and dumped his body into it – another unfortunate victim of the Civil War who died in secrecy and intrigue. We were not gagged, but we were instructed to keep quiet or we would have a club to the head to quiet us. Kensington was not one to listen to orders, and he was livid about his situation. He wanted to tell everyone how he was being set up for a crime he did not commit. Kensington glared at Shepherd and me as we sat together. We had been through some adventures in both America and England, and we were now well-defined enemies. Kensington continued to tell us, the soldiers, and some people who gathered in the morning sunlight, about his mistreatment. He was beginning to get louder as he saw a group of people gather, and suddenly he felt a club fall on his kidney. He slumped in pain, and he was silent for the rest of the journey to Whitehall. The once proud

241

Kensington was now reduced to a sick and pitiful old man, subject to the whims and authority of any soldier who decided to humiliate or subdue him. How like Charles Stuart, I mused...

We pulled up to Whitehall to witness a gathering crowd. There seemed to be no secrets in London these days, and word had quickly spread that the King was in hiding, the New Model Army was in pursuit, and collaborators who were trying to hide the King were being brought in to be questioned.

We were taken into dark rooms to be questioned, each of us interrogated alone. I was questioned first, likely because I was seen as least culpable. I was treated with some respect and dignity. I wondered what the purpose of this questioning was, but I quickly determined that they had no interest in me. A visitor from America who had no dealings with any politics was not their target. I was going to be used to get at Shepherd or Kensington.

I was asked about my relationship with Joseph Shepherd – why was I visiting from America? Was Shepherd plotting to get Charles out of the country, since he had so many contacts on the Continent? What were my plans about going back to America? Did I have any idea about the whereabouts of Charles Stuart?

Such questions went on for a long time – I lost track of the time, and I was getting both hungry and tired. That, I am sure, is what they had planned for the questioning. They wanted to break me down somehow. I held fast, answering questions as truthfully as I could. Finally, I was released to get some food. I had not eaten in a day, and I was famished. Even the dry bread and thin soup I was offered tasted good to me.

The questioning for Shepherd and Kensington was not as easy. Shepherd was being treated shamefully, beaten periodically if he did not answer to the satisfaction of the questioner.

"Mr. Shepherd," said one of the brutes who questioned him, "tell us why you took in the fugitive Charles Stuart!"

He had heard this question numerous times by now, and he never wavered from the answer: "King Charles of England requested asylum at a place of healing and worship. It is in the best and highest traditions of Christianity to offer refuge for the oppressed, and to give help for the weak and broken people who seek it," he said.

"Damn you!" said the jailer. "Charles Stuart is an enemy of the English people, and you harbored him as he ran from justice. You are guilty of treason, and you will be hanged or beheaded!"

"He has no warrant against him, sir," said Shepherd.

"You would not know that, Shepherd. He may have had a warrant, and you did not know," countered the guard.

"You saw soldiers of the New Model Army approaching your Mission, you knew that they were after your fugitive, and you willfully hid him and allowed him to make an escape," said the jailer.

242

On and on this went for hours. Shepherd was hungry, tired, weak, and bleeding from the beatings he was receiving. He was terribly thirsty from the ordeal, and the jailer frequently took large draughts of water in front of him, keeping the jug just out of Shepherd's reach. Then he would laugh at Shepherd, humiliating him because of his now distorted looks, matted and filthy hair, and the clothes that hung in tatters. Shepherd remained silent except when being questioned directly. He refused to break in the face of these illegal proceedings. He waited and he prayed, but he made no other defense to the guards.

In the other room, things were going very differently. Lord Kensington spoke with the jailer who questioned him.

"Young man," he said, "I think you know that I have been set up by my enemies in this affair. I have no interest in defending Charles Stuart any more than I care about Oliver Cromwell or Parliament. But I do have money, and I am willing to spend it to, let us say, 'resolve' this situation."

The guard was quite used to bribes and expected such a response.

"And how much money will I get for helping you speak to the right people?" he asked.

"Son, I will give you £100 just for the simple task of getting Mr. Robert Tarleton to come here right now," he said.

The jailer did not blink, even though that sum was well more than a year's wages for him.

"Make it £150 and I will do it."

He had learned to never take the first offer. He also knew that, with such an offer, Kensington was rich as well as desperate.

"Off with you then, lad," said Kensington, once again feeling in control because his money could be used to do so. The young jailer left the room only after getting a note of debt from Kensington. He departed, leaving Kensington shackled to the wall.

I was kept in a dank room, which had a small window near the top of the room. This let in a little light, and it kept a little bit of air moving to lower the stench just a bit. However, human wastes, mold, and rotting garbage made the place foul almost beyond words. Yet, in my current state of exhaustion, I curled up to sleep. The day was almost over already – a day that had been wasted in questioning about things that I knew nothing about. I had protected Shepherd as best I could, even shading the truth when I could slant it to make him look as ignorant as me. I knew nothing about Kensington's involvement in the affair, and I never could make any sense of it. I knew that he was a friend of the Crown, but he had no personal liking or allegiance to anyone. I could hardly imagine that he wanted to help Charles Stuart, but I did not say that. I simply answered all questions about Kensington saying, "He is a man of means and cunning. I do not know what that man is capable of!"

243

Kensington's connections began to come through for him as money began to pass hands to the proper people. By the next day, Kensington walked away from Whitehall's holding prison. He had already found out that, indeed, Lady Kensington had arranged for his predicament. She had nearly gotten him killed, and perhaps had wanted that.

Shepherd alone remained in the horrid prison. I was released the next day, since they seemed to have a villain identified in Shepherd. He would face charges of treason for his role in harboring Charles and for allowing him to escape. I was consumed with fear and rage over this injustice. Shepherd had only taken in his King and followed through with the help he promised on his honor. At the time, Shepherd did not know for a fact that Charles was truly running from a legal warrant. In fact, it is still not clear whether there was a warrant at that time, but Charles acted as if his life was threatened, and, indeed, it truly was. Sorting this out in a court of law would be tricky, and the current political landscape was not in his favor. Day by day, Cromwell and the New Model Army took on the role of stable government, offering moral authority – something that the King could not do. Charles had made too many enemies with his perceived favor of the Catholic Church and his runaway taxing schemes. People wanted change, and change was going to happen. Those who stood in the way – Charles Stuart, Joseph Shepherd, and any MPs who were seen as loyal to the Crown – were going to be tried, and likely convicted.

I came home to Margaret and Edwin Carr and fell into their waiting arms. They sobbed with relief as I told them about the latest adventure I had with my friend Joseph Shepherd. This time, Joseph did not appear to be likely to survive it. I had a dream the same night that I was released from Whitehall. In the dream, I heard a strong but very gentle voice come to me from across the English Channel. I was in a ship, the *Intrepid*, I am quite sure. The voice said several times, "Where is Joseph Shepherd?"

"He is in prison," I finally said.

"What will you do to get him released?" the voice asked with rising volume.

"I cannot get him released. I am helpless!" I cried, now in despair.

The voice was not pleased.

"You can get him released, and you *must* get him released!" the voice concluded.

"I am just a common man. I have no power!" I said weakly.

Now the voice was getting angry.

"You act weak as a newborn kitten, but you have more power than you realize!" it said. "Joseph Shepherd has many friends. You must call upon them for him, and you must do this quickly!"

I awakened in a sweat. I was crystal clear in remembering the dream – something very unusual for me. It seemed so real that I almost did not regard it as a dream. It was direction! Quickly I called in Edwin Carr and young Jacob.

Margaret was mopping my wet head with a cloth, worried that I was losing my mind.

"You cried out in the night, saying that you were helpless and that you 'could not get him released.' What in heaven was going on with you, my dear?" Margaret asked.

"I must make a list of Joseph Shepherd's friends," I said.

"He has many friends," they all said almost at once.

"Yes, I know," I said, "but we must contact the friends of influence and power. Joseph needs help beyond what we can give, and I must make this effort!"

I started to write down the most obvious people who might intercede for Shepherd. William Harvey, well known and well respected, even if he had the taint of Charles Stuart, having been Royal Physician. Rene Descartes and his friend Queen Christina of Sweden, William Bradford, Henry Adams, Robert Boyle, John Milton. Even though Milton was a strong Cromwell man, he had great affection for Shepherd.

I immediately prepared letters to each of them, explaining the predicament that Shepherd was facing. He was going to go on trial for his life, and time was of the essence! Edwin Carr said that he and Jacob would get the letters on the first ships out to the ports needed to reach the recipients. A courier was hired to send letters to John Milton and William Harvey. We then simply fell on the floor to pray that the letters would reach open hearts and minds in time.

Chapter 56

The trial was set to begin in one week. This was the worst possible news, as it gave not nearly enough time to have Shepherd's friends of influence have a voice in his behalf. I contacted Thomas Rainsborough, a recently elected MP, and a leader in the Leveller movement. Rainsborough knew Shepherd well, and he jumped at the opportunity to defend him in court. No Royalist he, Rainsborough might strike a nice balance as the defender of Shepherd. He would be equally trusted or distrusted by the Cromwell people as well as the Royalists. I wanted to make clear that, even though Shepherd was a former Royal Physician, he was not a supporter of the Crown any longer. I wanted to establish Shepherd as essentially non-political, even one who departed from his past leanings (if indeed he ever had any "leanings" politically!).

Shepherd was languishing in the prison, and I visited him every chance that I was allowed. Indeed, the only time he got decent food was when I brought him something that Margaret had made. He was grateful for the visits and the food. I teased him that he would be just as pleased if he only got the food, not my visit. In fact, I said, "If Margaret were to be the one to visit and bring food, you would be happy as a lark!"

Shepherd managed a weak chuckle at this. He seemed resigned to his own death, but I would not allow such thinking. Shepherd had been offered freedom if he would produce King Charles Stuart. At this point, Shepherd had no idea where Charles had escaped to, although many heard rumors of his presence in Holland. I was fascinated that the local wrath seemed to be centered on Shepherd, not King Charles. Charles would eventually make himself known, and there would be battles with the New Model Army – most were quite convinced of this likelihood. But the anger toward Shepherd seemed out of proportion and out of place. Yet there were those who seemed to place upon Shepherd the mantle of treachery. He had ruffled some people in high places, and people like Andrew and Anne Kensington were happy to fan the flames of fury against him. As long as fingers were pointed at him, they were not pointed at the Kensingtons.

I told Shepherd that I retained Thomas Rainsborough to defend him in court. He seemed grateful about this, but worried that this might be detrimental to Rainsborough – to defend someone like himself who seemed so unpopular. I told Shepherd that Rainsborough was quite able to make that decision, and that those who opposed him were not in the majority – they were simply more vocal. Shepherd conceded that Rainsborough would be a fine choice, and he thanked me.

I left the prison discouraged. My rock-like friend, Joseph Shepherd, seemed resigned to his fate. He hardly cared to make a defense for himself. It seemed like he wanted to die! I mused upon the fact that Shepherd's influence had really changed me. It seemed like the energy that Shepherd had originally possessed, and had infused into me, was now departing him. I was now focused and motivated in a mission, whereas I had been drifting along before I met him. Now, it seemed, his energy, his life force, was diminished, and that he had given me a life, but he was now willing to give his up. I would not stand for that!

The trial began as expected. Witnesses were paraded forth claiming that Shepherd was a Royalist. He had been Royal Physician (*Assistant* Royal Physician to William Harvey, not the official Royal Physician, Rainsborough objected); he had harbored his friend and colleague, Charles Stuart, King of England, in the mission; he had harbored thieves and criminals in the mission over the years, so this was habitual behavior for him; and he had consort with the lowest wretches in London there; and he enjoyed the privileges of royal friendship, as he had influence with monarchs on the Continent. This they said to imply that he was a friend of absolute monarchy. Even his unusual forms of medical treatment were called into question as the prosecutor called upon some of the medical professors from Oxford to berate his "ignorance of traditional and standard medical practices" and his "disdain for experienced scholars in the medical field."

Rainsborough was able to deflect many of these peripheral issues, simply because they had no bearing on the current charges. The jury, however, was getting a picture of a man who was radical, unpredictable in his dealings, and one who simply scoffed at current convention, even the law. One thing Rainsborough could not deny, however, was that Shepherd had harbored the fugitive king, and he failed to cooperate with the New Model Army who pursued him.

I was called upon to testify about the night that Charles Stuart came to the mission seeking asylum on his journey.

"Dr. Greene," began the prosecutor, "were you and Dr. Shepherd aware that Charles Stuart was a fugitive from justice?" he asked.

"The king told us that Parliament had issued a writ ordering him to appear before them, but he did not indicate that he was under arrest, nor that he would be pursued by Parliament's forces," I said.

"What did he say?" he asked.

"The king told us that he *could* be compelled to appear before Parliament, but that was not the case at that time," I said.

It seemed that part of the case rested upon the nuance of whether the king was actually being sought because he failed to appear before Parliament, or whether he was simply avoiding that circumstance by running away. The king had told us that he *could* be compelled to comply, not that this was already the case. Rainsborough had neatly explained this to me, so my response was as strict as I could make it in stating that we did not see him as under order to testify. He was not a fugitive from justice, he had simply asked us for refuge, and we complied. He was planning to go to Colchester Castle, and that was not totally out of the ordinary for him.

"Dr. Greene," smiled the prosecutor, "are you a legal expert? Are you trying to make a legal argument defending your obvious behavior of harboring a fugitive from justice? We all know that you acted upon the belief that you were giving safe haven to a man who was under a legal order to appear before Parliament, and that he was simply ignoring, nay, *flaunting* that order. Such is the behavior of that man who believes that he is above the laws of England. That, Dr. Greene, is the crux of the current problem with the king – he believes that he is above the law! This has been a bedrock belief of English civilization since the Magna Carta! No one is above the law!"

The prosecutor had gone from questioning to pontificating. He had his audience, and I was simply the puppet whom he used to give himself a platform. He had no interest in answers; he simply wanted a pulpit.

"How might I answer such a question, if indeed there is a question in that sermon," I said, probably inadvisably. The jury and spectators seemed to like the response, as it drew a gale of laughter and hoots. The prosecutor, Sir William Lundly, did not take kindly to it, however.

"You will answer that and all questions truthfully, Dr. Greene. Please be advised that charges have not been dropped in your case, and such rude and disrespectful responses could result in your own trial!" he fumed.

"My answer, sir, is that I am not a legal expert. In fact, the law is something I cannot understand well, but I do respect it. Dr. Shepherd and I were simply responding at that time to a man in need who came to a place he saw as refuge, and we could no more turn him away if he were a beggar or, as it turns out, the King of England," I concluded.

Lundly had established that we took in Charles Stuart and that we had the intention of giving him safety from whoever pursued him. That is all he needed to do, but he had stretched out the questioning so that he could once again make a case for an arrogant king, and that those who helped him were of the same ilk. In some ways, the King was on trial in absentia through the trial of Shepherd. My insolent response was not helpful, and I regretted saying it. It was too late to retract it, so we were now clearly living up to a reputation of being arrogant scofflaws.

We were hoping beyond hope to delay and string out the trial as long as we could in order to receive some replies from the influential people who might be of help to Shepherd. Rainsborough used all the tricks he knew, calling witnesses from as far away as he could conjure up, and even begging the court for extra time due to the poor health that Shepherd now experienced. Rainsborough took some pains to detail how poorly Shepherd was being treated, and that the poor food, inadequate quarters, and the lack of sleep he experienced was shameful and taking a toll on the defendant.

The judge, Sir Thomas Ackley, was not unsympathetic. He granted us some time for Shepherd to receive medical care outside of the prison, allowing him to be treated at the mission hospital under the watch of guards. We were able to gain several extra, precious days of rest, as well as time to get additional support.

Shepherd felt much relieved when he was brought back to the mission. I saw him actually smile for the first time since before his arrest. We did not know how much time we had for him to recuperate, but whatever we had was a blessing. Shepherd began to eat and heal from his mistreatment at the hands of the guards. He was over fifty years old now (although, truthfully, I never knew his exact age, and he had never bothered to tell me) and healing came more slowly. The truly healing thing for him, however, was to be able to treat patients again. He simply could not be stopped from ministering to the needs of those in the hospital. In fact, as he began working with patients, I saw his entire mind and body change. He had renewed energy, became more talkative, and actually started to discuss his future.

Of course, this ended up working against him, since the guards reported back to Sir Lundly and Judge Ackley that the prisoner was "fit and healthy," in their modest opinion. One evening, about six days after he had moved back into the mission, one of the guards was attacked by one of the patients at the mission. People there knew what was happening, and they were very defensive of their "protector" Joseph Shepherd. One of the poor wretches who had been at the mission off and on for several years felt very protective toward Shepherd. He saw that one of the guards had fallen asleep, and he took that opportunity to run at him with a knife. He stabbed the guard several times in the head and neck area, and was ready to finish him off when the other guard swung his sword at the man and cut him down. The poor man died almost instantly from the blow, which nearly severed his head. The attacked guard, however, was seriously hurt.

Shepherd ran to the guard quickly. He saw that there was nothing to be done for the assailant, but quick action was needed for the guard. The guard sustained cuts to his neck, scalp, and ear. His ear was nearly severed, but the neck wound was what concerned Shepherd. He quickly applied pressure to the wound and he called me over to help sew up the wound. There was a great deal of blood loss, and we were not sure that we could save him. Shepherd's skill at such work was unsurpassed. He was able to staunch the flow of blood and tie off the vein that had been pierced. We worked as a team again, recalling our work on Kelley aboard the *Intrepid*, the Algonquin native, Achak, in America, and on Jacob Carr after his stab wound. Shepherd made quick work on sewing the guard's ear back, this being almost an afterthought, given that it was certainly not life-threatening.

249

After this attack, the judge and prosecutor were resolved to end this kindness to Shepherd. He was indeed much improved in his own health, and there was no need to expose guards to harm in this house arrest situation any longer.

Shepherd would be called upon to testify after proceedings resumed. Hoping to delay that testimony, and delay the trial as long as he could, Rainsborough took the unusual step of calling in the guards who were at the mission to testify. The guards, Micah Davis and Elijah Mays, were summoned to court. Davis, the guard who was the victim of the assault, was called to the stand. Sir Lundly appealed to Judge Ackley that this was an unusual and unnecessary tactic. What value could there be in calling the guards to testify? This was a defense trick, and Lundly would not stand for it.

"I object to this trick of the defense!" thundered Sir Lundly.

"Sir Ackley, Your Honor," said Rainsborough, "I am simply trying to establish the character of my client, which has been so impugned over the course of this trial by the Honorable Sir Lundly. I am attempting to show that my client acted well within the bounds of this court when he was shown the grace of recuperating in the mission hospital. The only way that I can establish that is by the testimony of his guards. Is this trial not about character, as the Honorable Sir Lundly stated in his questioning of Dr. Greene?"

Sir Ackley paused for just a moment and said, "I will allow it. I see no harm in it, and if it can further justice, we all benefit," he ruled.

Lundly sat down, clearly upset, but he managed a smile as he nodded toward the judge.

"Mr. Davis," began Rainsborough, "can you tell the court if Dr. Shepherd was in compliance with the law while he was recuperating at the mission hospital?" he asked.

"Yes he was, sir," answered Davis.

"Did he ever try to escape during his time there?" asked Rainsborough.

"No, sir, he did not," answered Davis.

"Did he treat you with respect and dignity during the time you were guarding him?" asked Rainsborough.

"Yes sir, he surely did," replied Davis.

"You were injured while you were guarding him at the mission. Is that true?" asked Rainsborough.

"Yes, someone tried to kill me. I was attacked by a madman there!" said Davis, now a bit shaken.

"And how did Dr. Shepherd respond to this?" asked Rainsborough.

"Why, he saved my life, he did!" said Davis. Some of the spectators and most of the jurors were hearing this for the first time, and they gasped. Rainsborough, in his wisdom, had not allowed this information to be shared as far as he could control it. He had wanted exactly this response of surprise, and he was pleased that this information was new to many people.

Rainsborough went on, in painstaking detail, to question Davis and Mays about how Shepherd had responded quickly with care and skill to save a man who was guarding him from escape. Rainsborough was able to establish something that many people already knew about Shepherd – he was a kind and thoughtful man who sought the best for all he came in contact with. This example was just one example of that, but it was powerful and very timely! This testimony also stood in contrast to the Oxford masters who tried to paint Shepherd as a wild and reckless man who did not display good medical practices. This man Davis was living proof of the opposite.

Then something strange and wonderful happened. Several spectators stood and demanded to be heard. One after another, people gave testimony, unsolicited, about how Shepherd had saved their life – whether it was a physical intervention, food when they were starving, or a shelter when they were cold. Julius Rosello stood and told about his own healing in Rome when he encountered Shepherd there with a friend, and also about his son Mario who no longer had seizures after treatment from Dr. Shepherd.

Then a young man stood from far back in the courtroom. There was a short time of stunned silence, and the young man began to speak.

"I was abandoned at the Mission over twenty years ago and cared for by Dr. Shepherd. A man who Dr. Shepherd took in, whose life Shepherd actually saved, was the same man who saved me from a terrible fire. This was a man whose name I have proudly taken, Jacob Carr," he said. "I am also the son of Margaret and Dr. Luke Greene. I beg you to consider what you are doing here. This man, Joseph Shepherd, has done nothing but good in London, and you want to hang him for harboring a fugitive king?"

Jacob broke down at that point and began weeping. Edwin, his uncle, stood with him and held him.

Judge Ackley finally restored order in the courtroom, but emotions were running high. Sir Lundly had been beside himself with rage at the actions in the room, but he had been shouted down, and he could not turn the tide that had arisen.

Judge Ackley finally recessed the court until the next day. He asked that Rainsborough and Lundly meet him in his quarters. He wanted no part of the display that he saw in the courtroom to be repeated in the future. Yet he would need to convene without the usual open court to which people had become accustomed. Any secrecy these days was held to be highly suspicious. Mob rule was not far from London these days, and Judge Ackley was going to make sure that it would not begin in his courtroom.

"Gentlemen," he addressed them in his quarters, "we must come to some resolution here so that we do not set off a riot. Justice must be served, but not at the expense of the lives of innocent people who will be harmed in riots."

Just as he was finishing his sentence, his bailiff burst into the quarters and asked if he could have a word with Sir Ackley.

"I have news!" the bailiff cried.

"Just tell the news!" said an exasperated Ackley.

"Charles Stuart is at Colchester Castle, and he has sent word to Cromwell that he would like to discuss his situation," concluded the bailiff.

Charles, no longer a fugitive and in plain sight, was willing to talk with the Rump Parliament and Cromwell. There seemed to be less compelling reasons now to prosecute Joseph Shepherd for an escape that was over.

Lundly was not persuaded that anything had changed.

"Shepherd's treasonous act is not mitigated by the fact that his crime was not successful," he reasoned.

Rainsborough jumped in.

"Your Honor," he said, "Sir Lundly may be quite legally correct in his statement, but may I suggest a bit of a bargain, shall we say?"

"Bargain with justice, Rainsborough?" said Lundly. "You are like the rest of these brigands that you associate with!" he sniffed in his best self-righteous tone.

"My bargain, if I may proceed, Sir Lundly, involves a plea of guilt by my client, but with the promise of mercy by the court. No death sentence, no imprisonment, but banishment from England. That way, we have no local martyr that the street people will defend like that fool at the mission tried to do. There are others who may do that if he stays. You saw that courtroom – some people are passionate in defending that man. Let us remove him, not by death, but by exile," he concluded.

Rainsborough was taking a risk in this tactic. He was not at all convinced that his principled client would accept the idea of pleading guilty. Even if he did, Shepherd would find it very difficult to leave his precious mission behind. However, if he did not make the move now, it might never work. Timing was critical in these things, and he had just come from a courtroom scene that could turn the tide for now, but such passion could not be sustained. Now was the time to get commitments.

Sir Ackley and Sir Lundly pondered the situation. Rainsborough had given all of them a way out with some kind of honor. They would consider it overnight and discuss it again in the morning. If Rainsborough could convince his client, he might just save his life.

Chapter 57

R ainsborough came back to Shepherd and me with the offer that he had just proposed.

"Brilliant!" was all I could say.

This was a way to save Shepherd's life and take him away from the harm that was rapidly enveloping England. Charles' offer to meet with Cromwell meant that he was so desperate now that he would try a last-ditch effort of a "plea" himself.

Shepherd thought for a moment and said to Rainsborough, "Thomas, I did not authorize such an offer."

My heart sank. Surely Shepherd would not turn down his only way out!

"So you are rejecting the offer?" asked Rainsborough.

"I need to pray about that, Thomas," replied Shepherd. "I suppose Lundly and Ackley need to as well, since they have not accepted the offer yet either."

Rainsborough was very calm about the whole matter. I think perhaps that he had anticipated this possible response from Shepherd, so he gave some space for Shepherd to wrestle with it rather than try to convince him of the wisdom of the offer. Rainsborough recognized that it might not have been his job to convince Shepherd, but to simply present the facts in a calm and reasoned fashion and let God convince Shepherd of its wisdom. Indeed, this logic was unassailable. Shepherd was a man of reason, not impulse. Further, no man would convince Shepherd of anything unless Shepherd truly believed it was God's plan – I had learned that over the years with him. So giving him the time to pray about it was another stroke of wisdom on Rainsborough's part.

Lady Anne Kensington heard the news about Charles making his arrangement with Oliver Cromwell, and she was unsettled. She had cast her lot with the Crown over the years, whereas Andrew had played in the courts of the Royalists and Parliament, as well as the New Model Army at times. In doing so, Lord Kensington had made enemies among all sides while he believed that he was simply making friends of all. His deals had made temporary friends, but, evidently, lasting enemies as well. He had managed to get himself out of Whitehall prison by calling in some financial favors and distributing money, but could his luck hold out?

Lady Anne was certain that Charles would be toppled from the throne and likely imprisoned. In her worst fears, she believed that he might even be executed. The same fate might well await her. She contacted Andrew and asked to meet with him at Sherwood Pub. Both were well aware of the treachery of the other, but in this time of crisis they were thrown together for a last chance of saving themselves.

"Whom can we rely on in this danger?" asked Anne as they met outside of London at the pub. "You have friends who have helped you get out of prison; who helped you?"

"There were several people who came to my aid," Andrew said, "and they were well compensated for it. Your little plot could have gotten me killed. Why should I do anything to help you?" he asked. "If you had had your way, I would have been beaten to death, not imprisoned at Whitehall."

"We can help one another now," said Anne, deflecting Andrew's obvious observation.

"And how do you propose to help me?" asked Andrew.

"I have friends who have arranged a safe retreat for me," she said, "but you have the ship that I need for the passage."

"And what do I get?" asked Andrew.

"You get to keep all claims that I have on your estate," she said.

"So, I profit after I die, having the ability to rest in the grave with the consolation that you cannot profit from my hard work," he said. "That does not sound very satisfying to me," he snorted.

"Yes, I expected as much," Anne said. "I will also pay you £10,000 for the use of your ship."

Andrew did not even raise his eyebrows at this offer.

"You are truly in need, Anne," he said. "Even if I wanted to help you, and I do not, it would cost you £25,000 for use of the ship, depending on where you want to go."

Anne had expected that this would be a difficult negotiation, because she was not in a position of strength. But she was in trouble. Her affiliations with the Crown had made her poison with her primary contacts. Cromwell had already put her on the list of "Enemies of the English People," so she was expecting to be arrested any time. While Andrew was not safe to entrust her fate to, he was about the only one with whom she could negotiate now.

"So that is your offer?" she asked.

"I did not offer it," said Andrew, now enjoying Anne twisting in the wind. "I simply said that would be the cost. I am not interested in offering you safe passage."

Anne was starting to panic, but she tried to maintain her composure. Now she understood why Andrew was willing to meet with her despite her attempts to destroy him. He would now try to destroy her or put her into financial ruin. He was willing to take risks in order to exact some revenge upon Anne.

"How do you know that I did not invite you here to kill you," Anne asked, her mood darkening.

"I fully expected that you did, my dear," replied Andrew. "I brought along twenty-five armed men who are not fifty yards from here."

"I only brought five, because I trust you so much," Anne said acidly.

Andrew laughed, and the tension was broken a bit.

"I have good reason not to trust you," he said. "I should have brought more men!"

"Now that we have that out of the way, perhaps we can begin to negotiate in earnest," Anne said, smiling.

Andrew darkened quickly.

"Just because we can still laugh does not mean we are not enemies, Anne," he said. "My offer to you is that you turn over everything to me – everything that you own, and I will consider providing safe passage for you to America, or to France, where you have lovers who may take you in. I want you broken in every way, and I will not rest until you are!" he glared.

Anne knew that she was beaten. Her bravado in trying to negotiate might have made her feel like she still had some power, but she now realized that her bluff and showmanship were not enough for the steely and relentless Andrew.

"Very well," she said. "I will deed all my holdings to you for safe passage and protection to France," she said.

Andrew grinned at his victory.

"I shall expect papers from your attorney by the end of the week," he said. "I can arrange passage by the end of the week also when I have reviewed your deeds and holding contracts."

Joseph Shepherd was thinking and praying about his decision on the court bargain proposed by Rainsborough. I came to visit him in jail, and he seemed to be in a very reflective mood.

"Have you considered your decision about the arrangement that Rainsborough has negotiated?" I asked hopefully.

Shepherd seemed not to even hear my question, as he was intent to talk about other things.

"Luke, I have never told you about how I ended up on the *Intrepid*, have I?" he asked.

"You told me about being in Egypt, then signing on with a trade ship, the *Herald,* I believe. I always thought that you had lost your memory of what happened because of the blows to your head that you sustained," I replied.

"I did lose those memories for some time, but I have recalled much of what happened over the years," he said. "I did not tell you about my life prior to Egypt, did I?"

"No, I do not know of your life before you were in Egypt," I said. "Please tell me about that. I am most anxious to know!"

"Before I came to Egypt I travelled around the Continent, working with some wonderful people. I was in Swabia with Johannes Kepler as he was formulating his experiments on optics. He was a true genius and a man dedicated to God. He believed that he could honor God by discovering more about His creation, a notion, as you already know, I happen to agree with. He was an amazing astronomer, coming up with ideas about the planets spinning on axes, the moon's role in affecting tides, designing better optical equipment for both astronomy and vision. We even worked on things like determining the likely year that Christ was born, and I am quite certain that we have established that reasonably correctly."

"Wait," I said. "You both worked on these things?"

"Oh yes, Kepler and I were very close then. I just wish things would not have gotten so troublesome with his mother."

"What happened with his mother?" I asked.

"She was accused of being a witch by the people in her town. She was a bit of a troublesome woman, very bright but also very eccentric and opinionated. She absolutely refused to recant her story when being accused of being a witch. In fact, she was completely innocent, but she would not accept the bargain that was offered to her when they could not prove her guilt. The townspeople had conjured up a plan to get rid of her, and she fell into a trap of making a potion that they said was from the devil. She was a woman skilled in medicinal herbs and plants, and I have used some of that knowledge in my own practice. Sometimes people are not ready to accept new practices, and they react out of fear. Interesting that fear often comes out looking like anger," he concluded.

"I have been thinking about her lately with this bargain that Rainsborough has tried to arrange. She had the courage of her convictions, and she refused to succumb to the tyrants who oppressed her. Can I do less than that woman? Johannes learned that trait from her, and he stayed strong in his convictions, even when he would have been safer to accommodate to the demands of those in authority."

"Joseph," I began, "I am most impressed that you worked with Johannes Kepler. Your genius never ceases to amaze me! I also know that is not why you told me the story, since the only thing that surpasses your genius is your humility. And I know that your sense of 'right' is much more developed than mine, but I too am a friend, and I have some advice to give. You lose nothing by agreeing to plead guilty to harboring a fugitive – you *did* harbor a fugitive – *we* harbored a fugitive. So plead to the truth of that and accept the mercy they are willing to extend. Is that beyond your values?" I asked.

"I truly appreciate your care for me, Luke, but truth is more complicated than simply agreeing to a bargain. If I accept that bargain, I am allowing them to keep alive a system of authority that is not legitimate. What they did to me was wrongful behavior. When Paul was in prison and then was released after wrongful procedure, he demanded that they acknowledge the fact that they had wronged a Roman citizen. He did that not for his own

256

purposes, but for the benefit of the young church, which needed freedom from oppression."

"You may be the most stubborn man I know!" I concluded. "I will return tomorrow to see if even God can change that stubborn mind of yours!"

Shepherd was right – fear often does look like anger.

Chapter 58

Back at our residence, as I talked with Margaret, Edwin, and Jacob, I told them of my encounter with Shepherd and my frustration with his stubbornness. Margaret and Edwin nodded in agreement. They too had seen his unbending will when he believed that a principle was at stake, and they had worried that it might be his undoing.

Then Margaret said, "You mentioned something about Joseph and Kepler's mother. What happened there? I don't understand what that had to do with Joseph going to Egypt."

It then dawned on me that Shepherd had never finished that story. We had become involved in his current distress, and he never told me what happened.

"I must be sure to ask him that when I visit him again," I said.

"Have you decided when you are going to return to America?" asked Edwin.

"I have been giving that some thought, Edwin," I replied, "but I think that depends on Shepherd's decision and the willingness of the court to follow through with Rainsborough's bargain. If they allow him to go into exile in America, we can take him back with us. It would really be an excellent solution. We could all be together again, and I am certain that Shepherd would like to see what has happened in America."

"And if the court does not allow it, or Shepherd does not agree?" Edwin said.

"We cannot leave him in his hour of need," I said. "We must fight for his release, or stand by him in his sentence."

Margaret began crying softly as I spoke.

"We must persuade him to accept a bargain if it is proposed, and we must pray that there indeed is a proposal," she said.

We nodded in agreement and finally drifted off to our rooms to sleep.

Early the next morning, Rainsborough came to the Massachusetts Bay Company quarters where we stayed.

"I have news!" he said. We looked at him and knew that it was good. "They have offered Joseph a reduced sentence of exile to America if he pleads guilty and apologizes to Parliament for 'obstructing justice' in harboring the King."

We looked somewhat downcast, and Rainsborough was shocked.

"Don't you understand?' he asked. "Shepherd will be free! He can go back to America with you if he simply complies with the court's request."

"We know Shepherd well. I am not convinced that he will do either of the court's requests – plead guilty or apologize to Parliament. If he continues to believe that he is right, he will do neither, even if it costs him his life," I said glumly. "I will visit him this afternoon. Pray that he has an open mind."

"Perhaps I should go with you?" Rainsborough said.

"No," I said softly, "I want to go alone."

I visited Joseph in prison that afternoon, and I found him to be in good spirits. I decided to delay talking about the arrangement that Rainsborough had succeeded in acquiring for him.

"Joseph," I began, "you did not finish telling me about how Johannes Kepler's mother had something to do with you going to Egypt. Tell me about that."

"Yes, I did not complete that story, did I?" he said. "I was in Swabia with Johannes, and I had been there several months, in fact. We were working on refining the Copernican theory about a heliocentric universe. Kepler was sure that the mathematics of the orbits of the planets made it clear that they, along with the earth, revolved around the sun. We had intuitively believed this because any other theory would be much more complicated to explain. He began writing a book about what the earth might look like from the moon, and it gave a perspective that explains how we might look *from* the heavens as opposed to us only looking out *toward* the heavens. It got me thinking about how we are so proud in our thinking that the earth must be the center of all the universe – all the planets, stars, comets, and heavenly bodies. The sun, as giver of life, can be at the center, much like God, the maker of life, should be at the center of our thought. The church cannot explain all of God's creation. Indeed, that is not the role of the church. God has given to us inquisitive minds, tools like mathematics to understand His wondrous creation. It is a shame that those who pursue thought outside the purview of theology are condemned.

"We began to teach and publish such ideas, and church people were becoming uncomfortable, then angry. We were being called heretics for pursuing our discovery of nature, which, in our opinion, are not antithetical to theology, but complementary. The more I see of the intricacy of creation, the more I see God himself. At the same time, Kepler's mother, Katherina, was being charged with being a witch. She liked to deal with natural, herbal remedies, and she prepared such medicines for people in the town. Her ideas are a bit different, and she can be a hard woman to understand at times. In fact, many found her to be off-putting and distant – a dreamer with eccentric ideas. When Bruno Marker died after drinking one of her remedies, she was charged with being a witch. She was a hard-headed woman and refused to recant a statement that she had made earlier about witchcraft. Even when she was granted freedom, she chose to pursue vindication from her charges. Kepler and I rallied to her defense, and we offended the town burghers to the point that we were also accused of witchcraft. Kepler's mother remained in a kind of house arrest, and Johannes was ordered to watch over her – under house arrest himself until his patron, Tycho Brahe, could help arrange a reasonable disposition to the problem. I was told that I must leave Swabia, but I was not given safe passage to any Christian land. Neither Catholic nor Lutheran nor Calvinist would come to our defense, rather my defense. So, I decided to go to Egypt. This Moslem country, pagan as they were, allowed me refuge because of Kara Mustafa Pasha, whom I had met years before in my travels through Macedonia. He had heard of our writings, and invited me to have asylum in Egypt with the intent of going to help rebuild the library in Alexandria – a grand vision of Pasha, but just that – a vision or dream. That was unlikely in a land where any knowledge outside the Quran was becoming dangerous. I went to Alexandria and quickly found that Christians, even under Pasha's protection, were in danger. Pasha himself was executed not many years later. I went to become a ship's physician, and you know what happened to me after that," he concluded.

As I listened to his story, the one theme I heard was that his stubbornness, and that of Kepler and his mother, had time and again stymied him.

"Joseph," I said," that is a fascinating story. Your travels and adventures rival that of Marco Polo, I do believe. But your journey seems to be one of running from things at times, not going toward a dream or goal of your own. What are you running toward, not running from?" I asked.

Shepherd thought for a long moment on that.

"My life is not one of running away, although I see how it may appear so to you," he said. "My life is about seeking God by learning about His creation, and using that to help His people. I find that God's people do not always take kindly to things offered to them. We are like frightened sheep who resist the care of the shepherd who only wants to save them from danger. When I took over the Franciscan mission, I found peace, but even there I encountered resistance for doing good. But I have learned, as Peter said in his epistle: *Having a good conscience; that, whereas they speak evil of you, as of evildoers, they may be ashamed that falsely accuse your good conversation in Christ. For it is better, if the will of God be so, that ye suffer for well doing, than for evil doing.*"

"Joseph, you are dedicated to doing God's will. Please do not let your stubbornness get in the way of that," I said.

"What do you mean?" asked Shepherd.

"Rainsborough just this morning told us that Judge Ackley and Sir Lundly have accepted his arrangement to have you plead guilty to the charge, apologize to Parliament, and you will be offered exile in America as punishment. You could come back with us to America. Surely you know that you can serve God's people there, and you will have me and Margaret and Jacob and Edwin with you, along with Henry Adams, and other friends.

260

Joseph, it is another new start! How often does God put such opportunities before us?" I concluded.

I waited as Shepherd listened to my plea.

"Yes," he said, "I had already decided that if the offer were given, I would likely take it. But I would only accept the offer if you were completely committed to it. My prayer had been that I would know it to be God's will if you were to plead that case with me one more time. It was somewhat like the 'fleece' that Gideon put out before God when he was called to battle the Midianites. I know you had pleaded with me once, but I needed confirmation that this was from God, not just my decision for my own benefit. God speaks to us in many ways, Luke, but I wanted Him to speak through you. I am convinced that He has done that. I am ready to accept the grace offered by the court, even though I believe that the process and tactics they used were wrong. The more important principle, as you pointed out, is that I must not let my pride stand before God's work."

We rejoiced at the turn of events when I returned to the Massachusetts Bay Company quarters. We planned to return to America as soon as we could arrange for all of us to finish our business in London. Gerry and Hancock had not met with Charles Stuart, since he was already on the run by the time they were to meet with him. They did meet with several MPs who showed some sympathy toward them and the cause of those in America. However, most of the House of Lords was indifferent to the needs of America, and some were actually quite hostile. They spent the rest of their time in London meeting with importers who had a taste for the cod that were abundant in American waters. Cod was becoming king in the trade world, and New England had the best cod and oysters that could be found on earth. Gerry and Hancock made friends with people who were to lead the way in increasing the cod trade.

We would be leaving in just a matter of three or four weeks, as we awaited the *Queensgate's* refitting, and a final passage list for the forty-some passengers who were awaiting their trip to America. Edwin and Jacob Carr were busy with planning for the trip, as it was now autumn, 1648. Shepherd was regaining his health, which had been almost broken in Whitehall prison.

Andrew Kensington had his eye on our voyage preparations also. He had revenge on his mind toward Shepherd, me, and especially young Jacob, who had "stolen" his vessel in America. Kensington never forgot a wrong, and his "patience" for revenge was legendary. Kensington had reviewed the deeds given to him by Anne, and he had arranged for her passage to France after having ensured that she would be a near pauper upon arrival in France. She would be totally in the debt and graces of Cardinal Mazarin and Louis XIV and the French aristocracy. Likely too old now to serve as a mistress, Anne would be challenged again to live on her wits and guile to survive the machinations of the French court. She had been equipped to do that over the years, but she was now a beaten woman – another victim of the wily Andrew Kensington.

The recent Treaty of Westphalia, which had just been signed, seemed to bring an era of peace to Europe from the religious wars. Shepherd seemed to be alternately baffled and agitated about the religious wars, which had plagued the Continent for the last thirty years. However, the idea of peace brought him some relief. Indeed, I was finding myself to be something that was very new – an American. Yes, I was English by birth and culture, but I was finding that what some called an "American Spirit" was capturing me. I saw value in a land that espoused religious liberty, a land where position and wealth were not the prerequisites for success, a land where ingenuity and risk were rewarded with financial gain and personal independence. Adams, Gerry, Hancock and others were believing the same things, and that is why they returned with us somewhat sullen when they saw that the English Parliament had no such thinking. The House of Lords was more than a little stunned that the upstart Americans would try to negotiate as equals on economic trade items such as cod, tobacco, molasses, and timber.

We boarded the "*Queensgate*" on October 27th, ready to sail back home. Home indeed! America was now *home*!

Chapter 59

Anne Kensington was adrift and hopeless in Paris. Cardinal Mazarin, her old protector, seemed to no longer have use for her. Indeed, he had agreed to house her in the palace and give her modest financial support, but she no longer had access to power and the means to live the life she was accustomed to. She was a kept woman, the role she had let people believe she was playing in the past while actually managing to exert great power and control. Now, she was that hated type that she had played, and she was miserable.

One day, she received a package from London. She was surprised to see that it was from Oliver Craft. She opened the package, which was filled with envelopes from all over Europe. Craft had taken the package from Whitehall. It had been addressed to Lord Rainsborough, who was now dead – killed at the hands of Cromwell's New Model Army. Craft decided to send it on to her, asking for only £100 for the service. Craft himself, now destitute, was trying whatever gambit he could find to live. He gambled on this, thinking, perhaps, that he had nothing really to lose.

The letters were from some of the finest scientists and crowned royalty in Europe. The letters had come too late to be used in Shepherd's trial, but, of course, they were no longer needed after the agreement Rainsborough arranged. One letter, from Robert Moray, caught her attention. Moray had written at the urging of Robert Boyle.

Moray was known in both English and French courts as both a scientist and a person of some influence. Shepherd had met him while serving King Charles, and had discussed with him ideas on the role of potassium nitrate in gunpowder. While experimenting with Moray one day with nitric acid, they had come upon a peculiar effect when they mixed it with some starch from plant material – it tended to explode! Fascinated by this, they worked at trying to understand why this happened, and they came up with a type of gunpowder that exploded, but with much less smoke and soot. Shepherd saw the likely outcome of this and wanted no more to do with it. He knew that this might make battlefields much more dangerous, and cannon much more useful. He asked Moray to keep this a secret with him, and trusted that Moray would do just that.

Secrets do not tend to stay secret, and word got out about this curious substance. Moray, to his credit, honored his commitment to Shepherd that he would no longer work on this substance. However, as a man of science, he kept notes about his work, and those notes came into the hands of people who saw a way to exploit it. To their chagrin, they lacked the knowledge of how to proceed. Moray had noted in his letter that Joseph Shepherd was a brilliant man of discovery, and that he should be considered a treasure to England, not a subject of imprisonment. While the letter was no longer necessary for Shepherd, Anne wondered if this letter might be of use to her.

What Anne did not know was that Moray's letter had been received at Rainsborough's office just after the trial. One of Kensington's men had stolen the letter, and Kensington became aware of the possible power of obtaining the formula of this smokeless powder. Kensington quickly set in motion a plan to find Shepherd and manufacture this miracle discovery. Kensington had decided to destroy the letter, lest it fall into the "wrong hands." Before he could do that, the letter once again disappeared, this time into the hands of Oliver Craft, who had the fortune to be in the right place when the Moray letter came up missing at Whitehall.

Anne's scheme also was to find Shepherd and coerce him to cooperate with those who could turn this discovery into a fortune. It would be of infinite value to her French hosts, and might get her back into a position of power. Now she just needed to track down Shepherd. The £100 was a small price to pay Oliver Craft for this information.

She and her estranged husband were both, unknown to each other, on the track of trying to find Shepherd, and she had no idea that Lord Kensington had already started his search for Shepherd, and that he had moved so very quickly on it.

264

Chapter 60

We set sail on a glorious morning from London. We had around forty passengers and a load of sterling from the Bank of England, the payment for the most recent shipment of salt cod and rum that the Massachusetts Bay Company had transported. Business was good for the Company, and the chest of sterling was proof of that. It was guarded by several heavily armed merchant seamen, who were becoming a security force of some renown. Edwin Carr was skilled as a captain, and young Jacob was becoming a first-rate pilot. Margaret and I were so proud of him!

We were no more than a few days out of London when Jacob spotted a vessel off our port side closing with some speed. England had no current enemies, but pirates were always a threat. The *Queensgate* was not a fighting ship, but she had two cannons on board as a response to such threats. While no match for a fighting ship, it was somewhat of a deterrent for pirates who did not care for a fair fight when embarking on their despicable trade.

"Keep steady west," said Edwin as he heard the report of a strange vessel approaching.

"Aye, sir," said the helmsman.

Jacob came to our quarters and sought out his mother. He wanted to assure her that all was well. Word had quickly spread that there was some excitement on the top deck.

"Is all well?" Margaret asked.

"Oh yes, mother," Jacob assured. "We do not know the business of that ship coming up on us, but it may be nothing to mention. Nonetheless, we are careful, and we aim to protect this ship and all on board."

Shepherd and I had been in such dealings nearly thirty years ago. Shepherd came to me and inquired as to my wellbeing.

"Joseph," I said, "we have been in this situation before!"

I smiled. Shepherd laughed.

"Indeed we have," he said. "Do you think these are pirates?" he asked.

"I doubt it," I said.

"Well, we do have a nice chest of sterling on board, and there are people here who could be taken captive and sold into slavery," he said.

"Yes," I replied, "but the sterling on board is a secret that we know of only because of Edwin and Jacob telling us privily."

"True," he said, "but any ship is a target for pirates on the open sea. It is more a matter of opportunity than of target, oftentimes."

The ship on our port side was making good gains on us. It was a smaller ship with a larger sail-to-size ratio, equipped primarily for speed, not transport. As it gained, Jacob and Edwin became more concerned. They were becoming convinced that the vessel was up to no good, and that preparations were to be made to defend the *Queensgate*.

The two cannon were wheeled into position and secured. The security force was in heavy action now. They had placed a number of loaded muskets at their command near the cannon. They had also brought up a brazier to heat up some of the cannon balls so that they could hurl at the enemy a red-hot ball that could ignite a sail. Since the "enemy" vessel was loaded with sails, a lucky hit could indeed start a damaging fire.

It was getting late in the day now, and tensions were rising as the mystery vessel approached. Fighting at night was not unknown, but it was very unusual. The wind began to pick up, and the *Queensgate* was picking up speed. The skillful hand of Edwin Carr became evident as he tacked masterfully into the wind and began to put distance between our ship and the rogue vessel. Soon, all signs of the intruder were gone. Perhaps they had left the fray, or perhaps they were just testing us, but through the night, the *Queensgate* was putting distance between herself and possible danger. By morning, we could no longer see the intruder vessel. Perhaps it was an innocent encounter, or perhaps the intruders were simply shown the deft hand of a veteran captain. In any case, the *Queensgate* had escaped possible danger, and we were grateful.

The seas were calm, and we were making good time for a westerly voyage. Gerry, Adams, Hancock, Shepherd, and I became deeply involved in a discussion about the fate of America. Shepherd had much more experience with European sovereigns, and he talked of the unease they had with the American experience.

"You all think differently than people in Spain, France, Sweden, Russia, and Prussia," he said. "You may not be aware anymore, because you have had some twenty-five years of a kind of freedom unknown to most people in Europe. You have begun to see the world in a light which is not even possible for most people on the Continent to even conceive of. The serfs in Russia have no hope of ever having land of their own. People in Swabia, Prussia, France, and many other lands are required to accept the religion of the ruler as their own or they are persecuted. In America, there is a way to follow one's own beliefs without succumbing to the demands of the ruler. Do you understand the gift that you have?"

"I suppose one never really appreciates what he has until it is taken from him," I ventured.

"Human nature," several muttered in agreement.

"Yes, so true," said Shepherd. "I believe that America has a destiny, larger than any individual's capacity to understand freedom. People seeking asylum in America, people such as me, are looking for our own interests. We

266

need to find our larger mission in making an America which is a haven for people seeking safety, asylum, or escape from shackles and poverty. What a mission to serve!"

We pondered on this as Shepherd spoke. Indeed, we came to America for our own needs for protection, freedom, independence from oppression – just a fresh start for many of us. Shepherd's vision for an America based upon such principles made it rise to an almost divine mission. Our collective desires for a freedom in America could merge into a system whereby people could, for generations to come, find on American soil the freedoms that were so elusive in Europe. It could be that "beacon on a hill" that John Winthrop had written about several years prior.

Gerry, Hancock, and Adams were strong men with vision. Yet I do not think that they had been challenged beyond the need for personal freedoms and economic freedoms until Shepherd made the case for a *system* that might perpetuate such freedoms for generations to come. A new order was needed for such a system, and these men could be the ones to influence those future generations.

The rest of our voyage proceeded smoothly. We saw no further signs of the mysterious vessel that had shadowed us early in the voyage. We neared Boston harbor, which seemed to have grown even in the short time we were away in England. A bustling fishing industry was growing as the market for cod grew.

Shepherd was stunned at what he saw. He became convinced that America would be in the forefront of new movements in commerce, religious freedom, and invention. He was anxious to see the home that Margaret and I shared, and I was excited to have him with me at my next lectures at Harvard. He was such a presence when he spoke that I was sure that the students would be fascinated by his views and his wisdom.

Within a week, we seemed to be almost back into a routine. Shepherd stayed with Margaret and me, and he met our grandson, John, now over two years old, as Anna brought him to our home in welcoming our return.

"Meet John Adams!" smiled Anna as she introduced her son to Joseph. "He is named for his father!"

Shepherd smiled as he lifted little John into the air with a swing of his arms. John squealed with delight at this, and Shepherd then grew serious.

"This little boy will grow to be a man with a legacy," he said. "His children and generations to come will be blessed by him."

I thanked Shepherd for his kind words, but Shepherd explained.

"A strong feeling came over me as I lifted this child. It was as if I heard God say that 'this child will lift a nation as you have lifted him in the air,'" he said.

267

"Well, I hope that you are right about that," I managed to say. However, all of us in the room later said that we were strangely moved by those words of Shepherd.

Chapter 61

A few weeks later I returned to my duties at Harvard. Teaching students about the medical arts was a very enjoyable part of my life. In order to teach about medicine, I strongly believed that one needed to practice it every day as well. Shepherd joined me in my practice as physician, and it seemed like our old adventures together were simply renewed but had never ceased. Shepherd told me of the latest advances he had learned while on the Continent.

We discussed William Culpepper's ideas about herbal medicine. Shepherd believed in the use of herbals, but disdained how Culpepper, and even Kepler, had attached any value to linking medicines to the zodiac signs. Shepherd discouraged me from using bloodletting as a cure for any illness, including fevers. Shepherd talked about the importance of dealing holistically with people, not separating physical, spiritual, and emotional health, but having our patients work toward health in all those areas. He reasoned that diet played an important part in maintaining good health, and he would write out a plan for each of his patients what foods might be most healing – much like he had done for King James so many years ago.

One day a slave from one of the tobacco plantations in Virginia was brought to us. The slave, known only as "Jupiter," was a fairly young man who looked much older than his years. Rarely did we know the age of the slaves – even they themselves often did not know their own age – so we guessed him to be in his late twenties, based upon his recollections of his youth. His body was ravaged with scars – a sign of an independent spirit that had been tamed with lashes. He had run away from the tobacco plantation and had found his way north through the help of some churchmen he encountered along the way. Reverend Amos Willis brought him to us when he found Jupiter staggering along the road near his church. Jupiter had been showing signs of fever, and he was seeing visions of angels and "hearing their beautiful voices." Reverend Willis did not know how to help the poor man, but he was unwilling to let him go on his way without help.

"I can do no less than the Good Samaritan," Willis said as he brought the slave into our "hospital," which was two small rooms added on to our home.

Shepherd began his examination by simply talking quietly to Jupiter, as Jupiter sat in a large chair. He asked the slave how long he had been travelling, what he had eaten lately, what kind of water he had been drinking, how much sleep he had in the past week, and whether he had any family.

Jupiter, though burning with fever, seemed taken aback by Shepherd's interest in him.

"Son, how can I help you if I do not get to know more about you?" Shepherd replied.

Jupiter began to weep as he replied to Shepherd.

"You is one of them angels I seen!" Jupiter said.

"I am not one of those angels," Shepherd said softly, "but I do mean to help you."

"Nobody ever ask me about my family," Jupiter said. "I don't know who my family is since I left my home on that devil ship. I was a boy, and I got took by these people and put on a ship. Most people like me died on that ship, but I lived. Got took to Charleston and sold to some evil men. Got took to a plantation somewhere, and I had to plant and hoe tobacco. I worked hard, but I hated everybody around me. When I been there a while, they seen how big and strong I was. They start calling me "Jupiter" 'cause I was big and strong. They told me I was "breedin' stock," and they put me with women. Told me to "go have some fun" with them and make some babies for them.

"I done what they said, but they started beatin' me more often. Somebody said those men was jealous of me getting to be with those women. They just beat me all the time. So I ran away, but they always caught me and beat me more. The last time I run, they do not catch me. I still be runnin' but I got sick. Been sick for a week or more now…"

He trailed off at that point and slumped in his chair. We carried Jupiter to a bed and covered him with a blanket. These were, at the time, the only things we could do for the poor man's benefit.

I looked at Shepherd and said, "Is there anything we can do for him? I think he is near death."

"He is surely very ill, Luke," said Shepherd. "I am not sure of what those 'visions' are, but they could be the result of his fever. Until we do a further examination, we can just try to keep him comfortable."

"We will be lucky to keep him alive," I countered.

Jupiter survived through the night. Shepherd and I took turns checking on him as he slept, and we were exhausted the next day. In late morning, Jupiter stirred, then sat up with a start, screaming and covering his head as if to ward off blows of unseen attackers. He was drenched in sweat, and it appeared that his fever had broken. We gave him water, and he drank copiously. Calmer now, he was able to relate the dream that woke him up.

"I was runnin' from them masters that always beat me. But then I slipped and fell, and they catch me and they start beatin' on me worse than ever. Then one man he raise his hand, and he got a gun – he gonna kill me, I say to myself. He cock the hammer and he aim, and he say, 'Lord Kensington is gonna pay me a bounty for killing your sorry arse. You ran away for the last time!' Then I wake up – I think. Is I dead?"

270

I began to laugh out of exhaustion, relief, and the absurdity of the question.

Shepherd smiled, "No, Jupiter, you are not dead. Perhaps your life has really just begun!" he assured the slave. "Now tell us, what is your given name? Jupiter is the name the slavers gave to you. What is your true name?"

"My name... my name is Chibuike," he said. He gave a faint smile, which showed several missing teeth, and gums that looked red and painful. He still looked somewhat muscular, but he was very thin, having evidently lost weight on his run to freedom.

"We will harbor you here," said Shepherd almost immediately.

I was not nearly as certain about the idea as Shepherd was. There was a fair amount of danger in harboring a runaway slave, mostly from the owners. The slave was property of another person, therefore harboring a slave was considered to be stealing.

"Joseph," I said, "I do not think it wise to harbor a slave under my roof. My family and my reputation are at stake. You too could suffer for this, since we both know that it is stealing to harbor this man from his rightful owner."

Shepherd looked at me with a withering stare, something that had never been directed toward me from him.

"Luke, you worry about your reputation when a man's life is at stake here. You would take in a stray dog who was wounded without question – indeed, I have seen you do just that. But you question whether you should save the life of this man?"

I could not respond to that. Shepherd refused to consider the consequences for himself for doing something that he believed was the right thing. Whether it was safe or legal were not the first considerations. Rather, the first consideration was, "What is right?"

Chibuike heard our discussion and responded.

"I don't want no trouble for you two. You helped me, now you can let me move on," he said.

"I do not know what Dr. Greene will do, Chibuike," said Shepherd, "but I will not allow a sick man to go out to his demise. I will travel with you to find a more hospitable place, if need be."

Shepherd had managed to shame me and offend me at the same time. He seemed to have a talent for that.

"Dr. Shepherd has not the means to help you, Chibuike. It seems I need to take care of both of you, so you will stay here while I consider what to do next," I snipped.

Shepherd smiled a smug little grin, and I broke into laughter that overcame my anger at the time.

"Shepherd, you always seem to get your way. Why should this time be any different?" I said.

271

Chibuike could not understand what just took place, so Shepherd, smiling, finally said, "Chibuike, we are under the care of Dr. Greene now, so we must stay and be good patients for him."

Chibuike nodded and smiled. We now had another member of the household, at least for a while.

Chapter 62

Sean Kelley and Chepi had heard that Shepherd was back in America. They were living outside of Boston on a small farm with Kimi, now twenty-three years old. Kimi was different after her encounter with the devilish Lehane. She was now quiet, reserved, and even timid around people. She feared to be with men, and professed that she would never marry or want to have children. She tended to her chores, helped with the farm, and showed unusual ability in understanding herbs, plants, flowers, and trees as natural remedies for illnesses. Some thought her to be odd or eccentric in this talent. For example, she would deliberately have people with pain in their bone joints be exposed to bee stings in the area of the pain. After a while, those people brave (or foolish) enough to have allowed this odd treatment swore that they had less pain, and that they would allow Kimi to continue to do this in the future for them. Kimi seemed indifferent to the whispers about her being strange, even perhaps being a witch. Chepi took great offense to such talk, and no one dared offend Chepi. She too was considered a mysterious woman, especially because of her Algonquin heritage.

Kelley, Chepi, and Kimi visited Joseph, Margaret, and me, and we asked them to stay for a few days. Shepherd had not seen Kimi since she was a baby, and he was delighted to see Kelley and Chepi. We talked for hours about life in England, life in America, and the future for all of us. Chepi, through her contacts in the Algonquin community, had been hearing more disturbing news about white men who were stirring up trouble. The Algonquin people were being devastated by the changes that were happening because of the presence of both French and English settlers and adventurers. Diseases they had never seen were wiping out whole clusters of Algonquin, forcing them to change the lifestyles they had had for generations. The presence of rum, more and more firearms, and the English practice of wiping out large swaths of trees for lumber were bewildering to them.

"These people ravage the land!" said Kimi. "We must live *with* the land." We had heard such talk before, but Kimi proceeded to say, "We also hear more about treaties and promises from the French and the English. They want Algonquin, Seneca, Wampanoag, Iroquois, and other peoples to align with them and fight the other side. I think they want tribes to fight their battles for them," she concluded.

Later in the evening, as the women were cleaning up after our supper, Kelley, Shepherd, and I were reminiscing about our old times together. Then Kelley told us of his worries for Kimi. She was a bright and feisty young woman, and perhaps no man would, or would want to, be a match for her. Kelley feared that she would be a spinster growing colder in her old age.

"She loves her mother and me," said Kelley, "but we will not be around forever. What will become of her when we are gone? I do not think that she can return to her own people. She looks at the world through Algonquin eyes, but she is considered a white woman by the Algonquin, and Algonquin by whites. I fear for what will happen to her."

"She is a skilled and intelligent young woman," said Shepherd. "I believe that she can make her way in the world without a husband."

"Well, she will need to," said Kelley. "I know she must find a life outside of her parents, but she is fearful of that despite her stern appearances to others."

I sensed that Kelley was asking us for something – an answer of some type – but I had no response to him. Shepherd, however, did offer something for thought, saying, "May I suggest that Kimi stay with us and help us as we provide medical care for the community? She is quite skilled at finding natural medicines, and she can be very valuable to us as we minister to the native population that we encounter who want our help."

Once again, Shepherd was volunteering me for something that I had not considered. Again, I was offended and angry about his presumptions upon me and our friendship. His talk about ministering to the native population was a surprise also. Yes, occasionally we would be asked to help with some Indians, but that was seldom, and certainly not worth adding on someone to help for just that. Not wanting to offend Kelley, I said that we would consider talking with Kimi, but made no promises of anything beyond that.

After the others retired for the evening, I asked to speak with Shepherd.

"Joseph," I began, "I have become weary of your arrogance that you may make plans for my future! First with Chibuike, now with Kimi. We cannot simply take in all the people in this country who have problems. Yes, God has blessed me with some resources to care well for my family, but it is not up to you to be volunteering them to others. You rely upon my friendship, and indeed it will always be there, but you cannot use it in order to simply make yourself feel better that you have alleviated suffering through your presumption of that friendship."

Shepherd looked straight ahead and said nothing for some time. He finally spoke.

"You are correct in your assessment, Luke. I have presumed upon our friendship to achieve what I would like to do, what I believe is right. I have no right to assume that you share those same ideas, nor do I have the right to speak with your voice in these matters."

I had gotten myself into a self-righteous anger, and I was spoiling for an argument to convince him of my position. I wanted him to feel uncomfortable and argue back. His response left me speechless.

Nonetheless, I continued, "I cannot have you putting me in these positions. I have resented this in the past, but I ended up acceding to your wishes. I will no longer do this, Joseph."

"Very well," he said, "I understand. Please forgive my behavior; I did not mean to hurt you, Luke."

With that he left the room and retired for the evening. I was left with having the winning hand, but no joy in the victory.

At some point in the night, Joseph had left our house. The next morning, we learned that he had walked down to the harbor and that he had been seen in the company of several men near Oldham's Tavern. Such information usually did not bode well. Oldham's Tavern was the site of veteran seamen who were looking for work on a ship. Edwin Carr never took men from there as he was trying to put together a crew. Other captains did secure seamen from there, often to regret it later when they found these men to be thieves and scoundrels. However, these men worked cheap, seldom asking for much in actual wages, and only wanted to be left alone about their past duties on ships. Past sins were not brought up by captain or crew. Only loyalty to the ship, and willingness to fight to defend the ship and its cargo, were really required.

We also learned that just two weeks before, a ship had docked that was smallish in size, but had large sail capacity. It was built for speed, but not much for large cargo. It looked like a raider ship, and it was registered to Lord Andrew Kensington's London & Western Trading Company. It was the same ship that had badgered us on our return trip to America.

Chapter 63

Kelley and I went down Oldham's Tavern to talk with people there about having seen Dr. Shepherd. The owner, Horace Oldham, was a large man with ruddy red complexion and a scruffy white beard. He had been a sailor at one time, but stories varied about his past. Perhaps he had been in His Majesty's service, but perhaps he had simply been a brigand who claimed such service. He was advanced in years, and he lived alone in a room in the back of the tavern.

"What do you fellas want?" he asked.

"My friend and I came to buy a drink and to talk with you about some events of last evening," I said. Surely I knew that I would get no information without overpaying for a drink of rum.

"What do you want to know?" he said. "You know I don't know nothin' that goes on around here," he preempted.

"Let me buy my drinks, and then we can decide if you know anything or not," I said. Oldham knew what I meant by that and he became a little more agreeable. "How much for two rums?" I asked.

"I reckon three shillings a glass is fair, but four would be a might better," he winked. I handed him ten shillings and he poured us the drinks.

"There was a ship that came in a couple of weeks ago from the Western & London Trading Company," I said. "Did any of the crew come in here last night?"

"I get a lot of sailors come in here," he said, "and I never ask them what ship they serve on."

"Was there any disturbance here last night? Anything that seemed unusual?" I asked.

"Not in here," he said, "but the constable came by after I closed up the place, and he was askin' about some ruckus down at the harbor. I guess he thinks that whenever there is a ruckus, the men must have come from Oldham's place!" he said laughing.

"What did you tell him?" I asked.

"Well, a nigger come by here with a wild story about some men who rough handling another fella, sayin' they was gonna kill him. That sorta thing happens some down at the harbor, so I didn't pay him much attention, but this nigger was upset and about to bust. Wanted someone to come and help. I guess he got to the constable, but the constable don't listen much to slaves. The Constable got himself a drink and left. Never heard no more after that till you come in here," he finished.

"Did the slave give any names of who was in trouble?" I asked.

"Yes, now let me think a minute."

He paused. He looked at me in a way that I knew that such information would cost another drink.

"While you are thinking, give my friend and me another drink," I said.

Kelley, however, had had enough of this nonsense.

"Oldham, I'll take another drink, but you best remember that name or I will come over that counter and break you in half," he said with very little emotion.

Kelley, while up in years a bit, was still muscular from his daily farm work. Oldham took Kelley seriously, for he quickly remembered the name.

"Shepherd," he stammered, "Joseph Shepherd was that fella's name."

"What else did he say?" I asked.

"That's all – just that this fella Shepherd was bein' roughed up a little. Niggers get excited about such things, don't they?" he smiled, trying to ease the tension that Kelley had introduced.

"I can get kinda excited myself, Oldham," said Kelley. "I get excited when people don't tell me the whole truth, you know, like if they know something else but don't tell me? I can get very agitated, and you just never know what might happen."

Oldham swore that he knew nothing more, that the slave had run to the constable, and the constable showed up at the tavern.

I left with a bad feeling that Shepherd had once again found trouble, or it had found him. "We must find Chibuike," I said to Kelley. "I would guess that he is scared out of his wits, and he may have run off himself. We will go back and tell the women what has happened, and then we will try to find Chibuike."

Upon returning to the house, I found Margaret crying as she and Chepi and Kimi were discussing what they had just heard. Chibuike did finally return to our house, finding the courage to show himself to other people. He naturally feared for his own life, and, in fact, told us that he had overheard that very thing – a threat upon his life. But it was much worse than that…

277

Chapter 64

Chibuike was having trouble telling his story as he alternately wept and shuddered as he recalled what he had heard the night before. He had just begun telling of his encounter with the sailors from the London & Western Trading Company. The sailors had been drinking, and in their drunken ramblings they revealed much information. Their ship, named the *Cove*, had indeed docked about ten days earlier, and had unloaded a small cargo. That cargo was muskets, the finest French muskets that money could buy. They were headed, Chibuike understood, for French traders and hunters who could use them for weapons, or use them for trade with Indians. Chibuike had happened upon the group outside the Oldham Tavern, then quickly realized that he would not be safe if they saw him. He had hidden in a shed behind some bales of straw, which were used to refresh the filthy floor of the tavern at irregular intervals. He then heard the men enter the shed with a man whom they had captured and bound. He then peeked up just long enough to see that the victim was his protector, Joseph Shepherd.

Chibuike said he had scuttled behind the straw, fearful for his life. He heard the conversation now that the three men had with Shepherd, and relayed it to us in fits and starts.

"The one man say to Dr. Shepherd, 'Lord Kensington asked us to bring you along with us. Now, you come with us or we kill you, and we don't much care which one it is. But Lord Kensington thinks you may have some worth to us alive,' is what he said. Dr. Shepherd, he don't say nothin' back to them, so the other one says, 'If you don't come with us, we gonna kill you, and Dr. Greene and his family, and even that nigger and squaw he got at his house now. He say, 'We seen them all there tonight. We was outside the house ready to burn it down. We decided that having Dr. Shepherd alive would be better, since Lord Kensington tell us that we can get a ransom for him. He is a big man in England, and the people there want to talk with him about some things he done. Got some letters from all these people – kings and princes and such – that say he got to come there and work for them.'

"Dr. Shepherd, he say to them, 'I will go with you, but you must not harm Dr. Greene or anyone in his house.' Then he say, 'And do not try to extort money from them, or from anyone else, a ransom for me.' Then they say, 'We gonna do what we want with you; you ain't in charge here!' Then Dr. Shepherd, he say, 'I am no good to you dead, and we all know that. Promise me that Dr. Greene and his house are safe, and I will go with you.' Then they

278

took him down to the wharf, and I start to run back here. Nobody seen me. I'm good at runnin' and hidin'," and he had a faint smile on his face.

"Horace Oldham said that you had told the constable what happened, and the constable went to Oldham's tavern to ask about anyone seeing the disturbance," I said.

Chibuike looked dazed.

"Dr. Greene, I don't go near the constable. I am scared of that man. He might take me back to bein' a slave. I don't trust him or hardly anybody. Why would Mr. Oldham say that?" he asked.

"I don't know," I said, "but there is more going on here than we think."

I had suspected that Chibuike would stay as far away as possible from the constable. This now confirmed my thinking.

The women were crying, and Kelley and I were beyond fury. We were not going to allow Shepherd to be taken without a fight. Kelley and I gathered some men we trusted, and told them that we needed some help for Dr. Shepherd. Kelley and I were not young men any longer, but this outrage inspired us! We gathered a group of about fifteen men in just a few hours, and we headed down to Oldham's Tavern. Clearly, there had been some things that did not seem right, and Oldham's story about Chibuike and the constable was a good place to start. Kelley was glad to have another chance to confront Oldham, and I had to encourage him not to act too rashly too quickly. However, my heart was really not in that, since I too wanted to bash that devil's skull if he were really involved in some plot against Shepherd.

Kelley and I walked into Oldham's Tavern near dusk. Our little band of friends were waiting just outside the tavern, but out of view. As we walked in, Oldham began his brash posturing.

"You two ain't had enough excitement?" he said as we walked in.

"We just wanted to come in for another drink," I said calmly, but Oldham knew that was certainly not the case.

"I ain't got any more information for you two, so a drink is all you'll get from me," he said.

"I do not want any more of your information, Oldham," I said, "because I would not trust it to be true."

He squirmed a bit, but blustered and fumed. "You callin' me a liar?" he said.

Kelley could no longer constrain himself.

"We all know that you are a liar, Oldham. I just came for a piece of your hide," concluded Kelley.

Oldham's eyes grew wide. A man who was in the shadows came out and lunged at Kelley with a knife. Kelley saw him at the last second and stepped aside as the man lunged. The man hit the bar in front of Oldham, and Kelley drew his own knife and slashed the man's arm almost to the bone. The attacker howled in pain, and Kelley kicked the wounded man straight in his stomach. He dropped to the ground with no breath in him, and he was gasping for air. As soon as the men outside heard the ruckus in the tavern, they rushed in with knives, clubs, and pistols drawn, ready to wreak havoc with anyone foolhardy enough to challenge them. Oldham was stunned and, for once, speechless. The attacker began to finally draw a breath, and one of our men grabbed him and bound him with a chain. He was bleeding badly from the knife wound, but I saw that there appeared to be no likelihood that this wound was mortal, so I decided that a bleeding man might act as a good deterrent to more violence.

Indeed, Oldham quickly regained his voice then and blurted, "Are you fellows mad? What are you doing attacking my brother that way?"

"I really wanted to attack you," said Kelley, but that bastard had to be first. But you'll be next if you don't start telling the truth."

Oldham saw that he was seriously outnumbered, and that we had found that he was lying to us. I thought that Oldham was going to be forthcoming at this point, but Kelley went over to him and grabbed him by the collar and shoved him into the wall.

"I would cut your throat right here, but Dr. Greene would not have it. But I will beat the truth out of you right now," said an enraged Kelley.

Oldham was now in fear for his life, it appeared, and he told Kelley, "I will tell you everything I know!"

One of our men piped up, "That should not take too long!" and the laughter served to ease some of the tension that gripped the tavern.

Kelley backed away from Oldham a few paces, held up his knife, and said, "Start telling the truth, Oldham!"

Oldham took a deep breath and began to talk.

"Back last week, these men from Kensington's company came to the tavern. They had just entered port a few days before, and they said that they had a deal for me. They said that Lord Kensington had paid them to track down Joseph Shepherd and get him back to London. He had gotten ahold of letters from all over Europe about Shepherd and the things that he had done and some discoveries he had made."

Oldham said that he knew of Shepherd, and he knew of me, and he told these men where they could find us. When Shepherd wandered into Oldham's Tavern after leaving my house, unable to sleep, Oldham thought that he had been delivered a treasure. He notified the sailors through his brother Sam (now the worse for wear thanks to Kelley), and the men tracked down Shepherd near the tavern. Chibuike, who happened to be night-hunting for possum since he tried to remain scarce often during the daylight, stumbled upon the gathering on his hunt.

I found out later that Kensington had gotten hold of these letters which we had requested during the trial: the letters from Rene Descartes, Robert Boyle, the Queen of Sweden, King Christian of Denmark, Blaise Pascal, and

280

many others. Kensington, however, was only interested in one letter. A letter from Robert Moray was about a new kind of gunpowder that did not produce a cloud of smoke when it exploded. Shepherd had found some way to make this powder, and nobody else could apparently do it. Robert Moray, in whose letter these things were discovered, had given full credit to Shepherd for the discovery, even though he had written of the discovery of this new explosive powder in his notes.

"Where are Kensington's friends now?" I demanded of Oldham.

"I swear to you I don't know!" said Oldham, fearful for his life.

Kelley was not convinced of that, and he landed a tremendous blow to Oldham's stomach. Oldham fell to the floor and promptly vomited. He was in misery now, and Kelley would not relent.

"You tell me where Dr. Shepherd is or you will never get up from this floor!" Kelley roared.

Oldham tried to regain his breath, and I intervened.

"Sean, hold back just a bit and allow the man to breathe," I said.

Oldham was on his hands and knees and crawling through his own vomit trying to get to his feet.

"All I know," he said feebly, "is that those sailors were headed back to their ship. They were going to head back to England as soon as they could to get Shepherd back there to Kensington. That is all I know," he sputtered. Oldham then fell on the slippery floor, grabbed at his chest in pain and cried out. Then he lay there motionless. I rushed over to him and saw a tinge of blue coming to his lips.

"Dear God," I muttered. I listened to his heart, and I took his wrist to measure his pulse. Shepherd and I had learned this from Santorio at Padua during our brief trip there. We had found this skill very useful in our practices, and now I was desperately hoping to find a clear pulse. I could not.

Chapter 65

The constable had met with Kelley and me about the death of Horace Oldham. He had died on the floor of his own pub with Kelley, me, and a handful of our friends, who had confronted him and then witnessed his death. Oldham's brother, Elmer, had been seriously wounded in the fight with Kelley, and he had asked the constable to charge Kelley with murder. I had attested to the fact that Oldham had died of natural causes. While no charges were brought on us, Elmer Oldham became a sworn enemy who vowed to avenge the death of his brother.

Our son Jacob had been seeing Jane Smith, whose family had come over on the *Mayflower* in 1620. Jacob wanted to settle down and have children, much like his sister Anna. They were married in early winter, soon after Shepherd was taken captive and whisked away from us. We loved Jane and her fiery spirit. She expected that Jacob would forego his sailing career if he were to be serious about having children with her.

Indeed, Jacob had been considering starting his own business, and he took in his brother-in-law, John Adams, as his partner. Adams was an astute businessman, schooled in the law. Jacob knew sailing and commerce from the Massachusetts Bay Company, and, together, they began a shipbuilding business with an eye toward capitalizing on the burgeoning cod industry. Jacob believed that the inexhaustible cod population around the bay could feed the world. His technique for salting the cod to preserve it was something he learned from Chepi and Kimi. The amount of salt needed to be just right to correctly preserve the freshness and flavor of the fish, but not so much as to destroy the flaky flesh of the cod. Kimi and Chepi had kept this skill for themselves from their Algonquin heritage, but they shared it with Jacob because of their trust and affection for him.

Chibuike was learning a trade as Kelley took him in to help him to learn about hunting and farming. He was a very hard worker, and grateful for the opportunity which we had given to him. Kelley entrusted Chibuike with a musket for hunting. It was indeed rare for a former slave to be given access to a firearm, but Kelley had no real hesitation in allowing this. In fact, Chibuike became a rather skilled hunter, and he was able to bring in more game for our winter larder. Chibuike was helpful to not only Kelley and Chepi, but to Kimi, who became fond of him. He was the first man that Kimi actually had trust for. Chibuike also talked with Kimi about his interest in healing roots and herbs, talking with her about his native plants in Africa that had medicinal qualities.

I felt ashamed often when I thought about how I had resisted Shepherd in his compassionate efforts toward Chibuike and Kimi.

I was now sixty-one years old and, while slowing down some, had retained a large degree of my physical health. Here again, I needed to credit Shepherd, who had ideas about the value of physical exercise. Most physicians and professors advocated rest as a way to preserve the body. Shepherd however, in his typical paradoxical ways, suggested that daily exercise was essential for good health, as well as a diet that included many green vegetables and less meat. He was routinely ridiculed for this type of thinking, but he seemed to have little regard for criticism when he was convinced that he was right about something.

"One needs to live with oneself," he would say. "If you know who you are and what you believe, you will not become simply what others desire you to be," he would conclude.

So with Shepherd in mind, I continued my daily exercise, which usually was vigorous work in the garden, repairs on my house, and long walks to my work settings rather than riding my horse.

I believed that it was important to chronicle family journeys for future generations. America, I believed, would be that "beacon on the hill," and those of us who came here from England should write out that story as it was unfolding. Much like Shepherd referenced the Bible as a chronicle of faith, so journals, diaries, personal reflections, and historical works should be passed through family generations.

I had this discussion with both Jacob and Anna. Both agreed that such writings would be great ways to preserve the history of our family, and also could be of value to people even outside of our family, even with the knowledge that our family history might not be of impact or interest outside of those who followed in future generations of the Greenes, Carrs, and Adamses.

So, with this in mind, Jacob and Anna promised to preserve family history by writing their family story, and also to make this a heritage and expectation of future generations. I was so pleased that they respected my wishes and had even agreed so readily to this solemn pledge. I believed that our family story would persevere for generations to come.

I was, however, considering my future generations in this new land. America was clearly now my home, and I doubted that I would ever return to England. If indeed Shepherd was being taken back to England against his will, I would have been willing to take on the task of another trip back to help rescue him. More realistically, we would write to our friends in England who could be of more help in tracking him down, as well as the brigands who had captured him.

People at the Massachusetts Bay Company in London would be my first contacts. Jacob Carr and John Adams could secure more help in London than I could at this time. Indeed, they had already begun to try to contact people in London who could be of help when the next ship left Boston harbor.

Chapter 66

The sailors of the *Cove* had bound Shepherd and had taken him down to the harbor under cover of darkness. They had a day's head start on us in absconding with Shepherd. They likely planned to sail at night and be safely beyond sight of land before dawn. Shepherd, true to his word, offered no resistance to them in exchange for the promise that no harm would come to the Greene extended household.

Edwin and Jacob Carr were alerted about what had happened. We figured that we might need to pursue the *Cove* to try to save Joseph. Edwin and Jacob said that they had no access to a ship of the Massachusetts Bay Company for at least a week, perhaps two weeks, due to refitting. The type of ship required for this venture would also need to be fast, and able to fight if it were to come against the *Cove*. No such ship was available.

We decided to go down to the harbor in hopes of finding the *Cove* before she headed to England. Our little band of warriors was ready for action, and Kelley in particular. Despite his advancing years, and his bad leg from the old injury on the *Intrepid*, he was still a man of action and courage.

When we reached the harbor, we saw no ship that matched the description of the *Cove*. There were several fishing boats, and one ship from the Massachusetts Bay Company that was being refitted for service. A few fishermen told us that they had seen the ship we described a few days ago, but she had slipped away one night, and she was well on to the ocean by now. Once again, Shepherd was headed to England without me, but this time not of his own accord.

While out at sea, the *Cove* made good time. Clear but cold late December days were fine for sailing, but there was always risk of a winter storm. Sailors spent their time repairing the inevitable leaks, sewing torn sails, etc., but mostly they were bored and they drank. Discipline on ships such as this were only as good as the Captain's leadership and command. This was not an English ship of the line. It was more a combination raider/trader ship – a type that Kensington had practically invented.

The captain, Mr. Morley, was stern and weathered. Scarred from not only smallpox but some facial wounds from a sword, he was somewhat unpleasant of appearance. He evidently tried to compensate for his ugly appearance with an ugly disposition. This, of course, seldom produces the desired effect, but Morley was a man not to be disputed with.

One day, Morley was bragging to the men about his way with women. He went on to talk about all the women around the world with whom he had shared a bed. One of the crew, Eli Curtis, began to laugh hysterically. Indeed, he had been drinking, and his loose tongue was to be his undoing. Curtis uttered between laughs, "You mean to say that some woman would actually would want to be in the same room with you, much less the same bed?"

The rest of the men around Curtis heard the remark and started to laugh. Morley glared at Curtis, then drew his knife out of its sheath. He moved on Curtis with the knife. Curtis, with no weapon, turned away from the raging Morley, but Morley kept coming. No one moved to stop Morley, and Morley lunged at Curtis with the knife. Stumbling out of the way now, Curtis ran out of room, and Morley stabbed Curtis in the back as he tried to escape. Morley pulled at the knife, but Curtis's muscles had enclosed around it, and Morley could not easily withdraw the knife from the back of the wounded Curtis, who now fell on to some rigging. Curtis lay wounded, the knife protruding from his back as a grisly reminder of Morley's uncontrolled rage.

Curtis was seriously wounded as he lay in pain and shame, helpless to remove the knife, and unaided by the rest of the crew. Morley withdrew to his cabin, and only then did some men come to Curtis's aid. The man who served as ship physician, Mr. Davies, was untrained and not particularly competent. He withdrew the knife from the bleeding wound with some effort. He then found a rag, placed it on the wound, and tied another, larger cloth around Curtis's torso to keep the bandage in place.

He sat Curtis up and gave him a draught of rum to calm him. Curtis was in a good deal of pain, and he drank the rum greedily. Davies and one other man helped him to a bunk below deck and placed in the space that Shepherd occupied. More rum finally dulled the pain and allowed a fitful sleep for Curtis.

Shepherd was bound and chained to a bulkhead as Mr. Davies moved Curtis below deck. Curtis awoke much later to see Shepherd hunched over him, trying to tend to Curtis's wound.

"How did you get out of those shackles?" questioned Curtis.

Shepherd smiled.

"I have been free from them the whole time," he replied. "I simply slip them back on when I hear someone coming here."

"You mean you are free whenever you want to be?" asked the puzzled Curtis.

"Yes, you could say that. I am always as free as I want to be," said Shepherd to the bewildered Curtis. "I slip those shackles back on to allow the crew to feel at ease with my confinement. I am no risk of flight. I have given my word to Mr. Morley that I would go to England with this ship, and I mean to keep my word. Unless God provides some other answer, we will all return to England together. However, it appears that you are in some trouble. What happened?"

Curtis related his story to Shepherd, but the pain was worsening, and Curtis was drifting away from his narrative. Shepherd asked if he could be of help to Curtis, and Curtis just nodded. Shepherd unwrapped the cloth from Curtis and found the area around his back to be filthy with clotted blood, dirt, and bits of cloth. Curtis looked to be turning pale, and Shepherd suspected that there might be some internal damage, not just a wound in the muscles of his back. Curtis then coughed heartily, and blood dripped from his mouth.

Shepherd now believed that there was almost certainly some internal injury to Curtis, likely a punctured lung. Shepherd had seen this before, and decided that he needed to take action to relieve Curtis's suffering and perhaps save his life. Shepherd rummaged through his area and found that Mr. Davies had left his medical bag in the corner as he was moving Curtis. Shepherd saw in the bag an instrument that resembled an awl. He carefully cleaned the instrument and punctured Curtis's side between his ribs. He then inserted a thin copper tube that he had found on a makeshift still the men used to make "sailor's rum." Upon inserting the tube, air from Curtis's chest was released. Shepherd decided to leave the tube in for a little while to help relieve the painful pressure that Curtis was experiencing. Curtis had mercifully fallen unconscious and was now at some level of rest, albeit fitful at times.

Shepherd heard stirring as someone was coming below deck, and he slipped his chains back on. Mr. Morley had come to check on his victim. Morley moved close to Curtis and saw the tube protruding from his side.

"Good God in heaven, what is this!" screamed Morley. "Who did this to you? Did Davies do this to you?"

Curtis was still unconscious and unable to respond. Morley then looked at Shepherd.

"Did you do this to him?" he asked. Shepherd remained silent. Morley went over to Shepherd and kicked his leg. "Answer me, man, I am talking to you!" screamed Morley.

Shepherd remained silent as Morley raged.

"Are you trying to kill this man?" asked Morley.

Shepherd had to restrain himself from commenting on the incredible irony of that statement, but he again remained silent.

Morley left to go above to ask Mr. Davies if he had put a copper tube in Curtis's side. Upon reaching Davies, Morley screamed at him, "What are you doing to Curtis, sticking a tube in his side?"

Davies was dumbstruck.

"I did no such thing!" he proclaimed.

"Well, go below deck and see for yourself!" he said.

Davies went below with Morley and saw Curtis lying on his side, apparently asleep. He saw Shepherd shackled to the bulkhead with his head down, possibly also asleep. He then saw the thin tube of copper sticking in Curtis.

287

"Mr. Morley, I tended to Curtis with utmost care, wrapping a bandage around his wound. I gave him rum and laid him below deck. I did nothing else," he concluded.

Morley took Curtis by the arm to rouse him, and Curtis began to stir.

"Oddest dream I ever had," he began groggily. "I seen Shepherd moving about freely, then he comes over to me and I dreamt he was the one that stabbed me again, this time in my side," he said, almost laughing. "I felt some better after he stabbed me though, not like the first time in my back – that hurt like hellfire!" Curtis then allowed a little chuckle amidst his pain. "What is this in my side?" he then shouted. "My God, he left the knife in me!"

Shepherd then finally spoke.

"Yes, I put that tube in Mr. Curtis in order to relieve his pain and help him. Indeed, I believe that it has," he concluded.

"Well take it out of him now," said Davies. "The poor devil is scared out of his mind!"

Shepherd reluctantly agreed and gently removed the tube.

"I may need to reinsert this," he told Curtis, "but it will help you more than it hurts you."

Davies scoffed and said, "You'll have no more to do with this man. Heaven knows the harm you have already caused him!"

Morley was amazed at what he had just seen, but he was also enraged about Shepherd's deception.

"You removed your shackles even though you promised you wouldn't cause trouble. Then you stab a copper tube into an injured man and you say nothing. You are an arrogant rogue, just like they said about you. You cause trouble wherever you go. Now you are going to get shackles you can't break, and a taste of the lash as well!" concluded the raging Morley. "But that comes later, Shepherd. That will be a public lashing tomorrow. Always good to have the crew see discipline at work on a ship," he laughed. "Discipline at work!"

Chapter 67

The next day, Morley assembled the crew of the *Cove* and chose Argus Hurst to be the man to wield the whip on Shepherd. Hurst was an especially cruel and possibly deranged man who relished inflicting pain on others. His reputation as a sailor included some battles with Moorish pirates off the Canary Islands. He had been dismissed from the King's service after having beaten a pirate to death who had been captured in a sea battle. Hurst had gone into service with Kensington after escaping hanging for thievery outside pubs where he would find drunken patrons in the alley, rob them, then beat them savagely. Hurst wanted the opportunity to have free reign for meting out his cruelty on someone. Morley knew Hurst's tendencies, and picked him to administer the lashes to Shepherd. The number of lashes determined by Morley was to be twenty, administered to Shepherd's back as he was tied to a mast.

Many of the crew were uneasy with this punishment, knowing that Shepherd had simply acted out of compassion toward Spencer. Morley wanted more compliance from his crew, and for Shepherd to be incapacitated for the rest of the voyage. When Shepherd had been secured to the mast, Morley told Hurst to begin the lashes. Hurst seemed to grin as he reared back for two fast, sharp blows from the lash to Shepherd's back. Shepherd grimaced as blood splattered from his torn back. Hurst gave another hard blow to Shepherd's back and more blood splattered. The crew raised no voice of approval as Morley had seen in some past commands. Some turned their head as Hurst struck again and again. Shepherd faltered and lost control of his legs, unable to stand. He was now just hanging by the leather straps that secured his hands to the mast.

The sky, which had been somewhat overcast, now grew darker, and a sudden gust of wind whipped the sails, tossing the *Cove* violently. Hurst lost his footing, fell hard on the deck, and he cursed loudly. He rose to his feet only to fall again as wind whipped the sails and waves crashed the deck, causing slippery footing. Morley was enraged that his show of discipline seemed to end so quickly. Morley was forced to dispatch his crew to stations to secure sails and equipment on the ship. He told Davies to untie Shepherd, tend to his wounds, and secure him below deck.

Shepherd was in a great deal of pain. Davies untied Shepherd from the mast and quickly took him below. The weather now was turning quite ugly. The skies, once leaden, now were almost black. Lightning lit the blackish backdrop in the sky and rain started falling in sheets. Winds were now sustained, not just gusting, and the crew was working feverishly to roll up sails so that they were not shredded, and to save the ship from being torn apart.

Chaos ruled the *Cove* as cursing sailors tried to secure tattered sails. Morley was screaming orders to sailors who could not hear anything over the howling wind and rain. Hurst, still trying to get a secure footing, crashed into a spar, and fell yet again. This time he landed unconscious on the deck. A sudden heave of the *Cove* sent him flying off the deck into the roiling ocean. He was quickly carried away from the reeling *Cove* and was never seen again.

Below deck, Davies tried to apply salve to Shepherd's ugly wounds. The rolling ship did not allow for such treatment, however, and Shepherd thanked Davies for his efforts.

"The conditions do not allow for such treatment now, Mr. Davies," said Shepherd. "Go help with the work to save the ship."

Davies agreed and left Shepherd unshackled below deck. Efforts above deck were not going well as the winds continued unabated. The *Cove* was in serious danger now. Drifting at the whim of the winds, she began to take on water. The *Cove* was breaking up from the stresses of nature. A terrific noise overcame even the howling wind as the small ship succumbed to the shearing winds. The *Cove* had split nearly in half!

Sailors now panicked as the ship was disintegrating beneath them. Several men fell from the masts into the raging sea. Most were crying out to God, screaming for their mother, or were cursing their fate until the end. Morley, screaming to no avail, was felled by a toppling mast and killed instantly. Ultimately, all above deck perished as the ship began to break apart. Below deck, Shepherd saw water rushing in, and he scrambled up the ladder toward the top deck. As the ship heaved its near final groan above water, Shepherd spotted a small boat that was still lashed to the aft of the ship. It was used at times for sailors to venture out to fish for more provisions when food stocks were getting depleted.

Shepherd found a knife on the nearby body of Mr. Morley. He seized the knife and cut through the ropes holding the little vessel. Shepherd simply jumped into the little boat as the *Cove* broke completely apart. As the *Cove* spun about in the storm, the little boat fell into the sea with Shepherd clinging on the oars, which remained lashed inside the boat. The storm, now losing strength as the evening approached, splashed salty water onto the torn back of Shepherd. It was both pain as well as relief to him now as he lay exhausted on the floor of the boat. Gradually, the storm gave way to calm, and Shepherd could look up at the sun starting to appear as it was dipping below the horizon. The last bits of debris of the *Cove* were now outlined on the setting sun. Shepherd gave thanks for his miracle rescue as the sole survivor of a maritime tragedy. The skies began to clear as nighttime approached. Night fell on the sinking *Cove,* each half of the broken vessel sinking at its own pace. Shepherd finally had some peace, secure in his little boat. As it drifted lazily in the now calm waters, the small boat seemed to dance in the moonlight...

Epilogue

Anna Adams and Jacob (Greene) Carr were true to their word, and they kept lengthy and detailed journals, which were passed down through generations. Over the years, these journals were a source of delight for children, grandchildren, and even more generations that came.

Anna and John Adams' children did indeed have an influence on future generations as Shepherd had predicted when he picked up little John Adams. Their lineage produced two presidents, John Adams and John Quincy Adams, scholars, writers, and historians. Through the distant influence of Dr. Greene, this lineage produced some of the best documentation of American history to date. Charles Francis Adams, descendant of John Adams, became a great chronicler of American history – a history that depicts the strong love of country and dedication to faith that marked the early American landscape.

Jacob (Greene) Carr continued in his partnership with his brother-in-law, John Adams, and his "uncle," Edwin Carr. They became very successful in the shipping business, developing new contracts with Spain, Portugal, and Holland for salt cod and oysters, and beaver pelt. He had three sons and one daughter, Margaret Eliza Carr, who married John Madison. Margaret Eliza Carr's great-great-grandson, James Madison, had a large hand in writing the American Constitution, and became the fourth President of the United States.

Anna wrote not just of her family, but of Kelley, Chepi, Kimi, and Chibuike. Sean Kelley died in 1665, having seen his beloved wife Chepi die at the hands of Elmer Oldham some two years after Kelley had inadvertently killed Elmer's brother in the Oldham Tavern. Elmer Oldham died at the end of a hangman's rope soon after he murdered Chepi. However, Elmer Oldham's sworn revenge murder of Chepi seemed to take the heart out of Kelley. He later recovered somewhat after he moved in with Luke and Margaret Greene. He lived out the rest of his life in peace with the Greenes and continued to be a mentor for Chibuike.

Chibuike and Kimi married and were threatened with banishment from the community for miscegenation. It was only by the efforts of Kelley and Greene that they were allowed to continue to live at the Kelley farm in relative peace. They wanted no public attention and were content to live out their lives on the farm. While publicly shunned and shamed, and periodically threatened with being tried as witches, they also ministered their herbal remedies and medicines to people in very private, discreet, late-night encounters. People who railed at them in public would come to their cabin in the dark of night seeking relief from various maladies, and they were never turned away.

Chibuike and Kimi had a daughter, "Little Kimi," who married "Prince" Attucks in 1688. They had a daughter, Nancy Attucks, who bore Crispus Attucks in 1723. Crispus Attucks became the first casualty of the American Revolution when he died in a hail of British musket fire at the Boston Massacre.

Herbert Wesley returned to England, but never forgot his time in America. He had returned to England to care for his ailing mother, and he was never able to return to America. His progeny, however, would share that love for America, and later would help to shape and transform it. He and his wife had seven children, and two of his great grandchildren, John and Charles Wesley, founded a great spiritual movement which changed the Old and New Worlds with great revivals of faith.

Anne Kensington was in some despair when she heard nothing from those who were to bring Shepherd back to France to develop the smokeless gunpowder. Moray refused to work on the discovery out of deference to his promise to Shepherd not to work further on this dangerous substance. Smokeless powder would not be developed for warfare for another 150 years.

Anne was to try one more scheme to sustain herself in the French court. Anne had become involved with some of the disgruntled nobles engaged in what later became known as the Fronde of the Nobles. Her plan to give information and support to this group, which hoped to overturn the monarchy, became hopelessly entangled in the intrigues of the court. Those whom she trusted exposed Anne, and when Cardinal Mazarin found out he had her jailed. Within a week, she was scheduled for the hangman's noose. Seeing that her final scheme had failed, she decided to die by her own hand. She obtained arsenic from one of her court contacts and ingested it. She died rather slowly, with acute stomach pain and intestinal bleeding. This "friend" had given her enough to kill her, but not enough to kill her quickly. Even to the end, Anne evidently made poor choices in friends.

Lord Andrew Kensington met a grisly end as well. Even though his health had been failing for years, he managed to stay around long enough to continue to wreak havoc among those with whom he did business. Martin Crane and Edward Elliot, the old *Intrepid* shipmates, who had been cured of the plague, had been working for Kensington on one of his merchant ships. One day, as Kensington was overseeing a shipment of tobacco being unloaded on the docks, he ordered Edward Elliott to be beaten with a cane for stealing some of the product. Crane, a lifelong friend of Elliott, defended him, stating that Elliott was innocent. Kensington came forward toward Crane, and both then set upon the old man. A huge brawl then broke out among the seething

292

dockworkers. In the melee, Crane stabbed Kensington repeatedly in the stomach. As Kensington lay helpless on the dock, the workers stopped to view the writhing old man breathe his last breath. Ironically, his death had a calming effect on the workers. They did not even give him the dignity of a burial, but threw his still-warm body into the water, where he floated briefly in view of gawkers who did not seem to mourn his passing.

Oliver Craft's health had completely deteriorated after he had contacted Anne Kensington with the letters he had taken from Rainsborough (and Lord Kensington). He was found on the street near the Jacob Carr Mission coughing blood and shaking violently. He was taken in by Sister Clarice, who ministered to him that night. He lived just two weeks longer, his last days being comforted by the loving hands of people whose former mission he had burned to the ground many years prior.

Dr. Luke Greene continued to do what he loved until the end of his life. He taught at Harvard College until he was nearly eighty years old. He incorporated many of the ideas he learned from Joseph Shepherd into his classes, but he lost status and credibility with the other professors and the educational community as he befriended and defended slaves and Indians. His staunch defense of Chibuike and Kimi drew much criticism, and his published works on medical advances such as inoculation, sterile field for surgery, anesthesia, and proper nutrition as part of health were largely discounted and forgotten in the years after his death at age eighty-three.

Luke's beloved Margaret died one year after Luke, having been cared for by her son Jacob after Luke's death. Margaret wrote her own journals, as requested by her husband, and they have been passed down over the generations since her death. She lived to see her grandchildren become successful and generally prosperous. She had the sorrow of burying her beloved friend Chepi, but also the joy in helping to raise "Little Kimi," who was a prize to her.

Despite the unfortunate discounting of Joseph Shepherd's influence and knowledge, by virtue of Greene's lost credibility, Shepherd's influence was felt in many other ways. His ideas about inoculation were intriguing to Dr. Jenner, who continued to discuss the ideas with his friend Harvey. At first skeptical, Jenner wrote of the ideas in his own journals, and his great-great-grandson, Edward Jenner, finally popularized the concept, which had been around in theory for hundreds of years, in 1796.

Shepherd's intuition and insight into the circulation of the blood in the human body influenced and encouraged William Harvey in his signal work *De Motu Cordis*. Shepherd's understanding of surgery and anesthesia were passed on in literature, which later revealed a lineage of knowledge that can be traced back to his influence and practices.

Shepherd's work with Galileo and Kepler helped reinforce our understanding of heavenly bodies, the role of the moon on earth's tidal actions, and even the idea of the vastness of the universe, completely unknown up to that time.

Finally, Shepherd's ideas about freedom and self-government were realized through the efforts of William Bradford and the Mayflower Compact, and Adams, Gerry, and Hancock, whose progeny were instrumental in forming the United States Constitution and Declaration of Independence.

Some of the editing of this journal you have just read was actually done by Joseph Shepherd himself. He affixed his name to many of the entries, clarified details, made annotations and observations, but never attributed dates to these writings. This book has been compiled over the years from many sources. While mostly from Dr. Greene's first-hand accounts, many of the passages have been filled in by Joseph Shepherd, and others who knew the Greene family.

We do not know how or where Joseph Shepherd acquired access to this journal, nor do we know where he went after the shipwreck of the *Cove*. However, we are grateful for his assistance in compiling this record.

Final Editor unknown…

Author's Note

Many of the characters are fictional, including Joseph Shepherd. I have endeavored to give a "backstory" to some of the great thinkers and inventors, asking the reader to consider those people who may have played some hidden or untold part in the creative process of those whom we have identified as geniuses.

I used the words "scientist" and "science" through most of the book, recognizing that the name more typically used in the 17th century was "natural philosophy."

Some language used is reflective of the time, and may be considered disrespectful at times. Please be assured that such language was used only to reflect the attitudes of many people of that time, and is not intended to portray any disrespect by the author.

I have attempted, as one of the themes of this book, to portray Joseph Shepherd as a man of faith as well as a man of science. His insistence on the compatibility of the two disciplines is important to highlight, especially in the 17th century where the Church dominated thought and often disallowed scientific pursuit. The scientific age, really just beginning around that time, saw the start of the relative decline of the Church's influence, and the rise of rationalism. That transition was the start of major cultural changes in Western society. Now, in modern times, the transition is complete. Science has dominated contemporary thought, and has often discredited the role of faith in understanding a complex and interrelated world.

The character Joseph Shepherd is complex and enigmatic as well. My hope is that the reader will embrace him, consider his adventures and influences, and perhaps follow him on his next journey.